HARRY HERON:
NO QUARTER

*Book Three of the
Harry Heron Series*

Patrick G. Cox

Harry Heron: No Quarter
Copyright © 2017 Patrick G. Cox

Ebook ISBN: 9781946824042

Harry Heron: No Quarter is a work of fiction. Any resemblance to actual events, locations, or persons living or dead is coincidental. No part of this book may be used or reproduced in any manner without written permission from the publisher or the author except in the case of brief quotations in articles or reviews.

The Harry Heron Series

Harry Heron: Midshipman's Journey
Harry Heron: Into the Unknown
Harry Heron: No Quarter
Harry Heron: Savage Fugitive
Harry Heron: Awakening Threat
Harry Heron: Hope Transcends
The Harry Heron Series eBook Boxed Set

OTHER BOOKS BY PATRICK G. COX

A Baltic Affair
Limehouse Boys
Magnus Patricius: The Remarkable Life of St Patrick the Man
Captain James Heron: First Into the Fray

Part One – Fleet College

Chapter 1 – Fresh Start
Chapter 2 – Shades of the Past
Chapter 3 – The Yotties
Chapter 4 – Lacertian Cadets
Chapter 5 – Ingenuity
Chapter 6 – Frustrated Attempt
Chapter 7 – Hornet's Nest
Chapter 8 – Our Own Resources
Chapter 9 – Interference
Chapter 10 – Skulduggery
Chapter 11 – Der Große Kurfürst
Chapter 12 – Suspicion
Chapter 13 – Sabotage
Chapter 14 – Seeing Double
Chapter 15 – Death on Camera
Chapter 16 – Enquiry
Chapter 17 – Back on Track
Chapter 18 – Firing Exercise
Chapter 19 – Bad Judgment
Chapter 20 – Regatta Week
Chapter 21 – Against Wind and Water
Chapter 22 – Time to Move On

Part Two – Fleet Deployment

Chapter 23 – New Ship, New Challenges
Chapter 24 – Ferghal's Oneupmanship
Chapter 25 – Outward Bound
Chapter 26 – Pangaea, Again
Chapter 27 – Convoy to Seraphis
Chapter 28 – Diversion
Chapter 29 – Ambushed
Chapter 30 – Survivors
Chapter 31 – Consortium Strikes
Chapter 32 – Engage the Enemy
Chapter 33 – Farewell to Hell
Chapter 34 – Breakthrough
Chapter 35 – Surprise
Chapter 36 – Unwelcome Passengers
Chapter 37 – Fight or Die
Chapter 38 – No Quarter Asked, None Given
Chapter 39 – Taking Command
Chapter 40 – Long Way Home

HARRY HERON:
NO QUARTER

Part One – Fleet College

Chapter 1 – Fresh Start

Harry was so focused on sailing the Bermudan sloop that he thought nothing of the boat following some distance astern, but something about it registered a feeling of disquiet in his mind, and he glanced back at it now and then. This feeling amplified when the boat came up astern at full speed then slowed, apparently content to follow Harry through a crowd of small dinghies and pleasure craft. Harry dismissed his sense of unease with logic. This was, after all, a busy waterway, with the approach to the yacht harbour at Bangor, or across the Lough at Carrickfergus, and, of course, the many large and small vessels entering or leaving Belfast itself.

"We'll have to tack again to achieve the approach to Bangor," he remarked to Ferghal. "I shall hold this course until we are level with the channel buoy."

"Aye, aye, Cap'n," Ferghal said with a grin, saluting Harry. They had been friends since childhood, though Harry's station was a notch above Ferghal's, something Harry never gave a thought to. Sometimes Ferghal still struggled to understand that now they were equals in the eyes of society in the year 2206, a very different world indeed from the one they mysteriously departed in 1804.

Harry was becoming concerned with the boat following them. Glancing astern, he frowned. "Our shadow is with us still, gaining a little. Under power he has no reliance on the wind, but his machine does not appear to have the speed to shorten the chase."

Ferghal looked back at the boat and assessed its speed. "Not yet, but when we tack, he may take the shorter route."

Harry considered this. "So he may, but I do not see a reason to be concerned. He just sits in our wake at present."

Harry's guardian, Commodore Heron, had been very explicit before the two young men set out on this jaunt. If they noticed anyone or anything behaving in a manner that was out of the ordinary, they were to contact him immediately.

Watching the following boat, Ferghal let out an uneasy breath "I like him not. We should not have left Sci'gara ashore. She takes her guardian duties very seriously, does that astute Lacertian, and Sci'genza will give you one of her respectful lectures, I think."

Harry grinned. "No doubt I shall get a lecture from the Commodore as well. His lectures are far easier to suffer than Sci'genza's politeness, though her lectures are endurable because of her alien beauty, strange as it is." He glanced at the hefty channel marker buoy as they swept past it. They were clear of other craft and had this part of the Lough to themselves, but the boat shadowing them persisted on their heels like a dog intent on its chase.

Making a decision, Harry said, "Ready, Ferghal? Let's tack now."

Putting the helm over, Harry swung the bow through the eye of the wind while Ferghal and the pair of youths hired in Bangor brought the foresail smartly across and sheeted it home. The boat surged forward on her new course, responding well to the wind on the new tack.

"They've altered course," Ferghal called out. "I think they steer to cross our path."

Harry checked. "You are correct." He paused. "Damn. Contact the Commodore."

"The link is jammed. There's no way to make contact with the Commodore or Security." Ferghal glared at the boat. "They are closing fast." He noted its increased speed and the men clinging to the grab rails along the side of the wheelhouse. "Four of them, armed. And we are not." Ferghal flexed his shoulders. "What do ye plan?"

"From their approach, they will attempt to pass close alongside and board as they do." Harry thought quickly. "Pass the mainsheet to me here, and warn Maurice and Donald I will gybe as soon as these rogues attempt to board us."

"Aye. We've not much time. Two or three minutes at most." Ferghal casually passed the tail of the mainsheet onto the compass binnacle. He signalled the two youths forward. "Stand by for a little old fashioned sailin', lads. We've unwanted visitors. Just take care o' yourselves."

"Here, stand off!" Harry shouted at the approaching boat. "You're endangering us."

One of the men laughed and said something over his shoulder to the others. Addressing Harry, he shouted, "You can't outrun us in that sloop. You might as well give up."

"Go to the devil." Harry luffed slightly, causing the sloop to cross the track of the approaching boat. As he expected, the other boat's helmsman bore up, increasing his speed just enough to put his boat in the position he wanted. The gap closed rapidly.

"Stand by, Ferghal. Are they ready to use their weapons?"

"Doesn't look like it. They cling to the rail."

"Good." Harry glanced over his shoulder. "Stand by."

The pursuing boat surged up alongside, and as soon as the two hulls touched, the men leapt. Harry put the sloop's wheel hard over, reopening the gap. One man grabbed the rail but missed the deck, falling into the water to drag alongside. The other three made the deck.

Harry was counting on these men not knowing that the gybe would bring wind across the stern of the boat, and the danger that posed. Tripping the mainsail from the jam cleat, he let the mainsheet run free as they rolled under the helm, and the sloop continued her turn.

Ferghal threw himself flat as the mainsail changed sides with a lurch, the rigid boom along its bottom edge slamming unchecked across the deck. Two of the intruders saw it coming. A third man, his attention focused on helping the man in the water, failed to see the danger until it was too late, and it caught him square in the chest as the wind filled the sail.

One of the men lunged toward Ferghal just as Harry put the helm hard over in the opposite direction. Once again the boom slammed across, almost catching the fourth man as he heaved his companion aboard. The launch, having attempted to follow Harry's manoeuvres, was now right across the sloop's bow.

The boats collided, and a bellow of rage accompanied by the sound of breaking glass drew Harry's attention. He laughed when he saw Maurice retrieve the spinnaker boom and prepare to use it a second time on the man in the other boat's wheelhouse. Donald, he noticed, was laying into one of the men, and Ferghal had already flung one overboard and was lunging toward another to give him the heave-ho as well. That man chose to leap overboard rather than smack the water with the force Ferghal's muscles would propel him, and when he plunged in, he had to swim for his life as the two vessels ground together then parted before the launch sped away, apparently out of control.

The last of the attackers also leaped overboard and swam for the motorboat, which now sat idling in the water.

"The comlink is active again," Ferghal announced. "I've contacted security." He grinned as Maurice and Donald joined him, having finished tending the sails.

"That was a handy bit o' use o' the spinnaker pole," said Harry

Donald smiled, his face ruddy from the bit of fun they'd had. "Aye, it was nothin'," he said, shrugging his shoulders. "I could do it in my sleep if I had to!"

Maurice laughed. "They'll find they've another problem soon. He tossed a length of cable into the cockpit. "Snagged it with the snaphook. Didn't expect t' whole throttle unit t' come away. Someone didn't take care o' t' boat properly."

"Looks like the police are after them," said Harry, catching sight of the patrol boat speeding past. "Just as well, their mate won't be coming to pick them up in a hurry."

Ferghal clambered out of the cabin. "We're not taking water, but we've damage for'ard. The owners'll not be happy." Seating himself, he studied Harry. "We were lucky, my friend, but we might not be so lucky next time, and I have a feeling there will be a next time."

"I'M GIVING THEM BOTH THE YACHT MASTER TICKET." Captain Montgomery, chief examiner for the Maritime Qualifications Board, leaned back in the settee. "Frankly, I think young Harry could probably take command of a cargo hauler. Ferghal's a superb seaman, but he needs a little more confidence in command." He sipped the tea. "Incredible story, and I think their experience at sea in the wooden walls is evident in their advanced skill level. Harry was twelve when they went to sea?"

The Commodore nodded then shifted his position, wedged as he was into a corner of the settle against the heel of the yacht and the slight pitch as she beat back to port. "His own choice, he says. Nearly drove his parents to despair the way he tells it. His father was a Major in the Fusiliers and the holder of the farm and the house we live in." Smiling, he glanced at the open hatch. "The Major did his best to dissuade Harry, I gather, and Ferghal took it upon himself to follow where Harry led. Ferghal's father was the Major's groom, according to the records we've dug up, and Ferghal helped in the stables when he wasn't being schooled."

"Unusual for the son of a groom to be sent to school in those days, wasn't it?"

"I don't know the full story, but it appears Harry was a handful, and his father decided that Ferghal was a steadying influence in his early years. They were involved in some sort of scrape after the rebellion in 1797, and Ferghal saved Harry, then Harry managed to rescue Ferghal, and the Major decided they should be schooled together. He hired a tutor and set them both to work." He laughed. "And to keep them where he could watch them, I think. They seem to have a way of attracting trouble on occasion."

"Typical Irishmen then." Captain Montgomery laughed. "Hallo, we must be on approach."

"You're right." The Commodore stood as the yacht's angle changed, and he was forced to grip the edge of the table as she heeled in the opposite direction. Overhead the sails rattled briefly, then the light through the hatch changed. Both men made for the hatch as the boat came to a stop with a slight bump. They emerged on deck to find both boys securing the mooring lines to the jetty with the sails already down.

"I'm impressed." Captain Montgomery looked forward to see Ferghal lashing the mainsail, but he directed his question to Harry. "You sailed her onto the jetty with the wind in this quarter?"

A puzzled frown crossed Harry's forehead. "Of course, sir." Realization dawned, and he blushed. "Oh, I forgot — the boat has a mechanical engine."

A splash farther along the quay drew their attention.

"Someone's fallen in!" exclaimed the Captain.

The Commodore frowned. "Doesn't look eager to be rescued," he observed as the person surfaced and swam determinedly toward the harbour entrance. "Damned strange direction to swim if you've fallen in." He touched his comlink. "Security." After a pause, he gave his location, adding, "We've something unusual — a swimmer making for the sea, not the shore, after apparently falling in from the quay. If you've anyone handy, you might want to find out why."

"THE DEVICE WAS INTENDED TO ALLOW SOMEONE to redirect the module." The Commodore's anger showed. "The man they pulled out of the sea claims it was an attempt to make contact with Harry and Ferghal for an interview."

"You don't believe that, I can see." Niamh watched her brother pace the room. "What else have your security people told you?"

His back was to her as he stared out of the window at Scrabo, crowned by the tower built to honour a long dead Lord Castlereagh. "The man is known to them, a private investigator apparently, one who's been involved in activities that interest them. You know their usual form — never tell anyone anything if they can avoid it. They did let slip that he is known to be working for an agency associated with the Johnstone Pharmaceutical Group. That bunch are always involved when something nefarious happens, it seems."

"Right you are." Niamh joined him at the window. "So they haven't given up."

"No, nor will they until someone exposes their fraudulent research operations and puts an end to it." Clasping his hands firmly behind him, he added, "I've been assured this man's activities are at an end. They've enough to bring charges on several matters unrelated to Harry, and they'll increase their surveillance on the boys. Someone, and they know who, is very keen to get their hands on Harry in particular, with Ferghal as a bonus." Turning, he summoned Herbert, his android butler, and ordered a whiskey. "The enquiry is postponed again, which works in our favour. We can get the boys settled into the Fleet College. They will be much more protected there."

HARRY HEFTED HIS HOLDALL AND ATTACHÉ CASE from the baggage space of the transport module that had brought him and Ferghal to the College. He still found this mode of transport fascinating, having grown up in the age of horse-drawn carriages. It seemed astonishing that he could simply contact a central control unit and request transport to any destination.

The College architecture was an interesting blend of old and new. Set on the shores of a huge lake, the original buildings formed the heart of a large and extensive complex. He took in the vista, paying particular attention to the ornate facades of the historic buildings, reminiscent of the grandeur of a long gone Empire.

Automatically he checked the small pen-like device that he and Ferghal carried with them everywhere, which allowed them to block out the link to any AI they were near. While it did not completely shut off the link, it did reduce the distraction it caused. It also helped hide the fact that they had the unique ability to link to any AI when they needed to.

"What think you, Ferghal?" Harry grinned as his companion studied the campus map they'd received. "It's bigger and grander than I expected, but we'll manage, I think. Are we in the right place?"

Ferghal's expression revealed that he was even more nervous than Harry was.

"Aye, Master . . . I mean Harry. We'll find our feet, I'm thinking." Ferghal grinned to relieve the tension. "If I can find the entrance for the likes o' us, that is!" His booming laugh startled a few cadets who passed by. "The Commodore says we've a lot to learn yet, and this spell at the College'll give us a chance to get a wider perspective on the Fleet." Ferghal made a wry face. "I think I'm needing classes in how to be a gent."

"I feel adrift in this new world too, Ferghal. We're in this together. I have no greater advantage than you have." Harry clapped his friend on the back. "We both have to walk in there and greet our fellow College mates who have grown up in an era four hundred years in advance of our own childhood years. No wonder we feel lost!" They laughed again.

Recovering his bags from the pavement, Harry grinned as he shifted his weight. "Well, let us see if we can find our way to the officer of the day and report aboard. Who knows, we old-fashioned sailors might have something to teach these mates."

Ferghal hefted his bag and equipment. "Right you are. We're cadets now. Officer's College, here we come! Let's steer to starboard. The entry port for us lies there."

Harry looked at the entrance Ferghal indicated. "That looks like our way right enough. Away, boarders!"

Ferghal laughed at Harry's use of an expression from their time in the navy of Admiral Nelson. "At least our arrival on these decks will not be opposed — I hope."

"Aye." Harry grinned. "And there is not the same stench with it. Do you recall the first time we boarded the *Billy Ruffian*?"

"I'm not like to forget that stench," acknowledged Ferghal.

"I do not mind admitting that I sometimes wish for a return to those days when everything was familiar," said Harry.

"True, 'tis a right strange world we live in now, but I'm enjoying entering this College more than I did boarding the *Billy Ruffian*, climbing the tumblehome with the line for your chest and my bag while trying to discover where I was allowed to enter the ship. The entry port was not for the likes of me then, but here, I can walk right through the front door wi' the best of 'em."

Harry didn't quite know how to respond to Ferghal's plain honesty, and the two fell silent as they neared the building. Reaching for the door, Harry was almost knocked down when it was thrust open with some force. A well-built youth in the uniform of a midshipman barged through it, pushing Harry aside.

"Get out of my way," the newcomer snarled. He stormed past then stopped and turned around to stare. He planted his feet in a wide stance and crossed his arms. He looked Harry over, sneering. "New here, aren't you? Well, you'd better learn to keep out of my way or you won't last long."

Harry bristled, his fiery temper rising. Ferghal took a step forward, squaring off with the youth, and Harry signalled him to stay out of the argument. He felt there was something familiar about the midshipman. Trying to place it, he said, "I know you not, Mr—"

Harry waited for affirmation, but the youth just glared at him, looking as though he couldn't be bothered to give Harry his name.

Harry continued. "You may be assured that I did not intentionally impede your passage."

"You'll learn my name soon enough, you posh little jerk," snarled the large midshipman. "And you'll stay out of my way if you know what's good for you. How did you put it so properly? Oh yeah, if you dare to impede my passage."

Having just endured yet another dressing down for his treatment of a fellow classmate, the bully was in no mood to suffer any cheek from a newcomer. Even his Divisional Officer's recent warning couldn't hold Eon Barclay's temper in check. He hated this place and he hated the Fleet. He was only here because he had to be. His father and uncle had insisted on it and arranged this assignment for him. Damn them both.

"I won't stay out of your way," said Ferghal quietly, his tone deadly serious. "I'll seek you out if I have to." He squared up again to show he meant it. He had no clue what "posh little jerk" meant, but he could tell from the tone that it was an insult. He hated bullies and had almost intervened on Harry's behalf on *Spartan* more than once, risking being hanged for mutiny, the standard punishment in those days.

Barclay shifted his gaze and noted Ferghal's broad shoulders and well muscled build. He modified his tone somewhat, but not his expression. "I'm not talking to you, Irish." He glowered and folded his arms across his chest again, giving an unspoken invitation for either of them to take him on.

Ferghal's eyes blazed. He would have said more but Harry spoke first.

"I know your sort. You do not frighten me, sir, and I do not like being abused for no reason but to appease your ego."

Something familiar about the face and the look of this boy nagged at him, but he couldn't quite place it.

"What do you mean, my sort?" spluttered the big midshipman clenching his fists. "You'll learn not to mess with me, you proper little twerp. Why don't you talk like a real man and not like some butler named Jeeves in an old movie."

Harry ignored the insult, partly because he had no idea what this bully was talking about. "I have served with one such as you, and he was as big a bully as you are. I endured his floggings in the Gunroom, mastheading and being triced up in the ratlines for his ego, but I'll not stomach it in this place from anyone but an officer. You have the same attitude as that bully, but he could not cow me, and neither will you. Have no fear, I shall not seek your company unnecessarily, and I hope that you will do me the same courtesy." He retrieved his bags.

"Come, Ferghal, we must report to the Officer of the Day." Ferghal was still glowering at the speechless midshipman.

Stepping past the bully, Harry sensed rather than saw a fist aimed at his head. He ducked instinctively, and the fist whistled over him as he turned swiftly, his attaché case catching the bully squarely in the groin.

"I beg pardon," said Harry, with a calmness that belied the temper he wanted to unleash.

The youth turned a sickly shade as he staggered and fell to his knees clutching himself.

"Do you wish to call me out?" Harry taunted. "Ah, I see you have other things on your mind. Perhaps later."

Ferghal grinned as he followed Harry through the entrance. "You've made a dangerous enemy there," he remarked as soon as the door closed behind them.

"I know it," responded Harry. "But I could not allow him to strike me, nor you to strike him for me. If there is trouble from this encounter, it is my trouble and not yours." For all his cool appearance, it worried him to have got off to such a bad start, and it stirred the memory of his long dead adversary on HMS *Spartan*. It was unnerving to him in this place that seemed so calm and orderly on the surface.

He stopped at the registration desk, placed his bags on the floor, and saluted the Master Warrant Officer who stood to greet them.

"Midshipmen Heron and Cadet O'Connor reporting as ordered, Master."

"So I see, sir." The Master Warrant Officer's face was impassive as he studied the pair before him. Noting Harry's tidy mop of dark brown hair and Ferghal's thick shock of red hair and muscular heft, which made Harry's build seem smaller, he sized them up with interest. A thirty-year veteran, he'd seen a lot of budding officers in his time, but uniforms apart, these two were something different. It was obvious in the way they carried themselves.

"I noticed your incident with Midshipman Barclay. Don't try it again. Do you understand me, sir?"

Harry flushed. "I understand, Master. To whom should we report?"

"You have your joining instructions with you, I presume."

Harry produced his data card.

"Very good, sir, place your card in this slot, please. Thank you. Midshipman Henry Nelson-Heron. Any relation to Commodore Heron, sir?" Before Harry could answer, the Warrant Officer exclaimed in surprise. "This data card must be wrong. Says here you were born in seventeen eighty-nine! That can't be right. Damned networks have screwed up again."

"I'm afraid the information is correct, Master," replied Harry.

"Ah!" The Master Warrant Officer gave Harry a piercing look. "I should have remembered. You're the midshipman who fought off the Consortium crew to escape their underground labs, and then you built and sailed a ship from an island on Pangaea. It was all over the news." His glance covered Ferghal. "Well, I'm damned! Never thought they'd send you gentlemen here. Weren't there three of you?"

"Danny has been sent to school in Dublin since he is too young to join this Fleet" said Harry. "And it seems our heroic story has been a little exaggerated, Master. Ferghal and a number of others did most of the work. We only rigged the ship. I just navigated them home." He grinned.

"Well, well, our Mr Barclay had to pick on you two. I think I'm going to enjoy watching you gentlemen this semester." He gave Ferghal an appraising look. "I hope you haven't brought that sword with you, Cadet O'Connor."

It was Ferghal's turn to redden. "No, Master, the Commodore said it wasn't appropriate here."

"Well, thank God for that," laughed the older man. "Now gentlemen, a few rules for you to follow. Absolutely no fighting with your fellow officers no matter the provocation, and there will be some. I am Master Warrant Officer Winkworth, and I am the Master Warrant for your class this semester. You are junior officers, but while you are here, I am the law. Your Divisional Officer is Lieutenant Haäkinen. He is expecting you as soon as you have deposited your duffel in your cabins. You, Mr Heron, are in Cabin Two Zero Two on Deck Zero Two and you, Mr O'Connor, are in Cabin Two Zero Four alongside him. I will warn you that Mr Barclay is in Two Zero Three, opposite you, Mr Heron. Don't let him provoke you. Report to Lieutenant Haäkinen as soon as you are ready."

Once they were out of earshot, he strolled over to the Royal Marine Colour Sergeant. "This should be fun, Jim. I think we will have some interesting times this semester. That pair were the lads from Pangaea — the ones transported four hundred years into the future by that accident in the Indian Ocean Transit Gate."

"Oh?" exclaimed the Colour Sergeant. "My oppo on *Vanguard* said they were quite a pair. Took on a squad of Marines using knives, axes, and fire extinguishers." He laughed. "The word is they escaped from some high security facility after contaminating the food replicators. The older one, O'Connor, is the bloody devil himself when he's in a fighting mood, according to the lads who trained him. The Mid's a very cool fish in a tight spot as well. I hope Mr Barclay crosses them again. That will be entertaining, to say the least!" They both laughed. "Has O'Connor got that sword with him? What did they call it — a cutlass, I think?"

"No, thank God, or so he assures me. I think I'm going to have my hands full as it is based on the fire in his eyes — that I couldn't miss." He paused. "But I'll keep an eye on them both — odd pair, those two."

"O'Connor broke a guard's neck barehanded during their escape, then made the cutlass in a replication unit and used it on a villager when the fool tried to attack him. Took the fellow's arm clean off and damned near his leg as well." Hesitating, he added, "Never batted an eye, according to the Mid who was here last month. I wonder if I can get him to train some of my lads to use a weapon like that. Never know, it might be a handy skill to have."

Chapter 2 – Shades of the Past

Harry turned sharply at the outburst of a rude exclamation, half expecting another attempt at assault. "Where do you think you're going?" Eon Barclay demanded to know.

"To my assigned cabin, since you ask. You have some objection to that?" Once again, the resemblance of Eon Barclay to someone he knew tugged at his memory and stirred up a nebulous sense of anxiety, but he responded calmly, meeting the other's eye. Then the name surfaced a memory. Barclay! That was the connection — this must be a descendent of that other Barclay who had been the Gunroom bully aboard HMS *Spartan*. Surely a mean streak could not run in a family for so many generations, or could it?

Scowling, Barclay thrust his face closer to Harry's. "Think you're so damn smart, don't you? What's the name? What division?"

His own anger rising at being addressed like this, Harry bit back the urge to tell this bully to mind his own business. "Heron. Britannia Division." His annoyance prompted him. "And who enquires? What is your name and division?"

"None of your damn business. Just stay out of my way."

"It is my business to know whom I am addressing, especially when I am merely answering a question. You demanded to know where I am going. I see before me a man wearing the same uniform and displaying the same rank as mine, yet you demand my name and business as if you're a senior officer. Not only that, but you made this demand without introducing yourself first. As to staying out of your way — well, that will be determined by which classes we must attend and which other activities we must engage upon. Now, since I have made myself known, perhaps you'd do me the same courtesy."

Glowering, Barclay clenched his fists, aware that the exchange had attracted witnesses. Through the anger driving him, the name belatedly sparked a warning. "Oh, so you're Heron, are you? Well, I'm Barclay, Dreadnought Division." He glanced at the audience. "I'll be watching you. Put one foot wrong, and I'll—"

"I do not meekly accept attempts to assault me — particularly from behind, as you tried to do when first we met." Harry stood firm. "Good day to you, Mr Barclay. My cabin is on this flat, so if you would care to move aside, I shall install myself in it."

Barclay made a big show of reluctantly stepping aside.

When they reached their cabins, Ferghal muttered, "A fine start to College life, eh, Harry." He breathed out slowly, his eyes on the man glowering at Harry.

"You know we dealt with his like on *Spartan*," Harry said, shooting a quick glance at Eon. "Same surname, too. We'll have to watch this one. See you in a bit." He went into his cabin.

"It didn't take Eon long to make a new enemy then," said a voice behind Ferghal, just as he put his hand on the keypad to his cabin door. He turned to see who spoke.

"Hi, I'm Keiron Whitworth, and I've come to escort you and Heron to our Divisional Officer."

Ferghal nodded. "That'll be welcome. Who is that fellow?" As if in answer, Barclay slammed the door to his cabin.

"Eon?" Keiron sighed. "A burden we all have to bear. You must be O'Connor, and I gather that was Heron." He held out his hand. "For my sins, today I'm the Divisional Go-fer. Welcome to the Yotties. Stow your gear while I make my number with your friend."

THE WALK TO LIEUTENANT HAÄKINEN'S OFFICE proved a long one, made simpler by Keiron's demonstration of the system used to navigate the massive campus.

"If you enter the department code and a room number, it displays the building and a green line to follow." Keiron handed a tablet to Ferghal. "Here we are. I better rush. I've another newbie to round up. See you in the dining hall later."

As Keiron hurried away, Harry read the door label and eyed the lights on the indicator. Applying his knuckle to the door, he made a brief staccato knock. There was no response, and he was about to knock again when the door slid back to reveal the Lieutenant, his hand still on the switch. Harry stepped back in surprise, recovered quickly, and saluted. "Sir. Midshipman Nelson-Heron and Cadet O'Connor, at your serv—I mean, reporting, sir."

The Lieutenant smiled. Returning the salute, he stepped back. "Come in, gentlemen. You'll find using the door pad is the usual way now, Mr Heron." Taking a seat behind his desk, he signalled them to chairs facing him. "So, you are the famous Heron and O'Connor," he continued in slightly accented but otherwise flawless English. "I think you've heard about the College and what will be expected of you here, is that correct?"

"Yes, sir," replied Harry.

"Good, then I won't waste time going through it all again. As you're aware, most of what you will get here is the opportunity to develop your abilities with the goal of commissioning aboard a ship of the Fleet." He glanced at his desk display. "I see from your reports that you have done very well in getting the underpinning knowledge. You'll build on that using our simulators and by participating in real-time exercises to develop your knowledge and abilities in the required fields."

He observed their reactions. "You bring a range of experiences most of your classmates don't have, which may or may not help in what you'll be doing here. You'll discover that the competition among your fellow midshipmen and cadets is quite fierce and sometimes a little rough. Some of it will be in good fun, and some of it will be aimed at testing your limits. The line between what is acceptable and what is not is very thin indeed, but the way to know the difference is to consider the setting within which you're tested. If it is during an official exercise, that is part of your training. If it is outside of those parameters and during your free time, it is most likely a bullying tactic. Don't let yourselves be provoked, and don't let anyone bully you. The Fleet won't tolerate bullies here or aloft, at all."

He held their gaze. "I expect that you will know the signs and how to deal with it should it occur."

Harry gave a wry smile, wondering whether the Lieutenant knew of his encounter with Barclay.

"I think so, sir."

Changing the subject, Lt Haäkinen said, "I understand that you are both able to use a direct link to the AI network. That will give you a distinct advantage during your studies here, so it's best not to make that known to the other cadets and officers, or you'll be seen as having privileges not earned. I gather it is not the usual link provided to senior officers by the Fleet."

"Aye, sir," replied Ferghal for them both. "At first it was, but since the Pangaea laboratory incident, Harry's been unable to switch it off, and mine is now doing a similar thing. Surgeon Commander Myers on *Vanguard* thought it was because of something called a gene splice the Consortium people did to us."

"I see." The Lieutenant hesitated. "According to your medical records, they performed an illegal genetic modification on you both. I gather you have been given a briefing on the implications of that."

Harry glanced at Ferghal. "I think we may have the general idea, sir. Surgeon Commander Myers did try to explain it, and I looked up the information on genetic engineering, but I confess neither of us fully understands it." In this Harry was being a little reticent. While he now understood what a genetic splice was, he also knew that the particular gene that had been modified governed the body's ability to heal itself and regenerate lost or damaged parts. It worried him that no one knew the full impact of this on a human subject, and he was very much afraid that it might result in unwelcome changes to his person.

Lieutenant Haäkinen nodded. "It's best not to show off that ability. It won't be easy." He grinned. "You will make a lot of enemies very quickly if you get too cocky with it."

"Aye, sir." Harry glanced at Ferghal. The Commodore had been quite definite about this. "Our guardian made it very clear that we should not exploit it, sir, and we have a device that allows us to block the connection."

"Good. Then I can leave it at that." He consulted the desk display. "You are in Britannia Class. It's the group to which we assign all the midshipmen and cadets who have specialist skills, or who have already shown particular abilities." He swiftly outlined the programme, making sure they understood it all. "One last thing: if you have difficulty with anything, I expect you to discuss it with me."

"Aye, aye, sir," they replied in unison.

A smile flickered as the Lieutenant nodded. "Good. I understand you had a contretemps with Midshipman Barclay on arrival. Fighting is forbidden and punishable under the discipline regulations. Don't let him provoke you. If he persists in doing so, I want to hear about it."

"Aye, aye, sir." Harry shifted uneasily, aware that his instinctive response to Barclay's well-aimed fist could be considered fighting.

"See you do, please." The Lieutenant frowned as he consulted his display. "I see you're required as witnesses at the enquiry to look into the events that brought you here. Are you prepared for that?"

Harry spoke for them both. "Aye, sir. It was supposed to have been held two months ago, but was postponed."

"So I see. Unfortunate, the timing, but there it is. You'll be notified about transport and so on." He stood. "Right, that's it, I think. Better grab some dinner and meet the rest of the class. Just enter the words *dining hall* in your tablet."

"I DON'T SEE WHY I HAVE TO BE SADDLED WITH THIS." Eon Barclay kept his voice low as he addressed the holographic image. "I want out of this dump. With our family's connections, why can't I have a position like Stuart's with one of our subsidiaries?"

His father looked weary. Why did one son have to be so difficult when the other was so easy-going? "Eon, we've been through this many times. Your uncle needs you in the Fleet for reasons that have been explained to you. He'd have used Stu if he could, but your brother is on the surveillance list." Holding up a hand, his father signalled he wasn't finished when Eon tried to interrupt. "It will be well worth your while, and it isn't exactly fusion science. Heron's cabin is directly opposite yours. How hard can it be to keep him under surveillance?"

"That's not the point. There are loads of others here who could do this. You don't need me for it."

"We do. You're in a position to be closer to him and that wild Irish O'Connor than any of our other operatives because you're in classes together and on exercises with them. Damn it, Eon, at least make an attempt to stay on your uncle's good books. He pays you very well for the information you supply him — more than it's worth, I should think." His expression hardened. "You know the family trusts have large investments in several of the Interplanetary Consortium companies, and the current problem of their being unable to trade with the Confederacy, the WTC and the North American Union is causing some serious cash flow problems. If you want to be part of the restoration of all of that, stay where you are and do what you're told."

His expression surly, Barclay nodded. "Okay, okay, I get the message, but I hate the Fleet. I hate the way they order me around, and I hate having to play this stupid role. As soon as there's an opening, I want out of here."

"That's better. And you have my word. I'll talk to your uncle about getting you something more in line with our standing in society once you've done what we require of you." The elder Barclay smiled. "I'm assured it won't be long before the Consortium forces have achieved our primary objective. Then we can force the Confederacy and others to accept our terms and enjoy the rewards."

Slightly mollified, Barclay nodded. Without a goodbye, his father closed the connection. Eon scowled as he recalled the humiliation of crumpling to the ground from Harry's well-aimed counterattack to his groin.

"I'll get mine, Mr Harry-bloody-Heron. The hell with whatever my father says."

DURING THEIR WALK TO THE DINING HALL, Ferghal wasted no time getting back to what Harry had told him before their meeting with the Lieutenant.

"That Barclay fellow — you reminded me earlier that we dealt with his ancestor, or someone of the same family, on *Spartan*. He is exactly as the one we knew." Glancing about him, Ferghal added, "We're safe from prying ears here. So what's to do? At least I am no longer in danger of being hanged if I deal with him the way I want to."

Harry leaned closer to Ferghal to speak more quietly. "The Barclay who bullied me on *Spartan* was of the Raholp Barclays and my senior in the Gunroom. This one is not. Do not intervene on my part, Ferghal. You may not be charged and hanged for it, but this is my trouble, not yours, unless he makes it so. I think we may find this new Barclay is as difficult as the old one. There is a resemblance, though I could not place it at first."

"So you think this Bar...." Feghal lowered his voice, which was always at a level best described as booming. "This Barclay is the great great — however many greats — grandson or nephew as the one on *Spartan*, and he's just as ill tempered? What are the odds?" He laughed so loud is resonated off the corridor walls, and Harry laughed him, their tension eased.

Harry quieted. "Yes, it seems this bit of bad luck has followed me here."

"Tread warily, Harry. If he is of the same mould, he will not rest until he has made trouble for you."

Joining them, Keiron caught the tail of this exchange. "If it's Barclay you're talking about, you're right. Take care, that family have money and political clout — enough to get a lot of his antics forgiven or overlooked, if you follow my meaning." When they were at the dining hall entrance, he said, "I'm off the leash now, and it's dinnertime. Follow me to the trough! You've the rest of the class to meet."

Chapter 3 – The Yotties

Harry inhaled the savoury aroma of food. "It smells a great deal better than the boiled salt beef or pork did on *Spartan*. I confess, though, my stomach sometimes craves simpler fare than the foods we now enjoy."

"Mine too." Ferghal's nervous gaze took in the large refectory with its cacophony of conversation and laughter. The tables were arranged in a diagonal pattern, each one sporting an emblem identifying a class. "But I would not thank anyone for returning me to the rancid stuff from the casks after three years in the hold and God knows how long before that in a warehouse. And I would not wish to be deprived of such delights as the ice cream and other sweetmeats we now have for our pleasure."

Harry laughed. "Aye, I hear you, but do you not miss the wine and the rum?"

"Aye, there is that." Ferghal nodded, a grin flickering.

Keiron looked surprised. "You guys drank rum and beer? But you must have been underage!"

"We did not drink the water unless it was boiled for tea or mixed with rum. It was pretty foul after weeks in a cask, and drinking it meant days spent doubled over in the head — not a pleasant experience!" His sense of humour prompting him, Harry added, "And there were things living in it sometimes."

Catching his friend's lead, Ferghal said, "Aye, and I do not miss the stench of bilges or the slop bucket."

Harry nodded. "And we no longer have to endure the smell of the commode while we dine." Catching Keiron's horrified expression, he laughed. "The nose soon adjusted."

Keiron led them to a table occupied by a number of midshipmen and cadets, and they took their seats. "These are some of our fellow sufferers." To everyone at the table, he added, "Our latest additions, Ferghal O'Connor and Harry Heron."

"You're joking," said the midshipman next to Keiron. "Not *the* Heron and O'Connor?"

"I'm sorry?" Harry frowned, feigning mock puzzlement. "Which Heron and O'Connor should we be?" He smiled to set them at ease.

This raised a laugh from the others, and Keiron intervened. "I think what Howard means is are you the infamous Heron and O'Connor from the *Vanguard* and the Pangaea battle?"

Harry reddened. "The very same."

"Wow! I heard you guys had a bad time of it when you were taken prisoner and sent to that underground lab run by the Johnstone Group," said a very neat young woman. "How did you escape? We heard you caused absolute havoc at the facility."

"Yeah, tell us the gory details." Howard grinned. "Which one of you carved up the villager with this thing you call a cutlass?"

Everyone laughed, and Harry and Ferghal reddened in embarrassment at this barrage of questions. They tried to make light of their part in it, mindful that the pending trials of the Consortium prisoners could be compromised if they said too much. Harry was relieved when Ferghal intervened.

"Well, he asked for it. He tried to use his plasma pistol, so I stopped him."

"But how did you fellows get out?" demanded a youth named Senzile, who spoke with a lilting African accent. "We heard that you were pretty deep underground in holding cells."

"Our friend Danny got into the ventilation ducts. He is much younger and smaller than we are. Johnstone's AI network had gone a bit mad, so we really just walked out. Sub-Lieutenant Trelawney led us out and down the hill, and you've probably heard the rest."

Wanting to divert their attention, Harry indicated the model of a small and rather neat looking ship with the name HMY *Britannia* emblazoned on its base affixed to the table. "What ship is this? She is patently not the old First Rater we knew, nor is she a ship of the Fleet."

"That's the old Royal Yacht," replied Keiron. "She was famous in the latter half of the twentieth century. She's still preserved at Leith in Scotland, and that's a pretty good model of her." Eyeing Harry thoughtfully, he explained, "It's why we're called The Yotties by everyone else here." He paused, his mind still on the previous tack of their conversation. "We heard that you were tortured. Is that true?"

A bit surprised at the sudden shift in topic, Harry hesitated before replying. "Yes . . . that's true." He gave Keiron a brief smile. "I'd rather not talk about it if you have no objection."

"Fair enough." Keiron winced as the young woman dug an elbow into his ribs. "I'm sorry to be so nosey." He grimaced as she jabbed him in the ribs again. "Bad, was it?"

"You don't know when to stop, do you," she said to Keiron. "Ignore him, Harry. I'm Elize, by the way, and I have the cabin next to Ferghal's. I was on the flagship when you guys set off that blast in hyperspace. It freaked out the comms and the engineering people, and weapons went right off the board. What did it look like from your end?"

"Like a small sun," replied Harry, a forkful of food halfway to his mouth. He remembered all too well the terrible beauty of the night sky filled with brief bright stars as ships and men died in the battle over their heads. It was not a sight he was likely to forget. "It flared into existence and winked out again moments later. We saw it from the cutter as we sailed to Pangaea City." He smiled to hide his very real sense of horror at the destruction that had been wrought. "I'm afraid we were rather distant spectators to most of it."

Keiron interjected. "We heard about this boat you chaps used to escape the island. Must have taken a fair bit of work to convert a cargo hulk into an ocean-going sailing ship." His face lit up in a huge grin. "Hey, I've just realised — with you fellows in charge of our sloop, we have a chance of winning the Class Cup in the Regatta this year."

The amusing and lively chatter continued through dinner and into the evening. In the course of it, Harry told his new friends about their adventures under sail and the escape from New Caledonia. Ferghal imparted some of the details Harry skipped, and the group formed the beginnings of a plan for tackling the inter-class competitive events.

Toward the end of the evening they witnessed a small disturbance at an adjoining table. Harry looked across to see Barclay browbeating a smaller midshipman.

"Typical," said Elize, her expression one of utter disgust. "How he's managed to stay in the service this long, none of us can understand. He must know somebody important."

"Or he must be related to someone important," Keiron countered. "If he keeps pushing his luck like that, he won't be here much longer no matter who his daddy is." He turned to Harry. "I saw you facing him down in the cabin flat. What was that about?"

Before Harry could reply, Ferghal interjected. "We met Mr Barclay outside the entrance today. Lieutenant Haäkinen warned us not to follow his example, and the Master Warrant at the desk said we should mind how we deal with Barclay, didn't he, Master Ha . . . Harry." Outwardly calm, Ferghal's anxiety at fitting into his new station in life betrayed him into using his childhood form of address toward Harry.

"That he did now." Harry smiled, and with his hand raised as if swearing an oath, he adopted a formal tone.

"I promise all present that I shall mind my step and my temper." Everyone chuckled, and the moment of tension passed.

Howard looked interested. "Hold on — are you chaps saying you've already managed to have a run-in with *the* Barclay?"

"We collided at the door, and I'm afraid my attaché case found a rather tender target when he attempted to strike me." Harry waited a beat for perfect timing. "He crumpled to the ground in quite a bit of pain, I might add."

Keiron and the boys grinned, and Elize tried unsuccessfully to stifle a giggle, which became infectious, and soon they were all doing their best to hold back their laughter with no success. The obvious display of mirth drew the attention of others in the dining hall. Some watched with grins on their faces, others with curiosity, and the perfectly behaved ones looked disgruntled because they weren't having nearly as much fun at their table.

"Oh, God!" gasped Keiron shaking with laughter. "No wonder he was spoiling for a fight. He'll hate you for that. Better watch your back. He does have some friends and cronies, and he's good at getting even. God, Harry, you and Ferghal are going to be a breath of fresh air."

Elize put her hand to her chin and pondered. "I wonder if he's suffered serious damage from your well-aimed attack?" She grinned and winked.

Laughing, the Yotties pushed back from the table and headed toward the door talking and bantering. Midshipman Barclay watched them depart, his eyes burning with plans for revenge.

HARRY SLEPT BADLY AND WOKE FROM A NIGHTMARE in which the Court of Enquiry had become a different sort of court presided over by a scowling figure in laboratory garb who handed down a ruling that his new status was cancelled, and he must be returned immediately to the laboratory. With this, and the still troubling memories of the indignities he'd suffered on Pangaea in mind, he was shocked to find, when he reported to the swimming pool with the others, that he was expected to engage in mixed swimming.

"We swim with the ladies?"

Ferghal leaned close and murmured, "And why are they wearing only their undergarments — not that I'm complaining." His face reddened so much it matched his hair. Their shocked incredulity amused their companions.

Elize spoke up. "Yes, shippers, this is how we do it in 2206. You'll get used to it. Besides, we're all covered — at least the important bits are!"

This reminded Keiron of something humorous. "I wonder if Barclay has recovered from meeting you? Do you think he's feeling better now?" He grinned, and they all laughed.

Seeing no alternative, Harry and Ferghal reluctantly changed into swimming trunks and joined the rest of the class poolside.

As the women joined them, Keiron practically snorted back laughter to smother his amusement at Harry's attempt to look anywhere but at their toned shapely figures so clearly defined in their swimsuits.

Elize took the initiative again. "Do you fellows swim? It's a good way to keep fit." She leaned closer to Harry. "Relax. You'll get used to this." She gave his arm a gentle nudge with her shoulder.

Before Harry could respond, they were interrupted by the arrival of the physical training instructor.

"Right, ladies, gentlemen, double to that end of the pool, please. Then I want four lengths, in your own time. At the double, now!"

Realising that Harry and Ferghal had not understood the order to mean run, Keiron said, "Double means we run!" and he took off for the far end with the two close behind.

Despite the fact that Harry and Ferghal had spent many months aboard a sailing ship, neither were strong swimmers. Harry was somewhat better in the water, having had more freedom to swim on the voyage through the South Sea and along the New South Wales coast, but Ferghal struggled, as he'd had less opportunity and practice due to the restriction of the discipline imposed on him as a member of the lower deck.

As such, Harry enjoyed swimming and found it stimulating, but he quickly discovered he lacked both technique and confidence. Ferghal was far less comfortable in the water than Harry, and struggled manfully toward the far end of the pool.

The instructor soon spotted their lack of ability and called them aside. "Now then, gentlemen — your swimming needs a bit of work, doesn't it?"

"Yes, Warrant," said Ferghal, embarrassed. He would rather engage in a race to rig a seventy-four-gun ship than disport himself in this way.

"No worries, gents," said the instructor, his accent completely foreign to the pair, although it had a familiar sound. "A bit of instruction, and we'll soon have you up to speed."

Midshipman Barclay chose that moment to pass by. "You'll have your work cut out then," he sneered, speaking to the instructor as if they were of equal rank. "Fossils don't float, and they don't learn much either."

Harry felt his face flush as his temper flared. He despised the stupidity of these attempts to belittle him and Ferghal. In his view, the world was too often spoiled by those who sought to impose their will on others. Before he could respond, the instructor intervened.

"Thank you, Mr Barclay, I'm sure you've a need for another two lengths. As fast as you like, please." Watching the scowling midshipman depart, he added under his breath, "Drongo!" He turned back to Harry and Ferghal. "Now, Mr Heron, you need to work on developing your stroke. Some exercises will do it. Mr O'Connor, we need to work you up to a proper swimming stroke. Report to me here after class this afternoon and we'll draw up a programme. For now, let's just get you a bit more confident in the water."

Unnoticed, a lithe Saurian figure watched as Barclay walked away scowling. Unbeknownst to him and to everyone else at the College not directly connected to Security, the Lacertians had inserted several of their people into the grounds to guard the two young men they knew as the Navigator and the Sword Wielder — Harry and Ferghal. Their ability to blend into the background made them difficult to see, and their speed and phenomenal ability to cling to vertical surfaces gave them an advantage where their presence was unsuspected.

Sci'genza watched the retreating figure with predatory focus, assessing him. The Navigator had already shown himself capable of dealing with that one, but there were others here he would not find so easy to escape. She reported her thoughts to her superiors.

Chapter 4 – Lacertian Cadets

"Eon, there's a new development. A complication. Our plans have to change." The older Barclay paused, the uncertainty in his face plain in his holographic image.

"I knew it," Eon spat. "It's alright for you and Uncle. You don't have to deal with all the bull crap discipline here, and being nice to a bunch of nobodies just because they're wearing rank!" His scowl deepened. "You want complications? I'll give you one. There's a rumour that some of those lizard slaves are lurking around the College, and more are coming as cadets."

"That's what I was calling about." His father passed a hand over his face. "Damn it, Eon, pull yourself together. The Lacertians aren't slaves. It was a massive mistake under the previous board to use them that way. And now they've a mutual aid and development treaty with the WTO, the North American Union and the Confederacy. They're sending a party of cadets who will train with you."

"Like hell they are! I don't want any of those damned snakeheads near me." Eon drew a deep breath. "Not after what happened to Liam at the Johnstone facility."

"Liam's death was unfortunate. Now put it behind you. We have far more important matters to deal with. Your Uncle Sean wants to know the timing of the training cruise you'll be sent on.

There is a great deal he needs to prepare." His father's bitter expression showed. "That, surely, is not too much to ask of you."

"Easy for you to say. You don't have to share a classroom and the accommodation flat with the man responsible for Liam's death or with these snakeheads."

Losing patience, the older Barclay snapped. "There are much bigger things in play here than you imagine. Now do as you're damn well told. And don't do anything stupid that could get you thrown out of the Fleet either. Your uncle's counting on you being where he needs you for now. Don't screw up. You know what Uncle Sean is like when someone does."

Eon knew what his father meant. Reluctantly, he backed down. "Okay, okay, I'll do it, but if those snakeheads—"

"We'll worry about them. Just keep your nose clean and do what you've been tasked with. If everything goes to plan, it'll all be sorted out in a few months."

THE ARRIVAL OF SIX LACERTIAN CADETS AT THE COLLEGE caused something of a stir. Saurian but human in physiognomy, they were deceptively slight in build and very reptilian in appearance. They possessed the ability to camouflage their bodies in a manner that allowed them to vanish in plain sight, an ability Harry and Ferghal's protectors used to considerable advantage.

"They've been placed with us Yotties," Keiron told his companions, "and accommodated on our flat. Eon isn't pleased. I hear he's protested about having to put up with seeing them." Laughing, he added, "Got a right bollocking from the Commander.

Elize grimaced. "He needs an attitude adjustment. Trouble is, short of a brain transplant, I doubt you could give him one."

"So when do we get to meet our new classmates?" asked Howie.

"This evening, probably. They're on a crash orientation for the rest of the day." Senzile paused. "You know, I'm sure I've seen more of them around the College. At first I thought I was seeing things. A bit creepy really."

Looking up from the letter he was reading, Harry said, "There are others here. I see Sci'genza regularly. She's always around when we're on any training exercise." The others looked at him like he was out of his mind. "You haven't seen them?" he asked, surprised. When he was met with blank stares, he admitted, "They are pretty good at not being seen when they don't want to be."

Elize glanced furtively around the lounge. "Are any of them here now?"

Ferghal smiled. "Right behind you, Elize. Hello, Sci'genza. Are you sailing with us tomorrow?"

The others gasped in amazement as the Saurian moved into view, the realisation that she'd been in their midst startling them. She made the Lacertian gesture of greeting. "I salute you, friends of the Sword Wielder and the Navigator. The newcomers would be better suited to your vessel, Navigator. I will remain ashore."

THE SAILING VESSELS ALLOCATED TO THOSE INTERESTED in developing skills in this field were unlike anything Harry or Ferghal had encountered before. Broad-beamed monohulls with a single mast, the boats were quite shallow in depth between deck and bilge, and fitted with foils on which they rode above the water and achieved undreamed of speeds under suitable wind conditions.

"The boat can be sailed in displacement mode, of course," the sailing instructor told them. "But if you're racing, your best speeds are achieved riding the foils."

Taking notes, Harry studied the hull form and the foils, noting the twin bilge keels and the manner the yacht rode in the water.

"These are the boats used for the Class Cup races, sir?"

"Correct, Mr Heron. I believe you hold a Yacht Master's ticket?"

"Aye, sir. Gained in a displacement hull though. I should like to explore these craft if opportunity serves." Hesitating, he indicated the foils. "I should think a touch different to what I have sailed to date — and faster."

"Faster, certainly." The Lieutenant laughed. "From a handling perspective, not too different. You'll soon get the hang of it."

Harry did, even surprising himself. The rig and sail plan was efficient and relatively simple to manage, though he found it irritating that a network managed the sails for him, something he could have done quite well on his own. When he had the feel of the boat, he soon showed his mastery of this new skill.

"Whew," Keiron remarked as they secured the boat after returning from a sail. "I don't think I've seen anyone turn off the SailComp before. It got exciting there for a bit."

"The SailComp wanted to reduce sail all the time. The boat could carry the extra sail." Harry paused. "This may go against what you know, but I hope you can see that I am correct in this assessment."

Keiron and the others nodded. Without a doubt, whatever Harry and Ferghal demanded of the boat, it complied readily, right down to their having sailed it straight onto the pontoon mooring.

Elize laughed. "Okay, you were right, Captain!" She sketched a salute. "I'll admit I didn't know these boats could do some of these things, and the rush I got from the speed we logged on that reach just now . . . whew, that was exciting!"

"Our slave-driving Captain apart, I'm enjoying this more than anything else here," quipped Senzile. Clapping Ferghal on the back, he added, "Was he always like this?"

Ferghal laughed. "Worse! A real tyrant, our Captain Heron. Wait until he whips us into a crew. It'll be flogging round the fleet afore he's finished."

His cheeks burning, Harry joined in the laughter out of embarrassment more than humour. Senzile's home was in the part of Africa that Harry had known as the Slave Coast in the 1800s, and the remark about slave driving touched a nerve, as he would never do such a thing. Perhaps, he thought, he had been a trifle too demanding of his crew, several of whom had not sailed before this.

"Midshipman Heron, report to Lieutenant Haäkinen." The pipe interrupted a rare stand easy.

"Your sins about to catch up with you, Harry?" Senzile gave Harry a friendly nudge as he stood to respond.

With a grimace, Harry nodded. "I've been expecting this. The enquiry is at last taking place, and I am summoned."

"The enquiry? Oh, you mean the one about the problem that brought you here. Ferghal was telling us about it."

"Yes. I can't think why they want us to attend, unless as some sort of specimens — not a role I am happy to accept." With a frown, Harry made for the door.

"I should think not. Good luck with the Lieutenant."

"THE ENQUIRY IS SCHEDULED FOR NEXT MONTH, MR HERON. I have orders for you and Mr O'Connor to be available as witnesses. You'll be collected and taken to the location the day before you are required to testify."

"Thank you, sir." Harry hesitated. "I do not understand what we may add to any enquiry into the malfunction of a device we had no knowledge of at the time, so why would they wish to hear from us?"

"The enquiry has a broader remit. The malfunction of the Indian Ocean Transit Gate is a part of it, but the larger matter is what was discovered on Pangaea." The Lieutenant tapped his tablet. "There is, as you know, what amounts to a civil war between the jurisdictions the Fleet serves and the group known as the Consortium. Certain of our political representatives and a lot of bureaucrats are doing everything they can to label the Pangaea situation an anomaly and to block any further investigation. What you and Ferghal uncovered in your escape could be vital in getting to the truth of it all."

"I see, sir." He didn't relish the prospect of having to speak about his time in the laboratory. "Have I any choice?"

"Afraid not, Harry." Aware of the midshipman's reluctance, he added, "If it's any comfort, Commodore Heron and his sister will be here to accompany you and O'Connor. They will stay with you until you return to College — hopefully only a couple of days away, or you'll miss a lot of tuition."

"EON, WE NEED YOU TO ATTACH THOSE TRACERS to Heron or O'Connor, preferably both. We don't want either of them to reach the enquiry and give their account of events on Pangaea. Make sure you plant the trace. A special team will deal with it from there."

"It's not that easy, Uncle," Eon whined. "I've tried several times, but he's never alone."

"Damn it, Eon, it's a simple thing to do! They're small enough, damn it. Hide it in something he always has on him if you can't get it into contact with his skin. Get one of your friends to do it if you can't." The older man in the hologram leaned back, his flushed face truculent. "Find a way. Those two must not reach the enquiry. Is that clear?" The hologram vanished.

Furtively, Eon stowed his unregistered comlink, checked to make sure he was unobserved, and left his place of concealment. "I'll get Miles or Laschelles to do it," he muttered to himself.

Sauntering between the neatly trimmed hedges leading to the boating facility, he failed to notice the shadowy figures drifting along the hedge behind him. There was nothing magical about the Lacertian ability to be unseen. Their scales refracted light when they adjusted them, and their skin tone changed to match a background in much the same manner as an earthbound chameleon.

Eon turned his head suddenly, sensing that he was being watched and followed. He stared at the hedges and could see nothing, though on the edge of his vision, something didn't appear right. He walked on, failing to notice the shadow that didn't match those cast by the hedges.

Behind him, the Lacertian appeared briefly as she changed position, vanishing and blending with the hedge on the other side of the path.

Wrapped in his thoughts, Eon hurried on. He smiled as an idea formed in his mind. Changing direction, he sought out his cronies.

DESPITE THE EXTRA COACHING THEY RECEIVED IN THE ART of swimming, Ferghal still floundered, and Harry hadn't quite got a smooth rhythm. The morning swimming sessions were not among their favourite activities, but they persisted doggedly.

Harry had completed one slow length when he became aware of someone swimming close beside him, in fact crowding him as he stayed in his lane. Alert for some mischief, he was taken slightly unaware when the swimmer gripped his leg, pulled him back and made a stabbing movement toward his groin. Rolling swiftly aside and breaking free, he avoided most of the contact but swallowed a large amount of water. The other swimmer dove underwater and darted away as Harry swiped water from his eyes and coughed to clear his lungs. Furious, he looked round to see who it was, and saw Barclay laughing at the other side of the pool.

A disturbance in the water ten yards away drew everyone's attention. A swimmer seemed to be struggling and appeared injured. The smile died on Barclay's face when Ferghal emerged from the surface spluttering with fury, treading water and barely keeping his head above water. Their Lacertian guardian ripped through the water and hoisted Ferghal onto the poolside before Harry could reach him.

Coughing and retching water, Ferghal struggled to recover his breath. Clearly very angry, he protested as he moved into a sitting position. The other swimmer seemed to be in even more serious trouble. Another member of Harry's class swam to assist the second man, bringing him to the side of the pool with some difficulty.

"You humans have a strange sense of humour, Navigator. Do you wish me to assist the Sword Wielder's attacker?"

As the swimming instructor helped Miles out of the pool, Harry noticed, not without a little satisfaction, that his friend's attacker seemed to be having difficulty breathing. Retching water and bile, he looked very sick indeed.

Climbing out of the pool and kneeling to check on Ferghal, Harry asked, "What did you do to him?"

Before Ferghal could reply, the instructor joined them. "Mr Heron, Mr O'Connor, stay here. Mr Galika, get Mr Miles to the first aid station." He looked across the pool. "Mr Barclay, a word with you, please." His tone made clear this was not a request.

Watching this interchange with interest, Harry looked at Ferghal. "What did he try?" he said in a quiet voice.

"He came up close and struck me betwixt the legs, then he tried to hold me underwater."

"How did you respond?" asked Harry. He could feel his temper rising.

"The same trick Colour Sergeant Nelson taught me on *Vanguard*, the point of my hand under his ribs," replied Ferghal, making an upward stabbing motion with his open hand, palm up, fingers rigid.

The instructor returned to where they waited, his expression serious. "Now then, gentlemen, I will have to report this to your Divisional Officer. I saw what happened, so neither of you can be blamed for starting this, but you may have done Mr Miles rather more damage than we think, Mr O'Connor. Get dressed and carry on to breakfast, and don't let Mr Barclay or any of his friends provoke you into anything more. Clear?"

"Aye, aye, Warrant," growled Ferghal. He had struck out in self-defence to prevent what he was convinced was an attempt to drown him, and he felt aggrieved and a little resentful at the warning.

"Very good, Warrant," echoed Harry, idly rubbing a sting on his leg. He worried that his friend might be in trouble, and a meeting with Barclay would likely end with one of them hurt. He hated this sort of underhand dealing. As the son of a gentleman, he had been taught from the cradle that no gentleman ever behaved in a dishonourable manner, and to Harry, the actions of Barclay and his friends were beyond the bounds of honourable behaviour. His fury drove from his mind the question of why they had both been attacked while in the water. His instinct was to seek a showdown, to call Barclay out and demand satisfaction, but he knew that was no longer considered acceptable, and he found that very frustrating.

The instructor interrupted Harry's thoughts. "Mr Heron, I saw who tried to pull that stunt on you." He considered Harry's expression, and knew what that look of smouldering rage meant. "If you saw him too, let me advise you to stay away from him. It's a matter for the Commander, not for you."

Chapter 5 – Ingenuity

Eon Barclay confronted his crony. ""Did you plant the trace? The survival exercise is the perfect time to deal with them."

"I think so. Are you sure the thing will embed itself in his skin?"

"Yeah, if you did it as I showed you. He'll think it's an insect bite." Barclay looked round. "What happened to Miles? It looked like he tried to get creative. Did he plant the trace?"

"Not sure, but O'Connor jabbed him with his fingers just below the ribs. The medic thinks his spleen might have ruptured if the water hadn't softened the strike." Midshipman Laschelles scowled. "O'Connor's bloody fast and strong. Don got lucky, and before you say it, no, I'm not going to take him on in the fencing. Heron I can cope with. O'Connor has no finesse, and he just doesn't understand the concept of giving up unless he's disarmed or wounded, and you don't get a chance when he comes at you like a bloody madman."

Barclay nodded. He'd already learned this the hard way in the unarmed combat exercises. He still had the bruises to show for it. It wasn't so much the throw that Ferghal achieved, though that had been bad enough, but the follow through. He'd had to sit out the rest of the session recovering from it. Ferghal had been cautioned to remember he was in training and not supposed to kill his partner.

Laschelles hesitated. "You didn't tell me those Lacertians were friends of his. One of them almost got me after I planted the trace."

Barclay shrugged. "But he didn't get you, and the trace is planted, so it doesn't matter."

"I still don't see what you wanted them tagged for." Laschelles eyed Barclay warily.

"None of your never mind. My uncle's got people who will deal with those two from now on. They won't be testifying at any enquiry, and we'll be rid of them. Bloody fossils. Belong in a museum."

Laschelles held his tongue. He didn't know what had set Eon against Heron, and he didn't care to ask. Eon's family connections were powerful people, and his own family had links to the firms the Barclay family controlled. It paid to keep them sweet. His record with the Fleet wasn't good enough to ensure his success. Barclay's connections might be essential to his future.

THE FRENETIC PACE OF THE FIRST WEEKS SET THE PATTERN for the rest of the course. The class settled into the routine and formed the friendships and study groups that provided the peer support they needed. Harry and Ferghal struggled at first, especially in the classroom. In part it was the technology, but a larger part was the distraction of the AI link. Harry soon realised it was better to use the blocking device and take copious notes, which he then sorted out in the quiet of his cabin during his free time.

But where they really set themselves apart was in the practical exercises. Their early training at sea gave them an advantage over their peers.

"How do you fellows manage to do this so easily," gasped Keiron after a gruelling session on the obstacle course set with climbing nets, crawl ditches, tunnels, crossing spaces on lines and bridges, and scrambling up angled slopes and walls. "You seem to go up those scrambling nets and across those rope bridges as if you have an extra pair of hands and feet each."

Ferghal laughed. "If you had been chased around the rigging of a man o' war by a boatswain's mate with a starter, you'd soon learn to do it our way."

"I hate that single line crawl," groaned Elize. "And you went along it hand over hand," she protested to Harry. "Weren't you afraid of falling?"

"No . . . why should I be?" Harry was genuinely puzzled by the question. His mind flashed back to the voyage across the Great Southern Ocean in HMS *Spartan,* with the life and death struggles in the rigging as they fought the sails, the gales and the dizzying spiralling of the masts. They had lost two midshipmen and several hands to the storms. The old saying of "one hand for the ship and the other for yourself" came to mind. Suddenly it dawned on him that none of his companions had ever experienced anything like that. He softened his reply with a grin. "At most I would have fallen about ten feet. As Ferghal said, our experience clambering around the rigging in a seventy-four gave us confidence for this kind of exercise. But you excel at tasks which we have not the skill for."

This theme was picked up again when it came to combat training, as neither of the pair fully understood the concept of "going through the motions" in any form of combat. To their way of thinking, close combat was life or death — an attitude stamped upon them in their early days at sea where death had many forms, and no quarter could be expected in the heat of any battle.

"Ouch," groaned Howie, picking himself up after being thrown over Ferghal's hip in a classic wrestling move. "Do you always play for keeps like that?"

"Sorry," Ferghal said, and he winced when he heard the yelp of pain from a class member whom Harry had just disarmed, but he couldn't help grinning when the instructor hurried over to assess the damage. "It comes hard to remember that this is a sport. In our day, if you were this close to an enemy, it was life or death."

"Well, I'm damned glad you aren't waving a weapon around," grumbled Howie. "You fellows are pretty near lethal without any. I'm black and blue after that."

Harry knelt next to his fallen adversary and surveyed the damage. "I'm sorry, Haslar, but I appear to have dislocated your shoulder. Don't move. I will summon the warrant officer and ask for a medic to attend you." He stood then hesitated. "I really am most sorry. I do not seem to be able to adopt this way of not completing a throw."

"Damn it, Harry," gritted the other as the medic arrived. "Knowing you're sorry doesn't make my shoulder hurt any less. That wasn't a recognised hold and throw. I suppose I should be grateful you were only trying to disarm me."

"It's not a bad dislocation, sir," said the medic. "I'll ease it back into place then take you to the medical centre to be checked just to make sure." Turning to Harry, he inquired, "Mr Heron, isn't it? Hold your colleague steady for me while I manipulate his shoulder, please — thank you, sir." A gasp escaped Haslar Grundon when his shoulder popped back into place.

"Mr Heron, Mr O'Connor," called the Master Warrant Officer. Harry and Ferghal stood at attention before him. "Gentlemen, your methods are very unconventional, and at this rate, you'll have eliminated most of the class before we are finished. I'm moving you into a coaching role so you can teach some of your classmates a bit of your aggression — controlled aggression, I might remind you, so don't kill anyone. This is about learning to defend yourselves, not eliminating the opposition to gain promotion. Got it?"

"Aye, aye, Master," they chorused, abashed.

Harry muttered, "All these rules! If I am not to fight to win, what is the point of fighting? I may as well surrender and save us both the effort."

This remark got him another telling off from the instructor.

In fairness, it was not all one sided. Both had at different times been bested by others in the class, usually when they acted in overconfidence, and both had learned some hard lessons in the process.

Ferghal confided to Harry. "Just when it seems I have begun to understand the way things are done here, I find I have not understood something as I should."

"I too," agreed Harry, rubbing a bruise on his arm. "I cannot bring myself to attack a woman no matter how frequently I am told they are the same as us and perhaps more deadly. I simply cannot strike a woman." In this he was stating nothing less than the truth. Harry had real difficulty with the concept of launching what he considered an assault upon a lady. It was foreign to his notion of honourable behaviour, something no gentleman would ever do. And he paid for it in bruises sustained in the unarmed combat sessions, the most recent of which he had received from Elize.

"Aye," agreed Ferghal. "It goes against all we were taught. My Da' would take the whip to me if I laid a hand on any woman in anger."

Ferghal fell silent as his mind drifted to a rather shapely young woman named Siobhan Stevenson who had captured his interest. As smart as she was beautiful, she was specialising in environmental engineering. He flirted shamelessly with all the female cadets, at first to their surprise and then their amusement, but Siobhan was unique enough to quell his interest in others, for the time being.

When he introduced her to Harry, Ferghal said teasingly, "Siobhan is wanting to know about the climate in our times."

Catching his friend's mood, Harry grinned and said, "You mean the lady is interested in the way the land was ever boggy, and the ice froze on the roads, and when it melted, we slogged through filth and mud, and the women's skirts were ever tinged with dirt at the hem?" He grinned. "Ah, the joys of our old Emerald Isle — the grass was always green because it never stopped raining."

"Get away, the pair of you!" She laughed. "I'm Siobhan Stevenson," she said, extending her hand to shake Harry's. "Ferghal keeps telling me about the beauty of County Down. I would love to see it one day," she added with a wink to Ferghal.

"We can certainly make that happen!" Ferghal said with his usual boisterous enthusiasm, and they all shared a laugh.

Chapter 6 – Frustrated Attempt

Harry and Ferghal enjoyed the survival exercise. Their knowledge and skills — much of it gained in landscapes and conditions almost identical to the terrain chosen by the instructors — made it even easier. Looking at the latest offering of gulls' eggs, mushrooms, small fish, berries and dandelion leaves, Elize commented, "How do you guys know about this stuff? I've never seen anyone catch fish like that."

"It's practically a feast compared to what the others found," exclaimed Keiron. "I heard some of the Dreadnoughts complaining that we must've had food caches hidden."

Senzile laughed. "We're being shadowed by a couple of instructors checking we haven't got supplies and a replicator."

"Good luck to them. Here we go — a feast fit for the High King at Tara." Ferghal removed the fish from its wrapping of leaves after taking it off the small and almost smokeless campfire that Harry had built using pieces of dead wood, some moss he'd cut from a bank that burned with a bluish flame, and wood shavings.

The four midshipmen accepted the portions Harry passed round. "As soon as I've eaten, I'll relieve the sentries," Keiron declared. "I can hear their stomachs complaining from here."

Elize laughed. "All I can say is I've learned more about survival in the last twenty-four hours than in all the lectures we had in preparation." Wiping her hands on the grass and rinsing them in the stream a few yards off, she said, "Come on, Keiron, time to let the others get some food."

FROM COVER NEARBY, OTHER EYES WATCHED THE GROUP. "Heron is the one on the right. O'Connor is the heavy built redhead to the left of the woman next to the fire. Use the tranq darts as soon as those two are out of sight."

"Clear, Leader One." The speaker breathed in the aroma of roasted fish. "That smells damned good. Never had rations like that on my courses."

"Don't think they get them on these either. Those two are pretty good at foraging. I have no idea how they caught those fish without any equipment."

The leader slid deeper into cover. "Kat, Sonja, Mick — we'll take out the main group and grab the two we want." He pulled out a tablet that displayed a map. "They've got two sentries, one here and the other in this direction. Work round and neutralise them. We'll take this lot down as soon as you confirm you've tranqed the sentries."

"You're the boss." One of the team eased carefully into a better position as the first three slipped away, their camouflage uniforms blending with the vegetation. "I don't get why we have to take them alive — we could just waste them and be done with it. If they're dead, they can't testify."

"True, but we've been told to take them alive and deliver them to the client." The leader smirked. "And that's why we're being paid a premium."

"I'm not complaining — there's seven of us against a bunch of youngsters. Piece of cake."

The four stalkers moved closer to the group round the small fire. The leader positioned himself and prepared the tranquilliser projector he carried. His team were all professionals, one-time Special Forces from various nations, ruthlessly efficient. He checked his map display. The trace devices showed Harry and Ferghal exactly where he could see them. He smiled when he saw Harry scratch his leg absentmindedly. *Soon that "bug bite" will be the least of your problems, kid.*

"Sentries down." The voice in his earpiece was calm. "All clear."

He keyed his link. "Go."

HARRY FELT THE STING IN HIS SHOULDER, and his instinctive reaction to brush off whatever had stung him ended in a limp arm swing as he slumped to the ground unconscious. Elize collapsed across him as Senzile fell, spilling his freshly served food. The fourth member of the team fell against Ferghal, taking the dart aimed at him. As she knocked him off balance, he fell, but being the only member of the team still conscious, he was also the only witness to the arrival of four Lacertians.

"Stay down, Sword Wielder," said one of them. "Do not move."

As suddenly as they appeared, the Lacertians faded into the landscape.

Ferghal heard a plasma discharge followed by a brief cry of pain. "What t' divil?" His eyes darted across the visible landscape from his prone position.

"Abort! Abort!" the leader of the stalking team ordered into his link. Cursing, he wriggled backward then used his infrared goggles to spot any concealed Lacertians. Quickly he shed his Special Forces camouflage gear revealing the outfit of an instructor, and slipped on an armband proclaiming him to be an exercise director. "Damn, damn, damn," he muttered. Where the hell had the Lacertians come from? They weren't the cadet group obviously. He'd taken care to make sure they were in a different area entirely.

Two more instructors joined him. "What the hell went wrong? asked one of them.

"Damned if I know." A stealthy movement caught his eye, and a Lacertian stood before him.

"We have summoned the medics, Commander." The Lacertian made the gesture of salute their people used, but its eyes bored into him. "And your defenders of law. Two of the attackers are dead, another survived, and another escaped."

The leader maintained an air of nonchalance. "Lieutenant Alberts, go and check." He looked up as a Medivac skimmer passed over them and settled close to where Harry's party had camped. Moments later, a second and then a third arrived escorted by two troop carriers that discharged their Marines as they settled. The Marine Captain saluted. "Commander, we've a report some of the students were attacked. Apparently an attempt to kill them."

"What?" The leader hoped his genuine alarm would be read as concern for the students. "We were just checking on the teams now. The Britannias were our next check. Where are they?" He glanced up as Lieutenant Alberts returned looking sick.

"What's happened to them?" the leader demanded.

"One of the students is dead — took two of the tranq darts, at least that's what the medics think. And three more dead — look like special ops of some kind. One of them died just before the medics got here." He gestured as if checking his pockets for something. "Pity. Might have told the Red Caps something."

A Royal Marine major arrived with two Warrant Officers in tow. "Seems someone was trying to take out Heron and O'Connor. We've sent out a recall to all student teams and instructors. The exercise is terminated, and this entire area is under quarantine. The forensics team is on its way." He held the Lieutenant Commander's eye. "The three attackers the Lacertians took down are all instructing staff."

"What?" The Lieutenant Commander feigned surprise. "You're sure?"

The major's gaze didn't waver. "Yes, so as a routine precaution we'll need to know the exact position of everyone on this exercise in the last twelve hours."

HARRY RECOVERED CONSCIOUSNESS IN A MED-UNIT. His eyes focussed on the face of the MedTech next to the bed. "Where am I?"

"Easy, Mr Heron. You took a tranq dart. Lucky they got you back here pronto and got a counter dose into you.

"Tranq dart?"

"Yes." A Surgeon Lieutenant joined them. "They obviously meant you to be out of it for a long time — the dose would have knocked down an ox." He checked the monitors. "Did you see who put the dart into you?"

Harry's mind was fuzzy, and then he remembered. "I thought it was an insect sting, sir."

The Lieutenant finished his checks. "Yes, that's the whole idea They make those darts so tiny that you think nothing of them, but you should be feeling fine now. Your system is clear of the drug — the fastest I've ever seen that happen. Typically, a man of your size and build would have traces in your system for several hours yet, but you're all clear ... amazing."

Sitting up, Harry glanced round at the other members of his team, all of them semi-conscious. "There were eight of us. Six of us are here. Where are Ferghal and Selina?"

"Midshipman Schaaber took two darts, one probably intended for Mr O'Connor." The Lieutenant paused. "The overdose killed her. The Investigation Branch are treating it as a homicide. Cadet O'Connor is supplying them with details. He is the only surviving eyewitness."

LIEUTENANT COMMANDER ARI VALLANCE DID HIS UTMOST not to show his concern at the presence on the College of the special investigators from the Security Investigation Branch, dubbed Crushers with some justification.

"So the College has been placed on Security Code Red," he said with an air of casual interest. "An overreaction, surely."

The Head of School thrust his hands behind his back. "Command and the Director don't think so. The three killed by the Lacertians were all on the staff here, and the Crushers think there are more sleepers."

"Do they know who they're working for, sir?"

"The Consortium, apparently. Damned if I know what drives people to join that mob."

Ari Vallance shrugged. "Money. People will do just about anything to claim the bounty Johnstone Research is offering."

"Possible, I suppose. Damn. It disrupts everything."

More than you think, thought the Lieutenant Commander. The Head of School was a full Captain, but he preferred the life of an academic to that of "chasing about the universe," as he put it.

"How long will the alert last, sir?" Vallance asked.

"As long as the IBs take. We'll just have to run as normal an operation as possible until this is over."

"Quite right, sir. Will do."

Chapter 7 – Hornet's Nest

The Surgeon Lieutenant dropped the small sample container on the desk. "I found this embedded in Heron's calf. He thought he'd been bitten by something."
The security officer picked up the container and stared at the minuscule object inside it, a small amount of skin still attached to it. "A homing trace? How long did he walk around with this?"

The Lieutenant wrinkled his brow. "He said he first noticed it the day after the incident in the swimming pool. That was the day Cadet O'Connor put a midshipman in a med-unit when the fellow attempted to dunk him, most likely in an attempt to embed something like this in him too. Whoever did the same to Heron succeeded."

"Who tried to dunk him? Was it the same person who did this to Heron?"

"I didn't ask. O'Connor's waiting outside. He'll be able to tell you."

The investigator touched his link. "Bring in Mr O'Connor, please." To the Surgeon Lieutenant, he said, "I'm betting we'll find one of these on O'Connor." He placed the container in a clear plastic evidence bag. "I'd appreciate your retrieving it if he has, and I'll need a statement from you as to where this one was found and how it was recovered." He looked up as the door chimed. "Come in."

The door slid back and Ferghal saluted, glancing from the man in civilian dress to the Surgeon Lieutenant, unsure of the person to whom he must report. He played safe and addressed the Lieutenant. "You sent for me, sir?"

Glancing at the investigating officer, the Lieutenant nodded. "Yes. Actually, the Captain did."

A brief smile flashed across the investigator's face. "I don't always wear a uniform, Midshipman, so no worries. Sit down."

"Aye, aye, sir." Ferghal took the chair indicated. He was still angry at what had happened, and suspicious of everyone and everything as a result, but he kept a closed expression.

The investigator indicated the evidence container. "The Surgeon Lieutenant found a tracer on Midshipman Heron. I want to know if you have one. During the last three or four days, have you felt something like an insect sting? Has anyone attempted to touch you on the back, arm — anywhere?"

Ferghal frowned, thinking over the past few days. "Aye. In the swimming pool." He hesitated. "And on the wrestling mat. Both o' them regretted it." He broke into a grin.

The Surgeon Lieutenant looked at the investigator. "Midshipman Miles required treatment for severe bruising of the diaphragm and torn muscles in the upper abdomen. Midshipman Mustermann got a dislocated shoulder and concussion."

The investigator's face remained blank as he studied Ferghal's broad frame, the powerful musculature showing through the uniform jacket. Only his eyes showed his amusement. "I see. Where did they touch you? Have you noticed any irritation in the area?"

Ferghal's frown deepened. "Aye, sir. Just inside my thigh. Looks like a bite o' some sort."

The intelligence officer nodded. "Lieutenant, I'd appreciate your taking a look. If it's what I think it is, I want words with Miles and Mustermann."

"WE'VE GOT A PROBLEM, SIR," SAID THE MEDTECH. "They've found the tracers planted on Heron and O'Connor, and now they're trying to work out who planted them."

"Not our problem. The team that planted them don't know us and therefore can't expose us." Lieutenant Commander Vallance waited while the technician examined his eyes.

"That's a relief." The MedTech paused, checking his results. "Pity we lost some of ours. Where did those damned snakeheads come from? The place is crawling with them."

"Damned if I know, but I think they've been here a while. We should have been warned they were involved." Vallance wished he could communicate with his Consortium handler and have this out with him. "I'd have taken a very different approach if I'd known."

"Should have just killed the pair. This business of trying to take them alive is garbage." The technician packed up his equipment. "All due respect, sir, but if it's about making sure they can't testify, we should just kill them."

"I agree, but the top people want them alive — something to do with a gene splice they got." Pulling on his jacket, he prepared to leave. "So far we're not under suspicion. Keep your head down until this blows over. I'm expecting a visit in the next couple of days with new instructions. After that, we'll see."

"MR HERON, MR O'CONNOR, MY OFFICE PLEASE."

"Aye, aye, sir." Harry responded for them both, gathering his tablet and notebooks. He and Ferghal followed the Lieutenant, one of their instructors. Harry felt nervous at being summoned like this. The recent attempt to capture him and Ferghal had shaken them both, and the uncertainty surrounding who could be trusted was unsettling.

"Is there some problem, sir?"

"Nothing major, Mr Heron." The Lieutenant sat behind his desk. "Take a seat, gentlemen. There's been a change of plan. I'm to see you two off immediately to the enquiry. I've a transport waiting, and the security detail are in place."

"But we've nothing packed, sir. Have we five minutes to fetch our kit?"

"No, but you won't need anything. Everything will be provided for you. It's essential that no one knows you've left."

Something about this made Harry uneasy. Only an hour earlier he'd received very specific instructions concerning their transport to the enquiry site. "This is not in accordance with the written order we received an hour past, sir."

"I know." The Lieutenant pushed a tablet toward Harry. "These are the latest instructions. Check your orders tab. I expect it will have been updated as well. But don't delay, please. As you can see, my orders are labelled urgent." Pretending to study the tablet, Harry used his internal link to connect to the College network, and asked if there was a change of orders for himself or Ferghal.

"Negative, Harry," the AI responded.

"Any update on my existing orders to attend the enquiry?"

"No. I have received no change of orders concerning you."

The tablet in front of him seemed to have all the correct information, which he found interesting in light of what the AI just told him. "I had best check my orders again, sir," he said, returning the Lieutenant's tablet. "They were very explicit." He fished in his holdall and withdrew his own tablet, making a show of checking to buy some time. "I have no change at all, sir." He handed it to the Lieutenant. "As you can see, sir, the final paragraph is rather definite."

The Lieutenant studied it and nodded, his expression serious. "So it seems. What about you, Mr O' Connor? Any update?"

"No, sir. My orders are the same as Harr . . . as Mr Heron's, sir. We're to leave the College only under escort of a security team who carry the code to activate the clearance seal accompanying our orders, sir."

The Lieutenant frowned. "Stay here. I'll have to check this out Something's obviously gone adrift. You should have received this change of orders." Collecting his tablet, the Lieutenant hurried out shutting the door behind him.

"I like this not, Harry." Ferghal's face showed his suspicion.

"Nor I. The AI has no knowledge of orders for us beyond what we received this morning."

The door opened and two men burst in, weapons at the ready. Without a word, they fired, and Harry and Ferghal collapsed.

A MedTech entered, checked them both, and administered an injection into the neck. "That'll keep them quiet for the next few hours. Getting them off campus is going to be a bit of a trick though."

"We have that worked out." The Lieutenant was back with two large sail bags. "Wrap them in these and get them loaded. I'll bring the boat party round."

HARRY'S FAILURE TO KEEP AN APPOINTMENT FOR A TUTORIAL caused an alert to be raised a lot earlier than the abductors anticipated.

"Damn. Stow them in the cabin. We'll play this off the cuff." The Lieutenant glanced at his companions, all dressed as if for a sailing session. "Haul some of the gear on deck and set her up for sailing."

"Hope none of those damned snakeheads are in on the search, one of the team commented, a good-looking youth who'd discovered that fencing with Harry or Ferghal was not quite the pushover he'd thought it would be. He had mixed feelings about this opportunity to get his revenge for a humiliating defeat on the fencing piste that had dethroned him as the College champion. It was one thing to pull a stunt that would get Heron and O'Connor into trouble, but this was altogether more serious if they got caught.

"We've taken care of any Lacertians we could find. You can see them with infrared lenses if you adjust them properly, and we know where their cadets are." Laughing derisively, the Lieutenant added, "The group leader has them running after phantoms on the far side of the campus."

"So how are we getting these two out of here?"

"Not our problem. We get them up the lake and leave them for a second team. They'll get this pair off the campus and deliver them." The Lieutenant paused, watching the approach of a group of security branch operatives. "You know your roles. Stick to the script."

"They'll want to search."

"Let them. Just make sure those sails are piled over the bags." He stood as the security team approached. "What's up, Barry? Have we lost someone?"

HARRY CAME TO IN COMPLETE DARKNESS AND REALISED his wrists and ankles were bound. Tape covered his mouth, and he had a pounding headache. As he wriggled, he made contact with someone else in the same situation.

The now familiar sound as if someone were speaking softly in the background of his hearing told him an AI system was nearby. Listening carefully, he recognised it as the network that served the

Weapons School. Linking to it, he searched for an indication that Ferghal was also linked, and he found him.

"Ferghal, we must work ourselves free. Can you move?"

"Aye, though I am bound. Are you?"

"Aye. Can you release my hands? Or perhaps I release you?"

Ferghal wriggled into position, and Harry repositioned himself to meet his friend. Groping fingers explored each other's wrists.

"Damnation," said Harry. "They've not used a line. There is no knot."

They lay still.

"Where are we?" Ferghal asked.

"Somewhere in the Weapons School, I think, but not a frequented part if the silence is an indication." Harry focussed on a command to the AI. The lights came on but remained dim, exactly as he requested, and revealed a circular space occupied by a large generator unit, a host of shielded tubes and pipes, and the training ring of a heavy plasma projector.

Ferghal recognised it instantly. *"We're in one of the training turrets on the testing range."* Struggling round, he spotted what he wanted. *"There's the maintenance kit. If I can reach it—"*

"Someone comes! Feign unconsciousness. Perhaps we may find a means of escape." Too late, Harry remembered the light, which went out even as the door opened.

LEAVING THE SLOOP AT HER JETTY, THE TEAM GATHERED their gear. "They'll be collected by an outside team. Disperse to your usual posts." Picking up a sail bag, the leader smiled. "That went better than I expected."

One of the team nodded. "Easy money. They won't cause any problem for anyone once the Johnstone lot get them back."

The leader nodded. "Yeah. It's funny though — I think they have AI implants. O'Connor must have. Sometimes in class you can see he's adrift, then suddenly he's alert again."

"I know what you mean," said another of the team. "I heard they did something to the Johnstone AI on Pangaea — changed the program or something."

The leader glanced at the speaker. "You heard right, and that's one reason Johnstone is so keen to have them back. They did a gene splice on them, and it's affected them in a way they didn't expect. I heard Heron can talk to the AI, and I think O'Connor can too."

"That explains a lot." The speaker glanced at the others. "Bloody useful to be able to do it though. Do the collection squad know that?"

"Probably. Not our problem though. They should be on their way by now. Team One had the task of drawing off the Lacertians, and if they've done that successfully, the pair will be off site already." They stopped as armoured Marines stepped from cover.

"Remain absolutely still, Lieutenant, gentlemen. You are all under arrest. Any attempt to retrieve a weapon or to make any move we construe as hostile will result in your death." The security Captain paused. "Sergeant, secure them. Full search of their gear and full strip search once you have them in cells. I want them kept in isolation until I interrogate them."

The Sergeant secured the Lieutenant's wrists with handcuffs.

"You can't get away with this — sir."

"Can't I, Mr Crossley?" said the Captain. "I think you'll find I can. Espionage is not something we take lightly." His scornful gaze swept over the group, taking in the terror on the faces of the four midshipmen. "Yes, gentlemen, espionage. Minimum jail term is around twenty-five years, I believe. Sergeant, take them away."

Chapter 8 – Our Own Resources

Fighting to avoid the tranquilliser shot, Harry and Ferghal lashed out with their feet, and the smallness of the space worked to their advantage. No one escaped the thrusting and pounding of their boots. Even so, it was a very unequal struggle. Harry was the first to be overcome, but as the tranquilliser took effect, he managed to give firing commands to the turret weapon using his link to the AI.

The whine as it powered up and charged to full strength lent desperation to the abductors, and Ferghal, held down by three strong men, joined Harry in oblivion.

"Get them to the transport," said the leader. "We have to get out of here before anyone comes to check the reason this thing is powering up." The training mechanism engaged and the turret trained. "What the hell? I thought this thing was inoperative!"

"We better disable it. According to the power indicator, it's fully charged and armed."

"Impossible from here — no access to the AI or the targeting system. We don't know what it's targeting, and I don't want to be around when the bloody thing fires. There's a damned good reason there's no vegetation within a hundred yards of these installations."

The pair nearest the door lifted Ferghal and promptly dropped him as the projector in the turret fired pulse after pulse of incandescent plasma toward a target.

"Someone's shopped us," said the leader, swearing under his breath. "This damned operation has gone sour. Plan B. Get them in the ground transport before it gets caught in the heat flux this'll build."

By sheer chance, Harry's choice of target was the team's escape transport. As the drug had taken effect, he'd looked for something to aim the projector at to attract attention, and had chosen the one thing on the range that looked out of place. The sleek stealth craft was now rapidly becoming nothing but a ruin of incandescent molten metal, the remains of its crew already ash.

The all-terrain ground transport sped off with its cargo just ahead of the Weapons School team's arrival to shut down the malfunctioning turret. Meanwhile, the Consortium team were so focussed on reaching their back-up hideaway that they didn't notice when a passenger latched on.

The Lacertian had moved with the incredible speed of her race and attached herself precariously to the rear access of the ground transport. There wasn't much to grip, not even with her retractable claws, and she struggled to hold on as the transport hurtled from the firing range.

THE OPEN DOOR, THE TRACKS AROUND THE TURRET glacis and plinth, and the signs of a struggle alerted the Master Warrant Officer in charge.

"Command, we have a problem. Alert security — the abductors have been and left. They'll be on a ground transport." He laughed sourly. "Their aerial vehicle got the full benefit of the projector."

The whine of the coolant pumps as the deactivated turret was disarmed made him move to a quieter position.

"Whatever set the emplacement in action isn't clear here. There's been no access to the control unit. The instruction has to have come through the AI."

A TechRate approached. "Better come and take a look, Master There was someone in the flyer and a Lacertian on the outside of it."

The Master Warrant Officer swore. Over his shoulder, he called into the turret. "Is the projector deactivated fully?"

"Confirmed." A weapons specialist emerged and walked with the pair toward the remains of the target. "I've isolated it completely." He frowned, puzzled by what he had discovered. "These turrets aren't designed to develop full power, only enough to mark a target, but this one ran up to full power and then into auto firing. It took the entire command team to get in, override the firing codes and get it to the cease fire."

Arriving at the wreckage, the Master Warrant grimaced. "Bloody weapon is enough to rip holes in a starship! This little HST didn't have a hope in hell against a full strength pulse. Hell, even the usual ten-percent pulse for the target range would have done some damage."

Several transports bearing the Fleet Security markings drew up. "Well, not our problem now. Don't interfere with anything. If you do, the Jaunties will be all over you." The Master Warrant turned away and walked to greet the officer dismounting from the leading vehicle. This was going to get very ugly.

WHEN SCI'YAWEZI SENSED THE VEHICLE SLOWING, she prepared to dismount. This was a professional team, armed with infrared goggles, which would negate her ability to rely on her natural camouflage. The vehicle was almost at a standstill as it aligned with the open doors of a large structure. She made a decision, dismounted, and darted very swiftly to a hollow space within a low-growing clump of bushes.

The Consortium leader frowned. "That's odd. According to the lift drive reading, we just shed some weight. Soon as we stop, combat dismount and blanket the whole approach with stun pulses."

"If it's one of the snakeheads, we should burn it."

"Want to tell everyone we're here? Don't be stupid. Right. Doors open — Go!"

The four men tumbled out and came up firing. Advancing in short sprints and fanning out, they swept left and right, blanketing the entire area with pulses from their weapons. Birds tumbled out of trees, squirrels fell, and small ground-dwelling creatures collapsed in the onslaught of neural-disrupting electrons.

One targeted Sci'yawezi and she collapsed, her skin changing briefly to a grey-blue colour before she appeared to blend into the ground on which she lay. Only her yellow eyes remained visible to an astute observer.

The Consortium agents stopped firing and carefully scanned the area with their goggles. "No sign of anything this side, Leader."

"Nothing this side." The speaker stood above the clump of bushes beneath which the Lacertian lay paralysed, almost treading on her.

"Good. Two Alpha, stay on watch. Let's get the pair unloaded and ready for pick-up. Another team is on the way. I want to get the hell away from here before anything else goes wrong."

"WE HAVE A LEAD ON HERON AND O'CONNOR — at least we think we do. Lt. Sci'yawezi's comlink has been traced." The Commander rubbed her forehead. "She was paired with Lt. Sci'kalina and must have managed to attach herself to the transport the abductors used to get away from the turret. We have a pair of teams on their way to the location." She pushed her chair back from the desk with more force than necessary. "Now I have the lovely task of dealing with the bastards we have in custody that got Heron and O'Connor to the Weapons Range."

"A pity about the Lacertian." Lieutenant-Commander Vallance followed the woman to the door. "The second team were observed by one of the Lacertians who alerted the others. The sail bags tested positive for DNA from Heron and O'Connor. If that turret hadn't malfunctioned, they'd have got clean away."

"Probably." Something about Vallance bothered the security officer, and she made a mental note to run a background check on him. "Lucky malfunction though." She studied him with a casual air. "I'd appreciate your remaining available — there's bound to be something arising from this interview that I may need to clarify with you."

"Of course. Anyway, so you mentioned that the comlink signalled their location."

The commander smiled, her hand on the door control. She knew what he was fishing for, and she wasn't taking the bait. "Yes, but you'll forgive me if I keep that to myself. Not that I doubt you, of course, but given the current situation, I only trust my people, and even some of them on a need to know basis."

Hoping his concern didn't show, Vallance frowned. "What? Oh. Of course." He nodded vigorously, over-emphasising his agreement in doing so. "I'll be on the link if you need me."

The door shut behind the commander, cutting off the brief glimpse of the six men and women seated under guard in the room beyond. For a long moment he stared at the door then walked away, making for the Staff Wardroom. He needed a drink, but he couldn't risk dulling his wits until the damned security people had gone. How the blazes had that turret been activated? Placing his cap on the table in the anteroom, he signed the register acknowledged the android steward and ordered a tonic water coloured with angostura bitters.

Dropping into a chair, he picked up a tablet and tapped the news link, pretending to read while thinking furiously. Could the Lacertians have activated the turret? Did they have the codes?

THE ABDUCTORS REMOVED HARRY AND FERGHAL from the vehicle and replaced their manacles with humane restraints. They carried the pair to a small chamber and placed them on the floor.

"They'll keep there for the moment. Four Alpha, get rid of the transport. Three, help me rig the beacon for the collection team. Then we can get the hell out of here."

Feigning unconsciousness, Harry listened. He waited until the footsteps had receded before he rolled over, the last traces of the drug making his head spin. To his annoyance, he was strapped into a body harness that clamped his arms to his sides and his legs to each other. Ferghal was in the same bind, and they were both firmly gagged. Their only advantage was they were alone, for now. The men who'd brought them here had left or were out of earshot.

In his head he could hear a household management system like the one at Scrabo, little more than a means to control the internal environment — lighting, doors and security. Seeking a bit further he found an observation system. Through this, he discovered that their abductors were preparing to depart.

No, my friends, I think not. He planted a command to seal all the doors to the part of the structure that two of his captors were in. Unsurprisingly, the two men responded by attempting to escape, and Harry had the satisfaction of watching their attempt to open the door without success, and resorting to their weapons to get in by force.

The response masked developments outside the structure as a hypersonic transport arrived. It had barely landed and powered down its drives when the outer door to the partly buried structure closed, denying the collection team access.

"What the hell?" exclaimed the leading agent. "Something's wrong. Get back to the flyer." She keyed her comlink. "Power up. There's a problem."

"There's a problem, alright." One of her team pointed to the road. "Vehicles coming. Fleet security markings."

The leader nodded. "We're out of here. Back to the flyer." She followed her companions to the access ramp, and with no prior warning her body lifted into the air and crashed into the next man.

"What the hell?" The third man dropped to one knee and took aim at the fast moving Lacertian as she vanished into the flyer.

"Hold your fire! Shit! Come on, we'll have to deal with the bloody snakehead inside." She raced toward the flyer, leaping over her fallen companions and preparing her weapon. "Use the stun setting, and for god's sake, don't hit the pilots!" She almost lost her footing as the flyer lifted, lurched to one side in a half turn, and slammed into the ground.

Too late her weapon caught Sci'yawezi, and the Lacertian collapsed as smoke filled the cockpit.

"Shit! Shit! Shit!" the leader spat, surveying the damaged controls and the dead pilots. Furious, she changed the setting on her weapon and killed the Lacertian where she lay.

"Do not attempt to lift off!" The amplified voice boomed inside the cabin. "We have a weapons lock, and your flyer will be disabled. Throw out your weapons and surrender."

She looked at her companions. "They've nothing on us apart from attempting an unauthorised landing in a controlled area." She kicked the Lacertian's body. "We were simply defending ourselves when that snakehead attacked us. Follow my lead — we'll be clear and away in forty-eight hours." Reaching the door, she threw her weapons out. "Keep your shirts on!" she taunted. "We're coming out, but we want our legal representatives! We were attacked by a damn snakehead, and it killed our pilots and damaged our flyer."

Chapter 9 – Interference

Unaware of developments outside, Harry realised that he and Ferghal had a problem. Their captors had almost succeeded in blasting a way out of the room they were trapped in when Ferghal frantically signalled something. The door! He tried to get the network to close it, and realised he could no longer hear the system. Simultaneously, the lights went out, plunging them into darkness.

For a moment Harry lay still, trying to make contact with the building management system, but it was completely unresponsive. In the darkness he could hear their captors swearing and see the bursts of plasma fire they were using to burn their way out of the room he'd trapped them in.

And then he heard someone slithering toward him and knew that it was Ferghal. Sensing what Ferghal intended, Harry humped his body toward his friend, startling himself when they collided. Groping with the limited movement in his hand, Ferghal found Harry's arm.

Harry wormed himself into a better position and waited.

With an effort, Ferghal worked his way downward until his fingers found the restraint holding Harry's wrist. More movement put him in a position where his fingers could find the fastening pins. It took him several attempts to figure out how to release the locking clip and prise the strap free.

Harry made to return the favour, but Ferghal stopped him, working his way to a new position from which he could free the cuff securing Harry's elbow.

With one arm now free, Harry ripped off the tape covering his mouth and quickly freed his other arm, then removed the tape from Ferghal's mouth before freeing his arms. Sitting back to back they released their legs, then they stood.

"Now we will have a reckoning," Ferghal whispered. He wrenched a heavy metal stanchion from its anchorage. In the near darkness, he could just make out Harry signalling him to take cover. He said a quick prayer of thanks for having worked in the dim lighting on the lower gundeck of HMS *Spartan*. It had given him excellent night vision, as had the hours spent on lookout duty.

The soft sounds of stealthy movement reached their ears, and Ferghal prepared to attack whoever stepped into the room. Sensing his friend's preparations and intentions, Harry made his own plans. He knew there were at least two men and possibly more in the building.

Several things happened at once. A man cautiously sidled through the doorway, and Ferghal attacked. Only the agent's lightning-fast reflexes saved him from immediate serious injury. He leapt back, his plasma projector taking the blow aimed at his head. The blast of plasma missed Ferghal but partially melted his jacket and burned a hole in the wall behind him. The force of the blow numbed the man's hand, and he dropped his weapon, desperately trying to recover his balance while fending off Ferghal's determined attack, but he collided with his team leader behind him.

Ferghal gave neither of them a chance to recover or to retake the initiative, and with Harry joining the fray, it rapidly became a brawl. Only an interruption saved them from Ferghal's pent-up rage and Harry's fury. Armoured security officers stormed in through a hole blasted in the vehicle door.

"Easy, Mr O'Connor!" The leading Marine stepped back as Ferghal whirled, the Consortium agent falling at his feet choking and bleeding. "We're on your side!"

"Easy, lads!" The Security Commander ducked as Ferghal snatched up his stanchion and raised it to attack. "Heron! O'Connor! Stand fast."

Harry paused in his attempt to rip his victim's helmet from his head without undoing the chinstrap. His battle rage ebbed as he took in the armoured squad surrounding them. Ferghal grounded the stanchion and glowered at the newcomers, willing to resume his attack if anything suggested a wrong move.

When Harry caught sight of several Lacertians, he let go of his victim, only then realising that his hands were bleeding, and his victim had blood streaming from his nose and mouth. His IR goggles appeared to have been smashed, causing damage to at least one of the man's eyes. Sucking a deep breath, Harry stood, and that's when he saw the damage to the man's shoulder, face and body.

To the commander, Harry said, "My apologies for our appearance, sir. I'm afraid we did not wish to comply with the plans these people had for us."

The commander nodded. "So I see." Over his shoulder he called, "Medics!" Securing his weapon, he moved aside, signalling his men. "Search the place and secure it. Mr Heron, Mr O'Connor, go with Lieutenant Sci'yenzile, please. She'll get you checked and see you get back to the College." He watched the medic attending Ferghal's opponent. "Took some of your annoyance out on him, Mr O'Connor?"

Ferghal's face hardened. "Aye, sir. I've no patience with those who are traitors, sir, and I'll have no truck with their paymasters either."

Watching him follow Harry, the commander said softly to his Lieutenant, "Another minute or two and I think both of them would have killed these fellows. When the medics have patched them up, secure them and take them directly to our High Security Unit." He smiled briefly. "These guys are some of their first division, so our pair either got bloody lucky, or these two were off their game. Either way, looking at what O'Connor's done to that one, I wouldn't want to be on the wrong side of him."

"PLANS HAVE CHANGED, EON. JUST KEEP YOUR HEAD DOWN and don't attract attention for now. Something went badly wrong with the attempt to snatch Heron and his friend. Your uncle's furious."

"Yeah, I know. Lieutenant Crossley and his whole team got taken — the snakeheads tracked them to the weapons range." He shrugged. "They still don't know why that turret activated, but it took out one of the snakeheads, and I heard the team at the bunker took out another. That must've been sweet to watch." Eon laughed.

His father frowned. "Don't forget we lost two of our best special ops teams and the embedded agents. It wasn't all guts and glory and watching snakeheads die." He took a long drink from his glass. "Now, pay attention. The Chairman is annoyed and wants answers, and the legal team are concerned. We will have one last chance to take them out of the picture. Your uncle will send someone to brief you. This will be your chance to show your abilities, Eon. It will take place on your training cruise, and you will be the key."

"At last." Eon grinned. "Don't worry, Dad, I can hack it."

"I hope you'll more than hack it. The stakes are going to be very high, and we can't afford any slip-ups. It's vital you don't stir any more suspicion or get yourself into trouble in any way. We can't risk having you under scrutiny now. That damned enquiry is exposing things we've worked damned hard to keep under wraps, and Heron in particular could be the key to exposing everything."

"Damn it, Dad, do you think I'm stupid? Don't worry. I'll pull it off."

"You'll need help. Preferably some people who know nothing of the real agenda. Those two friends of yours will be ideal. Can you trust them after the fiasco with their botched attempt to plant those traces?"

Eon snorted. "I'll put the wind up them. Crossley had four dupes helping him, and that's got Miles and Laschelles worried — especially after the Red Caps grilled them over the business in the pool. I'll deal with them. They'll do as they're told." He stood. "I better get back. My leave pass is only until nineteen-hundred." His familiar scowl lifted for a moment. "I better keep my nose clean. Trust me for once."

THE DAILY ROUTINE OF CLASSES AND PREPARATIONS for the Regatta were interrupted for Harry and Ferghal by a visit from a team of police who demanded they be delivered to a police station for questioning, a request that was categorically refused by the Fleet Security Service and the shadowy Fleet Intelligence Command. There followed a legal tussle, and finally an agreement the pair could be interviewed at the College, but only in the presence of a legal representative appointed by the Fleet, and with officers from the Intelligence Unit present.

Harry faced an officer across the interview table, his temper strained as he found himself under investigation for criminal assault on his abductors.

"I fail to understand your purpose, Inspector," Harry stated. "Am I to understand that I am charged with attacking the men who abducted me?"

"Allegedly abducted you. It hasn't been proven that the men you attacked had anything to do with abducting you."

"I suppose you think I — we — secured ourselves in those bindings, and they were attempting to rescue us?"

"That's one possibility. We're still looking at all the options." He regarded Harry coolly. "We've run some tests using bindings like those you say were used on you, and the subject couldn't free himself. That leaves us with the possibility that you aren't telling us the whole story, or you had some assistance."

Before Harry could respond, his legal counsel intervened. "Are you suggesting Midshipman Heron is lying, Inspector?" His restraining hand on Harry's forearm warned him not to respond.

The Inspector shrugged. "You tell me, Counsel. We put one of our people into exactly the same restraints, and he could not free himself."

"Tell me, Inspector, did your test subject have a companion? You seem to have overlooked the fact that Midshipman Heron and Cadet O'Connor were in the same chamber."

Annoyance showed briefly in the Inspector's face. "Why is that an issue? They were both restrained. The restraints are impossible to escape. We've proved that."

"For one person secured in them, perhaps." The legal adviser leaned back. "Explain to the Inspector how you freed yourselves please, Mr Heron."

"Certainly, sir." Harry held the Inspector's gaze. "I worked myself close enough to Ferghal — Mr O'Connor — for him to withdraw the securing pin on the cuff holding my wrist and to release the cuff on my elbow. With my free arm, I released the cuff on his wrist and elbow. That allowed us to free our other arms, then our legs, and to remove the tape that secured our mouths."

The Inspector's face gave nothing away as he listened. "I see. So you claim that you freed your companion's wrist, and he freed you?"

"He freed my wrist and elbow, as I did for him. With an arm free, we did the rest ourselves."

"Why did you attack the men?"

Harry's expression was icy. "Should we simply have asked them to surrender their weapons to us?"

"You didn't know they were armed. They might have been there to rescue you. How did you know they weren't?"

The legal officer gestured Harry to silence. "Inspector, you have been provided with copies of all the information the Fleet rescue squad found and recovered. I suggest you accept it. The answer to your question is there." He paused. "Mr Heron and Mr O'Connor knew that the men were not there to rescue them, and that they were armed." He pushed a data chip across the table. "Any further information you may require will have to be authorised by the Advocate Admiral's department. The evidence concerning the abduction and the statements of the recovery team are there. Do you have any further questions for Midshipman Heron?"

The Inspector scowled. "A whole raft of them, but I see I am wasting my time getting answers. A charge has been laid in the local district court of serious assault on two men currently in hospital. As I can't get access to them due to their being held in a high security facility, I only know what is on the charge sheet concerning the assault."

The door opened, and the man Harry recognised as the leader of the rescue team entered. "Inspector, I think this little farce has gone far enough," said the man. "My boss wants a word, and I imagine the situation is already being explained to your superiors as we speak." He nodded to Harry and the legal officer, both on their feet. "Maurice, you'd better come with us. Mr Heron, return to your class."

"Aye, aye, sir." Harry had no idea what the man's rank was, but he was clearly used to giving orders. Saluting, Harry made for the door then paused. "I hope, Inspector, I have provided at least some answers for you."

Despite the awkwardness of the situation, the Inspector smiled. "I think so, Mr Heron. I think so."

HARRY COILED THE SHEETS AND TIDIED THE HALYARDS on the sloop. The training and sailing practice in preparation for the Regatta took his mind off the abduction and the legal row over their possible evidence. Even then there was no lowering of his guard on anything. Keiron, Elize, Howard and the others in the sloop crew found it frustrating, but did their best to understand his suspicion. It was especially hard for Elize, who'd formed an attraction for Harry.

The one benefit, as far as Harry was concerned, was that Eon Barclay was taking care to avoid him. This had not escaped the attention of their Divisional Officer, Lt Häakinen, who watched from the cockpit as the crew prepared to sail.

Keiron sought to set Harry at ease. "That business with Lieautenant Crossley still bothering you?"

"Yes." Harry's guard came up. "Yes, it is," he repeated defensively, and regretted it.

Keiron nodded. "I can see it's caused a problem for you, chum. We're all on your side if it helps to know that."

"Thank you, but yes—our abduction seems to have caused more than one problem."

"How's that?" Keiron asked.

"We are advised the enquiry is further postponed. There is some legal challenge arising from the means of our escape and the capture of our abductors." His expression hardened. "Apparently we stand accused of having used undue force."

"Bastards. What did they expect, for you to whimper, 'Please let us go and we won't hurt you'?"

Harry laughed. "Perhaps."

Elize watched as Ferghal swung aboard, coxswain by unanimous consent for the whaler racing team. "He's got his crew team in shape now," she said, hoping to distract Harry from mulling over Keiron's remarks. "Other teams have more muscle, but Ferghal's got a knack for making the boat work for the rowers."

Harry was grateful for her intervention. "Aye. He learned these and other tricks from men who knew the art of pulling a laden barge or cutter. Yon boat is a toy compared to what Ferghal's used to, lightly built and flimsy, with one purpose only — to race."

"True." She smiled at the mental image this evoked, a fast racing boat seeming like a toy to this young man who had learned to sail the "wooden walls," as the sailing ships were called in the nineteenth century.

Elize used her hand to shield her eyes from the sun. "Looks like we're all aboard now." She stood and dusted the seat of her trousers. "Are we going to sail this ship, Captain?" She winked and nudged him. "We've only got her for the next couple of hours."

"We'll sail then." Harry took command. "Everyone ready? Senzile, stand by to cast off forward. Howard, I'll want the foresail unfurled and sheeted home to windward. Elize, sheet home the mainsail on my order." Turning to Ferghal at the wheel, he asked, "Ready?"

"Aye, aye, Captain." Ferghal grinned, eager to get started.

From the cockpit, Lieutenant Häakinen waited for the order to start the small manoeuvring engine to leave the jetty. It never came, and he watched with interest as Harry checked the distance between the sloop and the other moored vessels, tested the wind strength and direction, and very obviously took command.

"Cast off forward. Let go aft but hold the after spring. Hold the jib to windward, Howard." Harry watched the opening gap between the hull and the jetty, then at the moorings to leeward. "Let go the spring, sheet home the jib and the main." The yacht gathered way swiftly and Ferghal caught her, steadied the helm and steered them clear of the moored vessels. "Very well. Let's see what we can do with her now." Harry gauged the wind and glanced at the log. "Stand by to extend the foils. Ferghal, steer east by south-south-east."

As he watched, Lieutenant Häakinen let his breath out slowly. "Now that was something I've not seen done," he told the security officer. "I've read about it, but wouldn't have attempted it myself."

The officer nodded. "You know the sail handling comp is disengaged."

"What? Then how are they doing this?" The Lieutenant checked as the whine of a pump told him the hydroplaning foils were being extended. "Well I'll be damned. Now this will be interesting,"

The yacht rose smoothly onto her foils and the speed increased.

"How does she steer?" Harry called to Ferghal. "Will she carry more sail? I've a fancy to see how she behaves if we press her."

Ferghal smiled. "She steers well, Captain. Let us press her and see."

The freshening wind gave Harry the opportunity to explore the performance of this unusual vessel to the fullest extent. At times his crew experienced exhilaration, and at others wondered if they'd be swimming home. Twice the Lieutenant considered intervening, but was forestalled by Harry taking action, which, while sometimes was not what the Lieutenant considered conventional, corrected the situation.

Securing the mooring lines once more, Keiron cast a respectful glance at Harry. "Damn it, Harry, a couple of times there I thought we'd break something, but I don't think I've ever had a sail like that. Fantastic! If we can get her to perform like that in the Regatta—oh yeah, I can taste the victory now!" He whooped

"You certainly pushed the boat to the limit, Mr Heron," said Lieutenant Häakinen, joining them. He had watched Harry on several earlier practice runs with these foil-riding sloops, but this, his first sail with him, had been different to what he'd expected. "You had us in the red range on the dynamometers for the foils several times."

"If we are to race, sir, then I must know her limits." Harry's face suggested he'd been testing more than just the boat. "I believe I have now found them. In conditions like those we have had today, these foils need constant adjusting." He grinned suddenly at a memory. "I do not believe they would have survived the storm I experienced off the New South Wales coast in *Spartan*'s Number Two cutter in '03. In sheltered waters such as these they do very well, but in the open ocean I rather think they will be a hazard."

"What storm was that? I don't recall any major storm reports off that coast in '03." The Lieutenant, a keen yachtsman himself, frowned. "*Spartan*? Oh. You mean 1803."

Before Harry could reply, Elize asked, "What sort of boat was that? Something like the one you guys built on Pangaea?"

"Lord no. The Number Two cutter was just over twenty-two feet — around six and a half metres — and open. She could ship six oars and carried a mast rigged with a sliding gunter for the main and two small foresails." Harry shrugged. "We'd been sent with the barge and the Number One cutter north from Port

Jackson to what is now called the Hawkesbury River estuary to prepare a preliminary survey and chart. On our return we were caught at sea by what they call a southerly buster." He smiled and glanced to where Ferghal was busy folding and stowing the sails. "I was fortunate to have a very good Master's Mate with me and some excellent seamen. It was quite alarming for some hours, but we survived intact and were able to assist the Number One cutter, which had lost her mast and part of her gunwales."

Sensing that he would not elaborate any further, the others made a mental note to drag the rest of the story from Ferghal if they could, and the Lieutenant to search the archives to see if there was any official record of the event. Now, with the boat secure, they disembarked and made their way back to the accommodation block to change and prepare for the evening sessions.

Walking beside Harry, Keiron said, "You guys always surprise the rest of us, Harry, and sometimes you scare us. Life is certainly not dull with you and Ferghal in command."

"I hope I am not too much the tyrant."

Laughing, Keiron punched his shoulder. "We'd soon mutiny if you were!"

THE POLICE INSPECTOR'S VISIT TROUBLED HARRY. Though he heard no more about the charge, the mere fact it had been made annoyed him. "What kind of society charges a man defending himself against an attacker, then charges him with injuring the attacker?" he demanded of Elize.

She drew away from him slightly. "Can't you let it go? Let the Security and Intel spooks handle it." She hesitated, wanting to say more, but not wanting to upset Harry. She never knew what might set him off. "You can't go round treating us all as enemies. We aren't. They've cleaned out the cell that was here among the staff, and none of us Yotties are playing for the other side."

"I am sorry, Elize. I no longer know who to trust, and this new attack upon us—"

"I can understand that, Harry, or at least some of it. As for the legal nonsense — well, the police are just doing their job. Someone laid a charge, and they have to investigate it, even if it is stupid."

Harry considered her words. "I shall do my best. I'm sorry." Smiling suddenly, he asked, "Shall we walk a while? Or do you wish to watch some fencing practice?"

Laughing, she linked arms with him. "The fencing might be the best way to get some of the aggression out of you." Glancing round, she frowned. "Have you and The Barclay made peace? I don't see him or his cronies baiting you these days."

Shaking his head, Harry grinned. "No such luck. Come on, then, let us see if there is a piste free and someone who wishes to try his blade with me."

Elize laughed. "I would take you on myself, but I have to report for a tutorial in ten minutes. I'll join you later."

"HEY FOSSIL!" LASCHELLES SWAGGERED OVER TO HARRY. "You think you're a swordsman? Want to try your luck with a class champion?"

"Are you challenging me?" asked Harry quietly. He didn't actively dislike Laschelles, but regarded him as a braggart and would-be bully. "If so, I am willing to accept it. Do you choose foil or sabre?"

"Sabre will do for me." Laschelles smirked. He believed himself more than capable of beating Harry, but planned a little fun to make a point of it. "I've got a piste reserved. Follow me if you've the guts for it."

Harry bristled, his temper rising at this calculated insult. "Lead the way," he said with a calmness he didn't feel. "We shall see how your sabre fares against mine." He noticed Laschelles' friends watching and smirking, and knew there must be some skulduggery planned. Deciding not to let this put him off, he prepared, now on his guard. After connecting to the electronic scoring system, he selected a sabre that suited his grip and balance and took his position.

For a few minutes he let Laschelles lead the attack while he gauged his opponent's skill and tactics. Then, when he had some measure of how the other fought, he changed his game from one of pure defence to an attack. At first he kept up the pattern of skilfully blocking Laschelles' sallies, and then he exploited opportunities to introduce his own feints, carefully exploring every opening. As he had been taught so many years before, he kept his eyes locked to his opponent's, even though partially hidden by the mask, something that seemed to cause Laschelles some discomfort as their blades flashed, clashed, locked and slid as each man looked for that all important opportunity to pass the other's guard and score a hit on the padded jacket, arm or helmet.

Where Harry had initially given ground, now he pressed his adversary step by careful step back along the marked piste.

Suddenly, Laschelles changed his own play, and moving through a beating attack, he forced Harry back, pressing in hard until their blades locked. Harry saw the look of triumph in his eyes and sensed what was about to happen. He danced aside, his blade disengaging and sweeping up and out to catch Laschelles' thrust even as the other tried to press on with his now foiled plan. From the corner of his eye Harry saw the obstacles that had been placed to trip him, and his temper flared.

Arriving at the fencing practice, Elize noticed that everyone had stopped their own practice to watch Harry and Laschelles. It was obvious that Harry had his blood well up. She watched in awe as his savage assault forced his opponent into a desperate defence.

Driving his attack home with fury, he forced Laschelles back, turning him so they changed ends. There was a flurry as blades clashed. Harry used the agility, speed and force learned in the harshest of schools, giving his opponent no room. Laschelles' defence became increasingly desperate, and fear showed in his eyes as he struggled to keep Harry's deadly attack at bay and avoid the trip hazards strewn at this end. The constant buzzes registering contact with his opponent's legs, arm or torso accompanied the ringing clashes of the blades and the exclamations of the spectators.

There was a gasp from the group of onlookers as Laschelles' sabre flew from his grasp in a parabolic arc as Harry's blade tore it from his hand. The buzzer sounded continuously as the point of Harry's sabre struck his opponent's chest directly over the heart, the blade bending in a dramatic curve as he pressed it home.

Holding his blade's point against Laschelles, Harry ignored the sounder, and tore off his mask. "When I engage with someone to fence for sport, Mr Laschelles, I do not then seek an advantage by arranging for the piste to be littered with hazards for my opponent. You consider me a fossil," he spat the word with venom, "but I learned the art of the duel as soon as I could hold a foil. What is more, I have killed men with a blade, not toys such as these, but a real blade while standing on a deck littered with more traps for the unwary than these paltry objects your friends have strewn about. You may call me all the names you like, but do not attempt to play foul with me. I'll not stand for it."

He disengaged his blade and turned to walk away even as a Sub Lieutenant hurried toward them calling for him to wait. He was furious and in no mood to discuss what had happened, but his sense of discipline and respect for his officers kept him standing while the Sub Lieutenant lectured them both on correct behaviour and sportsmanship, and then he acknowledged his dismissal with a curt, "Aye, aye sir," and took his leave.

Elize caught up with him at the door. "My God, Harry, is that how you fellows fought on that old ship of yours? I thought you were going to kill him." Her laugh sounded forced. "Have you really killed someone with a sword?"

Harry nodded. "Aye. Defending a prison ship against corsairs. Meeting her shocked gaze, he added angrily, "I was thirteen, and he was twice my size. I used my dirk to defend myself from the ratlines. No, it was not pleasant or clean. It was our lives or theirs." Stopping suddenly, he faced her. "They'd boarded our ship and would have carried us away as slaves along with any of the prisoners they wanted. I had my men use a swivel gun to clear the gangway, then more boarded. One of my men fell to the fellow's blade, and he'd have killed the other had I not done for him." He jerked his thumb in the direction of the fencing hall. "With a real blade I could have ended that farce in half the time, but I suspect that would have attracted something more than the Sub Lieutenant's lecture."

Chapter 10 – Skulduggery

Harry stared into the darkness. Sleep evaded him, driven out by his lingering anger at the betrayal of the abduction and Laschelles' trick on the fencing piste mingled with anxiety and a degree of disappointment. His budding relationship with Elize had clearly run into difficulties thanks to his own suspicions and wariness of everyone but Ferghal. Huffing with frustration, he tried to find a comfortable position on his back, to no avail. Not even the beautiful music he'd found through the AI helped distract his thoughts.

Idly he explored the latest assignment submissions and grades. Ferghal's looked very good, as did Keiron's, but his own had changed. They'd been adjusted downward since his last check a few minutes earlier. As he watched, they changed again, returning to their original mark.

Checking another file, he found that a notation had been added to his record, a decidedly unflattering comment casting doubt on his psychological state. Alarmed, he checked the origin, and was even more puzzled. It had apparently always been there.

Addressing the AI, he said, *"I do not recall this record. When did it arrive?"*

"These records are not authorised. The alteration was made by an unauthorised access, one that prevents my normal security routines from recognising it. Now that you have identified it to me, I shall alert my

maintenance officer. They will investigate it in the morning. The time and date of origin on this record are false. It was posted forty-two minutes and fifteen seconds ago."

Alert to some skulduggery, Harry asked, "Has there been any request for the release of this record to any other party? A legal request perhaps?"

"There has been. One arrived thirty-two minutes and seventeen seconds ago, but will not be processed until authorised with the resumption of office activity in six hours."

"When was the record altered? Was it before or after the request arrived?"

There was a fraction of a second's hesitation. "The request arrived ten minutes, two seconds after the alteration to the record. There is one for Ferghal O'Connor as well, and his record has also been altered."

Harry saw the pattern immediately. "Please restore the record to its unaltered state, and block any attempt to change it unless I have seen the change and know who is changing it." He hesitated. "Keep the altered records in a file only I can see — or better, can you forward them to my Aunt Niamh?"

"To change the records is contrary to my protocols, even though this record is unauthorised. I am required to alert my maintenance officer to such inserts and await their instructions."

"Correct. But the altered record is unauthorised — you told me yourself — and the request is from the people who have every reason to seek to discredit Ferghal and me. It may be released in this form to our enemy before your maintenance team can remove it. Our aunt is in touch with our legal adviser and will know how to deal with this.' Harry hesitated. "I need you to send an alert to the Fleet security officer investigating the attempt to abduct me as well."

For several seconds there was no response. "I have complied with your request, Harry. I have verified your suspicion as to the purpose of the alteration, and restored the record to the unaltered version I have alerted the Security Commander and forwarded the alterations and the disclosure request to Niamh L'Estrange."

With a sigh of relief, Harry relaxed. "Thank you."

"PHEW!" EXCLAIMED KEIRON AS THE CLASS EMERGED from another intensive session with Hugh the Unhinged, the students' nickname for the instructor in fusion reactors and weapons systems. "I'm really looking forward to the cruise. Anything to get away from the classrooms for a bit!"

"You can talk," groaned Senzile. "I reckon I've lost almost seven kilos with all this rushing about — and I have another two assignments to complete for tomorrow. All these instructors seem to think they are the only ones giving us extra studies."

"I wonder what ship we'll be sent to," mused Elize. "I heard there is a brand new heavy cruiser working up — the *Der Grosser Curfirst* or something — be interesting to see what she's like."

"Pity it's only a two-week cruise," said Howard. He punched Harry on the arm. "Captain Bligh here is bad enough with his demands on the sloop, and Ferghal's got us rowing like galley slaves in that whaler. I think he wants to water-ski behind it sometimes."

The group laughed.

Harry wondered if his friends knew the whole story of Captain Bligh and his epic voyage in an open boat as well as his supposed failures as a captain and colonial governor. He decided not to mention it.

Elize smiled at Harry. "How do you and Ferghal get through all the assignments so fast? I saw that you guys have handed in all the required work for this week already."

Harry shrugged. "I try to get them done as soon as they're assigned. That way the subject is still fresh in my mind, and Ferghal works with me some evenings doing his, usually while the rest of you are already in your bunks." He grinned, idly sketching a portrait of Elize on his pad.

Elize caught a glimpse of his sketch and recognized herself. "So, am I really that pretty, then?" She flashed a brilliant smile and made Harry blush, which delighted her even more. "Let me see!" She sidled closer, but Harry deflected and stuffed the small sketchpad in his pocket.

"An artist never reveals his work until it's finished," he said, returning her smile.

"I'll get that sketchpad one way or another!" she bantered.

Ferghal joined the group. "Master Warrant Winkworth says we are scheduled to join a new heavy cruiser for our training cruise next week." He grinned, unknowingly echoing Keiron when he said, "I shall be glad to escape the classroom for a bit and have some real work for a change."

"Don't bet on it." Keiron laughed. "Our schoolies will be coming with us and are bound to have plenty of teaching to fit in — and more assignments."

An exclamation from Elize drew everyone's attention. "Look at that!" She held up her tablet to show a photo in a news report. "Those damned Consortium pirates have hit another freight hauler, a Dutch registered ship, *Twee* something. According to this they seized her after booking a passage on her as passengers, then took control after she went into transit." She quickly skimmed the article. "And that's not all — they put the crew into a hold then opened it to space. The bodies were found by one of our patrols near Ephesus Minor only because one of the victims must have had a survival beacon."

"Those bastards!" Ferghal exclaimed. Being confined was all too recent in his memory, but at least he'd managed to free himself and live to tell the tale.

"There was a tablet with the First Officer's passenger list and manifest. Apparently this isn't the first time they've done this either!"

"They seem to be pretty ruthless when it suits them, is all I can say," exclaimed Howie. "Turns out they have a hell of a lot more ships than we thought. I heard they attacked a remote base in the Alpha Centauri Sector a couple of weeks ago and captured it. The damaged frigate that got away reported there was at least one starship and several heavy cruisers involved. You don't build those sorts of ships without someone noticing. And where is the money coming from?"

Senzile had been quiet to this point. "Yes, and the worst of it is no one seems to know exactly who is behind it or where they are based — or even what they are really after. My father tells me the City is saying that a commercial enterprise is trying to seize a monopoly on trade to the stars, but there's a rumour they are really after complete control of government. The bureaucrats and politicians are keeping very quiet about it."

"Up to their ears in it themselves no doubt," grumbled Keiron. "Look at this," he said, tapping the headline of another news report. "There've been several more ambushes of our ships. It says their forces seem to know exactly where our people are and the strength of our ships."

"So it appears," remarked Harry, peering over Keiron's shoulder at the report. "It's almost as if they are reading our signals." A loud voice interrupted their discussion, and they turned to see Midshipman Barclay bearing down on them.

"Heron, I've been looking for you."

"And you have found me, it seems, right where I belong." Harry eyed him calmly, his demeanour alert but relaxed.

"Well, not for much longer." Barclay's smirk betrayed that he considered Harry to be in some trouble. "Lieutenant Haäkinen has bad news for you and your sidekick." Barclay shot a withering glance in Ferghal's direction. "The Commander is not impressed with your message — and your latest assignments are trash as well. Good luck — you'll need it." He sneered with smug satisfaction.

Harry and Ferghal exchanged a perplexed glance. "What do you mean message? And what is wrong with our assignments?" demanded Harry.

"What I said, fossil. I quote: 'Heron and O'Connor's assignments are complete garbage, and I am not amused by the abuse of the comlink to send me impertinent messages' — our beloved Commander to your Divisional Officer." Barclay laughed. "Better run along to the Lieutenant, Harry, there's a good boy." He turned and sauntered away, obviously very pleased with himself.

"I don't believe that bastard," growled Keiron. "How come he's carrying the message anyway? How'd he get into the picture?"

"He's Duty Orderly today," said Elize, her eyes boring into Barclay's back. She hoped he felt her disdain. Even the way he walked with a cocky strut annoyed the hell out of her. "He must have been eavesdropping on the Lieutenant. He just can't resist having a go at you, can he, Harry? Pity you can't give him the lesson you gave Laschelles."

Harry didn't comment on the fencing incident. Instead, he said, "I suppose I had better go and see the Lieutenant, but I think it strange that he did not use the comlink to summon me."

LIEUTENANT HAÄKINEN GLANCED UP WITH A PERPLEXED frown as Harry entered. "Yes, Mr Heron?"

"Mr Barclay said you wanted to see me, sir. He mentioned a problem with my assignments and something about a message to the Commander."

The Lieutenant's frown deepened. "Did he? Very well — since you're here, we'll discuss it. Someone sent the Commander a message purporting to be from you. He was not pleased, but the Comms Department have traced it to an unknown source that doesn't carry your ID code. Just be aware and alert to this tactic. As for your assignments, you have, I believe, back-up copies?"

"Yes, sir."

"Good. We will leave the altered versions in place." He handed Harry a data chip. "Store your copies on this and give it to me personally." He smiled suddenly. "Oh, and you might like to ask the AI to alert you of any further attempts to interfere with your work. Tell Mr O'Connor to do the same. It will save us a lot of effort in future."

WEEKS OF TRAINING AND RUN-OFF COMPETITIONS honed the Yotties' skill afloat and on the drill competitions. They were determined to be the class that reversed the tradition that the Yotties took the academic and course prizes, but not the Regatta Cup. This coveted trophy was awarded for the best class performance in sailing, rowing, gymnastic display and the hair-raising Field Gun exercise. The last almost always went to the Field Engineers class, it having been revived as an exercise in a modified form and based on a popular and prestigious competition run by the former British Royal Navy.

The exercise itself had arisen from a long forgotten colonial war in the last years of the nineteenth century when the guns of a Royal Navy cruiser had been landed at a place called Durban. From there they had been sent, with their gun crews, overland on specially built gun carriages across the African terrain to relieve a besieged town called Ladysmith.

"We've a secret weapon in the Field Gun. With two Lacertians in the squad, we can't lose!"

"They're incredible." Ferghal grinned. "I've two in the whaler, and we've one in each of the dinghies."

Harry looked up from his chess game. "As Ferghal and I experienced first hand, their home planet is a bit more watery than Earth, and they are seafaring people." To his opponent, he added, "Checkmate in three moves. Would you care to concede?"

"What? Three moves?" Howie glared at the board. "Oh. Damn." He laid the king on its side. "I didn't see that coming.

Damn it, Harry, you sneaked that knight into place five moves ago, but I didn't see the threat until you moved the bishop. How do you do it? You're worse than playing against the AI."

"I hope not." Packing the pieces away, Harry smiled. "We've Hugh the Unhinged in fifteen minutes. I think we'd best hurry."

"Misery awaits." Howie smirked. "I'd been so engrossed in trying to beat you at chess, I'd actually forgotten about old Hugh. I wonder what he'll spring on us today?"

Chapter 11 – *Der Große Kurfürst*

The class disembarked from the ship's barge into the large hangar space of the heavy cruiser NECS *Der Große Kurfürst*. Smaller than a starship, the cruiser packed a very powerful armament and carried a squadron of interceptors. The ride from the College to the lift station and then to the platform dock had gone smoothly, and the transfer to the cruisers' barges was a simple evolution.

A commander watched as the Britannia and Dreadnought classes disembarked and assembled their equipment. Strolling forward he acknowledged the salutes of the two Lieutenants, with four of the cruisers' midshipmen following behind.

"Hello, Jaakko, still at the College, I see." He cast an eye over the class. "We will have to show them what it is really like instead of all that theoretical stuff you teach them."

The Lieutenant grinned. "With respect, sir, you were my Divisional Officer, and I can still quote your words when we went aloft for our training cruise."

"You have a most inconvenient memory, Jaakko. It will get you promoted one of these days." The Commander glanced about him. "Have you got your people split into groups yet?"

"Yes, sir, in accordance with the standing instructions."

The Commander laughed. "Of course, I trained you properly." Eyeing the classes of cadets standing at attention, he announced,

"I am Commander Scheer, Executive Officer. Welcome aboard *Der Große Kurfürst*. We are a heavy cruiser and the most recent addition to the Fleet. My assistants today are Midshipmen Arno Richthofen, Rudi Ecker, Hans Lange and Haakon Knutson. They will show you to your quarters in the midshipmens' berth and introduce you to the ship's stations."

Keiron nudged Harry. "I wonder if Richthofen over there is a relative of the Lieutenant Commander of the same name serving on *Ramillies*." He froze when the Commander fixed him with an enquiring stare.

"You have a question, Midshipman—?" The Commander waited for Keiron's name.

Keiron snapped to attention. "Whitworth, sir! No sir, I was just making an observation to Mr Heron, sir."

"In future, Mr Whitworth, I would appreciate it very much if you would refrain from talking while I am, as you gentlemen say, interrupting."

"Yes, sir," replied Keiron, trying hard to suppress a grin at the humorous way the Commander had made his point.

AS MIDSHIPMAN ARNO RICHTHOFEN LED THEIR GROUP TOUR, Harry paid particular attention to the Navigation and Weapons centres. The tour included a huge open compartment with a grassy lawn, flowering shrubs and other plants, which provided a natural environment for relaxation. Harry thought the official name interesting — the environmental lung space — but Midshipman Richthofen said everyone called it the park, which Harry also found curious.

"It's been found that we all need something like this for our mental and physical health, so they're adding vegetation spaces to older ships." Midshipman Richthofen paused. "It supplements the algae filter tanks and beds and is quite pleasant as a place to relax."

The tour continued to the power and reactor rooms then on to the flight control centre. Harry and the others began to get a good feel for the complexity of these vast ships, something Harry had appreciated aboard the *Vanguard*, but this ship, being half the size, really gave him the opportunity to appreciate just how complex it was.

He was gazing at the controls when he heard someone speak his name.

"Hello, Harry."

Harry turned. "Ute!" He glanced with surprise at the insignia of a Lieutenant on Ute's uniform. "Beg pardon, Lieutenant! I was just thinking about the *Vanguard,* and here you are. The last time we saw each other, we were aboard that fine ship."

Ute Zimmermann grinned. "So we were. Welcome aboard, Harry. I'm still getting used to it myself, being a Lieutenant and all that saluting and yes ma'aming." She grinned.

"Congratulations," Harry said, shaking Ute's hand. "Fine uniform." She now wore the rank markings of an Interceptor Pilot Lieutenant. "You might recall my friends Ferghal and Danny. Ferghal is with the Engineering group, and Danny is at school in Dublin. I thought you were still on *Vanguard*, ma'am."

"See, there we go with the ma'am already!" Ute laughed. "At ease, Mr Heron," she teased. "A month ago I got a signal re-posting me to the *DGK*. It's quite a challenge because she is so new. What's new with you? I expect you're having fun at the College and can look forward to being posted to a ship soon yourself."

"I hope so." Harry grinned. "We've completed our first three months, and when we go back, it will be for the run-down to the exams, and then there's the enquiry."

"Enquiry? Oh, that one. Hans and Paddy are on notice for that as well." Ute gestured round the Flight Command Centre. "What do you think of our ship?" To Midshipman Richthofen, she said, "Want me to explain the Flyco, Arno?"

"Thanks, Lieutenant."

Ute wasted no time pointing out the displays, communications stations, tracking systems and the monitors for the hangars and launching bays. "Well, that's it. Any questions?"

As no one had anything to ask, Arno thanked her and pointed his charges toward the door.

To Harry, Ute said, "With Arno guiding you round, you'll get a good run-down on the targeting and weapons arrays, but you don't want to fly with him in the pilot's seat." She winked. "He's a navigator, and his flying skills need a little work."

Everyone looked at Arno, who grimaced and said, "*Okay, okay, macht euch nur lustig über mich. Ich bin eben nicht mein Bruder!*"

The other midshipmen laughed, knowing exactly how Arno felt about the on-going competition with his brother, an exceptional pilot, but Harry didn't understand German, so Ute translated it for him. He didn't see the humour in it. "I think that's a bit unfair. It isn't as if we can all be interceptor aces. Some of us don't want to be."

"Touché, Harry." Ute laughed. "You are right, and we shouldn't tease him. Arno, it seems that Mr Heron may not be as impressed with us flybies as we'd like you all to be."

The midshipman smiled. "It isn't easy following my brother through the service. He is one of the flight leaders on *Ramillies* at present, and an acclaimed ace. I prefer operating the principal weapons targeting."

"Well, you and Harry should get along very well then, Arno," said Ute. "He helped us design the visual sighting aid for the interceptors at Pangaea."

Harry was glad that this observation was lost on the rest of the group, so focussed they were on the flight traffic control system and the landing control for the docking bays where a massive barge was entering the bay. He saw no need to talk about some of the things they'd done on *Vanguard*. As he joined the others, he was conscious of Arno's silent appraisal of him.

The group moved out of the Flight Control Centre, and Harry found himself next to Arno as they made their way to the next station on their tour.

"I've heard that you are a navigation specialist," remarked Arno. "They say that you are from another time."

"'Fraid so." Shrugging, Harry smiled. "My friends and I are here by accident, and we can't go back, so we have to make the best of it." He looked at Arno. "Is your brother really such a very good flyer?"

Arno glanced at Harry. "*He* thinks he is the best!" He grimaced "And he never lets me forget it."

Midshipman Barclay emerged from the Weapons Control Centre at the head of his group.

"There's nothing here for you, fossil. They don't use swords and bows and arrows on this ship." He sneered at Harry, adding in a remark directed at Arno, "Heron and his sidekick O'Connor shouldn't be allowed on board. They belong in a lab somewhere being dissected, or in a glass case on display so people can see what fossilised humans look like."

Harry flushed angrily, but Arno beat him to a retort. "You have that incorrect. Herr Heron is not the fossil; *es sind Leute wie*

Sie that need that treatment — as a warning to the rest of your kind."

His icy glare and the tilt of his head coupled with the tight-lipped sneer as he said this made everyone present feel as if Barclay had suddenly been caught in a freezer unit.

The midshipman accompanying Barclay's group smiled sourly. To Arno he said, *"Typisch! Ich erwische immer die schwarzen Schafe."* He signalled his group to follow him.

Those in both groups who spoke German laughed as Barclay flushed a deep red. Harry could only guess that something had been said that was not complimentary to Barclay, and was left wondering what it might be as the two groups parted. He was certain, though, that Barclay would retaliate, not to Arno who made the retort, but to himself, and he said as much to Arno, explaining that he was Barclay's favourite whipping boy. The other acknowledged that this was expected, but assured Harry that they would be on their guard.

The remainder of the familiarisation tour passed without incident, and the encounter with Barclay was soon forgotten as Harry focussed on everything he needed to remember to gain the maximum benefit from the cruise.

"MIDSHIPMAN BARCLAY, YOU LEFT THIS ON THE BARGE." Lieutenant-Commander Vallance held out a holdall. "I assume it's yours. It has your name on it."

Surprise almost made Eon Barclay refuse the proffered item, then he realised what it was. "Er, thanks, sir. I forgot it when we disembarked."

"You want to take more care of your belongings." The words conveyed a hidden meaning.

Eon's mind raced. Was Commander Vallance a part of this? Or was he just the messenger handing on something because it had been "found" on the barge with his name on it? All he knew for certain was that he now held the keys to the operation, and he must hand these over to another if that man gave him the correct password. "I will, sir. Thank you, sir."

"See you do." The Commander returned the salute and walked away.

With his habitual scowl back in place, Barclay walked to where his friends waited. "I've got the stuff. Now you'll see." He smiled suddenly and punched Miles on the shoulder. "You guys can look forward to a nice reward once this comes off."

THE YOTTIES SETTLED INTO THE SHIPBOARD ROUTINE aboard the *DGK*, as her crew had dubbed their ship. Curious as ever, Harry took the trouble to search the ship's data files for the origin of the name and discovered the fascinating story of the Markgraf of Brandenburg who had not liked Bach's music enough to employ him. As Harry loved the music of Bach — and revelled in being able to access it at any time — he had studied this and the rest of the Bach story with interest.

The navigating officer watched Harry plotting in the waypoints for a transit. "You enjoy the navigation, Midshipman?" he asked.

"Aye, sir. Working with the ship's mind is much easier than using a slate and tables."

"Slate and tables?"

"Oh, my apologies, sir. Aboard the *Spartan*, I did the calculations for latitude on a slate, but used the logarithm tables to simplify it."

The Lieutenant paused as he considered this. "You had no NavComp? What sort of ship was this?"

Realising the Lieutenant didn't know where he'd learned navigation, Harry explained.

The Lieutenant laughed. "I expect the calculus needed for our transits would be too complex for that."

Surprised, Harry blurted, "Oh, no, sir, it is a simple calculation if one understands the formulae and the process, especially if one uses the logarithms correctly."

"I'll take your word for it. But perhaps I'll set you a little exercise to test your claim later." Straightening, the Lieutenant studied the display. "Transfer that to the helm." Touching his link, he said, "Command, transit coordinates ready."

Chapter 12 – Suspicion

Ferghal felt a glow of satisfaction. The Electrical Engineer Officer, Lieutenant Commander Reuter, had a reputation for never considering any cadet's efforts as being good enough, yet he grudgingly complimented Ferghal on his skill after watching him work through a series of complex drills designed to test damage control procedures and ensure that the ship never lost power.

"Mr O'Connor, you seem to have a good understanding of the processes, but don't get too sure of yourself. One mistake could be disastrous for everyone."

"Aye, sir," responded Ferghal, flattered. "Thank you, sir."

"Don't thank me, Cadet. You've still got a lot to learn before you can be trusted to do this unsupervised. But you'll do well enough for now." He handed Ferghal a data recorder. "Report to your Divisional Officer and give him that with my compliments."

"Aye, aye, sir." Ferghal saluted and hurried away, oblivious of the amused expression on the officer's face.

"THE INSTALLATION OF THE DISRUPTION UNITS IS COMPLETE, sir." The Warrant Officer went through the motions of checking a work rota.

"Good. I have received the trigger unit." The Lieutenant grimaced. "That arrogant idiot who delivered it could blow the whole operation. Thankfully he doesn't know enough to be much of a risk."

The Warrant Officer nodded. "The big midshipman that almost botched the last exercise? Ja. Thinks himself better than he is. Daddy's important and has money, so he thinks he can pull rank that he doesn't have."

The Lieutenant shrugged. "If all goes smoothly, we will be with the Consortium soon, and so will he." Glancing round to verify that no one was within earshot, he added, "Make sure Giorgio is ready to join us in the escape pod if anything goes wrong."

"I will." The Warrant Officer hesitated. "Can it go wrong? I thought the idea was for us to disable the ship, they board and seize her, and we deactivate the disruptors."

"Yes, but that was before some of our people were transferred and replaced." The Lieutenant pretended to concentrate on a piece of equipment while a TechRate walked past. When all was clear again, he said, "Now it's just us and the four from the College. And I don't know which of the officers sent with the midshipmen are on our side. One of them must be, or he could not have brought the disruption unit triggers on board. He had to have been able to get past the security checks."

"But surely that doesn't change the plan. The devices are in place. Everything's a go now."

"Perhaps. We'll do our part. The rest is up to the *Almirante*."

THE GUNROOM WAS EMPTY, WHICH SUITED THE LIEUTENANT perfectly. Entering with his test instruments in hand, he checked the cabin allocations, walked to the cabin occupied by Harry and studied the plan of the air circulation ducts.

"Open the vent, Hans."

"Jawohl, Herr Lieutenant." The TechRate removed the grill.

The Lieutenant handed Hans a small device. "Push it as far as possible into the duct to the cabin, but not too far. We don't want him to see it through the grill."

Hans did as instructed then replaced the grill. "Done, Lieutenant. A good place to hide your hyperlink transmitter, but why this cabin?"

"It is the cabin of one of the pair who must be eliminated." Standing aside he paused while the android steward entered then stepped out into the corridor. When the door shut, he explained. "If the signal is traced before the *Almirante* engages, it will divert attention and convince our wonderful Captain the midshipman is a spy."

Laughing, the TechRate nodded. "Wunderbar!" He frowned. "Is there not a large reward for their capture? We could claim it once the ship is captured."

"We'll all share it once the capture is complete. It is too risky to attempt anything before then. Those Lacertian cadets are not here for training only. They protect this pair. Come, we must return to our stations before we are missed." Striding purposefully toward his office in AI Maintenance, the Lieutenant thought of his future, assured by the promised payment of a considerable sum for his part in this business, plus the promise of promotion to Commander in the fleet the Consortium was building. Yes, things looked good for those who accepted what the Consortium offered. All that remained was to send the signal confirming readiness at the appointed time, and when the *Almirante* appeared, to activate the disabling devices.

THE COMSRATE STARED AT THE SIGNAL DISPLAY. "That's strange. A hypercoms signal was just sent, but not from our transmitters. It originated from this ship, though."

"Trace the point of origin, and put a trace on the destination. Track the hyperlinks it passes through." The Communications Officer reached for his link. "Captain, we have an anomalous transmission originating from somewhere within this ship. I'm attempting to trace the source."

"Do so." Captain Haakon considered his latest briefing. "The security team think we have agents aboard from the Consortium. Do not discuss this signal with anyone. I wish to identify the agents."

Acknowledging the order, the Coms Officer cut his link. Nodding to the ComsRate, he said, "You heard. No discussion with anyone. Have you traced the source?"

"Only that it came from somewhere aft of Frame 150 and forward of the Weapons Control, sir. The message was too short."

"*Verdammt.* Okay. How about destination?"

"Hyperlink traffic makes it difficult, sir, but it seems to have gone to a deep space receiver beyond Seraphis." The man looked concerned. "The receiver is in Consortium controlled space, sir."

"Keep monitoring for more such signals. I want that transmitter traced." Studying a schematic of the ship section of the area identified by the ComsRate, he swore under his breath. This part of the ship housed the wardroom, the Gunroom, the Flight Command Centre — it was crammed with key systems and services. Without a definitive location it would take days to search. He advised the Captain.

"OUR PEOPLE HAVE EVERYTHING IN PLACE ON THE *KURFÜRST*. She's ready to be taken." The Captain of the Consortium cruiser leaned back as he faced the hologram of his fleet commander.

"Proceed with the operation, but be cautious. Haakon is a cunning commander. He won't surrender his ship without a fight."

"More fool him. I know Haakon. We were in the same class as midshipmen. As long as his ship is unable to fight or manoeuvre, it will not be difficult to force a surrender."

"You'll have to be the judge of that. She isn't up to strength on her Marine compliment, and she has around fifty cadets and midshipmen from the College on board for training." The Consortium admiral paused. "Including the two the Board want. Johnstone Research is offering a very large reward if they are taken alive, but don't take any chances doing that. The Board will be satisfied if they are killed."

"Very well, sir." The Captain watched the hologram vanish, and stared at the bulkhead for several minutes. He activated his link. "Number One, the operation is on. Assemble all HODs at twenty hundred hours for briefing."

"ANOTHER SIGNAL, SIR." THE COMSRATE FROWNED. "Got him. The transmitter is located in the Gunroom, sir."

"In the Gunroom? So it's one of the midshipmen. Verdammt traitor. Well, we have him now." He contacted Captain Haakon. "Kaptein, we have the location of the transmitter. It is in the Gunroom. I'm going there now to recover it and find out who is using it."

"Wait. I will send a security detail to meet you. I want to know whose cabin and how they are using this transmitter."

The search was thorough, but the searchers almost missed the simple box-like device in the duct. "We have it, sir. Portable hyperlink transmitter, set to send only on a frequency the Consortium use. It was in the air duct in the cabin of a Midshipman Heron."

Captain Haakon weighed the implications carefully. "Very well. Check the device for DNA traces and examine the access logs from that and all interfaces Heron has used. I want to know if he has accessed that transmitter through any system. Get Fleet Security on a private communications channel. Put it through to my office." The Captain left the Control Centre and arrived in his office just as his service android accepted the connection.

"Captain, your call to Fleet Security is on link. Shall I open the projection?"

"Thank you, SSU-01. At my desk." Seating himself, he addressed the hologram. "Lieutenant Van Damm?"

"Yes, Captain Haakon. What can we do for you, sir?"

"I need some information on two midshipmen in the College group I have aboard, Heron and O'Connor. Someone may be trying to implicate them in something close to espionage, and I need answers to some questions I have about them."

"I have to refer you to a more senior officer," said the security officer. "One moment please." Within seconds, an older man not in uniform appeared in the holographic display.

"Captain Haakon, I understand you need information on Midshipmen Heron and O'Connor. I will attempt to answer any questions you have. Please go ahead."

Aware the person he was addressing was very senior indeed, Captain Haakon gave a summary of what was happening and why he needed to know more about Harry and Ferghal.

"Very well, for your information only, please. They have abilities we don't fully understand but which are unique, a result of the gene splice, perhaps, or some other influence." The explanation continued, covering as much as the security service was prepared to release. "Does that answer your question, Captain?"

"I think it will have to do, sir. Thank you."

The senior officer smiled briefly. "Good. Just be aware that a lot of people are after them, and the Consortium has placed a reward on their capture so steep that it would balance the budgets of several countries. Good day, Captain."

The Captain leaned back in his chair. This conversation had answered one important question. He activated his link. "Send for Lieutenant Haäkinen and Midshipmen Heron and O'Connor."

CAPTAIN HAAKON STUDIED THE PAIR OF MIDSHIPMEN who stood at attention before him. "At ease, gentlemen. Mr Heron, do you recognise this unit?"

Harry glanced at the small oblong device on the Captain's desk. "No, sir."

"It was found in the air duct in your cabin, and it is — or was — linked to the interface to the AI there." He noted Harry's sincere look of perplexity. "It also has traces of your DNA on it."

"I cannot account for that, sir. It is not mine, and as far as I am aware, it has never been in my possession."

The Captain was already aware that the trace DNA his surgeon-commander had found on the device was probably due to airborne DNA from the occupant of the cabin. More intriguing was the absolute absence of any other DNA on the unit. He decided to take a different approach to get to the truth. "According to the access log, you do not use a manual interface unless you are under supervision. Why is that?"

"We have AI implants, sir." Harry glanced at Ferghal. "They were given to us on the *Vanguard* so we could access information. We needed it to catch up on knowledge we did not have when we arrived in this century."

Again, the Captain knew this from his contact with the Security Office. "But it does not function in the manner mine does, I am informed."

"Correct, sir. Something happened to it while we were captives in the Johnstone Laboratory on Pangaea. Now we have to use a screening device to shut out the AI."

"And they use a special code when they do access the AI through their links, sir," Lieutenant Haäkinen interjected. "It is unique and random, generated by the screening device they carry. The AI recognises them through it. Anything that does not carry that code is not from Heron or O'Connor, even if it appears to be from their interfaces."

"So I understand." Hesitating, the Captain studied the pair. "This is very difficult. Mr Heron, someone is trying to make it appear you are a spy or a saboteur, so I have no option but to make them think I believe that." He held up a hand to silence the protest he could see forming. "Trust me when I tell you we will ferret out the truth more efficiently with this ruse. I have no alternative but to order that you will, for the remainder of this cruise, not access the AI at any time unless it is under supervision. That goes for you too, Mr O'Connor. Lieutenant Hirsch and his specialist team are checking the system for any indication of sabotage. If they find nothing, I may reconsider."

"IT'S BLOODY RIDICULOUS!" KEIRON VOICED THE OPINION of the rest of the class. "I'll bet it's one of Barclay's stupid damn pranks."

"This isn't a prank, Mr Whitworth," Lieutenant Haäkinen snapped. "As to who's behind it, we don't know that either. In the meantime, Harry and Ferghal may only use an AI interface if one of you is there to supervise it. That's an order."

An angry murmur greeted this.

"I know it's unfair," growled the Lieutenant. "Life's not fair a lot of the time, and by now you know that. This is a serious business. All you need to know is what I have told you. I don't like this either."

"It's outrageous," protested Elize. "This means they are as good as under open arrest!"

"Yes, that is exactly what it means," said the Lieutenant. "But it allows us to protect them because now we know they will not be accessing the network. They're eliminated from suspicion. If anything happens, their actions will not have caused it, and we can set a trap for whoever is doing this."

Keiron was unconvinced. "Sir, I doubt the bastard who is behind this will risk exposure now. Why can't I go and beat the truth out of Barclay? We all know that he and his little toads tampered with Harry's work files at the College."

"Mr Whitworth, you know that can't be proved. And I most definitely can't overlook Mr Barclay accidentally encountering your fist, foot, or any other part of you. Is that clear?"

The Lieutenant's expression was grim. He despised this kind of business, a distraction foisted upon them by a bunch of troublemakers.

"The best thing all of you can do for Harry and Ferghal is make sure they have an ironbound alibi from now on. No," he held up a hand to silence the chorus of protests. "I will not discuss this any further. I will, however, tell you that Commander Diefenbach of the *Vanguard* has been contacted and has sent this ship's Communications Officer a special programme that will allow them to track the originator of certain access protocols. It will prove that Harry and Ferghal are innocent of any wrongdoing.

He paused.

"There is one more matter that is very important. Each of you will be assigned to a task for tomorrow's firing exercise. We are not certain that all the bugs in the system have been found, and it is essential that you are all alert for any, and I mean any, anomaly in any system you are monitoring. And I will add one more thing: you are under no circumstances to talk to anyone outside of this group about the restrictions on Harry and Ferghal, or why. We think the culprit may not be aware that we're on to this, and we don't want them to know what we suspect. Is that clear? Mr Whitworth, can I trust you not to take independent action?"

Keiron grumbled an affirmation of his compliance, and the group broke up to go to their next set of duties, Harry and Ferghal accompanied by Franz and Keiron respectively.

Chapter 13 – Sabotage

The restriction on accessing or using an interface with the AI meant Harry could not take an active role in the planned exercise. Instead, he was assigned an observer role with orders to shadow Lieutenant Grosmann at the manoeuvring plot table.

"Ready in Navigation, sir," reported the Navigation Officer.

"*Sehr gut*. Stand by."

Harry listened as Weapons Control confirmed that all was ready, the Scan team reported that the firing range area was clear, and Engineering confirmed that the hyperdrives were online.

The calm voice of Captain Haakon gave no hint of the tension he felt as he brought his ship into position for the full power firing trials of her main weapons.

"In position, sir," the ship's Chief Coxswain reported.

"Prepare to fire. Targeting, identify target." The Captain's orders stopped, mid-flow. "*Was ist das?*"

The three-dimensional display of the planets, asteroids and other objects visible to the ship's sensors vanished then returned without any of the normal annotations and information displays. Glancing at the console occupied by Frans Eberbach, Harry saw that instead of displaying the star chart for the system, it was blank. His mind raced as the Lieutenant tried to reactivate the star chart without success. Turning to the Navigating Officer, the Lieutenant said, "The system is not responding, sir. It is disabled in some way.

"Helm not answering, sir. We have no control from this station." The other display screens in the Command Centre went dark and inactive. Only the 3D view of space surrounding the ship remained, but without the identifying tags it normally showed for various objects.

The Captain linked to the Communications Officer.

"Manfred, we have lost all navigation display as well as the tactical and manoeuvring displays. What is the problem?"

"Something is jamming the system, sir," replied Lieutenant Commander Manfred Pösen. "It appears to be some sort of interference screen at local nodes. My men will have to search each node and find the cause of the problem, but it is blocking the system's ability to respond to the interfaces or to display data onscreen. I recommend a signal for assistance while I do this, sir. The ship will continue to function in failsafe mode while the system takes charge of essential controls to hold us in this position — provided it is not blocked from doing so."

"No, I don't want a signal. I suspect that is what someone is waiting for." The Captain paused. "Engineering, can you provide manoeuvring power and control of the propulsion systems without the AI?"

"Jawohl, Herr Kapitän. As long as we have control of the reactors, we can use the emergency manual controls to give you control of the propulsion systems. I will need time to disconnect the network interfaces and rig manual controls — say fifteen minutes."

"*Gut.* Do it and then stand by for further orders." Turning to the officers, the Captain ordered, "Mr Heron, Herr Eberbach, Lieutenant Grossmann, Lieutenant Haäkinen, follow me. We will manoeuvre the ship from the Observation Centre where we can see where we are going. Bring the navigation tablets." He activated his personal link. "Manfred, I will need you to keep the communication open between you, me, Engineering, and Weapons while you investigate the cause and restore the system. I am going to Observation and will command from there. I think we are being set up for an ambush."

"As you order, sir. There is some neural disruption of key nodes in the system, sir. We are tracing the source now."

"Do so, *schnell.* I think this is a trap."

In the open dome, with the stars and deep space visible, the Navigator set up her portable display. "Mr Heron, give me bearings on the nearest planets and moons. Hr. Eberbach, record them please." She paused. "Kapitän, without the AI, I do not have the means to calculate courses for micro transits."

The Captain linked to the Command Centre. "Bring the ship to full battle stations. I want Damage Control closed as well as all airlocks and main compartment doors."

"The weapons are inoperable, and the doors will have to be set manually, sir."

"Then do it, *schnell*. I do not think we have long." He contacted Engineering. "Have you transferred the drive controls to manual?"

"Ten minutes, sir, and we will have them ready. Manoeuvring, hyper transit and cruising drives almost ready, sir."

"Good. Stand by." To Lieutenant Grossman, he said, "*Sehr gut, Hannelore*, it is time to navigate by the stars. Herr Heron may assist you to bring us to this position." He handed the Lieutenant his tablet and nodded to Harry. "Herr Heron, I am told that you are very good with mathematics. What do you need to make your calculations?"

"Anything I can write on, sir," replied Harry, surprised at this question. His mind raced as he considered what he would need. "I will need to make notes for the calculations — but I do not have my logarithm tables here, and I will need them to do this, sir."

"Where are they?" demanded the Captain.

"In my attaché case in my cabin, sir. I could fetch them."

"*Nein*, you will remain here. Tell Herr Eberbach where the case is, and he can fetch it for you."

"As you wish, sir." The ice in Harry's voice showed his displeasure at not being allowed to do this himself. "Franz, my attaché case is stowed in my locker. I will also need the pad and pen on the desk, please. You will need my code to open the case."

The Captain interrupted. "Just bring the case, Midshipman. I trust Mr Heron. He may open it himself." He acknowledged Franz's salute. "Run, please — or walk very fast."

IN THE ENGINEERING CONTROL CENTRE, FERGHAL WATCHED in frustration as everyone around him did his or her part to bring the ship into the firing range designated for her exercise. Like Harry he was caught completely off guard by the disappearance of the engineering displays. The Engineering Commander was almost incandescent as the system malfunctioned, but he swiftly ordered his staff to switch to manual controls for all vital functions

Lieutenant Commander Reuter shook his head in doubt. "This is risky, sir. We could lose the ability to reconnect and restore control by doing this."

"Yes, but we could lose our ship if we do not," barked the Commander. "I want all essential services and controls disconnected now."

He answered his link then turned to his staff. "The Captain wants to manoeuvre by manual control. Herr O'Connor, help Lieutenant Commander Reuter — you too, Herr Whitworth. *Schnell, schnell!*"

In the process of disconnecting a part of the network's multicore harness, one of the Warrant Officers discovered a device that appeared to be independent of any part of the system. He called his Commander.

"Manfred, I think we have found a part of the problem, but now we may have a bigger one. This is sabotage, and it had to have been done by someone on board."

CALLING HARRY TO HER SIDE, THE LIEUTENANT POINTED to the chart display. "We need to calculate the waypoints for the helm that will take us clear of asteroids, the planetary gravity wells and so on. We will need to perform these calculations using the formulae I have here. I have heard it can be done, but I have no experience doing it since College." She studied Harry as he read the formulae, a frown on his brow. "Can you do it?"

"I think so, ma'am. If you can provide me with the relevant figures, it should be quite simple."

"I have the data. Where do you want to work?"

Looking round, Harry pointed to a cabinet next to the chart display. "This will do."

The Lieutenant smiled. "Sensible. Very well, let's prepare."

"The calculus is complex, ma'am, and the AI uses fifty-figure logarithms against my six-figure tables. I cannot be as accurate as the AI."

The Lieutenant shrugged. "That will be sufficient for our purposes. A thousand miles one way or the other should not be a problem as long as we keep clear of the planets." She hesitated. "In theory this is possible, Herr Heron, but it has only been done in classroom exercises — until now. We make history, I think."

She'd barely finished speaking when Franz returned with Harry's attaché case, slightly flushed and obviously worried.

"Sir, someone was in Harry's cabin when I entered the Gunroom — they were trying to break open this case, and I think they may have been trying to put something into it." Harry's head came up sharply, and he was about to exclaim his distaste for thieves and annoyance when the Captain cut across him.

"Can you identify the person? And why do you think they wanted to put something into it?"

"*Nein, Herr Kapitän,*" replied Franz. "I couldn't see his face. He was wearing a mask from a survival suit. He knocked me down and ran past me when I tried to stop him. But he dropped this." He held out a small device uncannily similar to the one Harry and Ferghal used to cut their connection to the AI, but with one significant difference. This one had a clamp.

IN AN UNOCCUPIED DAMAGE CONTROL STATION, a flustered and out of breath Midshipman Laschelles confronted Midshipmen Barclay and Miles. "Eberbach caught me in Heron's cabin. I don't think he'll be able to identify me though."

"Well, he didn't obviously," snarled Barclay. "Did you plant the device in Heron's case?"

"No, it was locked, and I couldn't get it open. Then I thought I could hide it in his cabin, but Eberbach came in before I could do it."

"Damn! So where is it now?"

"I don't know, I must have dropped it when I had to shove that damned Eberbach out of the way. What was so important about it anyway?"

"You bloody idiot. Now you've really bloody blown it." Barclay glared at his companion. "If it had been found in Heron's case, it would have got him into serious trouble. Damn you, Laschelles, can't you do anything right? Come on, we'd better get back to our stations before we're missed."

"Why are you so set on sabotaging Heron and O'Connor?" asked Miles, hurrying to keep up. "It's not as if they're that important."

"I've got plenty of reasons," retorted Barclay. "And I don't have to explain myself to you. Besides, I'm not the only one who knows that your father supplied the network log-ins and codes that you gave to Laschelles." Barclay glared from Miles to Laschelles. "You're both in this up to your necks along with me, so don't try to back out now. Both of you have too much to lose."

"Eon, I did my best! How was I supposed to know that Eberbach would be sent to fetch Heron's case?" Laschelles was almost in tears. "I'm just doing what my father told me to do. I'm trying to help you."

"Some help you are," snarled Barclay. Earlier he'd tried to talk to the man who'd received the activator that had now disabled the ship, and he'd been fobbed off with an order to mind his own business until the ship was taken. His attempt to plant the device in Harry's cabin had been a spur of the moment desire to take out his frustrations on his enemy. And now it had gone wrong.

He hurried off to join his classmates at their station, shadowing the main damage control party.

HARRY FOCUSSED ON THE TASK OF CALCULATING A COURSE using the coordinates the Captain gave him. Working quickly, he converted the figures to their appropriate logarithm and noted this on his pad, adding the integers and then adding, subtracting and converting back to the anti-logarithms.

Harry worked as fast as he could, careful to check his results, passing each solution to Lieutenant Grossman, who passed it directly to the Helm.

For her part the Lieutenant was fascinated as she watched. This was, as far as she could recall, the first time she had ever seen anyone using written tables and doing the calculations on sheets of paper. Mentally she made a note to find out how to do this herself when the opportunity arose.

The ship made a series of small near hyperspeed leaps to the first waypoint, then the next and then a third. Satisfied that he was now clear of the ship's appointed position, Captain Haakon ordered that a signal requesting assistance be sent, and he provided a coded set of coordinates for the rendezvous. Then, he ordered the next jump in the sequence according to Harry's calculations. As the ship surged, a lifepod ejected spinning in its wake.

Minutes later, a Consortium heavy cruiser dropped out alongside the lifepod, its weapons hot to fire. Frustrated by the absence of a target, the Captain ordered the occupants of the pod recovered, leaving the empty unit drifting in space. The three men had a difficult task to reach the open airlock on the cruiser, but as soon as they were in the lock, the cruiser vanished in another hyperjump.

SAFELY ACROSS THE SOLAR SYSTEM FROM THE POSITION occupied by the Consortium ship, Captain Haakon consulted the latest data from the scanners in the interceptors that formed a defensive screen around the ship.

"Ach! I thought so," he noted with satisfaction. "I was right. Someone was waiting for us to call for help." He activated his link. "Manfred, have you got the system back yet? We have visitors, and we will need to use our weapons very soon, I think."

"Ten more minutes, Kapitän. It is difficult because the devices are fitted to nodes, those that control our interfaces and displays. Removing them must be done carefully, as they could be programmed to destroy the node if tampered with, and there are a great many of them." He hesitated. "This will not be a simple operation. These things have been installed over an extended period but will have been activated by some form of trigger device. *Lieutenant* Marx, Warrant Officer Cantano and TechRate Drax are missing. I suspect they are behind this."

"Have the lifepod stations searched," ordered the Captain. "I will continue to manoeuvre on manual, but I think we're being followed. I want to be fully operational when we meet." The Captain paused. "One more thing, Manfred. We have recovered a device that might have the capability to signal the Consortium. I will bring it to you when we can resume normal operation. I want it analysed to discover who has used it and what its full function is.

The Captain ended the conversation then turned to the watching navigation team. "Now, gentlemen, calculate for me a course to jump us toward our visitor in three steps across this sector." He marked a series of waypoints on an erratic course that would be difficult for an enemy to predict. Harry bent once more to the task of calculating the courses necessary, his pages rapidly filling with his neat figures and the results. He handed these to Lieutenant Grossmann, and two minutes later the Captain ordered the first leap. The ship's hyperdrive pods flared briefly to send it on a long diagonal to a point just inside the orbit of Jupiter.

"Captain," called Lieutenant Haäkinen, as he controlled the optical arrays with Midshipman Eberbach. "The Consortium ship has jumped. He delayed and may have recovered something."

"Good." The Captain gave orders for the next jump, once more sending the ship on a parabolic swing to the edge of the Kuiper Belt where it stationed near Pluto-Charon. "Report enemy presence," he ordered as soon as the optical instruments focussed.

"Nothing on optical, sir," came the reply.

"Keep scanning."

"Sir," called Franz. "The electronic scanners are back online. I have a contact, sir, at our last position. A ship has just dropped out.

"Excellent. Next jump sequence. Commence." He contacted the Communications Officer as the ship leapt into her next course. "Manfred, are the weapons systems back online yet?"

"Yes, sir, but Navigation is still down."

"Keep working. We are about to engage the enemy. Get Navigation online and notify me when it is."

The ship dropped out in an empty sector of the solar system, and the scanners immediately identified several asteroids and a single comet.

"Captain, we have a ship on scan. Presumed hostile. She identifies as a Consortium heavy cruiser."

"Good," exclaimed the Captain. "He's taking the bait, and he doesn't know we're regaining control. Now, Lieutenant Grossmann, our final jump, if you please."

The ship surged into a microtransit then dropped out seconds later half a million miles from her previous position just as the Consortium ship vanished in a transit of her own. "Weapons, prepare to fire on the enemy as soon as he appears on screen. I want him engaged as soon as I close the range. Lieutenant Grossmann, Herr Heron — stand by for the next manoeuvre."

"Aye, aye, sir," responded Harry, already calculating the navigation solutions.

The Captain gave Harry a curious look. This youth was far more unusual than he had been told. He made a note to talk to him as soon as they had dealt with the present crisis.

"Target, sir. Consortium ship at our previous coordinates. He's locked his scan to us. He's jumped again, sir."

The Captain snapped his attention back to his ship. "Weapons stand by. Open fire as soon as you have a target lock."

The Consortium ship flashed into view a few hundred kilometres from their position.

"Lieutenant Grossmann, bring us to the position for firing."

As the ship slowed and swung, her weapons sent their brilliant beams of destruction arcing across the space between the ships. For the first time Harry, Franz, and at least one of the Lieutenants saw the awesome power of the plasma cannon and particle beam weapons as great bursts of energy tore chunks out of the Consortium ship's hull. The Consortium Captain reacted with commendable swiftness, his weapons returning fire even as his hyperdrive pods lit up and the ship leapt out of range to vanish into the singularity she had created.

The *Der Große Kurfürst* followed, leaping away from the scene of the engagement and placing herself almost a million miles from that position. But, instead of the expected return manoeuvre by the enemy cruiser, three ships dropped out between the *DGK* and the spreading debris, immediately identifying themselves as Fleet reinforcements.

"Herr Kapitän." The voice of the Communications Commander resonated throughout the observation dome. "The AI is now fully restored, but it insists there are still two nodes it is unable to access." His frustration was evident in his voice. "We have checked and double checked, but all our recorded nodes are clear and functional."

"Does the AI indicate where these nodes are? What are they controlling?"

"The two nodes are what it refers to as mobile units. One is in the dome, the other in Engineering, and neither is on my schematic. I'm sending someone to check the dome now."

"Very good, Manfred. Keep me informed." The Captain turned to his officers. "We will return to the Command Centre. Well done to you all. Mr Heron, your calculations were very interesting. Thank you for your efforts."

They had barely resumed their stations in Navigation when Commander Pösen arrived with two technicians in tow. He stopped and glared at the displays. "Alright," he growled. "Who has the mobile interface that is still blocked?"

The assembled team stared at him in surprise.

He didn't wait for an answer. "According to the AI, the mobile interface node that was in the dome is now here." His gaze swept the watch-keepers at their stations, taking in Harry, Franz and Lieutenant Haäkinen. "Come on, who has it? I haven't time for silly games, and I have another to check in Engineering."

"What is this, Manfred?" asked the Captain. "There is no portable or mobile device here, and we had nothing but the portable chart display and a tablet in the dome. Can the system not identify the unit properly?"

The Commander's face went through a moment of struggle. "It can. I shall ask it to identify the position on the schematic display. May I use your console, Siegfried?"

"*Natürlich!*" replied the Executive Officer.

Commander Pösen strode to the console and entered a series of commands. The screen filled with the schematic for the displays and consoles in the centre, each identified by a serial code. Just below the console identified as the one the Commander was using and shown as not connected to the network, was a single unit with a separate code that flashed on and off. The Commander turned with a triumphant look. "*Ich hab's!*" He stared at the schematic again then glared at Harry, who stood with his pad and books clasped in his hands, a puzzled expression on his face as his mind cast about for a logical explanation of the dread he sensed.

The Commander pierced him with a pointed stare. "*Was ist das?* Where have you hidden it?"

Harry glanced about him, making sure the Commander was speaking to him. Certainly he hadn't done anything!

"Hidden what, sir?" he asked, embarrassed that his face turned bright red as it always did when he felt singled out."

Lieutenant Haäkinen stepped forward. "Sir, I think it must be the device Herr Heron uses to block the AI, which he has been ordered to keep activated and on his person at all times."

"Let's see if you're correct, Lieutenant," said the Captain, somewhat doubtful of this possibility. "Herr Heron, please deactivate your device."

"As you wish, sir. " Harry put down his books and pad then reached into his pocket and withdrew his screening unit. He pressed the switch. Instantly the console display showed the mobile node reconnected to the neural net.

In his eyes and ears Harry was aware of the rush of data as the system tried to run a diagnostic scan in his head. He winced as it flashed code in his vision. He sent an instruction to the system that he did not need a diagnostic scan. Opening his eyes again, he said, "The system seems to think I am part of it, sir. It is trying to ascertain whether I am functioning correctly. I have told it that I am."

There was a long moment of silence as the assembled officers digested this.

Captain Haakon spoke first. "Let me understand this correctly You could have given commands to the system and run scans if I had ordered you to turn off that device?"

Harry looked surprised. This possibility had not occurred to him. The realisation sent a shiver down his spine. He was now part of the intelligence that ran this ship. Slightly stunned by this revelation, he stammered a reply. "I'm sorry, sir, I . . . I did not think . . . I mean, I did not realise . . . ." He stumbled to silence, at a loss to explain the turmoil in his mind as the full impact sank in.

"SO HERON AND O'CONNOR ARE A PAIR OF MOBILE NODES as far as the system is concerned. We could have used them to access it and bypass the devices the saboteurs installed. Is that correct?" Captain Haakon's fingers played with the data chip before him. "Why didn't they tell us they could do it? Heron must surely have known!"

"It certainly seems that the system regards him as part of its network," said Commander Pösen. "I have talked to him, sir. He simply did not think of it, and he was absorbed in doing manual calculations using pencil, paper, and logarithm tables so that we could make the necessary hyper transits since we had no access to the AI navigation system. We forget he is still very much a man from four centuries ago. I have no idea what is causing this interface. The neural links are not supposed to operate in this way — mine certainly does not."

"Nor does mine," said the Captain. "Yet these two are able to go into the system as if they are part of it." He paused. "Could they have triggered or disabled these devices?"

"It's possible, yes. I could test it with them. We do know the devices they carry were operational the entire time. The network activity log shows they were isolated before and throughout the period."

"That is so," interjected Commander Pösen. "At best they could have activated only the devices close to them. That would not explain how the rest were activated. I think there is another device available here — and we must not forget that we have an officer and two TechRates missing."

The Captain's frown deepened. "That is true. And the device Herr Eberbach found — have you analysed it?"

"Yes. It is another of these neural disruption devices. The Surgeon Commander ran a DNA check, which showed that it you had handled it as well as Herr Eberbach, Lieutenant Otto Marx and several others not connected with this ship. There are also minute traces that seem to be two of the passengers from the College, but they are inconclusive."

"I see," said the Captain. "So it appears that Marx may have the device that activated these. But he may not be the only person involved."

"That is correct, sir. It may be that the DNA is a result of handling by others before the unit was delivered." He consulted his tablet. "The DNA from the College could be from any of five or six people there — or two people on the ship now."

"Very well, hand it all over to the Security Service. They will have to sort it out." The Captain paused. "What have we learned from the lifepod that was ejected? Have we recovered anyone or anything from that?"

"Nothing, sir, but there was evidently some haste to evacuate the occupants because one of them damaged his survival suit in the hatch. A small piece of the suit was left on the locking mechanism." He smiled. "For the wearer's sake, I hope he was not too long in the vacuum."

Chapter 14 – Seeing Double

The *DGK*'s return to the huge docking station in geostationary Earth orbit met with a media circus. It got worse when the first people to board were members of Fleet Security.

"How was the ship damaged?" parried a persistent news reporter, eager to get the scoop.

The Security team brushed past him, but he was undaunted.

"There's a rumour of sabotage. Who's responsible?"

"No comment. Fleet will issue a report later."

"Looks like she's been in a battle — I recognise plasma burns. How'd it happen?"

"No comment." The stern man leading the security squad swept the crowd with cold eyes. "Fleet will release a statement in due course." Turning abruptly, he led the way through the boarding tube, his men closing rank behind him, with two armoured and armed men stepping aside to let him pass then turning to face the throng, their expressions unreadable as they hefted their weapons into the ready position.

The *DGK*'s Executive Officer greeted the visitors, saluting. "Welcome aboard, sir. The Captain has the pair you're here to collect in his quarters. This way please."

"Captain." Captain Haakon stood to greet his visitor. "We got your message. Midshipmen Heron and O'Connor have been isolated and are waiting for you."

"Isolated?" The visitor paused. "They're not under arrest." His frown lifted. "But it will fit with our plan. Very well, I apologise for the lack of courtesy, Captain Haakon, but, as you are aware, the situation is a bit tricky. There's been a leak, and now the media are on the dock demanding answers." His smile flashed and vanished as swiftly. "It serves our purposes very neatly — plenty of witnesses for what we have planned. Where are they?"

Touching his link, Captain Haakon said, "Jaakko, bring in Heron and O'Connor please."

The door opened, and Lieutenant Haäkinen walked in followed by Harry and Ferghal.

"Mr Heron, Mr O'Connor, sir," said Jaakko.

"Thanks, Jaakko. Mr Heron, Mr O'Connor, Captain Brandeis is here to escort you to Earth."

Harry nodded. "Aye, aye, sir. I believe the Captain has a code to impart."

Surprised, Captain Haakon frowned, but his visitor laughed. "I do indeed, Midshipman." He handed over a datachip. "I think you'll know what it means."

"Thank you, sir." He drew out his tablet and glanced at Captain Haakon. "With your permission, sir?"

"Go ahead."

Inserting the chip, Harry studied the image that opened. "Indeed, sir, I know what to do with this." Smiling, he showed it to Ferghal. "Admiral Popham's Signal Book. Repair on board."

Ferghal nodded. "Been a right long time since I've seen a hoist like that," he added with a grin. "Takes me right back to the *Spartan*."

THE NEWS MEDIA SCRUM BECAME A FREE-FOR-ALL when Harry and Ferghal stepped through the access port into the dock with their escort.

"Are they under arrest?" said one of the journalists.

"Was the ship sabotaged?" demanded another trying to push his way to the front.

"Don't answer that," snapped one of the escorts as he shoved the reporter aside.

"What's going to happen to them?" shouted another. "Hey, I recognise them — it's that pair they say are from the past, the ones Dr Sherring says are a danger to society!"

"Now watch them get it all wrong," Captain Brandeis growled. Touching his link, he ordered, "Marines, clear our route." To Harry he said, "Let them get a good look at you, but stay close."

"What are they talking about? Who is this Dr Sherring?" Harry gasped as he was hustled forward through the space the newly arrived Marine escort created.

"Some damned crackpot making a name for himself. Ignore them, Mid. Bloody journos. You can always rely on them to get everything fouled up." He snorted a derisive laugh as they reached the access to the transporter that would take them to the shuttle. "They say it's their job to keep the public informed — misinformed more like."

"Why do they think we've been arrested?" Ferghal frowned as he straightened his jacket and prepared to enter the transport car. It was all too clear in his memory what happened to men in his day who were arrested and accused of some crime.

The officer snorted again. "Fleet put out a statement that the scheduled cruise and the trial firing had to be curtailed because of an accident aboard." He shrugged. "Someone leaked that there'd been sabotage." He jerked his thumb in the general direction of the dock they'd just left. "Those vultures put two and two together and got five."

"I think I understand you, sir." Harry's frown deepened. "But it is most unpleasant to be considered a criminal. I'm sure Ferghal agrees with me."

The officer laughed as the transport slid to a halt. "There are worse things. It does serve a purpose, though — it will distract them while my people pick up the guys we're really after. Now then, gentlemen, another shuttle is going to take us to a safe and secure location once our decoys have led the pack in the wrong direction."

Ferghal's exclamation of surprise drew his friend's attention.

Harry looked in the direction Ferghal was staring, and was stunned at what he saw. There stood two young men, exact duplicates of himself and Ferghal.

"Amazing what a bit of facial remodelling can do. These fellows are going to keep the media and a few other people thinking that you've departed on the shuttle." He turned to their body doubles. "You've been briefed. Any questions? No? Right, you know your tasks. Join your escorts, and let's get going. We'll give the word to go as soon as we're set up."

Watching the doubles set off, Harry asked, "Will they always resemble us, sir?"

The officer laughed. "No, certainly not. It can be undone. Now it's your turn to get a new face. This way, please. This'll take about half an hour."

LOOKING IN THE MIRROR, HARRY COULDN'T HELP LAUGHING. The makeup and the prosthetic remodelling of his face had aged him and changed his appearance completely, nor did it end there. His hands had been fitted with thin gloves that aged his hands to match his face, and that also gave him new fingerprints. The makeup and partial mask were uncomfortable and felt very strange, as did the uniform, which he quickly realised was not quite as it appeared and had some kind of armour built in.

He glanced at Ferghal and laughed. "You look exactly like Eon Barclay!"

"Do not say so!" Ferghal tried to see his reflection. "Surely not!"

Studying him critically, the security officer frowned. "There's a resemblance, but it is mainly the build, I think. Never mind. I want you to change into the uniforms we have here. Then we had better get moving. Your body doubles will be doing their part already."

"Why is this necessary, sir? Surely we could simply board with our class and be removed from this place that way."

The officer hesitated. "A rather large reward has been offered for your elimination. To send you planet-side with your class would endanger them too. This way we hope to deliver you and everyone else intact." After Harry pulled on the Fleet Security jacket and checked himself in the mirror, the security officer said, "Ready? Let's go. Stay close to us, and do whatever we say immediately, without hesitation. Got it?"

"Aye, aye, sir," Harry and Ferghal responded in unison, and within minutes they joined the throng of reporters hurrying to watch the body doubles of themselves leave the station as taunts of "Traitors!" could be heard among the crowd.

"What on earth is happening?" Ferghal asked. Like Harry, he was finding the facial prosthetics irritating.

"We've had a tip-off." The officer lowered his voice. "Please don't say anything more than yes or no to anyone. Your accents and manner of speech are so unique that anyone will guess you're the real you."

Harry nodded. "Aye, aye, sir."

"That's exactly what I mean." The man smiled. "Look, it's important the newshounds don't realise what we're doing. You're about to appear over there with your escort. You'll be taken to a shuttle — or rather your doubles will be — and we'll tag along behind as if we're part of the crowd. While everyone's eyes are on the shuttle, we'll slip through the crowd and take a different transport."

It gave Harry and Ferghal a very strange feeling to see themselves surrounded by heavily armed and armoured Marines. The crowd exploded as the decoy Harry and Ferghal and their security escorts walked past the gaggle of reporters. The real Harry and Ferghal followed the armoured group escorting their doubles. Watching the behaviour of the news reporters, Harry found himself torn between amusement and disgust.

"This way, gents." Their escort turned them down a broad passage. "With a bit of luck that'll keep their attention focused on what we want them to see. Don't relax yet. We aren't in the clear. The fat lady hasn't sung."

Ferghal wanted to ask what this expression meant, but stifled the desire along with a grin at the humorous image it conjured as they joined a second group of security personnel.

"All set, gents?" Captain Brandeis said, and he acknowledged their nods of affirmation. To the security team, he said, "Good, the package is set up. You know your tasks, and you know the signal. Take your positions as we arranged. Alpha Squad, passenger transfer. Delta, arrivals. Golf to departures. Bravo, the College party will be assembling at Departure Gate Six. Let's go."

Chapter 15 – Death on Camera

It felt extremely strange for Harry and Ferghal to be among their classmates unrecognised and forbidden to speak to them. Seated in the transport with the security detail, they listened to the conversations around them, sorely tempted to intervene, Harry especially so when Elize spoke up in his defence when a few others said they'd doubted his integrity all along.

That made her blood boil, but she remained cool as ever. "I don't believe Harry or Ferghal fitted those devices. They couldn't have. They are honourable men, unlike some of you." She stared pointedly at Barclay.

"I agree," said Howie, "but we'll just have to hope the security people know what they're doing." He glowered at Harry and Ferghal, convinced he was looking at a pair of security officers.

Barclay got up to change seats, uncomfortable with Elize's glare, and sat directly across from Harry. "That's the last we'll see of Heron," he said to Laschelles. "Told you they'd be dealt with." He smirked.

When Harry tensed at that, pressure from the Captain's elbow reminded him that he was in disguise, and not to respond to the insult.

The loadmaster announced, "Seats, please, gentlemen. We're good to go as soon as you're seated."

Speaking directly into Harry's ear, the Captain said, "The other side have made their move. In a moment, all hell will break loose. No matter what you see or hear, do what I tell you, and don't react." He paused. "An assassin shot you both in front of the media crews. They've taken our bait. Now we close the trap."

Rigid with shock, Harry felt the blood drain from his face beneath the make-up and mask.

The shuttle pilot announced that their departure was on hold due to an incident in the adjacent dock.

The loadmaster approached. "Captain Brandeis, sir, the pilot's compliments, sir. He'd appreciate your joining him in Control."

The Captain stood and nodded to a Lieutenant the other side of Ferghal, and then he followed the loadmaster. The Lieutenant leaned close to them. "I'll order you two to secure the entry door in a moment. Stand each side of it as if you're guards."

THE BURST OF WEAPONS FIRE BROUGHT A MOMENT of shocked silence then screams as the security team responded. Directing their fire at two men on the edge of the press of reporters, the guards' bolts struck home. As soon as the men fell, the weapons were trained on the crowd, causing them to draw back, some alarmed, some angry. Huddling in clusters, some turned their cameras on the security troops pouring into the space, others focussed on the casualties. The haze of smoke thinned, but the stench of burned flesh wafted across the dock, and many looked decidedly unwell.

The tension was palpable. The body doubles lay sprawled on the deck partially obscured by the medics and security guards who surrounded them. The bodies of the supposed assassins sprawled against a bulkhead, one with a weapon next to his hand.

"In a horrific act, the two midshipmen suspected of sabotage have been killed by attackers." The news reporter dramatically directed his companion to the bodies of the fallen assassins surrounded by medics and armoured security personnel. His gesture brought a response from the security detail, and he made sure his gesture could not be deemed threatening by spreading his arms wide palms open. "The motive of the killers is unclear, but we will attempt to bring you more information as soon as possible.

The officer in charge of the security squad glared at the mayhem. "Sergeant, secure the area. No one leaves. No one is to approach the bodies!"

"Yes, sir."

The security officer noted who stood where. The assassins lay where they had fallen. Several more reporters and their assistants huddled against a bulkhead. Somewhat apart from the crowd stood a woman he recognised as the new anchor for a popular network, her assistants gathered around her, and a little to her right stood another familiar reporter, his tousled appearance his trademark, and his cameraman.

"Attention!" the sergeant bellowed. He waited until the noise subsided and his men moved into position. "This dock is now under total lockdown."

Stepping forward, the officer said, "Thank you, Sergeant." His gaze swept the reporters. "I will take no questions until I am satisfied there is no further threat." He glanced at the sprawled bodies of the two midshipmen, now being placed in containers. "Midshipmen Heron and O'Connor were not under arrest. They were being escorted to a secure facility pending their appearance at the Pangaea enquiry." He paused, allowing that to sink in. "My investigators will check everyone's credentials. Please cooperate. Refusal to do so will be taken as complicity in this murder."

A scuffle near one of the exits drew gasps and then screams.

"Everyone freeze, or I will detonate this!" The speaker was the thickset man with the tousled white-blonde hair. He seized the attractive news anchor and held her close to him. "This bomb is big enough to blow out this dock and everyone on it. Here's what's going to happen next, if you value your life. Security, put your weapons down slowly. Medics, load the bodies into the shuttle." He watched the security commander as two more reporters shed their pose and joined him. "And before you think of trying anything clever, they've also got triggers for this baby," he said, caressing the bomb.

ABOARD THE SHUTTLE, CAPTAIN BRANDEIS SURVEYED the seated midshipmen. "We have a serious situation in Dock Five. There has been an attempt to seize two of your comrades. As a precaution, we are going to do a full security check on all of you." He held up a hand. "That includes the instructional staff. Do not attempt to leave your seats, and comply immediately with my people's orders." Over their heads, he nodded in the direction of the Lieutenant. "Max, carry on, please."

The Lieutenant stood and delivered his orders. "You two. Take post at the entry port. No one boards or leaves. Move."

Harry took up the indicated position trying to look as if he knew what he was doing. Suppressing a grin, he thought of how often he'd mimicked his officers on the *Spartan* in the same effort to appear in control.

On the other side of the door, Ferghal took a similar stance, conscious of the stares of some of his friends and the glowers of others, particularly Eon Barclay and his friends. He wondered why Laschelles looked pale and Miles seemed frightened as the security men moved up the aisles, checking ID chips and running background checks through the AI.

Harry noticed the security team hesitate when checking a Lieutenant Commander's details. Then, apparently satisfied, they moved on.

"All clear, sir."

"Good." Captain Brandeis paused. "We'll be cleared to leave as soon as Dock Five is secured. There's been a further development there, but it is reported to be under control."

Ferghal watched as Barclay shot a furtive glance at him and Harry and whispered something to his companions.

THE SECURITY COMMANDER SIGNALLED HIS MEN. "We'll do it your way, mister." He unbuckled his weapons belt and lowered the lift to the deck while running an ID check on the blonde man. Reluctantly, his men removed their weapons as well. Moments later, the confirmation displayed in the commander's visor. Calmly he ordered, "Medics, load the bodies, please. They may as well have them. Dead is dead."

"The rest of you, on the floor. No one move." Staying close to the bulkhead, the three assassins and their hostage moved toward the shuttle. As the medics disembarked, the blonde man signalled his companions. "Check there's no one aboard."

The pair moved cautiously, their military training evident as they advanced, darting into the shuttle, then one reappeared. "All clear. Ready to go."

"Not quite." The leader indicated three reporters. "You three. Gather all the weapons and bring them to the shuttle."

The security commander noticed this with interest. Why summon reporters to gather the weapons? He recorded their faces and requested background checks. The woman "hostage" didn't appear to be making any effort to resist her captor. It struck him she appeared far too relaxed. He made a request to the AI, and an image appeared in his visor. Carefully he aligned it to the woman's face. The image flashed, and he recognised the match. Casually, he touched a concealed link on his belt as he remarked, "I hope you have a strong stomach, Ms Roach. Don't worry though, our people will have you back in no time at all."

A sharp intake of breath among the journalists was followed by screams as two Lacertians came into view seemingly from nowhere. Several of the reporters realised they'd been there all along; some would later acknowledge they'd actually been looking right at them but hadn't known it. One seized the woman, the other the man. There was a snap and a scream as his arm broke.

Ms Roach struggled in the iron grip of the alien holding her, trying desperately to reach into a pocket. With a ripping sound, the cloth tore and a small device spun out of reach.

Stepping forward, the security commander nodded. "Sergeant secure the prisoners." Turning to the shuttle he said, "Sci'Anatha? Are your prisoners able to walk, or shall I send the medics?"

Two more Lacertians emerged from the shuttle, one carrying and one dragging the two remaining assassins. The leader said, "No need, Commander. This one they may deal with. The other is no longer in need of their services."

"Pity. Still, we have three on murder charges, and three more on complicity at least." Addressing the stunned reporters, he said, "I will require all the data files from your cameras as part of my investigation into the murders of Midshipmen Heron and O'Connor. We will return the files once the Public Prosecutor's office has verified the records." Moving closer to the furious woman, he added, "Ms Roach, or perhaps I should say, Ms Schmidt, or was it Ms Ranford, or Ms Dunning? Never mind, I'm sure you'll be able to sort out who you are by the time we have put all the outstanding charges against you before the prosecutor."

Chapter 16 – Enquiry

Harry thought back on the week following the events that day with the assassins. *The strangest week I've ever experienced*, he mused, and then he remembered — *well, with the exception of the day we were catapulted four hundred years into the future.*

This was a strange new world indeed.

Accommodated in an apartment normally reserved for senior officers while they awaited the enquiry, he and Ferghal were well catered for by the android service units, but cut off from almost everyone except the security team guarding them. Pacing the luxurious quarters, he tried to make sense of the news broadcasts. Finally, he blurted to Ferghal, "I understand in part why the news of our deaths is being perpetuated, but why may we not see Aunt Niamh? I know she is here, and she is terribly distressed. So is Danny."

"Aye, the divil is in it now." Ferghal watched Harry and huffed out an exasperated breath. "Can you not stop pacing? 'Tis making me nervous just watching you."

About to snap an angry response, Harry stopped. "My apologies." He flung himself into a chair. "I can't stand this waiting."

"It is no easy thing for me either." Ferghal cast his eyes about, hating their confinement. This was becoming all too regular for his liking. "I know the Captain said our doubles were not killed, but I did not like having to watch them fall to the ground in an attack meant for us, and I cannot understand why this ... this *thing* keeps showing that scene over and over again!" He gestured toward the news hologram.

The door opened, and the boys leapt to their feet. "Captain," they said in unison, straightening their uniforms and squaring their shoulders.

"Good morning, gentlemen. At ease." Ushering in two men, the Captain smiled. "I thought you might like to meet the men you were impersonating while they impersonated you."

Harry stared, speechless. Ferghal broke the tension with a laugh. "Begorrah, now that takes the pot o' gold." Striding forward, he held out his hand to the man whose face he'd worn long enough to begin to think it his own. "I admire a man who stands in to be shot for another he doesn't even know. And thank ye that ye let me have my own face back."

The young man laughed and shook Ferghal's hand, wincing at the firmness of the grip, which Ferghal did not do intentionally. He was never aware of his own strength. "Next time you can take a hit from a neural disruption bolt. I'm just glad they didn't use a plasma burst. It wasn't a lot of fun, but if it brings these bastards down, I hope it was worth it, and you fellows will give them hell when you testify."

Harry shook hands with his body double. "Thank you for keeping us safe. Was it very bad—? I'm sorry, I don't know your name."

"I'm Peter. It's good to meet you finally. As Armand said, not a lot of fun, but we knew what to expect, and we had some help to take the worst of it. Still, I want to see those bastards squirm."

Harry laughed. "To be sure, we will do our best. I've a notion of what they're afraid we might reveal."

The Captain cut him off. "Don't tell us. Save it for the stand." Motioning them all to seats, he took one himself. "Now, the charade isn't quite done yet. As you know, the enquiry reopened yesterday. The Consortium people have challenged just about everything from the Fleet records of what was going on when the squadron arrived at Pangaea, but they haven't yet managed to invalidate the questionable activities you fellows exposed when you escaped from Johnstone's secret facility. What they have done is cast a lot of doubt."

Harry pondered this. "I see, sir." He paused. "When will we be allowed to see our family?"

"That might be tricky. You're due in court shortly, and you'll see them shortly." The Captain looked guilty. "Your guardian, Commodore Heron, knows the situation, but his sister Niamh L'Estrange . . . well, let's just say that I don't plan to be within earshot when she finds out."

The boys chuckled and exchanged glances. They knew all too well their aunt's fierce temper. Harry felt conflicted; he was angry that Aunt Niamh — in reality his twelve times great niece — had suffered this distress needlessly, and he was amused at the Captain's wariness of her expected reaction.

The Captain continued. "Unfortunately, we needed her unaware of the truth so that we could maintain the deception. That's also why you've been kept in isolation."

"So when do we appear before the enquiry, sir?" Harry asked.

"In a couple of hours. I've come to collect you. Peter and Armand are Special Ops, and they'll accompany you just in case." He paused. "But before that, we thought it best for you to see Mrs L'Estrange. She's with Commodore Heron in the adjoining suite."

THE WAIT TO BE CALLED TO ENTER THE COURT and take the stand made Harry fretful. Their presence was still being kept secret, but the three judges presiding knew of the subterfuge.

"Just remember, lads, this is not a trial," said Captain Brandeis "It is an enquiry to establish and confirm certain facts. They want to hear your story because your escape effort exposed a lot of things we never would have known had you not salvaged the core memories you brought out of the Johnstone facility." Captain Brandeis hesitated. "And there's something else. They seem to think you learned something that the Johnstone Group is desperate to keep secret."

Harry nodded. "So everyone says. I think I know what it is, but I will need to have those memory units connected to an AI to be able to show the court."

A look of surprise crossed the Captain's face. "I'll arrange it." Taking a deep breath, he sat back in his chair. "Now, I better tell you what to expect when you enter the court. It is like an auditorium. The judges will be on a dais in front of you. The three judges are at the centre, and they have writers and technical advisers on each side of them. In this case, some are senior officers from the Fleet. On either side of the dais are the legal teams representing various interested parties. The judges will ask the questions, but the lawyers may ask supplementary questions to clarify anything you tell the judges. You will be sitting facing the judges with the legal teams to your left and right. There will be large screens behind you so the public — in this case mostly reporters and people with a personal connection to these events — will be able to see everything you say, show or do."

"It sounds very crowded, sir." Ferghal's nerves made him fidget. His only experience of courts — four hundred years earlier — suggested oppression, injustice for the poor and judges who handed out harsh sentences for the least offence.

"The public gallery is a bit full, but the court itself is quite relaxed. As I said, this isn't a trial. It's a fact-gathering exercise. The lawyers are here to challenge any fact they think might prejudice their clients' interests. Remember, the main purpose of this enquiry is to determine what happened on Pangaea to trigger the sending of the Fleet force to stabilise it."

TWO HOURS DRAGGED PAST BEFORE THE MASTER AT ARMS arrived. "Midshipman Heron is called," she said to the Captain.

Captain Brandeis looked at Harry. "Ready, Midshipman?"

"I hope so, sir." Harry made sure his screening device was in his pocket, and stood to follow the Master at Arms.

"You'll be fine. Armand, go with him."

"This is going to be interesting," said their escort, a Master Warrant Officer. "The bench know who you are, but the court has not been told your name, so you'll be asked to state it."

She opened the door and announced, "Witness H, sir."

Trying to control his nerves so that his knees wouldn't feel weak, Harry walked into the court. The sharp intake of breath from one group of lawyers reached his ears. Stopping at the seat indicated, he faced the judge and bowed.

"Midshipman Henry Nelson-Heron, WTO Fleet?"

"I am he, my Lor — Lady." He realised just in time that the presiding judge was a woman.

She smiled and glanced at her papers. "Please be seated, Mr Heron." She watched him sit. "Let's get started. You may address me and the members of the panel as sir. It has been a very long time since we rejoiced in titles such as Lord and Lady."

A quiet chuckle rippled throughout the courtroom.

"Objection, sir!" One of the lawyers to Harry's left was on his feet.

"To what do you object?" asked the judge. "Surely not to the use of sir as a form of address."

Another chuckle ensued.

The attorney flustered about looking important. "I must insist on proper identification of this supposed witness the Fleet has stood before you today. Midshipman Heron was killed — we have proof in the form of news video of the assassination. This man could be an imposter produced by the Fleet to mislead you."

"I take note of your objection. I'm sure Mr Heron will be quite happy to provide us with proof of his existence." She held up a hand. "We have before us details of exactly what happened on the dock and how it was achieved." Addressing Harry, she said, "Mr Heron, I believe you are able to access an AI and converse with it."

"Yes, ma'am — sir." Harry swallowed, wondering what was coming.

"Can you do it here?" She turned to the fuming barrister. "I believe, Mr Lockerly, that Mr Heron's ability is unique. In fact, your clients acknowledged it was this ability that caused all the problems at a facility they had an interest in on Pangaea."

"It was, but Fleet might have—"

"I'd say that was fairly unlikely, Mr Lockerly, especially since we already know that the Consortium's people have been unable to explain the phenomenon or to successfully reproduce it in anyone other than Mr Heron and Mr O'Connor."

A hush fell on the court. Then, with every indication of reluctance, the barrister said, "Very well, sir, I will concede that, but I must insist on having the witness DNA tested as proof he is Heron."

"That will be arranged." She waited while he sat. "Mr Heron, the court would like you to demonstrate your ability to access our AI and to have it display the record of the evidence we heard from the third witness last Monday."

"The third witness, my lady — sir?" Harry withdrew the blocking device from his pocket and disabled it. Instantly, a rush of data filled his head as the AI linked to him. *"Good day, AI. I am asked that you display the testimony of the third witness the court heard on Monday last."*

"Good day, Harry." The soft feminine voice could be heard in his ears only. "Shall I display it holographically with sound?"

Harry nodded. *"If you please."*

Watching Harry, the bench and the legal representatives saw the nod, and were startled when the hologram of Captain Wardman appeared between them, and his voice filled the courtroom.

"The facility on the island of New Caledonia looked as if it had been attacked by a large assault force, sir. However, all the damage and casualty patterns indicated the attack came from someone on the inside and not from an external assault. The survivors and prisoners we took were all in a seriously psychotic state, and suffering from starvation and dehydration. Our medics discovered that all the food replicators and the water supply from the filtration and recycling system were contaminated with a mix of psychotropic substances."

"Thank you, Mr Heron, you may stop it, please."

"Aye, aye, my lady." Harry flushed when he realised he had once again forgotten to address the judge as sir. He hated sounding old-fashioned and out of place, but it was engrained in him from years of early training. Focussing again, Harry told the AI, *"Thank you. Please end the display."*

As the hologram vanished, a murmur ran through the court. The judge fixed the lawyer with her gaze. "Do you know of anyone else who can do that, Mr Lockerly?"

Reluctantly, the lawyer conceded the point. "I must still insist on confirming his DNA, sir."

"Mr Heron?"

"If you wish, sir." Harry remained seated while a court officer held the device to his cheek.

"The DNA is confirmed, sir. There is no doubt the person before us is Henry Nelson Heron, born Downpatrick, 20th May, 1789, registered a citizen of the State of Ulster in the North European Confederation."

"Thank you. Any further objections, Mr Lockerly? No? Then we will proceed. For the records, Clerk, please read the witness's biography to the court."

Rising, the Clerk activated her display and read aloud a brief resumé of Harry's career from his joining HMS *Bellerophon* in

Chatham in 1801 to his subsequent transfer to the seventy-four gun HMS *Spartan* and the voyage to New South Wales, the South Sea and the Indian continent. When she reached the final part of the record, she summed it up by saying, "HMS *Spartan*, HMS *Rajasthan* and HMS *Swallow* encountered two large French frigates and engaged them. During that engagement, Midshipman Heron, Boy Seaman O'Connor and Powder Monkey Dan—," she paused as a titter of laughter ran through the gallery, "and Ship's Boy Danny Gunn were caught in a time rift caused by the malfunction of the NEGSHIO."

The judge's expression was one of weary impatience. "Another one of those incomprehensible military acronyms. Clarify it for the record, please."

"Near Earth Gate Southern Hemisphere Indian Ocean, sir."

"Thank you. Is that a true record of your career, Mr Heron? It seems to have taken you to some very interesting places." She nodded at Harry's affirmation. "Now, Midshipman Heron, would you tell the court what you can recall of your arrival aboard the NECS *Vanguard* in 2204?"

Briefly, Harry told the court of how they'd found themselves in the hangar on the *Vanguard*, dealt with Ferghal's injuries, and searched for a way to return to the *Spartan*.

"Where you able to hear the AI on the ship?" The question came from one of the other members of the bench.

"No, sir." Harry grinned at the memory. "And when we did encounter people, we could not understand their manner of speaking. We now know they were speaking the modern form of English, but I thought they were speaking French with a very poor accent, as did Midshipman O'Connor. That explains his volatile response. It was quite well known aboard the *Spartan* what he thought of the Frenchies, as he called them, sir."

Another ripple of laughter broke the testimony, and Harry flushed, not having intended to be humorous.

"Earlier witnesses tell us you attacked a fully armed squad with fire extinguishers. Why did you do that?"

"We'd no notion of who they were, my lady, sirs, and I determined I would not allow them to harm Ferghal or Danny while I had breath to defend them. They were my men, and I was charged with their safety." The simplicity of this statement drew a murmur from the public gallery.

"Commendable, young man. Very commendable." The comment came from a senior admiral seated to the right of the judges. "Now, Mr Heron, we need to hear what you experienced when first fitted with the AI implant."

Harry frowned. It was difficult to remember that initially he'd only been able to ask for and receive information, and then only if he mentally framed his request in a specific manner. He explained this, adding that it had been an added pleasure to discover he could ask the AI to play his favourite music in a manner that he alone could hear it.

The questions continued, leading up to the moment he and his companions had been captured and taken to the secret research facility on the island of New Caledonia on the planet Pangaea. Now he was entering territory he did not like to think about, much less discuss in public.

"At what point in the experiments did you become aware of a change to your link to the AI? Was it immediately after you received the gene splice?"

"No, sir. At first I could only hear it when I asked it a question and followed the routine for activating the link. After the gene splice, I could hear everything in the network. I became aware of it while they experimented on me, and I could do nothing to control my own body, something I found very hard to accept. I have no way of knowing how long it took to reach the point at which I could access the AI network as I did to alter it, sir."

He paused, remembering the events with a pained expression. "While I was under the control of their drugs, the passage of time seemed endless. It was not until they stopped the drugs to allow me to recover that I discovered what I could do with my link to their system, and that's when I realised I was part of it."

"And what exactly did those experiments involve, Mr Heron?" asked a Captain quietly.

The court went very still as Harry stared at the desk in front of him. Then he looked up and addressed the Admiral. "Ma'am, I find myself still unable to speak of this, but if you will permit me to access the AI, I can, with its help, show the court what I saw." He hung his head. "Some of it fills me with shame."

"Very well." The judge glanced at her companions then at the legal representatives. "You may proceed, Mr Heron."

"Thank you, ma'am," said Harry, his face white with anxiety and shame. Focussing on the flow of data from the AI, he said, *"Please display for the court my recall of these events."*

There was a brief pause while Harry gathered his thoughts and recalled what he'd experienced. A gasp went up from the court as the holographic scene of his, Ferghal, and Danny's capture appeared in the space between the legal representatives.

It was followed by a confused series of glimpses of the interiors of vehicles, then of a tunnel and finally of a submarine vessel. Next came a glimpse of a room lit by overhead lights behind secure glass in a ceiling. Suddenly the face of a man snarling at the audience appeared. Several people winced as a hypodermic device was briefly visible, then the hologram vanished before displaying a laboratory. The audience watched in horror as Harry relived the torment of the experiments, seeing what he had seen, but spared the sound and the feeling. Finally they witnessed his struggle against the hallucinations and his escape when he saw Danny in the duct above him followed by Ferghal and the others releasing him.

After that, the hologram dissolved and the lights returned. Harry sat with his head in his hands, and the courtroom remained totally silent as if no one dared to breathe.

The whole had been seen from the perspective of the victim — Harry — a circumstance that left the watchers in little doubt as to the behaviour of the perpetrators. Some of the scenes had been sufficiently graphic to make many of those watching feel ill.

The judge broke the silence. "Mr Heron, that is one of the most distressing things I have ever seen — and I can quite see why you find it painful to talk about it. But what you have shown us explains a great deal, and it will be extremely valuable in the prosecution of those involved. I am sure you will be required to assist the prosecutors when they assemble the evidence they need, and I know that will cause you to relive the pain of this event yet again, but your help will be exceedingly valuable." She paused. "However, doing so may require you to return to the Pangaea site."

Her eyes rested on the legal team representing BarCor, all of whom were staring at their hands or the desk, refusing to meet the gaze of the court.

To Harry, she said, "Be assured that the Fleet will provide you with every support you need." She glanced at her companions on the bench. "For the record, Mr Heron, would you tell the court what you did when you discovered that you could give instructions to the AI?"

Harry raised his head, his face white. In a quiet voice he replied, "I directed it to place the drugs they had been giving me into the food replication and supply units for their personnel. Then I disabled the locks on the cells in which we were held, and my companions found me and released me from my bindings."

A murmur ran through the court, and for a moment it looked as if the BarCor team would demand a further question, but refrained.

"Thank you. During your escape, I believe you encountered the central core of the AI. You removed certain memory components from it."

"Correct, my lady . . . uh, ma'am . . . I mean, sir. We took the components that held the records of what they were doing to their victims there." He paused, struggling to suppress the desire to run away from this place and hide the shame he felt in allowing the court to see what he had experienced at the hands of the researchers. "I did not realise the importance of something that occurred while we were removing the data files. Another AI connected to Ferghal and me, and downloaded several files, then attempted to remove them from our memory. Those files contain a record of all the agents, individuals, bureaucrats, politicians and companies that funded, work for, or support the Consortium — and something else. It had to do with currency transactions and trade on the World Exchanges. The amounts involved were very great indeed."

This time the gasp of surprise quickly turned into an uproar as the legal teams demanded immediate access or withdrawal of this information.

Hammering the gavel, the presiding judge demanded silence. With order restored, she asked, "Do you still have that information in your head?"

"I do, my lady."

Lockerly was on his feet. "That must be inadmissible! No human memory of that nature can be allowed, sir. There's no precedent for it, and he could be making it up for all we know. He's a teen boy! Are we really going to trust his word? This is absurd!"

"Sit down, Counsel." The judge looked at Harry, noting the angry flush to his cheeks. "Are you able to upload those files to the AI here? Perhaps you can also tell us whether the source of this information might still have it."

Composing himself with difficulty, Harry let the AI retrieve his memory of the files. "It is done, my lady. As to the source, I believe it to have been a second AI unit located within the research facility, a more powerful one which was connected to other bases on the planet, I think."

Screens lit up with the retrieved data. "The files are unaltered, sir." The soft feminine voice of the AI startled several people. "Midshipman Heron's memory circuit is unusual but reliable."

"We will take a short recess while we consider this new information," announced the judge. She struck her gavel and stood, the court scrambling to stand with her.

The Master at Arms appeared at Harry's elbow. Steering him toward the nearest exit, she said, "This way, quickly, before the vultures close in. You look as if you could use some refreshment and a break. The coffee is actually good today, and we have some delicious sandwiches and cakes. Let's get you out of here."

When the court reconvened, there was a noticeable gap at the legal representatives' desks. Mr Lockerley and his assistants had gone.

"For the record of this enquiry," the presiding judge announced, "the investigation team on Pangaea confirm that there are two AIs in the Johnstone research facility. The second is in a command post beneath the facility." She paused. "Unfortunately, it appears that someone has inserted a very unusual block command into it that the researchers have been unable to overcome. To all instructions it responds by playing a very loud and persistent rendition of a marching tune called 'Hearts of Oak'. Smiling, she watched Harry as his cheeks flushed. "Your handiwork, Mr Heron?"

As the next order of business, Harry was instructed to download for the court the lists of names and organisations he carried in his head. When these were visible on a large holographic screen, they created an immediate stir.

"These will have to be verified against the originals as soon as they can be retrieved," declared a member of the bench. "Agreed," said the presiding judge. "However, I begin to understand why certain parties might wish to keep these unseen." She straightened "Thank you, Mr Heron. Now, back to your recollection of the situation on New Caledonia, please. I understand you found and released the Lacertian who goes by the title Sersan — their Chief of Chiefs."

The judge and the members of the bench prised from him the details of the actions taken to escape the Johnstone facility, and Harry's observations of the same. Finally, the judge asked, "Mr Heron, before we release you from what has obviously been a painful experience, we would appreciate it if you could tell us the reason your officer, Sub Lieutenant Trelawney, decided to escape from New Caledonia by boat. As everyone present is probably aware, he was killed in a recent engagement and cannot give us this information himself."

This news caught Harry by surprise. "I had not heard of the Sub Lieutenant's passing, ma'am—a great loss to the Fleet. He was a good man and an excellent leader. Concerning the reasoning behind our escape attempt, I believe it was because we were not certain that the Consortium's forces on the island had been completely neutralised, and we knew not whether our own forces could find us. I believe that Mr Trelawney felt that we should make every effort to reach Pangaea City. Since there were no aerial craft and no powered sea skimmers available, he examined some of the craft in the harbour to determine which was the most seaworthy. During our escape, the communications transmitters at their facility were damaged or destroyed. We could not find any working communications system, and thus we could not contact our own people."

A Marine officer interjected. "According to Sub Lieutenant Trelawney's report, you provided the design for a rig that enabled your party to sail a converted cargo hulk to Pangaea City."

"Yes, sir, it was a relatively simple task and one we were able to complete fairly quickly with the help of friendly settlers. The voyage itself was straightforward, although it would have been better had we had proper charts and instruments for navigation."

"Thank you, Mr Heron," said the judge. "I believe we can obtain the rest of that from the report and from your fellow travellers. I can see that recounting your situation in the laboratory has taken a considerable effort on your part." She glanced at the other members of the bench, who nodded their assent. "You are excused and may stand down."

COMMODORE HERON MET HARRY AT THE DOOR. "You did magnificently, but you look as if you need to recover." Holding the door, he motioned Harry inside. "I'll get us some refreshments."

"I am most sorry if I have caused you embarrassment, sir." Harry swallowed hard and accepted the tea. "I am ashamed of what was done to me. I can only think the Fleet will not wish to retain me now they have seen the experiments."

"Good God, what the devil gave you that idea? From what we've just seen, you did damned well to survive at all. What they did was forced on you, and we'll make them pay for every bit of it. Is that what worries you?" Harry shrugged listlessly, not a gesture he normally proffered. "Well, put it aside," affirmed the Commodore.

Harry sighed, his anxiety plain. "I cannot tell you how much I wish my mother, father, and brother had been here with me today." His voice choked with emotion. He took a quick swipe at his wet eyes and soldiered on. "Besides the dread of this enquiry, Ferghal and I have had to cope with certain ungentlemanly midshipmen at the College who delight in calling us fossils and other names. It is very tiresome and distracting, being mocked day after day. It is said we are nothing but curiosities — and that the Fleet indulges us because of you and our family's connections."

The Commodore was stunned at this flood tide of emotion. "Harry, put one foot in front of the other with your eyes set firmly on your aspirations. It matters nothing what offensive names others may call you. What matters is how you rise above that to be a man of integrity and honour, something you have already proved to be. Your father and mother would be proud of you, as am I." He gripped the youth's shoulders and squeezed gently.

That broke Harry's resolve, and all the tension of the day came out in a moment of quiet weeping.

Chapter 17 – Back on Track

The return to the College was a strange experience. Elize's gasp of astonishment brought instant silence to the class lounge. She was out of her seat and running toward Harry before she realised what she was doing, and almost reached up to wrap her arms around his neck in a welcoming hug but caught herself just in time. "Harry! Ferghal! We were told you guys were killed. We saw the news shows! But we're so glad you're alive, and then we heard you were giving evidence ... what the hell happened?"

Harry smiled, happy at her exuberant welcome. "I'm afraid reports of our death were a trifle premature, and perhaps a bit dramatic. You'll have to blame Fleet Security for that and our miraculous resurrection. So here we are again, we Fossils of the Fleet, at your service, milady." He bowed dramatically.

His quip broke the tension. Laughing, their friends gathered round them, bombarding them with questions, and Elize smiled and said, "Go on, you!" before getting that quick hug she wanted, as did Harry, though he would never admit it. His lingering look into her eyes before joining in the group camaraderie told her as much.

Keiron walked in just in time to catch the tail end of the raucous greeting. "So it's true." He grinned. "Barclay and his cronies are looking sick as dogs. Helping Security find answers, I think the word is."

"That calls for a celebration," one of the others cut in. "But why?"

Glancing at Harry, Keiron grinned. "It's on the news. Something to do with someone finding a list of Consortium collaborators, agents, spies, informants." His grin widened. "There's hell to pay in all the member states' capitals. Just about every contractor providing services from security to operational support is on that list. They're all Consortium fronts and surrogates."

"Barclay is implicated?" Frowning, Harry worked this out. "Oh You mean he is being questioned by Security. But why would he be involved? Was he also among those named?"

"Not directly," Howie interjected. "But he, Laschelles and Miles have been under suspicion for a while, and their families are on the list." He grinned. "Who cares? With you guys back, the Regatta's up for grabs again."

"Hell, yes!" said Ferghal. "Do the Dreadnoughts know? Let them try to beat us. I can't wait to put them in their place."

"I heard that," said Keiron. "They've been counting on taking the sailing and rowing events to save face after we beat them in drill and the obstacle course run, but that's not happening. I can't wait to see their reaction."

DEEP IN THOUGHT, FERGHAL HURRIED ROUND THE CORNER and only just avoided walking straight into Eon Barclay.

"Watch where you're going," snarled the bully. He was having a very bad day. While it was obvious Fleet Security had nothing concrete they could pin on him, they obviously knew something, and equally, made no secret they knew that his uncle was on the Board of the Consortium. He recognised who he was addressing — one of those damn fossils. "You lower deck scum. You don't even belong here at the College, and yet here you are getting in everybody's business, you and your 'Master Harry' Heron, you suck-up. I don't know what you told that stupid enquiry, but it's got my family into a load of trouble. I'd like to kick your ass four hundred years back to where you belong."

Bristling, Ferghal stood his ground, his fists clenched. "We've told them nothing but the truth. If that has damaged your family, then so be it. Raholp may mean nothing to you now, but it is not forgotten by me or by Harry."

Barclay's temper snapped. He'd only just learned recently about the enmity between the Barclays and the Herons over a parcel of land at Raholp in County Down, and he didn't like the accusation, true though it was. Unable to restrain himself any longer, he swung a punch.

Ferghal reacted faster. His punch connected solidly while Barclay's went adrift. Eon Barclay measured his length and slid several yards down the corridor, coming to rest on his back and out cold, his nose squashed and bloodied.

Appalled, Ferghal left his equipment where he'd dropped it and hurried to where Barclay lay. Having ascertained that his victim was unconscious, he quickly turned him on his side and placed him in the recovery position. Then he called for a medic. The corridor was deserted, not even an android present as a witness.

Ferghal contemplated his next move. He touched his comlink. "Lieutenant Haäkinen, please."

"Haäkinen."

"Sir, Midshipman O'Connor. I have to report that I have knocked Midshipman Barclay unconscious."

"Was it an accident?"

"No, sir. I hit him when he attempted to strike me."

For several seconds there was silence. "Where are you? Have you called a medic?"

"The Study Flat, sir." Looking at the door label, Ferghal added the level and door number. "I've called the medics, sir."

"Very well. Stay there. I'm on my way."

"O'CONNOR DEFENDED HIMSELF, COMMANDER. Nothing more. He reported himself and called the medics, even attended to Barclay while he waited."

"Even so, Mr Haäkinen, he hit Mr Barclay." The Head of School scowled. "God knows Barclay's been begging for it, but we can't condone it." He hesitated. "Since there were no witnesses, we've nothing to go on. Barclay maintains it was an accident and refuses to make a complaint — probably doesn't want to admit he bit off more than he can chew — and O'Connor has admitted the incident, which puts us in an awkward position."

"May I suggest, sir, that you leave it to me to deal with O'Connor. I think I know exactly how to punish him for his part, and I'll have a word with Barclay's Divisional Officer, and let him deal with that side. Between us we can sort it out without endangering discipline."

The Commander considered this. "Do it, Jaako. I'll put it on file. Make sure they know it is part of their permanent records."

"GEEZ, THAT NAVIGATION PAPER WAS A KILLER." Keiron plopped down next to Elize in the student lounge, and Ferghal sat next to him.

"You really hate writing papers, don't you Keiron?" Ferghal shoved his friend's shoulder playfully, but as usual, with a bit more force than he realised.

"Well, what'd you think of the Nav Paper, Bruiser?"

Ferghal grimaced. "I got there in the end, but I had to recalculate the final result twice! Hey, why are you rubbing your arm like that? Does it hurt?" He grinned.

Keiron made a great effort at rubbing the soreness out of his upper arm. "You've got a mean right hook, Fergie. Why don't you sign up for boxing classes and get it out of your system already?"

Everyone laughed and looked up as Harry walked in.

"So, how'd you do on the Nav paper, Heron old boy?" said Howie.

"It wasn't too difficult. I think I managed well enough." Harry grinned. "I struggled with the theory of artificial gravity, but you sailed through that one."

"True." Howie wouldn't admit how brilliant he was, and how easily all their subjects came to him. "Hey, at least all those dreaded papers are behind us now."

Elize changed seats to a comfortable chair, and Keiron moved down the sofa to make room as the rest of the Yotties joined them. "Finally we can forget about all this boring classwork and concentrate on lifting the Class Cup in the Regatta. That baby is ours, my friends!" He stood and made a great show of wielding a hefty trophy for a photo op, and he got the laugh he was going for.

Harry said, "When is the runoff for the Field Gun Run?"

"We're drawn to run against the Hood Class in the semis, and we're up on Friday." Keiron looked round. "Which means we need to get our final practice runs in today and tomorrow, team."

"The sailing is on Monday fortnight in the afternoon, and pulling is in the morning." Harry consulted his timetable. "Unless you wish to run a Field Gun practice, Keiron, we've time for some sailing practice this evening. Ferghal? Howie? Elize? Are you in?"

"Sounds great!" said Elize.

"Count me in," said Howie.

Ferghal stood and stretched, easing the tension out of his broad back. "I'm always ready for a bit o' sailin'. You can get me out on the sea any time!"

"Oh really?" Elize said in a friendly tease, winking at him in good fun, which elicited Ferghal's hearty laugh, and Harry shot her a jealous look.

"That's settled then," he said, all brisk and full of business. "I'll round up the others."

He didn't see Elize's small smile as she watched him depart, and admired for the thousandth time his tall frame and confident masculine stride.

THE FIELD GUN EXERCISE FASCINATED HARRY because it reminded him of being on the gundeck of the *Spartan* during the sea battle with the French, but without the fear for his life. He watched as Keiron and his team hauled on the trace lines to bring the specially adapted gun carriage and its limber into the start position.

"Ready?" he asked as Keiron resumed his position after checking once again that the eighteen members of his team knew exactly what to do.

"Ready." Keiron and his team took their starting stance.

Harry dropped his arm and started the timer.

The team responded like a well-oiled machine, racing to the first obstacle — a five-foot-high wall — to the turn at the end of the course. Hoisting the entire rig over the wall, they regrouped and raced to the turn. Now the second run began, back to the wall and then the "chasm" to be crossed. Up went the stay mast as the team stripped the wheels from the gun carriage. With the transfer wire rigged, Keiron and Howie shipped the "traveller" on the wire. The first pair, each carrying a wheel, travelled across, leaping off as the traveller reversed direction, and the next group slung the gun carriage from it and rode it across the gap.

As soon as it returned, the gun itself — all 900 kilograms of it — was whipped across again with more members of the team, and then the second set of wheels, followed by the limber, and the rest of the team. Now they raced away with gun and limber to the firing point, first passing the whole through a gap in another wall, then they separated the limber, turned the gun and went through the motions of loading and firing. Now with extra zeal, they reversed the process, with the manoeuvre of having to pass the gun through the gap then cross the chasm again, this time dismantling the spars and stays before scaling the final wall and clambering down the other side, back at the start point.

Harry stopped the timer as the gun passed him.

"Faster than your previous best."

Flushed and panting, Keiron nodded. "Not fast enough. The Engineers are faster." He addressed the team. "We need to improve our time on setting up and taking down the transfer stay, people. We lose time on it." He wiped the sweat from his face with his arm and grinned. "Still, we can beat just about everyone else. If we beat the Hoods, then we'll be up against either the Scheers or the Drakes, and the final round will be against the winner of the match between the Tirpitzes and the Engineers."

"We'll do it," Ferghal told him, flexing his shoulders. "Never you fear. I'm ready. I could do it again now. I'm not even tired!" Everyone laughed and gathered round the water canteen to slake their thirst.

FERGHAL'S PULLING TEAM WERE IMPRESSIVE in their racing whaler. The large six-oared boat —a "proper boat," as Ferghal called it when he laid eyes on it — skimmed through the water under his coaxing. With Keiron on the stroke and Ferghal as coxswain, the boat powered through the water, the mix of human and Lacertian crew a powerful one.

Harry's sailing team, with Ferghal as his helmsman, was generally thought to be the best the College had seen in a very long time.

Returning from their final practices, the Yotties gathered in their lounge. "It's all or nothing now." Elize joined the group. "I've heard they're tightening security for the Regatta. We're already swarming with Red Caps. Hope they're not going to spoil it."

"No chance of that. We're going to rewrite the record books." Howie threw himself into a chair. "Especially if Captain Bligh here sails our sloop as hard as he did on our last training run."

Harry coloured. Younger than everyone else, he sometimes adopted a very autocratic approach, something his companions teased him about. The insistence on perfection and instant responses to orders on the sloop was a touchy point with him. He'd learned aboard the *Spartan* the importance of a crew being able to perform tasks in all conditions and under all pressures by touch and feel as well as by knowledge. In that spirit he'd planned, rehearsed and practiced until everyone in the crew could perform his or her assigned tasks instinctively. Though they teased him about it, they had begun to appreciate his reasoning.

Now he retreated into defence. "If we want to win, we have to be disciplined on board."

Elize laughed. "You make that plain, Captain." She gave him a playful push. "Relax. We trust your judgement, Harry. None of us can make the boat do what you can. She responds to your touch better than anyone's," she added with a sweet smile, and enjoyed watching him blush again.

Elize was aware that Harry found her attractive, and she enjoyed the rather old fashioned and courtly attention he paid to her. She had a fondness for him and his proper manners, *something rare in a man these days*, she mused as she watched him. Like the others, she'd at first not understood his insistence that she be able to adjust the foils the boat sometimes flew on without the assistance of the automated system. Now she could do that with expertise, and she knew exactly how to do it in an emergency — as did everyone else, and every other task necessary to "flying" the boat under all conditions.

Unaware of Elize's scrutiny, Harry studied his programme. "We've to return to the *DGK* for the firing exercise we missed. It's programmed for two days before the Regatta. That will give us little time for our final training."

"True," said Keiron, "but it will have the same impact on everyone, so we'll just have to make the best of it. At least the exams are over!"

Chapter 18 – Firing Exercise

"All hands to stations for the live firing exercise."

The announcement sent the trainees scattering to their assigned positions throughout the ship.

"What are we going to do, Eon?" Laschelles asked as he and Barclay followed the rest of their class to the Damage Control Station.

"Nothing. Just keep quiet and act normal. They can't prove a damned thing, and if you hadn't lost the bloody neural disrupter I gave you, they'd have even less."

"But they suspect us. I heard Lieutenant Grossman talking to one of the Commanders. They don't know I speak and understand German. Anyway, they found DNA on that thing—"

"Not enough, or they'd have acted already. Now shut up, and for God's sake, man, get a grip."

"Mr Barclay, Mr Laschelles, we're ready when you gentlemen are." The Lieutenant Commander's expression was unreadable. "MWO Västeros will brief you. You're to work with his party for the exercise."

"Gentlemen, suit up, please."

Barclay glared at the warrant officer then realised the man had no intention of backing off. In fact, he looked quite capable of enforcing his request if necessary. "Yes, MW."

Miles joined them, his blanched face betraying his nervousness. "They must suspect us," he whispered. "The MW is Special Branch."

Barclay started to swear, then thought better of it. "Shut up and get rigged," he muttered under his breath.

"MR HERON." LIEUTENANT GROSSMANN INDICATED the vacant station next to hers. "You'll be assisting me with the manoeuvring plot." She waited as he took his place. "And this time we will have the AI do the calculations."

Recognising the gentle acknowledgement of his efforts during the recent crisis, he returned her smile. "I think it will be quicker than my efforts, ma'am. After all, it can perform all the calculations simultaneously and not, as I must, in sequence."

Laughing, she nodded. "True. But your method worked very well. I think the AI is concerned it has a rival. Now, let us begin. Enter these coordinates, please."

Harry set to work, aware as he did so of the flow of orders around him.

"Ready, ma'am."

"Very good." She accessed her link and reported, "Navigation ready, sir."

"Commence plot for La Grange manoeuvring."

Repeating the order, the Lieutenant nodded to Harry. "I'll do those. You'll find them interesting, I think." She plotted the waypoints using a menu displayed on a screen beside her. "These are supposed to give us a course that is efficient, avoids known bodies and gives the Weapons team the best chance of holding a lock on the target as we weave and dodge him in an effort to do the same."

Harry watched the stream of results appearing on the screen before him. "I see, ma'am, but with the alternatives and the permutations all dependent on your choices, how will the targeting controllers know which you have used?"

She finished her input and leaned back in her seat. "Good question, and the answer is simple." Making a further entry, she ordered, "Helm, accept the course orders, then link to targeting."

"Accepted, Lieutenant. Targeting linked and tracking."

"See?" She said, touching her link. "Command, courses plotted and targeting linked to helm."

Fascinated, Harry watched as the ship began its first manoeuvres. In the time it took him to blink, she vanished in a quick transit from her start position and flashed into a new position some ten astronomical units away.

"Target acquired. Firing!"

On the helm display, the beams of plasma lanced from the ship and engulfed the target, a large asteroid.

"Helm, next sequence. Commence."

Once again the ship vanished, reappearing on the other side of the asteroid and in a different aspect. The great beams of fire engulfed the asteroid again.

"Shift position. Adopt Pattern Three."

"Pattern Three. Commencing."

Harry watched, aware the Navigation Officer had skipped several of her original planned courses and adopted a later sequence. Once more the target acquisition was rapid, and the asteroid took yet another pummelling. Without a pause, the Lieutenant repeated her command, this time choosing an earlier sequence.

"Secure weapons. Navigation, plot course for Neptune. Prepare for the next series."

Acknowledging the order, the Lieutenant told Harry, "Go ahead, Mr Heron. Give us a course to Neptune, please."

THE FIRING EXERCISE PROVIDED AN OPPORTUNITY for all other departments to conduct trials of their own. Shadowing the Lieutenant Commander overseeing the power supply to the ship's weapons batteries, Ferghal was interrupted by an order to simulate a hull breech affecting the control room.

"Don survival suits! *Schnell!*" The Lieutenant Commander thrust himself into his suit then verified that Ferghal and the others were properly dressed. "O'Connor, with me. Rudi, transfer power to the secondary banks. We meet in the Emergency Control. Go!"

Hurrying to keep up, Ferghal dodged aside as a team from Damage Control lumbered past, burdened with their equipment. He grinned as he recognised Barclay with a tight-lipped Warrant Officer hard on his heels, and wondered what they were exercising. Engrossed in his thoughts, he collided with the Lieutenant Commander.

"*Was ist?*"

"It was an accident, sir!" Midshipman Miles, scarlet in the face was flustered. Two TechRates stood back to allow the Lieutenant Commander to peer into the cabinet. "No one warned me the fire fighting system was live. It went off when we simulated a fire, sir, as ordered, sir."

Lieutenant Commander Reuter struggled with his temper for several seconds. "Your name, Midshipman?" His voice almost produced ice, and the TechRates paled.

"Miles, sir. Dreadnought Class."

"Miles." For what seemed an eternity, the officer paused. "Return to your assigned station, report what has happened — no. He reconsidered. "I shall report it. You will accompany me and take no further part in these exercises. You are now a casualty — *und Sie beiden auch!*"

Miles followed, with a rueful glance at Ferghal. For a moment Ferghal almost felt sorry for the midshipman, but it was merely a passing thought, as he had to focus on the task of running the auxiliary system to power up the weapons.

Watching him, the Lieutenant Commander snapped, "O'Connor, take two men and deal with that mess in 302ANd."

"Aye, aye, sir." Glancing at the two men who'd accompanied Miles, he asked, "May I have these men, sir?"

Lieutenant Commander Reuter nodded. "Richter, Kosch, you heard Herr O'Connor." To Ferghal he said, "Get it sorted out and run a full diagnostic on it. Any problem, contact me."

"Aye, aye, sir." Ferghal nodded to the men and led them back the way he'd come. He asked the AI, *"What is the problem at 302ANd?"*

"There is a short circuit due to the extinguishing agent. You will need to remove the components, clean them, and replace the damaged elements."

Taking care to isolate the fire protection system, Ferghal opened the cabinet and almost whistled in surprise. "Damn, this extinguishing foam makes a mess." He eased himself out of it. "Mr — er — Richter? We'll need to dismantle the unit. Mr Kosch, clean the area so we can see the damage."

The TechRate nodded. "*Sehr Gut, mein Herr.* I will fetch the cleaner tools."

Ferghal turned to the second TechRate. "Have we access to a maintenance kit?"

"*Jawohl, mein Herr.* It is here." He indicated an adjoining cabinet. "It is this your colleague was looking for."

Extracting the kit, Ferghal frowned. How could Miles have mistaken the cabinets? Or had he simply not bothered to ask? Probably the latter. The indicators on them were clear enough. A thought occurred to him. "Why did Midshipman Miles need this kit? Was there some other task?"

TechRate Richter shook his head. "He did not say, sir. Our orders were to carry out a simulated response to a fire in the Node at 303ABn1. He said we should take the Maintenance Kit from here with us."

"So who opened and set off the suppression system in this node then?" Studying the casing of the damaged unit, he added, "That foam certainly got into everything — just as well it is protected by isolators."

"Der — the Midshipman, mein Herr."

Engrossed in his task, Ferghal grunted. "Well, what's done is done. Pass me the testing kit. We'll need a replacement neural junction I think."

TechRate Kosch returned with the equipment for removing the extinguishing foam, and at Ferghal's order, cleared it from the cabinet.

HARRY WATCHED THE PREPARATIONS WITH INTEREST. The flow of orders between the Command Centre, Navigation, Weapons Control and Engineering brought home to him just how essential each component of the ship's operation was. With his isolation device from the AI deactivated, he had the added advantage of being able to see and hear the AI at work.

"Shift position. Transit to Grid 4405 at plus 22 degrees. Target Asteroid 93-93-555-Jupiter-67."

Harry ran the calculation for the change of position, transferred the solution to the helm, and watched as the hemispherical 3D display revealed the asteroid looming close. Even as he registered this, the brilliant beams of the weapons flashed into focus.

"Micro-transit. New position Grid 4406-Left, negative plane 30 degrees."

As soon as Harry entered the coordinates, the solution appeared in his eyes before it showed on the screen, and without hesitation, he ordered, *"Transfer to helm,"* through his internal link to the AI.

The displays showed the asteroid hovering above and on the ship's starboard side. Even as the weapons fired again, the Captain's orders for the next shift in position arrived.

"This time let me see them before you activate them, Mr Heron." The Navigation Officer saw Harry's surprise. "You didn't with the last one."

"Aye, aye, sir." Setting to work, he found the solution and waited for the display as well as the order to execute it, aware that the AI considered this delay strange.

"THE EXERCISE WAS A COMPLETE SUCCESS." Captain Haakon swept the assembled officers with his gaze. "The Damage Control teams performed very well despite there having been a small accident when someone set off the fire extinguishing system in the main weapons power distribution module." He frowned. "It is fortunate that it could be repaired and that the auxiliary system cut in immediately. Commander Reuter, your comments please."

"Luckily I discovered it moments after it happened, sir. A midshipman apparently opened the cabinet unaware that it would set off the fire extinguishing system. Midshipman O'Connor was able to repair it immediately, sir. I have spoken to the Divisional Officer concerned."

The Captain nodded. He knew there was considerably more to it than his Engineering officer was prepared to say publicly. "Thank you, Jorgen. Navigation? The course transfer and transits were excellent." He paused, a slight frown creasing his forehead. "There was one, however, when the ship entered transit before the solution appeared on my repeater. Is there a problem with the system?"

The Navigation Officer smiled. "No, sir. I had Midshipman Heron on the plotting table. On one of the manoeuvres he allowed the ship to read his thoughts, and it acted on them immediately."

The frown deepened. "Have you talked to him since then? I know the ship sees him as a mobile node, but he must not let his thoughts become an alternative to proper command."

"I've explained it to him, sir, and he agrees. He wasn't aware that the ship considered his thought process a direct order."

"Hmm. Very well. Is it in your appraisal for the College?"

"Yes, sir."

Right, then we can leave it there." He turned to his Executive Officer. "Damage Control report, Dieter."

Chapter 19 – Bad Judgment

Security was tighter than usual during Regatta Week, which led to some frustrations and delays for the visitors, but most accepted the necessity with a reasonable degree of equanimity. Harry and Ferghal were delighted to find that their visitors included Chief Justice Theo L'Estrange and his wife Niamh with their friend Danny.

Ferghal greeted them with a smart salute and a smile at Danny's eager expression. "Welcome to the College, sir, ma'am. I'm to show you to your suite."

"Thank you, Ferghal. Is the Commodore here yet?" Theo noted Danny's eagerness. "You'd best show Danny round once you've deposited us before he strains his neck trying to see everything from here!"

Ferghal laughed. "Aye, Harry's with the Commodore. He'll be in the suite on the flat above yours."

Ferghal and Danny walked a few paces ahead with Theo and Niamh following. He was curious to learn more details of Danny's unwitting adventure. "What happened when those Consortium agents tried to kidnap you, Danny?"

"One of them had me almost into their transport when Sci'sinada took him down. It was a bit messy after that — not as bad as the gundeck on *Spartan* after grape shot, but close!" He grinned. "She'athe wasn't playing, and the guy that Sci'sinada took is going to be in the med-units for a long time." He smiled as

Sheoba fell into step beside them with a group of Lacertian guests. Danny added, "I wish I could move as quickly as your people can, Sheoba, and that vanishing trick is fantastic. I wish I could do that. I could dodge some of the boring classes then!"

Ferghal laughed, but Sheoba remarked in her sibilant hiss, "Then, Little One, you would find our ways harder, since you can never be still as we are taught to be."

"Now there you have the flaw in your wish, Danny." Theo gripped the boy's shoulder in a friendly squeeze. "Is this our suite, Ferghal? Then we shall be fine. If you've no other duties, perhaps you can show Danny some of the College."

HARRY STOOD TO ATTENTION AND SALUTED AS THE TALL and distinguished figure of Commodore Heron approached. "Sir!" he exclaimed. "I am ordered to conduct you to your suite and ensure you have all you require."

Returning the salute, the Commodore smiled. "I am delighted to have your company, Harry. It's lucky that my squadron is currently home for replenishment and maintenance, and I'm Earthbound for the enquiry." As they walked together, he said, "And this gives me the opportunity to check on you myself. The judge was very pleased with your evidence and conduct at the enquiry, by the way. I didn't have the chance to tell you, as you'd left by the time I'd finished giving my evidence."

"Aye, sir. They were afraid we'd miss too much classwork if we didn't return as soon as possible." Standing aside, Harry waited for his guardian to enter the suite. "I'm flattered that you have chosen to attend the Regatta and our Passing Out parade, sir." Harry smiled. "It has been a challenging course — even without the other distractions."

The Commodore laughed. "I wouldn't have missed it even if it meant giving up my command. I've been keeping a close watch on your progress, and your distractions have had us all worried. Still, your instructors seem to think you and Ferghal have done well." Studying his ward for a moment, he paused. "And I hear the Yotties intend to change the record books this year. As a Yottie myself, I felt I had to be here for it."

"We hope so, sir."

"Good. I hear the Yotties are showing great promise for certain races this year. I will be eager to see if you can reverse our sad lack of performance in sailing, pulling and the Field Gun exercise."

LIEUTENANT COMMANDER VALLANCE GLARED at the cryptic message on his tablet. This was getting out of hand. Didn't the damned fools know how tight the security here was? Did they have any idea how difficult this would be? Did they care? Deleting the message, he pocketed the device and stood. He was in way too deep to get out now. Even if he turned himself in to Fleet Security, the best he could hope for would be a plea bargain and a shorter sentence.

Well, too late now. He'd taken the money, and he'd delivered what they asked. His team had been the best. Now three were dead, two on the run, and just himself left at the College — and now this message from the Consortium could blow his cover completely. Walking briskly, he made for the reception and signed himself out.

"I'm going into town for some peace," he told the desk attendant. "Getting too full of top brass around here."

"I take your meaning, sir." The attendant was a retiree, a former TechRate who enjoyed his duties because they kept him in touch with his Service. He smiled. "Must be half the top command here, not to mention the Chief Justice, the Fleet Board and several other senior politicians."

"Quite. The gleam of gold braid is straining my eyes." Vallance smiled amiably. "See you later." He stepped outside glad to be rid of the confines of the building and its rigid structure — both external and internal.

Now to link up with the special team and get them in place. With the damned Lacertians everywhere, that is going to be a challenge — a big one. This whole damned thing has gone sour.

He walked to where he kept a small recreational vehicle. This whole plan was supposed to have been simple and straightforward Just recruit people with the right skills and talents. Make sure they were on board with the idea of bringing in a new world order — and God knew, in his opinion, it was needed — and in the meantime enjoy some rewards and benefits for their loyalty.

Then it got more intense. First it was acting as the inside contact for agents sent to deal with specific problems for the Consortium. He'd had a few qualms over that, but then there'd been a request that he arrange an accident for someone, with the threat of exposure if he didn't. Next, he'd found himself leading a special ops team — again reluctantly, but, as with everything else he did, meticulously planned, managed and executed for his controller in the Consortium.

Deep in thought, he failed to notice he was being followed.

The Lacertian noted his direction then moved swiftly. By the time Vallance reached his pride and joy, an expensive personal runabout, one of the Lacertians had planted a tracking unit on it.

After standing outside in the near dark for longer than he would've liked, Vallance felt relief tempered with foreboding as he watched a transport pod approach the gate on schedule. Stopping a little short, a light flickered.

Using his own device, he replied from his side of the gate. After the recognition signals were exchanged, he opened the gate and admitted the vehicle. It slipped past silently without stopping and vanished into the night inside the College grounds. Now he had to make sure he was where he was supposed to be next.

THE LACERTIANS SPREAD OUT AS THEY APPROACHED the site where their target had stopped. They did not know what they might encounter, but their orders from the Sersan were clear: guard Harry, whom they called the Navigator, and Ferghal, the Sword Wielder. Sersan had received intelligence that an attempt was to be made on the College, and Sci'Enzile had placed a tracer on the vehicle Lieutenant Commander Vallance used. She and the others had suspected him of involvement in the attempts against Harry and Ferghal based on their observation of his movements and who he conferred with.

Now she signalled her companions as he stepped out of his vehicle and appeared to be searching for something. They watched as a new vehicle approached, stopped briefly to exchange signals with the commander, then accelerated away. Ari Vallance watched it go then slid into his own vehicle and drove off along a different track. Sci'Anthe signalled her squad to follow the strange vehicle, and Sci'Enzile settled down to follow the commander.

Preoccupied with his own thoughts, Ari Vallance guided his runabout to his favourite lookout point. From here he could watch the whole stretch of the lake, the perfect place to wait for the team to return and report their departure.

THE CONSORTIUM INTRUDERS TOOK NO CHANCES. Leaving their vehicle in a concealed hollow on the far side of the lake, they crossed using self-propelled submersion suits, towing their device in its container.

The leader verified that his team were present. Stripped out of the suits, they appeared to be Fleet personnel, the leader wearing the insignia of a Commander. "Follow me. We'll get the package installed under the VIP stand."

The Lacertians waited, then the leader signalled one of her team to recover and sabotage the intruders' suits. Satisfied her people were ready, she signalled the rest to follow.

Moving with care, the Consortium intruders reached their target, as did their shadows. The Lacertian leader stepped into view. "You do not belong here."

"What the hell?"

The Consortium team were good, but the Lacertians were faster and stronger, especially in one-to-one combat.

Surveying the now prone intruders, Sci'scinada signalled her intentions. "We shall return these and their device to their masters."

The security cameras captured images of the brief disturbance in the water, but by the time the security patrol reached the dock, all was calm and the place was deserted. A scan using a patrol skimmer also turned up nothing, and the disturbance was put down to a school of fish.

The delay made Vallance nervous. Glancing round to makes sure he wasn't watched or followed, he left his vehicle and moved to where he could use his night scope to locate the team's vehicle.

"Shit! Those bloody Lacertians!" He hurried back to his vehicle, started it, and gunned it away. "Damn, damn, damn. I knew this would go sour. Shit!" Heading away from the College, he considered his options then swung onto the highway and made for the main gate. Better to be seen in the wardroom if anyone came looking.

SCI'SCINADA WATCHED HER PEOPLE LOAD the last of the captives into their vehicle. Another of her team busied herself with the device the intruders had brought with them.

"It is done, Sci'scinada, as you instructed. It will detonate when the vehicle reaches its base. The transport will return to their place of origin. The device is integrated with the destination."

"That is good." She regarded the captives. "We have spared you to return you and your device to your masters. It will detonate when you reach the place you came from. We wish you a pleasant journey."

Closing the door, she activated the transport's automatic homing system and set it in motion for its final journey. With that done, she and the other Lacertians returned to the lake, submerged beneath the surface with barely a ripple, and swam swiftly back to the pontoon, emerging to watch the security patrol checking all the moorings and boats.

Lieutenant Commander Vallance faced a quandary. He needed to alert his paymasters that his plan to vanish with the assault team had been thwarted. But that created an almost impossible problem. The heightened security during Regatta Week included the monitoring of all communications channels at all times. Even a short signal would be picked up.

Frustrated, he sought solace, somewhat morosely, in the wardroom.

Chapter 20 – Regatta Week

"The weather forecasts for the next several days are not good." The Commodore shook his head. "Pity. Even if they try to rearrange the events, it's going to be a case of same problem, different day."

"What are they going to do? Surely not still run it all." Niamh watched the wind bending the trees and whipping the shrubs.

"There may be some changes to a few of the events, particularly the sailing events." The Commodore's comlink chirped. "Commodore Heron," he answered.

"Admiral's compliments, sir. He'd appreciate your joining him immediately."

"On my way. What's his location?" He listened to the address and acknowledged it then ended the connection. "Damn. I wonder what this is about." Shrugging into his uniform jacket, he fastened it and tugged it into place as he made for the door, grabbing his cap on the way. "I'll join you as soon as I can." Absently he returned the salute of the junior cadet who was startled into a salute when the door opened, which he hadn't expected. "Looks like your escort is here," said the Commodore over his shoulder to Niamh and Theo.

"Come in, Mid, we'll be ready in a second." Theo invited the youth into the suite. "I'm Theo L'Estrange, and this is my wife Niamh."

"Thank you, sir. Cadet O'Reilly, sir, ma'am. I'm assigned to be your guide for today."

Niamh smiled. "Nice to meet you, Mr O'Reilly. Hopefully we won't place too many demands on you." She glanced at Theo adjusting his jacket, and Danny already at the door. "I think we're ready."

"JAMES, HAVE A SEAT." GRAND ADMIRAL CUNNINGHAM gestured toward a chair for the Commodore to seat himself. "The news will break any moment, so I'll get straight to it. There's been an explosion beneath the headquarters of Global Security Group's corporate headquarters — a big one. The entire building has collapsed, and there's collateral damage."

"Global Security Group? Weren't they implicated in the prison scandal?"

"Not directly, but the holding company was — and the whole lot are connected to Consortium interests. That's why they've lost a lot of their contracts to provide security services for several governments. There are suggestions that they had a black ops section as well, which is why Fleet Security have been monitoring them." The Admiral pushed a paper across the desk. "We think they made an attempt on this place." He tapped a finger on the paper. "There was an intrusion last night. Security found evidence of it this morning. Captain Brown of Security is discussing it with the Lacertian team that their leader Sersan insists on posting here."

"Ah." The Commodore frowned. "I understand. The Captain feels they've acted outside of their scope of authority." He knew the Lacertians had a rather direct view of their responsibility to protect Harry, Ferghal and Danny. "Could they be responsible for planting a bomb? It doesn't seem like their normal method of dealing with a threat."

"That's just it. It isn't the way they've worked in the past, and there's no indication they left the site. No, this is something else. We're certain they intercepted the intruders but let them go. At least there's no sign of their having detained them."

"Would you like me to have a word, sir?"

"Thanks, James, but I think we'll leave it to Brown and his merry band to unravel. For the moment, it's better you stay out of it. I do want you to alert your brother-in-law as he's going to get a call about it at some stage."

"I'll do that, sir."

"Good." The Admiral took back the sheet of paper and fed it into an atomiser unit. "Now, perhaps we better take our places for the first of the Field Gun runs." Rising, he picked up his cap. "By the way, Flags will have some new orders for you once the Regatta is over. I'm strengthening your squadron, but it can wait until you're back in the saddle."

"WHAT THE DEVIL HAPPENED?" MR BARCLAY CONFRONTED Ari Vallance on the grassy bank above the promenade overlooking the lake. He hadn't intended to be here, but events dictated his presence. The calm weather had already given way to a stronger wind creating a nasty chop on the water, making the sailing difficult. "The bomb was still in the vehicle when it returned to the office." He glanced round to make it seem like he was merely enjoying the view. "Took out the entire building and part of the neighbours on each side."

"Damned if I know, but I think it was the Lacertian security lot that intervened."

"What?" The man stiffened. "We knew they'd been involved with the failed attempt to recapture the two from the Johnstone lab, but our information said they'd gone. Why weren't we alerted they're still here?"

"You were. I sent several messages advising my contact." Vallance studied the racing dinghies through his binoculars. "Not only is the place swarming with their people, but half of Fleet Security is here with their elite Phantom Squad. I warned you people when I was contacted about this operation."

Mr Barclay made a pretence of watching the sailing. "That wasn't passed on. I expected the security to be tight, but I had no trouble at the gate."

Vallance smiled. "You have an invitation to attend your son's Passing Out parade, and you're evidently not on anyone's radar at present. Or, you are, and they're watching to see who you make contact with." He prepared to move away. "So it may be best if you meet and talk to as many of the staff as you can. I'll try to find out what happened to the team who were supposed to plant the device. I'm sure we'll meet up at the reception tomorrow evening."

Incensed at such a casual dismissal from a man he regarded as his inferior in both status and wealth, the elder Barclay controlled his anger and schooled his face. He had to admit, this plan made sense. He needed to deflect any suspicion if he was being observed

THE STRENGTHENING WIND MADE FOR AN EXCITING SERIES of races for the dinghy sailors.

"We've a first, two second places and two boats in the finals." Keiron studied the results on his tablet. "We're neck and neck with the Dreadnoughts in second place, four points ahead of the Agamemnons and three behind the Field Engineers."

"And the weather is turning nasty." Elize tucked herself into the corner of a sofa and hugged her knees. "Tomorrow's forecast is looking really bad. It was pretty tough sailing this afternoon."

"You did well though." Harry took a seat beside her. "You took first place in the final and a respectable second in your heat."

"I can say I've had a few lessons from a demanding teacher these last few weeks." She nudged him playfully, and shifted her position so that their shoulders touched, causing Harry to blush. "We're counting on you tomorrow, Harry. I just hope the sailing isn't cancelled by the weather."

"I'll do my best, but the weather may make it a dangerous enterprise. We need to have a clear win in the sloops, the whaler race and at least one other event to be sure of the Cup."

"They've changed the course for the whalers." Ferghal joined the group and seated himself heavily into a deep-cushioned club chair. "It will suit us well, though it will be hard pulling."

Harry would not admit it publicly, but he was far from certain he could beat the competition in the sloop race. Some of the others were superb tacticians and had the advantage of having grown up sailing vessels like these. The events of the last weeks had sapped his self-confidence, and the attempt to kidnap Danny coming on top of the attempts on himself and Ferghal had really unsettled him.

Ferghal noted Harry's intense look and lightened the mood. "We've the best pulling crew for the whaler," he said. "She's a bit light for a real boat, but she's fast."

"And we've the heaviest coxswain in the race!" retorted Keiron, tossing a sofa pillow at Ferghal.

Ferghal blushed as fiery red as his hair. "Well, you wanted me there, and you'd not let me pull the stroke!"

"All in good fun, old boy," said Keiron. "We wanted someone who could coach the rest of us and row the boat on his own!" Everyone laughed at this remark.

"You're a fine one to speak," Ferghal retorted, but his smile showed that he took it as a compliment.

Howie added, "With Sheoba, Sheanthe and you in the Field Gun team, I think Keiron's going to be almost unbeatable."

"We'll see!" said Ferghal.

"THIS IS GOING TO BE A TOUGH COMPETITION." The Commodore leaned into the wind. "The weather isn't going to improve until sometime tonight."

Handing their invitation cards to the smartly turned out cadet, Theo smiled as he watched the youth's dilemma as he weighed the need to salute a full Commodore and deal with a very senior member of the Judiciary of a member state. Mischievously he leaned closer to the midshipman and said, "He's with me," and winked.

"Yes, sir." The midshipman's lips twitched as his eyes flicked from the Chief Justice to the Commodore, lingering a moment on the ribbons adorning the senior officer's chest. He managed to salute. "If you'll follow me, Ms L'Estrange, Chief Justice. Sir?"

"Lead on, Mid." James Heron was impressed. The young man had managed to observe protocol and keep a straight face at Theo's teasing.

Leading the party to the stairs, he took them up and stood aside at the door to the VIP observation lounge. "Rear Admiral Lopata, the College Commandant, is receiving, sir." Snapping to attention, he saluted again.

"Thanks, Mid." The Commodore returned the salute. "Carry on, please."

Having exchanged greetings with the commandant, Niamh moved to the observation windows. "We'll be able to see everything from here, and it's great to be out of that wind!"

Danny sighed. "I wish I could be in the boats with Harry and Ferghal. I wouldn't care how strong the wind is. Dealt with much worse on the *Spartan* and still managed to sand the decks and carry the powder magazines. I miss being out on the water."

Glancing at the waves, Niamh nodded. "I know you'd rather be with your friends, Danny, but that will come soon enough."

Seeking to distract him, she said, "Oh, look there — are those the whalers Ferghal was talking about? They're getting into them now. It's going to be an exciting race!"

"LIEUTENANT COMMANDER VALLANCE, I'D APPRECIATE a moment of your time."

Looking up sharply, the Lieutenant Commander bit off the retort he was about to make when he recognised the speaker as a senior member of the Fleet Security Service. "Certainly. Can it wait? The pulling race is due to start, and I'm one of the safety officers."

The man nodded. "I'm aware. This won't take long. We're looking into an anomaly. Your DNA was among several traces found on a device recovered aboard the *DGK* — one of the devices used to disable the interface with the AI network."

"I'm afraid I can think of any number of reasons I might have handled such a device." With a shrug, he added, "I am, after all, a communications specialist. If someone brought me an item, I most certainly would have handled it. Is that so unusual?"

"Not really." The visitor produced an image display. "This is the one."

Feeling relieved, Vallance relaxed a little. "I think it is safe to say that I have several such items in our display in the class. It could be one of those, or it might have been one brought for examination here. Mine would not have been the only DNA on it if it came from here."

"As you say, Commander," the agent replied. "I have to talk to several more people before we can wrap up this investigation." He did have a number of other College people to talk to, but not necessarily about the device he was investigating.

Vallance tried not to look too relieved. "Well, if that's all, I'd better get back to my duties. Regatta Week is a bit of a nightmare — for you fellows as well, I should think."

The security officer smiled. "As you say. Well, thanks for your help. I'll be in touch if anything else crops up." He stood to leave then turned back. "Oh, yes, there's one more thing. We've reason to believe someone attempted to install a device under the VIP observation stand. You wouldn't happen to have noticed any strange events last night?"

Ari Vallance felt a sudden chill. He knew the Consortium had intended to blow the Fleet Board and top command to hell — and probably a sizeable number of the visitors and staff who would have been close by. "Attempted?"

"Yes. Can't say any more at present, but someone let a team in. They were intercepted and neutralised, but apparently got away." The security officer noted the reaction and the look of concern.

"Got away?" His link chirped. *Not a moment too soon*, Ari mused inwardly. "Lieutenant Commander Vallance," he answered

"Ten minutes to the start, sir. Captain's asking for you."

"On my way." He kept his voice casual. "I have to go."

"I won't detain you. I think I'll take some time out to watch the sailing later."

Vallance hurried away, wondering whether the item on the news about an explosion and the collapse of a multi-storey building in the capital was connected to the apparent escape of the team.

"Damn, damn, damn," he swore to himself. The security people were getting way too close.

Chapter 21 – Against Wind and Water

Ferghal and his team gathered at their boat for the whaler race. The wind had been steadily increasing all morning, and serious consideration had been given to cancelling both the pulling and sloop racing events. In fact, the final dinghy and skimmer events were postponed and then postponed again, with the announcement that they would be sailed late in the day when it was expected that the wind would ease. That left the rowing event and the teams assembled at the pontoon to prepare their boats and confront a lake that was a mass of white-topped wavelets. The course was moved to the windward shore of the lake where a lee was formed by the land, but this also meant that the wind eddied and squalled around the buildings and structures along its edge.

The safety officer checked they were all wearing the correct safety equipment including their emergency flotation vests.

"Infernal things get in the way, and they add extra weight," Ferghal grumbled when the safety officer had moved on to check the next crew. He shifted the vest on his broad chest and shoulders still not finding a good fit. "Right, into the boat, please. We're clear to get ourselves into position." He hefted a heavy oar he'd brought down to the boat. Unlike the standard oars, this one had a longer blade that was straight and without the feathered curve.

"Aye, aye, Mr Coxswain, sir," quipped Keiron as the six rowers took their places and checked the stretcher boards, eased the seats in their runners and shipped their oars.

Keiron watched with interest as Ferghal unshipped the rudder, stowed it beneath the sternsheets, then shipped a heavy rowlock in the sternpost and fitted his oar. "What the devil? How will you steer?"

Ferghal grinned. "With this — a steering sweep. Better than a rudder in these conditions."

"Is it allowed?"

"It is. I checked. There's no rule against it. The rules state there must be a coxswain, and he or she must steer the boat. I shall steer with this."

Shaking his head, Keiron laughed. "I'll be damned. Something new every time you take us out."

Ferghal grinned and checked that everyone was ready. "Cast off," he ordered. "Fend off the bow." Letting the bow idle clear, he said, "Give way, port." Using the sweep, he forced the bows further round until the boat was completely clear. "Oars, port — now, together. Give way. Keep it slow and steady."

He watched as another crew was thrown into disarray when their bow oar's life vest inflated after the boat shipped a burst of almost solid spray. Idling the boat into a suitable position, he ordered, "Oars all. Bow pair, hold us in position." He leaned forward, and just loud enough to be heard by the bow oarsmen, he said, "Disarm your flotation vests. Damned things will be a danger in this sea." Satisfied they'd done it, he added, "Now make sure everything loose is tied down or stowed where it will not come adrift. We cannot afford anything rolling about once we start."

WATCHING FROM THE SHORE, COMMODORE JAMES HERON noted with approval the way the boat rode the white-capped waves with Ferghal's sturdy figure upright, his feet braced against the motion and the long sweep oar making easy movements to which the boat responded almost at odds with the other boats struggling their way out to the start.

Turning to Harry, he remarked, "Ferghal makes it look as if he and his crew are out in a flat calm. I can see you fellows have a definite advantage here, Harry." He laughed. "I rather think the Yotties' reputation will never be the same again."

Recognising the compliment, Harry nodded and smiled. "After the launches and barges we were used to, sir, these craft are toys, and I doubt they can really keep the sea as a good boat should." His grin lit his face. "But Ferghal knows how to make the boat and the sea work together, sir. His crew will show the others a clear stern chase."

"I think you're right." Nodding as Theo, Niamh and Danny joined them, he added, "I've seen pictures of boats steered as he is doing. It seems to be very effective in these conditions. Some of the other coxswains are struggling to keep their boats dry." He raised his binoculars. "Right, the starter boat has them under orders. This should be interesting — but why has Ferghal opted to pull out to the end of the line like that?"

Harry took the binoculars for a closer look. "Oh, he's a cunning one!" He laughed. Handing the binoculars to the Commodore, he said, "See, the others are bunched already, but where he is, there will be clear room for his oarsmen."

"They're off!" exclaimed Danny when the starting gun fired, the smoke whipped away by the wind.

FERGHAL HAD THE BOAT GATHERING WAY TOWARD the start line when the signal sounded.

"Now then, me hearties," he called, leaning into the motion. "Keep it long and steady. Conserve your strength and pull together." He coaxed his team into a steady stroke, slowly building them up to a comfortable pace that sent the boat surging across the short chop. "Watch my face and keep your concentration on the stroke," he called. "Pull, out, feather, dip, pull," he called steadily, and his crew settled into the rhythm.

His strategy paid immediate dividends when they rapidly pulled themselves into a leading position ahead of the boats bunched on the shore end of the line. The steady rhythm sent the lightweight hull skimming across the waves, spray bursting away from its bows as it did so.

Behind them two boats entangled their oars and drifted across the path of another boat that had to change course to avoid colliding with them. With adroit skill, Ferghal shaved a small point and turned slightly along the shoreline using wind and waves to increase their speed without increasing the strain on the rowers.

Their lead grew from one boat length to two, then three, gradually opening the gap as the watchers on shore cheered the boat and crew. Ferghal knew that the crucial effort was yet to come, when the boat must turn on the distant mark and pull back to the starting point to finish. He focused all his attention on the boat and let the wind and water speak through his senses as he urged his crew on.

HARRY'S ATTENTION WAS DRAWN TO A COMMOTION at the promontory, and he let out a guffaw when he saw the Dreadnoughts' boat broach as the bow oar dug into a wave then fouled the next oar. Dragged round by this mishap, the boat shipped water and capsized. "Oh, famous!" he exclaimed. "That leaves the Dreadnoughts, the Terrors and the Gorgons out of the race altogether. Ferghal has only to finish now, and the race is ours."

"Blood-thirsty young devil, aren't you, Harry?" Niamh smiled as she watched her ancestor and ward, his face alive with the sheer pleasure of being involved in something he so clearly enjoyed and understood. "Gloating over your opponents' misfortune like that!"

He grinned at her. "It's not gloating, Aunt. The Dreadnoughts have Miles, Laschelles and Barclay. That is all I shall say on the matter."

Further along the gallery, Eon Barclay's father heard the remark, and turned his head to study Harry. Frowning, he made his way to find some refreshment. So that was the youth his brother was so keen to capture or kill.

The Commodore noticed the man's studied interest in Harry and his quick departure, and he made a mental note to learn more about him.

"Ferghal's turned!" called Danny.

"My God," exclaimed Theo, "He's taking a line right along the wind. Look at that boat fly."

Suddenly the boat was leaping through the water, spray bursting over its prow as it surged forward as if under some sort of power. Without breaking the rhythm, Ferghal avoided the nearest oncoming boat and the three remaining that followed.

"Steady now," he called to his crew. "We'll be wanting everything you have to finish. Keep it easy until I give the word." He altered course slightly to bring the boat close to the shore where the water was a little calmer and the assembled crowd and structures provided something of a lee.

Now everyone could see the effort being given by the rowers. The concentration on their faces as they kept their eyes on Ferghal was almost palpable even as he eased the boat around the point and began the final dash to the finish. To the crowd's amazement, he increased the pace and the boat accelerated as his rowers responded, every muscle straining as they maintained their rhythm, their eyes fixed on their coxswain.

"I think he's going for a record here," breathed the Commodore. "And what a record this will be."

The finishing gun fired, and the crowd burst into a wild cheer as the oars ceased their power stroke and eased down to a more leisurely rhythm. Heaving her head round with a few powerful strokes on his steering sweep, Ferghal allowed the boat to idle back to the shore seven or eight boat lengths ahead of their next competitor.

Ferghal grinned at his crew. "We did it. I told you it would be well with us, and we've done it!" He glanced at the scrutineers waiting on shore. "Rearm your flotation vests. I've a feeling they expect it." He watched as the crew swiftly and without fuss did as he told, making it look as though they were merely easing their muscles as they inflated their vests.

The boat touched the pontoon as Ferghal heaved the stern round with the sweep, and the bowman passed the painter to a scrutineer. The rest unshipped their oars and clambered out stretching and easing their muscles, glowing with pride and success as the retired and rescued crews gathered round noisily offering their congratulations.

Unshipping the long sweep, Ferghal joined them and shook hands with the scrutineer, a Lieutenant, who took a swift look at the boat and its equipment then held out his hand.

"Well done, Mr O'Connor. You and your crew have just made history. That was one of the best boat races I have ever seen."

"Thank you, sir." Ferghal smiled as his crew clustered round him. "But I didn't do it alone!" His team let out another whoop of joy, and before Ferghal knew what was happening, Keiron yelled, "Grab him!"

The six oarsmen grabbed Ferghal, hoisted him over their heads, and made a run to the end of the pontoon where they threw him out into the lake as far as they could to the applause and laughter of the crowd. Ferghal emerged spitting water and floundering to clamber onto the pontoon, hindered by his inflated vest and almost helpless with laughter. As he finally regained the pontoon, he grabbed Keiron's hand and dragged him into the water with him.

"So it's a mutiny you want to have, is it, Mr Stroke," Ferghal called, laughing down at Keiron spluttering in the water. "Well, I think we'd be evenly matched if we had to wrestle for it." He held out his hand and helped Keiron up, then shook hands with the rest of the laughing crew. "We showed them all, didn't we? And now we will take the sloop race as well. See if we don't."

LUNCH FOR THE CLASSES AND THEIR FAMILIES WAS SERVED in a large hall. Harry and Ferghal joined Danny, Theo, Niamh, and Commodore Heron at one of the round tables, just the right size for their group. Theo studied the schedule for the sailing races that afternoon. "Have you checked the weather forecasts yet, Harry? I understand the prediction is for as bad or worse than this morning's weather, though that didn't seem to hinder Ferghal any."

Everyone laughed and enjoyed easy conversation and friendly banter as they relished the delicious meal.

"Indeed, the weather is challenging, sir, but I think we still have a good chance against the others. I have checked our spars and rigging, and I think we have the ability to deal with a good blow." Harry grinned. "I fear the onboard boat management system may not approve of what I have planned. It will be wet and hard work, but it will be like old times for Ferghal and me. We've sailed in worse conditions, haven't we Ferghal? Much worse!"

"The pulling races were certainly an eye opener," remarked Niamh. "And the swimming. Your class seems to be doing very well."

"Yes, but the points are still very close. I suspect it will remain so right to the Gun Run." The Commodore caught a signal from Captain Brandeis. "Excuse me, I see I'm wanted. I'll join you again shortly."

"WE'VE CONFIRMATION THAT THE GSG HQ WAS DESTROYED by the device intended for here." Captain Brandeis handed the Commodore a glass, making a show of greeting a friend rather than relaying such important information. "Several of their agents are here, one on the staff we're trying to get the proof for." He lowered his voice. "Please make it look like we're old chums, sir."

"Well, well, fancy your being here, Marcus. How long's it been?" James Heron remarked for the benefit of the group passing.

"At least ten years," Marcus Brandeis replied in answer to the Commodore's deflection question. James Heron was still as fly as ever. He returned a greeting from another passing officer then leaned closer to the Commodore and spoke quietly. "That man over there is Brian Barclay and his son, Eon, a midshipman here at the College. We've an eye on them. They're connected to BarCor, and the head of that is on our wanted list. Eon is involved in something. We just don't have enough on either of them to make a move yet."

"The C-in-C knows?"

"Of course. He'd appreciate your company later." Allowing himself a smile, the Captain changed the subject. "He suggested after the main race this afternoon." He paused to allow the Commodore to acknowledge a greeting, then continued. "I understand young Harry's a demon in command of that boat. I expect we'll see some exciting sailing in these weather conditions."

"I've heard. I just hope he doesn't push himself and his crew too hard."

Captain Brandeis laughed, causing heads to turn. "From what I hear, he's very demanding of his crew and certainly pushes the boat to its limits. But you're right, he gives a lot of himself as well."

AFTER LUNCH, AS THE COMMODORE MADE HIS WAY to the VIP observation gallery, he was intercepted by the C-in-C's Flag Lieutenant.

"Sir." She glanced round. "The Commander-in-Chief's compliments. The attack on the GSG building is being reported as a terrorist attack." She hesitated as several guests passed them. "They were stakeholders in WeapTech, which complicates things. He's closeted with the Chairman of the Fleet Board at the moment but he'll join you as soon as he can." She smiled. "He said to tell you he's counting on the Yotties to give him some good news."

The Commodore smiled. The remark was typical of Grand Admiral Cunningham. "Thanks, so am I. Tell him I'll be here when he wants me."

"I will, sir." Something caught her eye. "Looks like Mr Barclay's headed this way, sir." She saluted then hurried off.

"Commodore Heron." The stocky figure of Mr Barclay stood in his path, giving him no option but to stay put and listen to what he had to say. "I'm Barclay. You may have heard of me."

The Commodore shook the proffered hand after a moment's hesitation. "Glad to meet you, Mr Barclay. I believe your son is in the Dreadnought class. I've heard from my ward of their acquaintance." He was struck by the thought that if the old saying of sons being like their fathers was true, Harry had been economical in describing the younger Barclay. "Would you care to walk with me? I don't want to miss the start of the sloop race."

"It's about to start? Good, good. Yes, I'll accompany you. My son is in the crew for his class. Should be the skipper, but he tells me he stood aside to give someone else a chance to star."

Hiding his amusement at this statement, the Commodore nodded. "Generous of him. You mentioned you had something to discuss with me." He indicated some seats. "This should give us a good view. Something to drink?"

"What? Oh. Yes, yes." He ordered a whisky from the android steward. "Yes, this business on the news — the entire building collapsed. Hundreds dead, they say. How was this possible? Surely Fleet Security is doing something about it."

Accepting the coffee latte from the steward, the Commodore nodded. "I expect they are, and no doubt I'll be briefed on the situation later. Not being in the Security Department, I don't know any more than what is on the news channels at present." He smiled reassuringly. "I have every confidence they will have their best operatives working to discover who is behind it, and will bring them to justice." He paused, watching his companion. "You have some interest is Global Security Holdings?"

"No! I mean, yes. Yes, as a matter of fact, I have a major share holding in them — part of my family's portfolio, of course. This is a tragedy. Shocking business."

Watching the boats preparing for the start of the race, the Commodore nodded. "All such atrocities are, of course." He decided to throw in a hook of his own. "I understand the security people managed to thwart an attempt by some group to target this event. I don't know the details, but it was, they think, aimed at some of our more important visitors." The manner in which his companion stiffened told him Barclay had been at least partly aware of this plot. He glanced at the lake again. "Ah, I see they are about to start."

THE WEATHER CONDITIONS WERE WORSE THAN ANY THAT Harry and his crew had practiced in. The decision not to use the flimsy modern sails with their Venetian blind structure was the right one, he thought.

"I know they are less efficient — we have proved that — but they are stronger and easier to handle in this wind," Harry told his crew. "And we will do this our way, by hand. I know it is hard work, but the automated system will work against us if we allow it to have control."

"You're the captain." Keiron laughed. "If you say do it the old fashioned way — then so be it."

"It will cost us a little speed," agreed Harry. "But I think we will make up for that in better handling and the ability to drive her harder." He looked at his crew. "Anyone who feels they would rather stay ashore than sail in this wind can say so now. I will not blame you, and we can find a replacement if need be."

Elize looked at the others then at Harry. "If you think any of us would miss this, *Mr* Heron, you've mistaken your crew." The others nodded in agreement. "None of us would miss this for the world. Now give us your orders and let's show them how we sail!"

The watching crowd were treated to a vintage performance as he sailed the sloop, the hybrid displacement hull with hydro foils she could deploy in the right conditions whimsically named *Sparrow,* off her berth under sails reefed to the merest scraps. On deck his crew worked like a well-oiled machine as they prepared their boat for the start of the race.

Harry hid his nervousness well, adopting the stance he had seen his officers adopt in the past: feet placed well apart, hands clasped loosely behind him as he stood on the windward side of the helm with his face neutral as he gave his orders. It worked well because the discipline required to maintain firm footing in this pose meant he had to concentrate on what was happening around him.

The boat idled to Harry's chosen starting position. He let the feel of the wind and the motion of the boat transmit itself to his senses through his feet until he became one with the boat. He needed to win this race, not just for the Class but for himself and Ferghal. His chest tightened with tension and determination as they waited for the start.

COMMODORE HERON WATCHED AS EVERY BOAT BUT HARRY'S set off under power and were well clear of the moorings before they set their sails.

He trusted Harry's judgment, but the *Sparrow* seemed to be at a disadvantage as she idled into position for the start while her opponents stormed back and forth jockeying for a prime starting position. When the starting gun sounded the five-minute alert, *Sparrow* set more sail and moved steadily between the other boats until she was in a perfect position when the start gun went. Like magic, more and more sail expanded on her genoa and mainsail, and the yacht heeled steeply, leaping forward, building a bone in her teeth and sporting a growing wake astern as she did so.

Several boats had misjudged the start and had to make rapid returns to restart, while *Sparrow* engaged in a tussle for the lead with the *Kestrel*, a boat manned by a very able crew from the Rodney class, and with the *Guillemot* manned by a crew from the Dreadnought class. Initially it seemed that their modern rig was more efficient than the *Sparrow*'s, and they drew slightly ahead, closing Harry out on the long beat toward the first marker buoy. But, as the boats drew out into the open lake and felt the full strength of the wind, their automatic systems reduced sail — and *Sparrow* stormed past, her mast bowed spectacularly as she did so.

"How is the helm?" Harry called to Ferghal.

"Very light, and I can feel the tremor in the rudder as she moves," Ferghal called back against the wind.

"Then she is overpowering," exclaimed Harry, instantly alert to the need to reduce the strain. Calling to Franz manning the reefing gear and Senzile on the mainsail sheets, he ordered, "Take another three turns on the roller reefing. Reduce the mainsail to the next reef mark." To Ferghal he said, "Tell me when the tremor eases."

"Aye, aye, sir." Ferghal grinned, and as the boat responded to the reduced sail, he called out, "Steady as she is. That's a good mark."

Harry grinned and glanced at the speedometer. Satisfied that he hadn't sacrificed any speed with his easing of the sail forces, his face creased in a satisfied grin when he saw that the other boats were well behind him. Turning his attention to the approaching buoy, he gave a rapid series of orders in preparation for the change of course. "We will round the mark and take a long tack close hauled. Then we'll tack again to bring us to the position to approach the next mark." Hesitating, he timed his order to perfection. "Ready all! Put the helm down. Headsails and sheets!"

The short tack put him in the ideal position for his next tack to the mark.

Shaving the marker buoy, he gave Ferghal the order to bear up, and soon the ship canted over at a steep angle as she drove to windward as close hauled as they could. In their wake the *Guillemot* and the *Kestrel* followed suit and crept up on them. Seeing this, Harry mentally kicked himself as he realised the reason. These modern hulls gripped the water better if they lay more upright.

To his crew he called, "Take in some of the genoa and another six inches of reefing on the main! Elize, deploy the starboard foils — just give us ten percent, please." He watched the result, feeling the tremor. "Now the port foils, the same mark." They all felt the boat lift and the speed change.

Sparrow responded rapidly, opening the gap between them and their pursuers.

Harry studied the wind and wave patterns to determine his next tack. Judging the moment with a practiced eye, he ordered the foils retracted and the helm put up. *Sparrow* rounded on herself, the sails snapping as they filled from the opposite side with barely a check in their speed. They stormed to windward, making another tack close to the windward marker, and then a short leg placed them on the mark with a quarter mile between them and the nearest boat, the *Kestrel*. This put them on a very broad reach, and Harry ordered the reefs taken out of the genoa.

"Elize, deploy the foils, please, fifteen percent forward and ten aft."

"Fifteen and ten, aye, aye, sir."

Once again the hull lifted, staying close to the surface, and the speed increased.

"How does she steer?"

"Light but well," Ferghal responded. "The log shows twenty-eight knots."

"Would the crew of *Spartan* could see this!" called Harry exuberantly to Ferghal, his whoop of pleasure drawing grins from the entire crew as the *Sparrow* stormed past the cheering spectators.

"Would that we had our ensign on show," called Ferghal, his muscles standing out as he strained to hold the boat steady on her course.

Harry checked his position indicators and verified their course for the buoy, then noticed that the fleet of yachts seemed to have been reduced. He called to Frederik Dornier, who was monitoring the comlink for the boat. "Frederik, were there not eight boats at the start?"

"*Ja*, but some have withdrawn."

There wasn't time for further questions as the third marker buoy was looming — and this, Harry knew, would be a dangerous turn at this speed, since it meant a gybe with the wind across their stern. Misjudged, it could spell disaster. He made several checks then had the genoa reduced again and took some more turns on the mainsail.

"Retract the foils."

Their speed dropped until he was almost on top of the buoy and then, in a flurry of orders and activity, they were round it without mishap and sail was again increased until the boat stormed across the start line to mark the beginning of her second circuit of the triangular course. His nerves forgotten, Harry saluted the guard boat as they crossed the start line on the new lap, the *Sparrow* rising to the foils as she tore through the water. He wanted to dance for the sheer joy of the thrill.

They had barely turned for the next leg when Elize called out, "Wreckage ahead! Fine on the starboard bow."

"I see it," called Ferghal. "It extends to leeward."

"We'll come about," yelled Harry, instantly conscious of the danger. "Stand by." His crew leaped to readiness, and he called, "Now! Helm a-lee."

The boat spun, her crew fighting to control the thundering sails as she swung through the wind. Then she was steady again, rising on the foils, and racing away from the wreckage, which Harry now saw was the partly submerged hull of one of the other sloops. He glimpsed a figure clinging to the wreck and felt a moment of doubt. He was torn between the instinctive feeling that he should turn back for the rescue and the desire to finish the race and win at all costs.

He yelled to Frederik, "Use the comlink and make a signal — survivors in the water at Mark B." To Ferghal he said, "We'll need to tack again." Looking over the transom at the receding wreckage, he added quietly, "It goes against every instinct to leave him there."

Frederik emerged from the cuddy below deck. "Harry," he called. "The course is shortened. This is the final circuit. The rescue craft are busy at the other end of the course. They ask how many we could see in the water."

Harry looked aft then at the pursuing sloops. He looked at his crew. "We're going back," he told them. "Reduce the mainsail please, Franz. Elize, retract the foils. Prepare to come about."

"We'll lose the race," said Senzile, and Elize nodded. "We will," she confirmed.

"Our fellows need help," said Harry. "We cannot leave them to drown. And there is no skimmer at hand. Stand by to come about. Ready? Helm a-lee."

The watching crowd saw the *Sparrow* reduce her sail area yet again, then turn and reverse her course. A gasp went up from the assembled Yotties. Then the public address system burst into life to inform them that the *Sparrow* had spotted someone in the water and was returning to pick up survivors. The crowd watched as the remaining four boats in the race slowly closed on her as the *Sparrow* approached the spot she had so violently avoided. The four boats avoided her as she manoeuvred, recovered several items and resumed her sailing, but now in a stern chase, albeit close behind the former tail ender.

FREDERIK FOUND HIMSELF BELOW DECK WITH THREE extremely cold and very wet members of the crew of the sloop *Bittern*. All of them were shocked that their sloop had been overwhelmed in a moment of poor handling that had resulted in the boat's catastrophic broach and dismasting. All her crew had survived, but some had swum clear of the boat and could not be seen.

On deck Harry and Ferghal worked with the rest of his crew to close the distance between themselves and the new leader, the *Guillemot*. Well before the next mark, they had succeeded in overtaking the *Peregrine,* whose crew sportingly cheered as they did so, then caught the *Kestrel* at the mark itself, managing, having achieved the right under the rules to do so, to force their way between the rival boat and the mark. Ferghal and Harry displayed nerves of steel as the other boat shied away from the threat of collision and allowed them to pass. That left the *Guillemot* to catch.

Harry called to his crew, "We will have to take a chance." He hesitated. "Elize, we depend on you to control the foils." He watched the waves, the wind whipping the crests into long white streamers, but, ironically, flattening them as well.

"Keiron, stand by to hoist the smallest spinnaker. And we will have to cut it loose when we have done."

He made sure Keiron understood his order before he joined Ferghal at the wheel. The strain increased, and the boat almost became airborne, its hull vibrating violently, under the additional power from the sail. He dared not allow the spinnaker to be fully sheeted home, but it lifted them clear of the water on the partially deployed foils.

In the cockpit, Elize strained on the manual adjustment controls to keep the hull just above the surface.

The spectators held their breath as they witnessed the titanic struggle to control the now heavily overpowered boat as it overhauled their rival. Harry's crew were aghast as they passed the leader.

They're trying to copy us," Franz exclaimed. "I hope they've practiced manual control on the foils and sails!"

Harry, straining at the helm with Ferghal, smiled grimly. "I hope they know the risk they take."

"Do we?" gasped Ferghal sweating under the strain.

They tore past the *Guillemot* yawing badly as her helmsman struggled to control his boat and Senzile fought to control their own spinnaker.

Harry judged the moment as the final mark loomed ahead. "Let go the sheets," he yelled. "Let them fly free completely!"

The sail streamed upward, tearing the released sheets from their fairleads to whip ahead of it.

"Franz — cut the halyard — let it go with the wind." He watched the sail blow free and clear. "Elize, retract the foils! Ready all for the gybe!"

They heard a shout from behind followed by a series of terrifying cracks and crashes as they began the gybe.

Harry dared not break his concentration, and when his crew turned to look aft, he bellowed, "Eyes in the boat. Concentrate — or we go the same way!"

Ferghal brought them through the gybe with a grunt of strain as the sails slammed across and the *Sparrow* leapt away from the mark to lunge toward the finish. When they were across it, Harry glanced back at what had happened behind them, but he leapt into action again. "Stand by to come about. Ready? Helm a-lee." As soon as they were on their new course, he drove all hands to reduce sail to the minimum until he could back the genoa and heave to in the spreading pool of wreckage that was the *Guillemot*.

Leaving Ferghal to hold the boat in position, Harry and Franz worked the sails to keep her hove to while the rest of the crew assisted the swimming Dreadnoughts aboard. A rescue skimmer retrieved four more, two clearly in need of medical treatment.

"Everyone is recovered, Harry."

"Very well, see to their comfort, please, Elize, Franz. Stand by. We're getting under way."

HARRY SAILED THE BOAT STRAIGHT ONTO HER BERTH without using the engine. It was not something he even considered unusual, as he had never had to use an engine for this manoeuvre, and it simply did not occur to him to do so now.

"Damn, now I see why you fellows beat us," remarked Jorgen Dinsen, skipper of the sunken *Guillemot*. He said it with a trace of envy. No mean yachtsman himself, he had never attempted such a manoeuvre.

"Everyone from the *Bittern* is accounted for and safe," Franz told them as they approached the berth. "But two of your crew, Jorgen, have been taken to the medical centre." As the adrenalin wore off, the crew realised how exhausted they were, and the full weight of the risks they'd taken sank home. A very subdued group returned to the pontoon.

Harry stepped ashore to find Commodore Heron waiting to congratulate him.

"I'm proud of you, Harry. Well done on your win, and your two rescues. That is the stuff that makes the Fleet the best there is. We never leave our own. We always come back for them, wherever they are and whatever the circumstances." He looked at the rest of Harry's crew. "Well? Are you all satisfied with his command? You've won the race — the first time the Yotties have done so, I believe. Are you going to let him get away with his having driven you all so hard?" He grinned, and they knew what he was prompting them to do.

"No, sir!" exclaimed Franz and Frederik in unison.

Before Harry could react, Ferghal, Keiron, Franz and Frederik had lifted him off the ground and carried him along the length of the pontoon to deposit him, without ceremony, off its end. Harry surfaced spluttering with laughter, just in time to see Elize and Senzile join the others in pushing Ferghal off the pontoon as well.

They swam ashore grinning from ear to ear and feeling the thrill of their achievement for the first time.

"THE YOTTIES HAVE DONE IT! WE'VE TAKEN THE CUP by two points!" Howie's shout of excitement stunned everyone in the class lounge until the news sank in.

"Finally, we showed 'em all!" said Senzile.

"Yeah! That's what I'm talking about!" Elize did a little victory dance over to Harry and hugged him, enjoying his startled look of surprise and embarrassment.

"Give us the details!" said Franz.

"The tally was for a dead heat between the Rodneys and the Britannias. It's up on the results board. The C-in-C decided the Yotties should have a bonus for the sailing event. Told the Commandant he'd never seen anything like it, and we should be awarded a bonus."

Another whoop of triumph shook the room, and everyone laughed so hard it hurt when Ferghal grabbed Keiron and did an Irish jig around and over the furniture to the melody of a bawdy old sea shanty.

Chapter 22 – Time to Move On

The perfect weather continued for the Passing Out Parade. The entire College paraded, every class and officer in full parade dress. Occupying an entire side of the parade ground was the tiered seating for the families, friends and visitors. At the centre were the saluting dais and the seating for the Fleet Board, the Fleet Command and other VIPs.

It was a proud moment for Harry and Ferghal as they marched out with the rest of their classmates, this being the first time they wore the dress uniforms of their service and their rank. Smarter than the normal working uniform, or the Number Fives normally worn, the dress uniform comprised a jacket of very dark blue-black that matched trousers of the same hue. Gold piping ran up the outer seam of the trouser leg. The cuffs of the jacket bore a thin gold braid looped into an intricate star pattern, and the collar was adorned with the familiar white patches enhanced by a double gold cord and button stud.

The raised saluting dais was crowded with senior officers in their full dress, the various ranks of seniority now evident in the braiding of sleeves and collars. Harry managed an aside out of the corner of his mouth to Ferghal and Elize, causing them to snort with stifled laughter. "With all that heavy gold brain on show, let us hope they do not topple to the ground when they stand." Just when they had regained control, he added, "Senior officers scrambling all over the parade grounds — imagine the sight!" He got an elbow from Elize for that one, but not without a cheeky grin

Master Warrant Officer Winkworth, marching beside them, managed to glower at him from the corner of his eye, and Harry adjusted his face to a mask of innocence, his eyes fixed on Keiron's collar ahead of him as they marched into position. Ferghal almost missed his step as he struggled to regain control, his broad back still shaking from suppressed laughter.

"Watch it, Mr O'Connor, no slacking on *my* class parade!" said Winkworth. "Whatever it is, it can't be that humourous!"

This almost sent Ferghal and Elize into paroxysms of laughter all over again.

Finally taking deep breaths and settling down, they listened to the Commander-in-Chief's address, Harry thinking to himself that perhaps the most remarkable difference between this speech and those he had heard on shipboards in his past was that he could actually hear this one clearly, thanks to the public address system.

Ferghal couldn't resist commenting on this. "Inspiring stuff, eh, Harry? I wonder if Captain Blackwood or our Admiral would have sounded as rousing had we been able to hear more than one word in ten, but then again, maybe it was better not to hear them! They sure could go on and on."

Now it was Harry's turn to snort, and Keiron's shoulders shook with suppressed laughter.

A cadet from the Dreadnought class chose this moment to faint. When he saw this, MWO Winkworth growled in a barely audible voice, "Britannias, don't you even think about fainting. I'll be after your guts for sausage-making if any of you even waver."

That almost sent them over the edge, and their snorts actually caused the Master Warrant's mouth to twitch in amusement.

Various prizes were awarded during the ceremony, and suddenly Harry heard, "Midshipman Ferghal Sean O'Connor, Britannia Class, for his score in the Micro Engineering Project."

Flushed with pleasure, Ferghal snapped to attention and went forward to receive his prize, while the officer making the announcements continued. "Midshipman O'Connor has excelled in his studies, a remarkable feat considering that he has had to adapt to an age of technology. He has shown remarkable resourcefulness on the practical exercises, and has taught us some old skills which we have found very informative."

Harry's delight at Ferghal's award turned to amazement when he heard his own name called. "Midshipman Henry Nelson-Heron the prize for Astral Navigation."

He snapped to attention and marched out even as Elize whispered, "Well done!"

"Good going, you devil," Keiron murmured as he passed, incurring another glower from the Master Warrant.

As Harry strode forward, the commentator continued. "Midshipman Heron is also receiving the Fleet Commendation for his part in manually navigating the cruiser *Der Große Kurfürst* when her command interfaces were sabotaged."

Harry's face was scarlet as he arrived at the dais and exchanged salutes with the Grand Admiral. He barely heard the Commander-in-Chief's congratulations and just managed a coherent reply. As he accepted the trophy, shook hands and saluted, he caught a brief glimpse of the pride showing in Commodore Heron's face. He set the trophy on the table set up to receive them until after the dismissal.

He returned to his place wondering anew at the fuss everyone seemed to be making about his having performed so simple a task in so ordinary a manner. It seemed to him a far less spectacular achievement than the remarkable things done with modern technology — or the ability to create such thinking engines.

He had barely regained his place when he strode forward again with Ferghal, Keiron, Senzile, Elize and Howard as each had led one of the teams or crews for the class.

"Ladies and gentlemen," the commentator's voice followed them out. "Today you see history being made. This is the first time the Class Cup for the Regatta has been awarded to the Britannia Class."

The Grand Admiral surveyed them as he returned their salute. He smiled and said, "Ladies and gentlemen, as a former Yottie, you may imagine the pleasure this gives me!"

There was an appreciative laugh from the onlookers.

"I do not think I have ever seen a class of Yotties so determined and so focussed, and that is saying something. I doubt any of us will forget the spectacular display this team provided in the sloop race, where the crew not only gave a demonstration of sailing in conditions which, frankly, were marginal, but pulled off two rescues and the most spectacular demonstration of iron nerves I have ever seen. I can only guess what it was like to be aboard her, and I suspect that those who were will never forget it. I understand the strain on the *Sparrow*'s fittings will mean an extensive overhaul, and our research teams are revising their textbooks concerning the strength of certain indestructible materials." He paused as a ripple of appreciative laughter went through the crowd.

"As for the man who commanded that crew — well, it speaks for itself that he not only crammed on more sail than anyone thought safe, but he judged it perfectly, and abandoned the sail when it had served its purpose. Skill and determination, knowledge and its application have been demonstrated by this Class in ways that have been refreshing and reassuring. Ladies and gentlemen, I think we may safely say that the future of the Fleet and of our society is assured as long as we have young men and women like these to carry on the best traditions, the best practices, and to offer the very best in leadership. Thank you."

The applause was deafening as he stepped down from the podium to shake each of them by the hand. Behind him the assembled visitors rose to their feet, the sound of cheering from their fellow classmates and their rivals adding to the noise.

The remainder of the ceremony passed in a blur, but as they broke away from the dismissal, Harry found the Master Warrant Officer alongside him.

"Well done, Mr Heron," growled the senior. "Quite a joker on parade, I noticed." The man's face was stern, but his eyes twinkled. "You almost had me laughing on parade, and that would never do. I figured you'd give us some interesting moments, and you didn't disappoint, I'm happy to say. Keep up the good work."

And with that, he was gone, leaving Harry speechless as Ferghal, Elize and the others clustered round him demanding to know what the Master Warrant had said.

AFTER THE PARADE, ALL THE CANDIDATES ASSEMBLED in the main auditorium to be presented individually with their certificates, and for the cadets, their Warrants as Midshipmen. Each candidate was handed a wallet that contained a data chip with orders for posting to a ship. Harry found himself wishing he had his tablet with him so he could read this information — and anxious to know where Ferghal's posting would take him. Not for the first time he wondered how he would feel if they were to be separated. He confided this to Elize as they sat waiting for the presentations to be completed. "I hope Ferghal and I are posted to the same ship," he whispered. "It will be very strange not to be together after all that we have been through."

"You'll have to wait and see, won't you? And I notice you aren't saying you'd like me to be on the same ship!" she teased. "I know I am due to go back to the *Vengeance*, so I suppose we won't be together, unless you're posted to that ship." She gave him an enquiring glance. "Will you write to me? One of your *real* letters in that lovely handwriting of yours?"

Surprised and flattered, Harry returned her smile. "Of course. But you must reply to mine." He had enjoyed her company and his flirtation with her, even if some of the others considered it so stilted as to hardly qualify as flirtation. He realised he was rather old fashioned, but he was fairly certain Elize liked that about him. He would miss her companionship when they parted, but he was also very unsure of how he should respond to a lady so obviously interested in his company. After all, in the nineteenth century, young men rarely got close to a young lady unless she was in the company of an older chaperone, always a woman. Furthermore, despite a great deal of searching through the Discipline Handbook he was not at all sure that it was proper for him to pay court to a fellow officer. It was yet another of the very confusing things he wrestled with whenever he was unable to sleep.

Eventually the assembly was dismissed, and Harry rushed to his room to get his tablet with Ferghal hard on his heels. Anxiously they inserted their data chips and used their security codes to access the orders. "I am posted to the *Leander* — Fleet frigate. What ship are you sent to?"

"*Leander* as well," breathed Ferghal with relief. "I was afraid they would send us to different ships now, but all's well. I can continue with you, Master Harr . . . I mean Harry," he finished, for the first time in months falling back to his old form of address, a sure sign that he had been deeply concerned about the possibility of their being separated.

Harry looked across to where Barclay was talking with Laschelles. "I wonder who will have the pleasure of their company in future. Not we, I hope!"

THE SMALL MAN LEANED BACK IN HIS CHAIR and steepled his fingers. His mild appearance and mannerisms belied a steely resolve. Not for nothing did the sign on the door to his suite of offices say simply Director of Corporate Security. Myles Campbell-Jones was deceptive. Outwardly the epitome of a loving family man, his desk displayed holographic images of his wife and their children, now all at top public schools in England. Soft spoken and always very polite, he was dressed impeccably, every stitch of clothing tailor made and perfect in its fit. Yet even this did not make him stand out, but seemed to enhance his very ordinariness. It was a carefully cultivated front, one that served him well. In meetings with outsiders he always let his number two do the talking, and most people fell into the trap of thinking that this mild mannered and innocuous little man was a nobody. In fact, after the Chairman, he was the most powerful man in the Consortium, the one man even the Chairman dealt with carefully.

And today, he was not pleased.

"Tell me again how this simple operation failed?"

"We don't know," his deputy replied, shifting uncomfortably. "All we have for certain is that the team apparently failed to return to the College to collect our contact there. There is nothing on the security scanners to indicate that anything may have gone awry, and there was no sign of any attempt to place the device. As you know, the intention was to detonate it once the boats had been manned so that we could be sure of the maximum number of casualties among the spectators, particularly among the Fleet Command Staff." He wished he were brave enough to wipe the beads of sweat from his forehead, but he didn't want to draw further attention to his nervousness, and he was afraid the Director would see it as an insult to the perfect temperature in the climate-controlled room. "All we know for certain is that the transport returned automatically to the garage it left from — and the device was still in it. When it detonated, the entire building collapsed."

"That is something else we will need to look into then," replied the small man. "That building was supposed to be impervious to the explosion from a device of that size." He touched a control and spoke to a secretary. "Have Mr Brandfort look into the construction contracts for the Global Security Group. I want him to look at who built their HQ and why it failed. If there was any..." he searched carefully for the right word "...misalignment between our specification and the construction, those responsible must be made aware of their error. If necessary, we will make an example of them. We cannot allow anyone to think we will accept sub-standard work. Thank you."

He turned his attention back to his deputy. "Let our agents at the College know that I am very disappointed, but at least they have delivered one useful piece of information. It seems that our targets have been assigned to the frigate *Leander*. I understand from Fleet HQ that she is part of a group taking a convoy to Pangaea and then to New Eden to do a survey. That will give us more than one opportunity to remove them, and if we can't, it would be very unfortunate if she were to be lost en route, would it not? See to it, please."

"We may have a problem at the College," his deputy reported. "It seems that Lieutenant Commander Vallance had a visit from Fleet Security and is now under surveillance. Our other operatives at the College want out as soon as possible in case he implicates them."

"Ah." The small man nodded. "Well, perhaps it's time to get him moved to a new post. I'll see to it. Is there any indication as to why he failed to warn us things had gone wrong?"

"Yes." The big deputy gave a sour smile. "It seems that the security clamp-down left them all unable to get a message out that would not be intercepted and traced. I suppose we should have anticipated that. Still, Vallance had planned to leave with the team and none of us anticipated them being intercepted. We still don't know how that happened. All I have is some garbled story about some sort of special ops security team."

MIDSHIPMAN EON BARCLAY MADE SURE THE PRIVACY SCREEN was activated in the public communications booth. He'd not dared to use his unregistered private communicator at the College. Now he addressed his uncle, a florid faced and rather corpulent man.

"I've been posted to a destroyer being sent to the Seraphis sector."

"Good. Cheer up, Eon. That will put you in a good position when we are ready to move you. Just keep your nose clean and it will be to your advantage soon. "Things will be moving very quickly in the not too distant future, and you stand to benefit."

"But what about Heron and the others?" Barclay scowled. "I wanted to see them pay for all the trouble they put me through, not to mention what happened to Liam."

"Liam was in the wrong place at the wrong time — and involved in activities you would do well to stay clear of. As for those boys, forget about them. They're not your problem. Our people will deal with them. Their survival is not important to anyone except Dr Johnstone, and he's out of favour at the moment."

"But there was a big reward for their return to Johnstone," protested Eon. "I could use that!"

"As I said, Johnstone isn't in favour with the Board at the moment, and they don't support his attempt to have those boys recaptured. So keep out of it. Don't mess this up like you did the other business. We don't need to upset the Chairman just now if we can help it. Is that clear?"

With obvious reluctance, Midshipman Barclay agreed. Privately, he vowed to take the soonest possible opportunity to exact revenge on those fossils. O'Connor would definitely pay for the humiliation he had forced on him, and so would Heron.

Part Two – Fleet Deployment

Chapter 23 – New Ship, New Challenges

Harry studied the frigate as the transport approached the huge docking station. Considerably smaller than any of the ships he'd been aboard since his precipitate arrival in this age of interstellar travel, she had a sleek beauty suggesting speed, power and manoeuvrability. Dwarfed by the orbital dock, she still managed to project the grace of a predator even among several of the Fleet's ships.

"She's a beauty," Ferghal remarked. "I hear the Engineering Commander is a tiger."

Harry nodded, his eyes on the weapons pods and the navigation array. "Aye." He grinned. "Or a bear. I heard she is known as Mama Bear. They say she takes care of her people though." Shifting his attention as the transport moved further round the dock, he pointed to some larger ships. "The *Darings*, I think, a new class of destroyer."

"Aye, and Barclay was assigned to one — the *Driad* — but he resigned his commission. No loss to the Fleet." Ferghal indicated a larger ship in the next berth. "The *DGK*. I wonder if we will have time to see our friends aboard her."

"We can but hope. I believe we are not due to depart for a few days yet. Perhaps we may also explore this dock station or at least a part of it."

The transport manoeuvred carefully, and with the slightest tremor slid into a vast open bay. Behind them the huge doors closed silently as the transport aligned with the deck.

The Loadmaster made the usual announcements. "Your dunnage will be available for collection at Security. Please proceed directly to Boarding Control. Have your ID and assignment orders ready. Transport to your ships will be assigned once you have cleared Security. Officers may disembark through the forward ports. All other ranks through the after ports." He sounded bored. It was obvious he had given these instructions many times before.

STEPPING THROUGH THE BOARDING PORT, HARRY and Ferghal found themselves in a wide-open space. Against the forward bulkhead was a large board on which were the Battle Honours of all the previous *Leanders* stretching back to the earthbound navy of the 17th Century. A Quartermaster, two TechRates and the Officer of the Day in Number One dress stood at allotted posts with two Marines in parade dress on sentry duty.

Saluting the Honours, as he'd learned was customary, Harry addressed the Officer of the Day. "Midshipmen Heron and O'Connor reporting in accordance with our orders, sir."

"Welcome aboard, Mr Heron, Mr O'Connor. I'm Lieutenant Orloff. I'm responsible for your welfare and development on this commission." She signalled one of the TechRates. "Show these gentlemen to the Gunroom and then to the Exec's office. I'll notify him you're on your way."

Saluting again they followed the TechRate aft then down a deck.

"The Gunroom, gentlemen. Your cabins are ready." The TechRate operated the door and stood aside. "I'll wait here for you."

"Thank you," Harry responded, returning the salute. "Lead on Ferghal. Best not keep the First waiting."

"Good afternoon, Mr Heron, Mr O'Connor." The android steward moved to meet them. "Service Droid 14 at your service, sirs. Mr Heron, you are assigned Cabin Four. Mr O'Connor, you have Number Six. Sub-Lieutenant Istafan is the Gunroom senior. She is currently in the Command Centre."

Harry grinned. The android seemed even fussier than Herbert the Heron family butler droid at Scrabo House. "Thank you. We are awaited by the Executive Officer, so we can make your acquaintance properly later, perhaps."

He was about to stow his kit when the steward said, "Leave your bags, sir. I will see them properly stowed. If the Commander expects you, best hurry."

The interview with the Executive Commander was brief. She wasted little time beyond the normal pleasantries, assigning Harry to the Navigation Department and Ferghal to Engineering.

"Captain Kirkham runs a tight ship, gentlemen, and I make sure it remains that way." Commander Philippa Sönderburg smiled briefly. "Your files indicate that you have some special abilities. Your Heads of Department will find good use for them." Her link chirped. "Carry on. You have your assignments."

The Navigation Officer acknowledged Harry's arrival with a grin after he returned his salute. "Mr Heron. Great, just in time. I hear you're a wizard at astro-nav maths. You can get to work with me immediately — we've to run checks on all these updates for the Pangaea system and another we'll be visiting."

"Aye, aye, sir." The Navigation Officer was younger than he'd expected, a Lieutenant Commander named Dalziel. Glancing round the Navigation Centre, Harry took in the position of the various operational stations including the helm and manoeuvring controls. "Where shall I work, sir?"

"We'll work over here on the 2D display." He led the way to the flat-topped display. "Easier to do plotting on this. We'll run a full check on the normal 3D once we've run through the calcs."

"Very good, sir."

"I've been told you've an AI implant. I believe it's a bit special. Can you access the AI and get it to display the latest list of updates?"

"Aye, sir." Harry switched off his blocking wand. A rush of code filled his eyes and ears. He addressed the AI in his head. *"Good afternoon, Leander. Would you display the latest updates for the Pangaea system for me, please?"*

"With pleasure." The pause was imperceptible. *"May I address you as Harry? If we are to be joined in this manner, I would hope to be a friend."*

Surprised, Harry nodded. *"Of course, Leander. I hoped we could be friends as well."*

The watching Navigation Officer saw Harry smile as he stared into space and wondered what he was doing. He was about to intervene when the display produced the updates he'd asked for.

"*Thank you,* Leander. *Do you mind if I remain linked to you while I assist Commander Dalziel?*"

"*It will be interesting to see how you do this. Please remain linked to me.*"

Nodding again, Harry turned to the Navigator. "*Leander* wishes to watch how I work on these updates, sir. Shall we proceed?"

Staring at his new midshipman for a moment, the commander frowned. "*Leander* wishes to? How exactly does this link work, Mr Heron?"

"I'm afraid I don't understand the exact mechanism, sir, but when my blocking device is switched off, the ship sees me as a mobile node, sir."

Letting out his breath in a soft whistle, the Lieutenant Commander nodded. "Ah." A memory stirred and his face lit up. "This is what the *DGK* people were talking about. Right! That's going to be extremely useful, Mr Heron."

FERGHAL SALUTED. "MIDSHIPMAN O'CONNOR, MA'AM. I'm ordered to report to you."

The small fierce-looking Engineering Commander studied him for several seconds before returning his salute. "So you're O'Connor, the man Commander Reuter on the *DGK* says can control the drives through his AI link."

"Er . . . aye, ma'am." Ferghal, all six foot four of him, suddenly felt like a small boy in the presence of this woman. "We did our training cruise on the *DGK*, ma'am."

She smiled suddenly. "So he said. And a right shower for the most part, but he seemed to think you were alright." Indicating a console, she said, "That'll be your responsibility once we get underway. In the meantime I have a list of checks and routines for you to run. Find Lieutenant Sci'Angelli — she's a Lacertian in case you don't know — and she'll put you to work."

"Aye, aye, ma'am." Ferghal turned toward his console.

"You've worked with the Lacertians before? You don't seem surprised to have one as your supervisor."

Ferghal smiled. "Met them first on Pangaea, ma'am. They sailed with us from New Caledonia to Pangaea City, an' they've a knack for being wherever Harry — Midshipman Heron — and me and Danny are—that's Danny Gunn, our powder monkey aboard the *Spartan* ... but he's away at college now."

Commander Behr leaned back, her eyes narrowed as she considered this. She was at first baffled by the term powder monkey then recalled the story of these three young time travellers. "So the rumour is true about some link between you and the Lacertians." Straightening, she smiled. "Carry on, Mr O'Connor."

LIEUTENANT COMMANDER VALLANCE SLIPPED INTO HIS SEAT at the bar. "Bring me a gin and tonic, please," he said to the android bartender. He wondered why he'd been invited to meet a representative of WeapTech, the supplier of most of the Fleet's weaponry. His posting to the frigate *Naiad* had been a welcome surprise as he'd begun to feel Fleet Security were getting too close and too interested in him at the College. He was keeping a low profile to avoid suspicion, and now this. He knew the woman from WeapTech wasn't just a specialist engineer.

The bartender returned with his drink, and before it departed, a woman stepped forward and took the barstool next to him.

"Commander Vallance? Good evening."

Ari studied the newcomer as she ordered a drink. He wondered what the real reason was behind this invitation.

Settling back into the barstool, she smiled. "It's been a while."

"It has been a while." He sipped his drink and pondered his next move. He played his cards close. "My last posting had its moments, but it's good to be on a ship again. How about you?"

"Oh, you know, here, there and everywhere. Always something needing my attention." Changing the subject, she said, "I hear your flotilla is heading out to Pangaea. You might be interested in a little opportunity there."

"That depends on the opportunity." Alert for some trap, he shrugged to appear disinterested. "I've enough on my plate without upsetting the Fleet."

"I expect so." She sipped her drink. "How is your son? I heard the medics had some new treatment they hoped would stop the degeneration."

Ari Vallance froze. How did she know? "It's early days. The source for the modified genes is not available at present."

She nodded. "Exactly. But they are going to be on Pangaea when you are. Something can be arranged."

His eyes narrowed. "It would be bloody risky. You know that planet has been turned into a major forward base. It's crawling with troops. What do you have in mind?"

"Me? I'm just the messenger. There are people in place, but they'd need to be steered by someone who knows the targets, someone who can pass on the word as to when they're accessible and where. It would be extremely lucrative, and it's an entirely private matter this time — no Board involvement."

He almost used an expletive to express his feelings on that matter but coughed to cover it. He'd damn well had enough of certain Board members and their overreach. "Yes, well, they've certainly made a mess of things so far. Who's involved in this?"

"Johnstone himself. He's offering a premium on the recovery of his assets, he says. You've the perfect cover for it. Legit reason to be there, good reason to know where they are." She hesitated. The next thing she said would seal the deal. "Johnstone will also pay for the treatment your son so desperately needs. He says it's the least he can do to repay you for your loyalty and service."

Vallance leaned back in his seat. His young son suffered an incurable degenerative disease, and the doctors' efforts had done nothing but slow it down. He needed a specialised treatment that was beyond Vallance's pay grade. This was a major reason he'd got involved in this mess to begin with. He would do anything for his boy.

He sighed with the weariness that only a beleaguered parent could understand. "Okay, let me have the details and I'll deal with it."

Chapter 24 – Ferghal's Oneupmanship

The invitation to send representatives from the Gunroom to the recommissioning Dining In aboard the *Der Grosse Kurfürst* provided a welcome interlude to the demands of preparing for a deep space voyage. Resplendent in their Formal Mess uniforms, the midshipmen joined the Wardroom representatives and the Captain for the brief trip to the *DGK*'s berth. A full side party welcomed them aboard.

Arno stepped forward to guide the guests. Saluting Captain Kirkham, he clicked his heels. "Sir, Captain Haakon's compliments. I am to take your party to the Wardroom."

Returning the salute, the Captain smiled. "Lead on, Midshipman. I know your brother, I think. Good to see you keeping up the traditions of the family." Indicating Harry, Ferghal and the others, he added, "Some of my officers are already familiar with your ship, I believe."

"Yes, sir." Arno nodded toward Harry and Ferghal. "Herr Heron and Herr O'Connor were with us for their training cruise, sir. Herr Heron had to manually calculate our transit solutions when the operating interfaces went offline."

Greg Kirkham had heard rumours of this feat, and now that he was in the presence of that young man, he glanced at Harry, who was engrossed in conversation with several of the *DGK*'s midshipmen. "I heard there was a problem with the interfaces. All fixed now?"

"Yes, sir. All is in working order." Arno held the door for Captain Kirkham then stepped inside and quietly told the rigid Marine Warrant Officer the Captain's name.

Stepping aside, he saluted as the Marine announced in a stentorian voice that filled the space, "Kapitän Kirkham of the *Leander*!"

ONE OF THE HANGAR BAYS HAD BEEN TRANSFORMED into a large dining hall for the event. The seating had been carefully arranged so that the *DGK*'s officers and midshipmen could mingle with the visitors from the *Leander* and other ships, with all the captains seated at the head table, which formed the long bar of the E-shaped design of the table arrangement.

Everyone wore the Formal Mess uniform, with one exception.

"Who is yon man?" Harry asked Arno, seated next to him. "The gentleman with the piratical look next to Lieutenant Commander Reuter." The man looked anything but happy.

"Herr Doktor Glasfiend, a scientist we have to take with us." He made a face. "He has some mad project that is supposed to overcome the Consortium interference screen. The Kapitän Leutnant is not happy with him."

"I can see that," Harry remarked, studying the man. Clad all in black, with the smallest eyeglasses he'd ever seen, the scientist seemed to have no idea concerning table etiquette at a function such as this. "He seems rather out of place here."

"He is a nightmare to work with," Arno retorted. "Very, very, clever, but sometimes." His expression said all that he couldn't.

"I think the Lieutenant Commander must be hard pressed to keep his patience then." Ferghal recalled all too clearly the engineering officer's insistence on everything being exactly right, and more especially, his lack of tolerance for anyone who would not work as a part of his close-knit team. Catching sight of his own new boss, Lieutenant Commander Heather Behr in conversation with another officer, he grinned.

"This Dr Glasfiend should be glad he is not dealing with our Engineering Commander. Mama Bear would likely devour him."

"Mama Bear?" Arno exclaimed.

Ferghal had to suppress his laughter. "That's what everyone calls her when she's not within earshot. We don't know if there is a Papa Behr, but she is quite fearsome when she wants something done." He paused and grinned, a witty remark coming to the fore that he couldn't resist. "I don't think I'd want to be her Papa Bear. Can you imagine being stuck in a den with her?"

Harry chuckled. "Her team must be the Baby Bears then," he said, dodging Ferghal's elbow.

Their companions laughed, and Arno said, "And what does she give you to do?"

"I am tasked with renewing some microcircuitry that wasn't up to her standards." He looked smug and very pleased with himself. "She has expressed her satisfaction thus far."

"Oh, really?" parried Arno. "And exactly how did she express it, Fergie old boy? You working that Irish charm on her already?"

Everyone laughed again, and Ferghal shrugged it off, concentrating on the prime filet, his face an expression of pure bliss as he savoured every bite. "I'll never tire of how well they feed us," he added, remembering to use his cloth serviette to wipe the corners of his mouth.

"What did she say to you about your cutlass demonstration for the Royals?" asked Harry, mischief showing in his face. He wasn't letting Ferghal off the hook that easily.

"That I'd best leave my carving knife in my cabin lest I be accused by the Consortium of breeching some convention." Ferghal set his knife and fork across the edge of his plate to take a sip of wine, and Harry noted with quiet pleasure his old friend's improved table manners, remembering the rough stable boy that Ferghal had once been. "Then I told her I'd taught some of the Royals at the College the art of how to properly wield a cutlass, and she said the Royals were menace enough, and now I'd made them worse."

His companions laughed, and the discussion moved on to the merits of the various ships, and speculation on the coming deployment.

Sub-Lieutenant Mariam Isfahan joined in, slightly troubled because her group, sat at the very end of the table and farthest from the head table, seemed to be getting the same service as the Captains and Senior Officers. She put it down to the presence of the Lacertian midshipmen in her party, and got on with enjoying herself.

Further up the table, Lieutenant-Commander Dalziel noticed that the midshipmen appeared to be receiving Captains' Table service from the android stewards. Curious, he mentioned this to his counterpart on the frigate *Hermione*.

"Am I imagining it, or is that group — where the midshipmen from the *DGK* are entertaining my lot and those Lacerations — getting Captains' Table service?"

His companion watched. "You're right. They've got some pull, obviously. I didn't think the androids could be persuaded to break protocol like that. Someone must have reprogrammed them."

"You're right, but why only that group?" Hoping he wasn't going to get the answer he thought he might, Bob Dalziel stopped a passing android. "Steward, who requested Captains' Table service for that group of midshipmen?"

The android paused. "Friederich Wilhelm instructed us to provide it, sir. Do you wish for more wine? I see your glass is low."

"Friedrich Wilhelm?" Both officers chorused. "Who is Friedrich Wilhelm?"

"*Der Grosse Kurfürst*, sir," replied the android, topping up their glasses. "He ordered that we take special care of his human nodes and their companions."

It took a moment for the meaning to sink in. "The ship ordered you to do this for its — what did you call them? — human nodes?" Dalziel leaned back in his seat. "Well, I'll be damned. Thank you, steward."

"What the hell was all that about?" asked his companion. "Human nodes? Who the blazes are they — or should I say what are they? Don't tell me we've now got cyborgs in the Fleet. I'm just getting to grips with the androids."

"Not cyborgs, no, but something unusual, I think." Bob Dalziel decided not to enlarge on this. It explained a great deal about the relationship *Leander* seemed to have with Midshipmen Heron and O'Connor. Mama Behr had remarked on it as well. He laughed. "I wonder if Fleet Command know the ship named itself after the original Great Elector of Brandenburg? Probably not."

The discussion dropped as the Executive Officer of the *DGK* struck the ancient bell and announced the traditional toast to the Fleet. There followed the usual Toast to the Ship introduced by a

Rear Admiral who spoke wittily, the reply given by an equally witty Commander, and then, with dinner over, the party began in earnest.

"PILOT SAYS SOMETHING ODD HAPPENED ON THE *DGK* at the Dining In." The Executive Commander relaxed slightly in her seat "He noticed that the androids were giving the full Captain's Table service to the table where Heron and O'Connor were seated. When he asked the steward serving his group why, it told him that Friedrich Wilhelm had instructed its human nodes be given the full treatment."

"Friedrich Wilhelm?"

"I looked it up, sir." Commander Sönderburg smiled. "Friedrich Wilhelm von Hohenzollern, Prince Elector of Brandenburg and Duke of Prussia in the 1600s, otherwise known as Der Grosse Kurfürst. Seems the ship has named itself after him.

"Well I'll be damned." Captain Kirkham leaned back in his chair. "Have you passed that on to Captain Haakon?"

"Had a word with his Exec, sir. He was quite surprised, but he thought it amusing." Commander Sönderburg continued. "It's not been made public, but when they had that problem with the controls during the training cruise, they discovered — after reverting to manual operation of the drives and the navigation — that Heron and O'Connor were somehow linked to the AI and could have done both functions through the link."

"I think I need to talk to Mr Heron." Captain Kirkham stared at the bulkhead. "I'd heard a rumour about this, and Pilot mentioned that Heron's updating of the star charts was a one-man show. The star charts appeared, the updates and corrections happened, but he didn't use the interface to do it." Pausing, he frowned. "On second thought, I think I'll take the opportunity to watch him at work, and then I'll talk to him. Mama Behr said something about O'Connor. I'll follow it up."

"MR O'CONNOR." LIEUTENANT COMMANDER BEHR beckoned Ferghal. "I've an errand for you. I sent MechWarrant Brunton to collect the final allocation of spares I ordered, but he says there's some bureaucratic problem. Get over to Dock Engineering Stores and sort it out."

"Aye, aye, ma'am."

"Take TechRate Klein with you. You'll need a stores transport as well." Her frown deepened. "I'll tell them you're coming." Under her breath she added, "And they better have the problem sorted by then."

Ferghal found Klein and headed for the ship's quarterdeck and the station gantry. Saluting the Honours, he led Klein onto the dock and requisitioned the small transport from the pool assigned to the ship.

Klein leaned close and said, "Any bets it's the usual problem, sir? Someone hasn't signed the right form in the right order." His suppressed snort of derision told what he thought of their needless errand.

Ferghal laughed. "Probably. They do love their forms. Worse than the purser on *Spartan* — he was convinced all the stores belonged to him, and he hated to part with anything, even the most rotten salt pork." Quietly he explored the dock station AI and found the stores system and then the requisitions. He frowned at the bulkhead when he saw the approvals displayed, and notices that the stores were to be redirected to a different ship. Armed with this knowledge, Ferghal entered the Stores Office.

"Yes, I have the spares your Commander has ordered, but I cannot release them unless I have the authority of my Director. They're reserved for another ship." The little bureaucrat had the sort of smug air that got under Ferghal's skin. "I have explained this at length to your, er, Warrant Officer."

Glancing at the Warrant's face, Ferghal saw the barely suppressed fury there. "But these stores are essential, and we sail tomorrow." Ferghal consulted his tablet. "And the order was made over a week ago, enough time, surely, for the proper authority to be obtained."

"Normally, yes." The supply clerk sniffed importantly. "Yes, normally," he repeated, as if needing to convince himself of the lie. "Unfortunately, the Director has been called to Earth for an important meeting. Until she returns next week, I can't get the reallocation and release signed."

Ferghal hesitated, controlling his temper at the blatant lie. "When did this Director leave the station?"

"Last night."

"Could she not have issued the authority before this?"

"Yours is not the only ship needing anything, you know. And priority is always given to the needs of the station—" The man cut himself short when he realised he was saying too much. "We have to prioritise. The ships' needs are important, but the station is undergoing some major maintenance at this time."

"I see." Fingering his link, Ferghal called the ship and left a message for Mama Behr. He suspected he knew what her reaction would be. "So you say the authority has not been issued and cannot be until next week? And we must therefore sail without the spares we require for the transit?"

"I have told you repeatedly. Now you are wasting my time, young man. I have a great deal of work to do."

Ferghal bit back his retort. An idea formed.

"Search," he inwardly ordered the AI. "*Engineering Requisition Leander 5771 slash 77.*"

"*Found. What do you require?*"

"*Authorise the issue of all items on the requisition.*"

"*The spares on this requisition have been reassigned.*"

"*To what ship?*"

"*The ACF Conveyor.*"

"*That is an error. She is not a Fleet ship, and cannot draw Fleet supplies.*" Ferghal considered. "*Cancel the reassignment and deliver the packages to this station, and copy the allocations to NECS Leander FAO Lieutenant-Commander Behr.*"

"*On what authority?*"

Ferghal hesitated then remembered the name. "*Flag Officer Du Plessis, Commanding Fleet Engineering.*"

"*It is done. The packages will be issued at your location in one minute fifty-eight seconds.*"

"*Thank you.*"

Ferghal cleared his throat. "Excuse me."

The clerk looked up, feigning that Ferghal had startled him out of deep concentration as he studied a supply list on his tablet. "What is it? I told you, I'm busy."

"So you did, sir, but I believe my requisition has been authorised." He indicated a display screen. "Perhaps you could check."

The man stared, unable to deny that there was indeed a series of pallet carriers trundling into his despatch station. "I doubt it, but—" He glared at his handheld reader. "Just a moment. I need to check this on the inventory. I haven't entered any authorisation."

"Perhaps your Director did and forgot to tell you, sir."

The Warrant and the MechTech stared at Ferghal then at the clerk.

"I don't understand it." The man turned back to the counter. "Authorised by Flag Officer Fleet Engineering?" His eyebrows rose and he paled. He was flustered now, and very unsure of what was going on. "The stores are all present according to the system." Impatiently, he waved at the pallets. "Take them then."

With the clerk still puzzling over the appearance on his screen of the necessary authority, the Warrant and MechTech Klein loaded the packages on a freight lifter just as Lieutenant Commander Behr stormed into the office. "Well, O'Connor," she demanded. "What is the delay?"

"Mr, er," Ferghal cast his eye quickly at the man's badge. "Mr Lane has been most helpful, ma'am. He discovered there had been an error. In fact, ma'am, I was about to contact you and inform you I apologise for having troubled you, ma'am."

Lieutenant Commander Heather "Mama" Behr was not often lost for words. On this occasion, though, she seemed to have difficulty. Her glare switched between Ferghal and the clerk. "So I came all this way for nothing. Don't let it happen again."

"Yes, ma'am," chorused the clerk and Ferghal while the MechTech had a coughing fit.

"What the hell's the matter with you, Klein? See the surgeon when you get back aboard. I'm not having you coughing and spluttering all over my Control Room! Now get that stuff over to the ship the pair of you."

MechTech Klein activated the maglift of the small freight transport and led the way, still spluttering as Ferghal followed his Commander. Behind him the clerk stared at his screen, puzzled by the authorisation. He knew it to be false, precisely because he'd arranged for these very stores to be assigned to the ACL *Conveyor,* a regular little fiddle his line manager was in on. The trick was to select a requisition submitted by a ship that was about to depart because it would not have time to query the delay. How had their foolproof system failed?

IN THE CORRIDOR, FERGHAL WAS SUDDENLY AWARE that the Lieutenant Commander was glaring at him and expecting an answer to some question he had not heard.

"Sorry, ma'am." He gulped. "I beg pardon, I did not hear you speak."

"I said liar!" she growled. "That man was never being helpful. I've had run-ins with him many times. He found an error? That's the biggest load of manure I've ever heard! He never agreed to release these items without some authority. What did you do? Out with it now — all of it."

He told her of his redirecting the already packed stores.

Passers-by in the long corridor averted their eyes and hurried past at the sight of an officer of the Fleet — Mama Behr, no less — leaning against the transport howling with laughter, tears streaming from her eyes.

Eventually she managed, "My God, you'll get us both court-martialled. It will be worth it just to drag that shower of worthless paper shufflers in to face the music with us. Oh my God, I had better tell the Captain so he can warn Flag and Flag Engineering of the bomb ticking away there." She shook with another paroxysm of laughter. "No wonder Klein looked so happy!"

Relieved by her response, Ferghal used his AI link again.

"Thank you for your assistance. I would appreciate your forwarding a complete record of all issues not made to the originating ships and delayed or declined requisitions to my ship, for the attention of Lieutenant Commander Behr."

"In progress." There was a moment's hesitation. *"You are an unusual node. What is your function?"*

"I am a human node assigned to NECS Leander. *Thank you again for your assistance.* Leander *will be grateful."*

FERGHAL TAPPED ON THE DOOR OF MAMA BEHR'S OFFICE. "You wanted to see me, ma'am?"

"So what is this list of declined or unauthorised requisitions? Mine is right there at the top marked declined. And they didn't even have the bloody decency to contact me!" She paused, visibly controlling her fury. "I know you told me you'd redirected the stuff and altered the authority, but what I want to know is how did you get these records of all the declined and redirected requisitions?"

Ferghal weighed up how to say what he'd done. "Um, privately, ma'am."

She stared at him, then her anger faded. "You've pulled a blinder, have you? Right, what did you do? Who else has copies of this?" She waved him to a chair. "Am I going to have Special Branch descending on me looking for you?"

"I hope not, ma'am. The clerk said his Director hadn't signed the authority to release, and wouldn't be back until next week. I, um, checked with the AI when he wouldn't reconsider in light of our departure. When I saw the authority had been given and redirected to a private ship, not a Fleet one, I told the AI to cancel the reassignment, reauthorise our requisition and reallocate the issue to us."

"And the clerk didn't know?"

"I did it through my link, ma'am. When he checked his inventories, the requisition showed it was authorised to us."

Mama Behr's expression underwent a transformation.

"Ma'am?"

"I'll be damned." She started laughing. "Oh, bloody hell. I'm glad you only gave the bull version on the station. There'll be hell to pay over this, and bugger all they can do about it — especially the stuff issued to contractors and non-Fleet ships! Well done. There's been a lot of this, obviously. I'll have to pass it to SO Engineering to investigate it further." She straightened in her chair. "Carry on, Mr O'Connor. I had better see the Commander immediately. Don't tell anyone else how you did this."

ACCOMPANYING THE NAVIGATOR AND THE CAPTAIN to the Admiral's briefing, Harry chose a seat next to Lieutenant Commander Dalziel in the lecture-style briefing room aboard the flagship. He watched and listened with interest as each Briefing Officer addressed the specific groups of specialists, though a great deal of it was of no consequence to his remit, which was navigation.

Sitting straight as the Fleet Navigation Officer took the podium, he made copious notes on his pad, to the amusement of his commander who simply made use of his tablet to capture and record the data. The amusement turned to fascination when the briefing moved on to dealing with matters unrelated to navigation, including stores, spare parts, repair facilities and catering. Bob

Dalziel watched as the swiftly moving pencil captured the faces of the Briefing Staff, the Admiral and the assembled Captains — all while Harry listened with apparent intense interest. The sketches of the Captains of *Dragon, Danae, Naiad* and *Lysander* appeared, and one of the Admiral and his Flag Lieutenant, all of which captured their likeness and personality in a few deft pencil strokes, each labelled with the name.

The convoy coordinator took his turn at the podium. Harry stopped sketching to write a few notes, and Bob Dalziel turned his attention to the speaker, making a mental note to ask for copies of the sketches afterward.

The convoy coordinator consulted his tablet then glanced around the room to make sure he had everyone's attention. "You'll have ten freighters and a colonist transport to take out to Pangaea. Details of all the ships and their cargo manifests are in your orders pack. The situation with the Consortium is getting worse with every day that passes. We have no time to lose. Several of the non-treaty governments here on Earth are actively supporting them, apparently in return for weapons and ships."

A murmur of anger stirred among the Captains, quickly suppressed.

"This means that not even our own system is safe from incursion. We haven't had a direct attack, but we've been the target of several scouting missions. They seem to be testing our preparedness and assessing our defences. We have to keep a substantial force in readiness. Meanwhile, they strike at colonies and unescorted freighters whenever it suits them."

"Something is badly wrong if their ships are coming off unscathed," remarked one of the Captains.

"They aren't," said the Admiral, "but they have well established facilities, and they're diverting just about everything they need from our own stores." He stood to speak, and the convoy coordinator stepped aside to give him the podium.

The Admiral continued. "Gentlemen, there is no point in trying to fool anyone. The Consortium's fleet is considerably larger than was permitted under their charter. In fact, it is three times that, and growing larger thanks to some very innovative conversions. Our current intel suggests they have enough ships of the starship category to pose a significant threat, and those are supported by at least the same number of heavy cruisers plus frigates, destroyer class and landing ship platforms capable of supporting planetary landings."

He allowed the outraged protests then held up a hand for silence. "There has been a serious breakdown in the arrangements for monitoring their building programme, and certain governments on Earth are directly supporting them in their aims, but that is a matter for the politicians and the Fleet Board to sort out. Your task is to get your convoy to Pangaea intact."

For the *Leander* officers there was the additional information that they would first take the convoy to Pangaea then another group to Seraphis, and finally a research ship, the *Beagle*, to a planet called New Eden.

"Interesting name that," commented Captain Rafferty. "Sounds like paradise. What sort of place is it?"

"Interesting is not quite the word most people use for it," replied the Admiral. "It's no paradise, although it is full of vegetation. A very wet and warm place, but the oceans are so shallow they would be a joke anywhere else."

"THOSE SKETCHES ARE VERY GOOD, HARRY," Lieutenant Commander Dalziel remarked after the briefing. Keeping his tone casual, he asked, "What do you do with them when you've finished each sketch? Why do you need them?"

"Sir?" Harry coloured slightly, wondering if this was a mild reprimand. "I keep them for my journal. They remind me of who I have met among so many new faces. And, of course, they illustrate my letters to Aunt Niamh."

"Aunt Niamh?" Remembering why the unusual name was familiar, he said, "You mean Mrs L'Estrange? Commodore Heron's sister?"

"That is correct, sir." Harry grinned. "Actually, she and the Commodore are my great-niece and nephew twelve times removed, but it seems a little rude to remind them they are my juniors."

Bob Dalziel let out a guffaw. "I expect so! I can just see the Commodore's face if you did." He paused. "I'd like some copies of those sketches for my own logbook, Harry, if I may. Just a word to the wise, though — take care to keep things like that secure. You never know who might find it useful to go through your notes."

Chapter 25 – Outward Bound

"All hands to stations for undocking."

The announcement emptied the Gunroom. Harry hurried to the Navigation centre with Sheoba the Lacertian in company, and stopped as he noticed that, if she were not in uniform, she would be almost impossible to see. "Er, Sheoba, do you normally blend into the background like this? I mean, I know you do it when you wish to hide, but why here?"

She stopped. Slowly her head and hands came into view. "My apologies, Navigator." She made the gesture of respect. "When I am excited, I blend into the background. Does it disturb you?"

He smiled, returned the salute and continued walking with her. "Not really, but it does look very strange to see a headless body walking to its station." He raced up the stairs and paused at the entrance to the Navigation Centre. "Are you excited by our departure?"

"It is something I have looked forward to, yes." Stepping aside, she motioned. "I will follow you, Navigator."

Laughing, Harry took his place at the Navigation console and logged in as Sheoba took her place next to him. "Remember to keep yourself visible, please. We would not wish to distract the Coxswain while attempting to enter the transit gate in company."

"Ready, team?" Lieutenant Commander Dalziel looked round the Navigation Centre as each station reported ready. "Great stuff.

Here we go then." Activating his link, he reported, "Navigation closed up, helm manned, manoeuvring on standby, sir."

"Stand by. We'll be undocking and using the tugs to clear the dock. Once clear we will move to the assembly position. We're the lead ship through the gate."

"Standing by, sir."

The 3D display showed the dock along the starboard side and ahead, and a sister frigate and her tugs to port. A slight shudder in the deck accompanied the long boarding tube disengaging and retracting.

"Manoeuvring, stand by. The tethers are being released now."

"Tugs have us, sir."

The dock slid away as the ship drew clear of it. The tail of the long arm they'd been attached to slipped to starboard, and the ship swung to port.

"Tugs releasing. Tugs clear. Thirty second pulse on starboard manoeuvring thrusters." The ship's backward motion checked, and the swing to port increased. "Twenty seconds port thrusters. Stop thrusters."

The ship steadied. "Helm, steer forty-five degrees left, positive angle five degrees. Twenty seconds thrust aft thrusters."

"Ship will be on station in four minutes, sir," Harry reported, tracking their position on the large navigation display.

"Very good. Give me a mark at two minutes thirty."

The seconds ticked by. "Two minutes thirty seconds, sir."

"Forward thrusters, fifteen-second pulse." Watching the ship's position relative to her gathering convoy, Bob Dalziel waited until the glow of the thrusters vanished before he activated his comlink. "On station, sir."

"Well done, Pilot. As soon as everyone is in position, we'll lead our sheep into transit."

From his station, Harry watched the display, noting the ships gathering astern. Slightly beneath them and now well off to starboard hung the huge orbital dock, and beneath that loomed a great slice of the planet Earth — home. The sight of it from this vantage point gave him a strange yet exhilarating feeling.

THE *LEANDER* AND HER CONSORTS DROPPED OUT in the system of Pangaea Alpha exactly on schedule, with their small convoy intact and just inside the asteroid belt that Harry and Ferghal recalled from their earlier visit to the planet. Studying the planet and its three moons as they approached, Harry found his mind in a sort of emotional turmoil. He had not expected this reaction, and he was lost in his thoughts as the memories of the last time he visited Pangaea came flooding back.

The Lieutenant Commander noticed Harry's pensive expression. "Looks pretty from out here, but I expect it has a few ugly memories for you, eh?"

"Sir?" Harry almost jumped in his seat, he had been that lost in his thoughts. "Er, yes sir, it does. Ferghal and I first walked in the void on the inner moon, the smallest, and it was the first unearthly world we walked upon as well."

Bob Dalziel knew of the midshipman's ordeal at the hands of the Johnstone researchers. "Good memories are the ones to hold on to."

Harry stayed silent for a moment, not trusting his voice, which was threatening to break on him. "As you say, sir." He focussed on his work, plotting their approach to orbit, and took refuge in the maths and the star chart as a welcome distraction.

Allowing himself a peek at the scanner images he saw three orbital platforms and a number of Fleet vessels including a starship and several transports in orbit or attached to the docks. Half listening to the conversations around him, he focused on directing the helm and manoeuvring. The course and approach were straightforward enough.

I can't keep running away from this, he thought. *Distasteful as it is, I shall have to confront my own fear of this place, or it will continue to disable me.* Suppressing a shudder, he flexed his shoulders. *But not today,* he told himself. He set to work running the next series of calculations for braking, and passed these to the Coxswain's console.

Watching, Bob Dalziel nodded to his second-in-command. "Relax, Caryl, I've been monitoring his solutions and handling on my monitor." He indicated his screen. "Have you noticed that half the time he isn't using his manual interface? He only does so when he remembers we're watching. It's as if he's trying not to be different and to do it as he thinks we expect him to. Heather Behr tells me that O'Connor does this too. A bloody useful trick, I think, especially since he's twice as fast as the rest of us and a heck of a lot more sensitive with the controls too."

"I wondered about that," replied the Lieutenant, equally as quietly. "I know it's supposed to be a result of what that Consortium lot did to them, but sometimes it's a bit creepy when you ask him to calculate a course solution and it just appears on your screen. I hear there was a question as to whether he could have been used on the *DGK* to get past the Consortium blocking devices. It looks as if that would have worked."

The Lieutenant Commander's comlink chirped. "Navigation," he responded.

"Bob," the Captain's voice was clear. "We'll be lying off Orbit Dock Three until further notice. We're ordered to take position at North Cardinal Fifty-Two by Two at fifty miles. Bring us into that spot, please."

"Got that sir, North Cardinal Fifty-Two by Two at fifty miles." He looked across at Harry. "Did you hear that, Harry? Bring us onto Orbit Dock Three at the coordinates given, please."

"Aye, aye sir."

The ship altered course and decelerated rapidly. Unaware of the scrutiny of his officers, Harry concentrated, oblivious to the fact that he had not used the keypad interface for several minutes as he went through the required steps in the navigation routines and subroutines.

Finding the solutions, he manoeuvred the ship by relaying the course corrections and orders directly to the helmsman's screen and to Engineering. He could sense Ferghal manipulating and controlling the ship's propulsion system. Occasionally they swapped mental comments as they passed commands to each other, and they found comfort in the brief contact.

Harry withdrew from the system and turned to the Lieutenant Commander to find himself under that individual's interested gaze. He flushed slightly, wondering why they appeared so interested in his work.

"Ship is on station, sir."

"So I see, Mr Heron, well done. But tell me, when you were unable to access the networks on the *DGK* through the manual interface, couldn't you have reached it this way?"

"Pardon, sir?" Harry looked surprised then embarrassed as he recalled the Captain's order to always at least appear to use the interface. He hesitated. "I'm sorry, sir. Captain Haakon ordered me not to access the AI network. I did not think of the consequences of what I had done until later."

Bob Dalziel laughed.

Harry grinned nervously. "Captain Haakon seemed to think that I had deliberately withheld my ability from him, sir. I shall use the manual controls in future if you prefer I do so."

"There is no point in doing that if it's easier and more efficient for you to do it this way." Bob Dalziel stood. "Frankly, I wish I had that ability." He laughed. "My interface skills are a little erratic."

LIEUTENANT COMMANDER VALLANCE LOOKED UP SHARPLY as the shadow fell across his table. He frowned at the sight of his visitor.

"What do you want?" he growled in irritation.

"Come, come," said the newcomer, his grin making him even more annoying. "I've a message for you. Bert said to tell you he's in on this operation. All you have to do is identify the targets and leave the rest to us."

"Fine. Tell Bert to stick exactly to the plan. No getting creative. Tell him this is his last chance. He sticks exactly to the script and gets the targets to the rendezvous for collection. No distractions, no deviations and definitely no side excursions. This place is swarming with troops, and if he tries anything, anything at all outside the agreed plan, they'll be all over him before anyone can even sneeze."

The visitor looked angry. "Bert won't be happy about it. He likes to do things his way."

"I don't care what Bert likes or doesn't like. If he can't comply, the deal's off." Vallance huffed in frustration. "There is far more at stake here than his ego. Tell him it's straight down the line or not at all."

"I'll tell him." The visitor made to leave.

"Do so. And remind him that if it goes wrong, he's on his own with a large price on his head."

The visitor scowled. "And on yours!"

"That's where you are wrong, my friend," said the Lieutenant Commander, carefully anonymous in his casual outfit. "My cover is solid, but you and your friends will be deeper in shit than you can imagine if you try anything clever on that score."

Chapter 26 – Pangaea, Again

Marcus Grover looked up in surprise. "Good God, it is you! I'd heard you were coming, but had to see you for myself to believe it."

Harry grinned. The settlement of Urquhart had grown and changed since the expulsion of the Consortium from Pangaea. It now boasted several additional accommodation domes and a new leisure industry.

"Indeed, Mr Grover. We are here on leave. We are assigned to your establishment for accommodation and to meet Captain Stotesbury of the Advocate Admiral's Office. I am glad you appear to be thriving now."

"As you say, Mr Heron." Marcus smiled. "I must say I am surprised to see you, though. I should have thought you'd seen enough of this place and of us." Offering his hand, he added, "I hear your boat trip went well — only one attack from a Pleurodon. Shaking hands with Ferghal, he asked, "You do know there is a price on your heads. The Johnstone people want you fellows badly and there are some who won't hesitate to turn you in. I hope you have protection."

Harry took the proffered hand and smiled. "Yes, we did have an interesting passage. I will say that I would not have chosen to spend my leave here, with respect to you and your family. But," he shrugged, "it seems the Fleet has some arrangement with you, so here we are."

The hotelier nodded. He could appreciate the youth's feelings. "Yes, I was lucky. We got some development funds, and I managed to persuade the Governor's office to let us build this place, then along came the Fleet Recreations Office and booked it solid." He noted that Harry seemed older — more than his nominal age suggested — and he stood a lot taller than he remembered. "But I am forgetting my manners, Mr Heron. Please sign in." He noted several soldiers and a transport. "Your escort?"

Harry laughed and nodded. "I think so. Advocate Captain Stotesbury is coming, and it may have something to do with his investigations. We will be joined by some others from our ship as well." He grinned. "Perhaps we could have the best rooms for arriving early!"

Marcus gave a shout of laughter. "I like your nerve. You've got it." Nodding to Ferghal, he added, "There'll be one or two looking to stay out of your way then. I think Stepan Glinka will probably take to his bed and stay indoors until you leave. Terrien Hurker won't be too eager to go out while you're in town either."

He escorted them to their rooms in the best wing of the hotel, across the hall from each other. "These two are the best in the house." He winked, adding, "We'll give the Advocate Captain the end room. It's a good room, but it doesn't have the view yours has."

CAPTAIN STOTESBURY'S ENQUIRIES REQUIRED FAR LESS TIME than Harry feared. A brief visit to the Johnstone facility allowed him to confirm the location of the events and experiments. It also allowed him to unlock aspects of the second Consortium AI he had inadvertently isolated in their escape. Back at the hotel, he told Ferghal that he wanted to visit the home of the Glinka family and assure them he bore no ill will.

Ferghal hesitated. "Do you insist that we call upon Master Glinka?"

Harry understood his reason for uncertainty. "I do. I have heard he is recovered, but disabled." His smile flickered across his face. "He suffered badly for defending his home and family, my friend. You need not accompany me if you do not wish to."

Frowning, Ferghal shook his head. "And let you fall into some new mischief? No, I shall accompany you, though I feel no remorse for having nearly killed him."

THE VISIT DID NOT GO QUITE AS HARRY HAD HOPED. Stepan Glinka was sullen and clearly afraid, his wife nervous and uncomfortable. Ferghal, however, diverted the children and quickly lightened the atmosphere. By the time they left, Stepan had relaxed. At the door, he shook their hands, adding, "Mind how you go. A few here will be glad to see the bounty in their hands. You should not wander round without an escort."

Harry smiled. "Thank you for the warning, but I think we are safe enough. Our path takes us back to the hotel, and the Marines are everywhere." His gesture swept the landscape between the residential domes, currently devoid of any other human presence. "It is but two hundred yards to the entrance to the hotel dome from here." He bowed slightly to Mrs Glinka. "We may not have the opportunity to call again. I hope things go well for you both."

They had not gone far from the Glinka household when they met Lieutenant Commander Vallance.

"Well, well, Heron and O'Connor, isn't it? What brings you here?"

"A rest period, sir," Harry replied politely. His instinctive feeling of unease struggled to overtake his natural courtesy and ingrained respect for the man's rank. "We have been sent on leave for a day or two."

"Of course," the older man said, obviously making an effort to sound casual. "Staying at Grover's hotel, I suppose."

"Indeed, sir." Harry sensed the man was trying to keep them talking. "I beg pardon, sir, but we have another engagement and must be on our way."

"Of course." Vallance smiled. "I expect Captain Stotesbury will want your services up at the facility."

Harry was about to deny this when something rang a small cautionary warning in his mind. "As you say, sir." Two could play this game of false politeness to dig for information. "And you, sir? Posted to a new ship or to the school here?"

"Just finishing some leave. My ship will be joining your squadron in a few weeks." The Lieutenant Commander exhaled and looked about him. "Time I got out of the classroom. Working in the field is much more productive. We'll meet again, I'm sure." He resumed his walk and made his way to a transport vehicle. He boarded, and it sped off in the direction of the harbour. From his seat he made a call on his link. "They're on their way. No escort." He cut the link. "Little fools."

Harry watched the departing transport and quickly assessed the situation. "We'd better hurry, Ferghal, before the Captain discovers we have no escort. Something about that man Vallance doesn't sit well with me."

"Aye, with me either," Ferghal said.

They continued at a brisk pace in the direction of the hotel when they heard a door open in a nearby residential dome, and a woman emerged.

"Looking for something?" she asked.

Recognition flared in Harry's mind. "Good day, Mrs Hurker. Thank you, no, we are simply passing by." No sooner had he spoken than a burst of firing erupted from two domes away. The world spun and he collapsed, unaware that Ferghal was already down.

Mellia Hurker stepped aside as several men in a variety of military coveralls and equipment ran out and grabbed the downed pair.

"Take them round the back and put them in the transport. We don't have much time to get them away to the holding." The men scurried to comply. "Their security escort will be along in a minute." She watched the men drag Harry and Ferghal toward the back entrance.

"Put cuffs on my husband and me, then stun us. That'll delay the pursuit," Mrs Hurker ordered. When the men hesitated, she said, "Do it now! What are you waiting for?"

They did as they were told then hurried to the transport vehicle waiting behind the dome. As soon as the doors were shut, it lifted and sped off, skirting the town before disappearing into the trees even as a security detail burst through the front door of the house to discover Mellia Hurker and her husband restrained and unconscious.

A Sergeant entered from the rear. "They got clean away, sir. I've called for reinforcements and transport trace scans."

The Lieutenant nodded. "There'll be hell to pay over this. Damn." He looked at the medics reviving the Hurkers. "The whole damned thing stinks of a set-up."

"Agree, sir. I'll have the forensic boys run this place over. Something's not right."

"Good idea." He nodded toward the Hurkers. "Take them down to the cells — call it protective custody. Then get one of the interrogation team to get their story. I'll take the rest of the men to search for the route they took."

"WHAT DO YOU MEAN SOME OF MY PEOPLE were abducted?" Captain Rafferty fumed. "Who is it?"

"Midshipmen Heron and O'Connor, sir." The Marine Major let his annoyance show. "They apparently went out to visit the Glinka family and didn't inform us."

"How the blazes did that happen? Never mind, does Captain Stotesbury know? Do you need any assistance from my ship?"

"The Advocate Captain knows, and he's furious. He's on his way back now. If you can do a deep focus scan of the whole island, it may turn up something. We think — no, the indications are that the Hurker couple facilitated the kidnap, and we know who took Heron and O'Connor."

HARRY REGAINED CONSCIOUSNESS BOUND AND PRONE on a dirty floor. His hands were restrained behind him with metal cuffs and his ankles were similarly secured. He tried to free his mouth of a strap of thick tape by scraping his cheek against the floor, but finding this impossible, he focussed on figuring out where he might be.

In the darkness, he could hear someone struggling nearby. Certain that it must be Ferghal, he focussed on his link to the AI, and could hear the communications of a household network.

"Turn on the lights in U3," he ordered. The lights came on, and he saw Ferghal a short distance away. The room appeared to be a storeroom, but the state of it suggested it was not much used.

"Ferghal, do you hear me?"

Wriggling to face Harry, Ferghal nodded, grunting through the tape covering his lower face. *"Aye, I hear you."*

"We must free ourselves. I will try to get my hands in front of me." Wriggling round he managed to get into a seated position then contorted himself until he could get his arms beneath his body and finally, with a lot of effort and some damage to his wrists, to his front. In triumph he pulled the tape clear of his mouth. "Ow!" he exclaimed. "Damnation, that hurt."

Working over to where Ferghal lay, he whispered, "Access the network to discover where we are and who guards us. I will remove the tape so we may speak normally. Have a care, it is a powerful glue and stings as it comes away. It will hurt, but I'll make it quick. Brace yourself."

Ferghal nodded, and Harry ripped the tape off in one quick move.

"Bloody hell!" Ferghal exclaimed as soon as his mouth was freed. "Did you have to make it hurt that much?"

Harry grinned. "Best to get it over with quickly."

Ferghal wasn't convinced on any account. He looked around at their confinement. "Now you see the folly of your starts, my friend. Visiting a former enemy is one thing, a noble desire perhaps — but we should not have gone unescorted." He rubbed his sore face and listened to the network. "There are five here, two in one room and three more in another, and more elsewhere, but I'm not sure where." He grunted, contorting his body to get his hands in front of him. "Let me but lose these irons and there will be a reckoning for Mr Hurker and his Jezebel wife." He glowered at Harry. "I never wanted to see them again in my entire life, but I went along because you asked me to."

"Now is not the time or place to argue about this." Harry sighed. "Very well, I was misguided in my intention, but let us take stock and get free before we wrangle over the rights and wrongs!"

"And how do you suggest we remove these?" growled Ferghal, holding up his manacled wrists. "Have you some miracle key concealed upon your person?"

"No, I do not," snapped Harry. "As well you know. Now help me search these cases. There must be something we can use."

The search produced several items, but nothing with which to remove the manacles. With these restricting their every move, escape was impossible. Ferghal's anger increased as his frustration mounted. "There is nothing here but rubbish and broken tools." He kicked at the boxes to emphasise his point.

"You are right again," said Harry, his temper fraying. "I think this place must have been abandoned by its rightful owners, and these scum are using it because it is vacant."

The sound of footsteps approaching made them pause. Harry signalled. "Quickly, take a place at the door. I will lie on the floor."

Ferghal shuffled to a position beside the door as Harry lay down and ordered the network to douse the lights. A moment later the door slid back and a man looked in. Seeing Harry apparently unconscious on the floor, he stepped further into the room and scanned his eyes around, his weapon held loosely in his hand.

Ferghal swung a pipe and made a solid connection as Harry ordered the AI to shut the door. The man grunted and folded, his weapon falling into Harry's lap as he collapsed. Realising that a second man was trying to operate the door, Harry commanded the network to lock it and refuse any command to open it. He activated the lights, and Ferghal gave their victim a *coup de grace*, knocking him senseless.

Wriggling free, Harry said, "Let's see if he has a key to these shackles." Picking up the fallen weapon, he studied it. "I'm not sure that we could safely attempt our release with this, but if all else fails...."

"Do not even think it," growled Ferghal. "He has no key on him, but I did find this." He produced a small device. "Now this is more like it — a laser saw. At least this can cut the links that restrict our legs, but I want rid of the cuffs as well, and for that we need the key."

Activating the device as he spoke, he cut through the links joining Harry's wrists and ankles then waited while Harry did the same for him. The second man had by now ceased to hammer on the door and call his companion.

Nodding toward the door, Ferghal said, "We will have to move quickly, else he will return soon with more of their kind."

"We have a pistol now," said Harry. "There is another room beside this. Perhaps if we can gain access to that we may buy a little time."

"Then let us move," Ferghal growled. He commanded the AI to open the door and darted into the short passage with Harry hard upon his heels.

A man appeared at the top of the stairs and shouted, "Hey! They're loose." He fired a bolt, and the pair threw themselves aside. Harry snapped off a shot, and the man ducked behind the corner of the wall.

From somewhere else a voice shouted, "Use the stunner, you fool. We want them alive! Johnstone won't pay for dead meat, and if he doesn't get here soon, they will be our only negotiating chip."

Ferghal crouched in a doorway and ordered the network to open the door. He slipped inside and Harry followed.

"Now what?" growled Ferghal. "We're trapped. Unless...." He eyed several long cases. "Now, this is more like it, if those hold what I think they do."

Harry had a thought. "I will alter the AI so that it makes things difficult for them. If I can make it so they must peer into darkness to see us, it will give us an advantage."

"What about us?" snapped Ferghal, attacking one of the cases. "Of what help is it if we cannot see our own way?"

"It may be we can make it difficult for them. I will explore what I can do with this network console." Harry studied the environmental controls and quickly deduced what to do. He sent the temperature plummeting to freezing on the upper floors. Then he operated the doors to every room, opening and closing them randomly and overriding the occupants' attempts to adjust anything or stop them.

Behind him Ferghal searched among a collection of heavy cases, breaking them open and tearing out the contents with frequent grunts of annoyance or hopeful interest. Hearing someone on the steps, Harry leaped into the corridor and snapped a shot upward. The plasma sizzled as it screamed along a wall and a man stumbled then fell headlong down the stairs to crash into Harry, knocking him sprawling.

The man recovered first and managed to get to his knees, raising the very thing Harry dreaded — a stun pistol. In desperation Harry lashed out with his feet and made a solid connection with the man's body, throwing him back along the short corridor and sending the stunner sailing into the room from which Ferghal now emerged, a heavy weapon in his hands.

Another man appeared at the top of the stairs and raised another of the stun weapons. Ferghal fired the weapon he held. His aim wasn't perfect, but it didn't have to be; the man died instantly, and Harry snatched the second stunner as he retrieved the fallen pistol projector and raced up the stairs after Ferghal. Finding themselves in quite a large space, they charged across it to a position from which they could command the doors that gave access to it.

A door opened and a man peered round it carefully. The blast from Ferghal's weapon took out the wall adjoining the door, and the man missed death by the merest fraction, saved only by his reflexes. "You can't get away!" he shouted. "Give yourselves up. Our people are on their way."

"We'll see about that," shouted Ferghal. "For now it's just the three of us here. Who has the key to these cuffs? I want it now!"

Harry spotted a movement out of the corner of his eye and ducked. Raising the weapon in his right hand, he snapped off a shot. His target froze then slumped to the floor. Harry looked at the weapon, amazed at what it could do. To Ferghal he shouted, "That will hold him! You said there were five, and we have two below, a third dead, this fourth I have disabled, and that leaves just our friend in there."

He accessed the network. All the remaining doors in the building snapped shut and sealed.

"I have sealed all the remaining doors, Ferghal," he called across the room, "and if you're suddenly feeling very cold, it's because I've lowered the temperature as well." Ferghal stepped closer to assess the situation as Harry explained further. "There are more here, but they cannot leave the rooms they occupy and must freeze – as we will if we do not get out soon! But we have another problem. Once we are free of this place, we must find transport or be recaptured. I have sent a signal to our people, but I could not tell them our location. I hope they can trace the signal."

"Well," said Ferghal, "I know where one man is who can tell me. Give me cover and I will persuade him." He fired another blast through the damaged door of the room sheltering the man who had urged their surrender, and then he darted across the intervening space and flattened himself against the wall next to the door. "You in there!" he called. "Come out with your hands up and empty, or I'll come in and burn you out."

"Okay, okay," the man called from within. "I'm coming out. Don't shoot." He emerged, his hands raised and empty, and Harry stepped forward to disarm him. Using a short section of rope he'd found in one of the open storeroom boxes, he tied the man's hands behind him.

"Search his pockets," said Ferghal. "One of these bastards has the key, and I want free of these damned cuffs."

Someone began hammering on the door at the end of the short corridor followed by the sound of a small explosion and angry voices. Hope flickered in the man's eyes then dimmed when he saw Ferghal's expression harden.

"I have the key," he gasped. "It's in my weapons pouch." He indicated the belt Harry had removed from him. Harry found the key. Seconds later they were free of the handcuffs.

Harry checked the network to determine who was attempting to break through the outer door.

"Damn, Ferghal we are undone, I'm thinking — it seems to be more of their sort, no doubt come to fetch us away."

"Let them come." Ferghal hefted the weapon he was holding. "I have a fancy to see what this beastie does to a group in a doorway!"

"Wait," Harry said. "We can't take on everyone we meet. Let us first try reason." He activated the external communicator. "I am Midshipman Heron, and I am now in control of this dome. Identify yourselves immediately."

There was a solid round of swearing from the group outside, and Harry watched through the AI. Then a small rather swarthy man stepped forward. "Open the door, kid. I'm Bert Lowe, leader of the Commonwealth Resistance, and you are surrounded. You can come out quietly or we'll blast our way in and take you out the hard way. Johnstone will pay handsomely for you if you come quietly, and the Consortium will pay if you get killed. Either way we win. Your call!"

"Not exactly," replied Harry. "I have contacted the garrison, and they are on their way," he bluffed. "Your people are secured here, and we have their arms. You are eight men. We will certainly take at least four of you with us. Which four is up to you."

There was a hasty conference outside, which Harry listened to The leader said, "You're bluffing. There are five of my people inside there, you can't hold them and take us on."

Harry was about to respond when there was a heavy explosion and shouts from the men outside.

"Damn, it's the bloody Marines!" the leader shouted, and weapons fire commenced.

Harry opened his mouth to speak then collapsed, caught by a stun beam blasted by the fifth member of the gang, the man they'd left unconscious in the storeroom. Ferghal looked on in horror, a bellow of rage breaking from him when he saw the man and the weapon swinging toward him. When he fired the plasma rifle from the hip, the first bolt burned away the man's arm, and the second killed him.

Ferghal dropped to his knees and cradled Harry. "Harry, I am sorry — don't die on me now. Harry, speak to me!"

The firing outside died down, but Ferghal was too distraught to notice until the outer door blew in and several armoured troopers stormed inside. Major Brydges took in the scene at a glance. "Medic," he called. "See to the Mid."

Gently easing the distraught Ferghal aside, the medic knelt next to Harry. Quickly checking the paralysed young man for a wound, he looked up and said to the Major, "No damage, sir. He's been hit by a stunner. I'll have him up in a sec." He applied a small device to Harry's neck. "A shot of neurostim will bring him round."

Ferghal breathed a sigh of relief as Harry's eyes flickered open and he smiled weakly.

"Major, sorry to have been a nuisance, sir." He caught sight of Ferghal. "You were right, my friend. I was careless."

"Just take it easy, sir," the medic interjected. "I've given you a dose of neurostim, which will reverse the effects of the stunner, but you'll feel unsteady for a bit."

Relieved that Harry was recovering, Ferghal gave the Major a full account of everything that had happened. He watched as the medic helped his friend out to the transport. He felt guilty over his bad temper earlier. Harry was the brother he had always looked up to, the one person he trusted in this strange world of 2206, and it had hit him hard to see his friend fall, apparently lifeless, to the floor.

"MIDSHIPMAN HERON! OFF CAP." HARRY REMOVED HIS CAP and stood rigid at attention in front of the Captain's desk. To his left, Lieutenant Commander Dalziel saluted.

"Midshipman Heron, sir."

Commander Sönderburg, standing to the Captain's right, studied Harry. "Midshipman Heron, you were aware there was a bounty on your capture?"

"Yes, ma'am."

"You had instructions not to leave the hotel without an escort?"

"We were told it was advisable to have an escort outside the main domes, ma'am."

"Midshipman Heron is correct, sir." Lieutenant Commander Dalziel interjected. "The order states that he must be escorted outside the settlement limits. They were not outside those limits, sir."

The Executive Commander checked her record. "Accepted, sir. However, given that they were specifically warned, and knowing there were people in that vicinity hostile to their presence, Mr Heron showed an unfortunate lack of judgment."

Captain Rafferty kept his silence while he watched Harry, his expression closed. "I agree, a distinct lack of judgment, Mr Heron. It has cost the Fleet, the Marine contingent and your colleagues a lot of effort to recover you and Mr O'Connor. Were it not for the fact it uncovered a nasty little nest of Consortium operatives, and brought the Advocate Captain's team some useful information and some new informants, I would consider a court martial." He watched Harry's face pale. "However, I have decided to issue a reprimand on this occasion. You placed yourself and Mr O'Connor in danger by not considering the threat you were aware of, and that placed some hundred Marines in danger of enemy action while recovering you. Do not let it happen again."

"Midshipman Heron. On cap. About turn. Dismissed."

The three officers watched the door close behind Harry.

The Captain smiled. "I have no doubt that lesson has been learned. I'll leave him to you, Pilot. I'm sure a little extra duty won't hurt. Anything else, Phil?"

IN THE OUTER REACHES OF THE SOLAR SYSTEM, A STRANGE triangular ship shimmered into view. It lingered long enough to register on the frigates' collective scanners, but not long enough to be scanned. On *Leander*, a brief spike registered in the signal carrier, but no message was received.

In his cabin Harry awoke suddenly from a deep sleep. The sensation that someone or something had been trying to enter his mind kept him awake for a while. It left him with a lingering memory of a strange and very alien landscape.

What manner of dream was this?

He asked the ship to let him hear some soothing music in an effort to put it from his mind.

When he awoke in the morning, he felt more alive and refreshed than he had in a long time. As he lay quietly pondering this, he realised that surviving yet another attempt on his life had set him free of the fear he had wrestled with for so long, the fear of being captured again and put through the abuse in the laboratory. All of that was a thing of the past now. He had a new confidence that bordered on recklessness, and his sense of self and honour had been fully restored.

When Harry shared these things with Ferghal, his friend reminded him that their abduction had been a result of Harry's insistence on visiting their former enemy. It seemed Ferghal was having a hard time letting this go.

"An enemy remains an enemy," he said firmly as they argued over this for the umpteenth time. "Hurker is but a pawn in his wife's hand. Surely you must admit that."

"I do not deny it," argued Harry. "But that is not a reason to make no effort to make our peace with them." He smiled at his friend. "And we made that effort, and their response gave us an adventure, did it not?"

"Adventure?" snorted Ferghal, exasperated. "So it's adventure you're wanting? Well, as to that adventure, Master Heron, here's what I think on it – pure folly!"

"It can never be folly to attempt rapprochement," declared Harry firmly. "And was it not yourself that was boasting of your destroying half the dome with the biggest projector you could carry?"

Ferghal laughed. "Aye, that was a bit of fun, but you'll not admit the error, I can see that, nor yet concede how close we ran to losing all. Yet," he held up his hand to silence his friend. "I'll confess it seems to have given you release — and yes, I did enjoy the havoc I wrought." He studied Harry for a quiet moment. "Damn me, Harry, you'll be the death of us both, but you've stood by me through every scrape, and I'll not abandon you while I've breath either, but do not expect it of me to hold my tongue if I think you wrong in future, for I won't."

Harry hesitated, his face serious, then he smiled. "When did you ever hold your tongue if you considered me in the wrong? No, my dearest friend, never do that, and I will not abandon you for as long as I have breath either. I am sorry that my good intentions led us into danger, but I did and still do believe that it was right for us to try it."

Their conversation shifted to the shared feeling that they were constantly being watched, and for Harry, this was particularly strong whenever he had time to retreat to the observatory dome and sit contemplating the vastness of the universe. The image of the strange landscape remained strong in his mind and came to him unbidden whenever he was alone. How he missed being able to share his experiences with his father.

Chapter 27 – Convoy to Seraphis

"*Aurora* to escort. Take stations for transit."

"Acknowledged," said Captain Rafferty. "Pilot, bring us into position, please."

"Manoeuvring, sir." Feeding the coordinates to the helm and propulsion controllers, Lieutenant Commander Dalziel brought the *Leander* into her assigned position. On the displays, the cruiser *Aurora* and her consorts changed position to take the lead and to flank the convoy, while *Leander* and her sisters formed the close escort.

Watching, Harry was struck once again at the apparent ease with which the convoy formed and held station — so vastly at odds with the wooden sailing ships and convoys he'd seen from the *Spartan*.

"Link helms."

"Helm linked."

"Transit in four, three, two, one — transit."

The singularity formed by the massive gate projectors flashed into existence. The transit drives on all the ships lit up, and then the displays blanked as the ship passed from normal space into transit and hyperspace.

"Next stop, Seraphis — Consortium pirates notwithstanding," remarked Bob Dalziel. Seconds later, the displays revealed the ships against the swirling grey backdrop of hyperspace. "Mr Heron, you have the plot."

"Control, Scan. Unidentified contacts detected at extreme range, sir."

"Bearing?"

"Starboard bearing zero eight five degrees horizontal, positive angle zero six zero degrees closing, sir."

"Can you identify ship types?"

"Negative, sir. We have them only on passive scan. They are using a screen against visual."

"Damn. Can you get an indication of size from their emissions? How about numbers?"

"Six contacts, sir. Two of them large ships, the rest either freight haulers or destroyer class ships based on the drive signatures."

"Keep tracking," Greg Rafferty commanded. "Sound off action stations. Get me a link to *Aurora*."

The urgent sound of the alarm provoked a rapid change of personnel at posts in the Command Centre and elsewhere, and the crew responded. The few minutes of apparent chaos were replaced by a stillness broken only by operators reporting their systems online and ready.

"Ship closed up. Weapons manned and ready," the Executive Officer reported.

"Good. What have you got, Weapons?" Captain Rafferty settled into his chair, his focus on the battle display.

"Definitely Consortium. None of our ships are fitted with that screen." The Weapons Officer grimaced. "Okay, at least we can still use the passive scan to target. Activate the visual sighting program. Weapons closed up and active, sir. We'll have to use the passive-visual sighting system unless the cruisers can knock down that screen."

"The Escort Leader wants us to hold our fire until they show themselves. Target and track until they fire. Then give them hell." The Captain paused. "Can you get some idea of what types of ships they are from your targeting system?"

"Looks like two heavy cruisers and either four cruisers or four large destroyers, sir. They may be converted freight liners — that would give a similar signature."

"They're pretty confident of themselves." Captain Rafferty frowned as he studied his displays. "Six of them against seven of us. Even if they have the firepower...." Using his link to the AI network, he searched for a report on the latest attacks on convoys. "Damn. I knew I was missing something. Get me *Aurora*."

"*Aurora* on link, sir."

"Carl, my people think we're up against two heavies and four destroyers, but I've just checked something from the latest hit on a convoy. I think we're seeing two heavies, but the other four are carrying remora barges. They'll try to come in close, so I need you to keep the cruisers off our backs. They'll use the remoras to board and capture the freighters while distracting us with their cruisers. We can expect to be targeted by some of the remoras as well. Even if they can't board us, they can cripple us while they take over ships in the convoy."

"You beat me to it, Greg. I agree. At their closing rate, we estimate they'll be in position to initiate their attack in thirty minutes."

"It'll give away our ability to track them on the passive — but I suggest we shoot as soon as they make a move. If we target the mother ships as a priority—"

"Good idea. I'll issue that instruction."

"THE ENEMY SHIPS ARE SEPARATING, SIR. The two largest are coming straight on, but the smaller ships are ... Sir! The smaller ships appear to be breaking apart!"

"That's it. Bloody remora carriers. Weapons, open fire and concentrate on the remoras. Leave the cruisers to *Aurora*, *Penelope* and *Hermione*."

"Target remoras, yes, sir." The weapons officer checked his displays. "They're still screened. Targeting by visual on passive scan. Engage individual targets. Commence, commence, commence."

The first bursts of plasma lanced toward the spreading cloud of attackers, the calm voice of the weapons officer directing his batteries to specific targets.

"Mother ships are dropping their screens, sir. Confirm two heavy cruisers and four remora carriers."

"Make that three. Who bagged it? Well done, main battery. Nail another of the bastards." Pausing, the weapons director studied the targeting plot. The targets were now plainly visible on all his displays, confirming the intelligence that the anti-scanner screen prevented the enemy from using his own targeting scanners. "Close-range defences. Four remoras coming our way. Don't let them attach."

"They've managed to get some of their remoras on the freighters, sir."

"Damn. Which ones?"

"*Castle Derwent*, *Morwenna*, *Eastern Star* and *Mornington* are all signalling they have boarders, sir."

"*Castle Derwent* and *Eastern Star* just dropped out, sir. They've been taken by the looks of it."

"Helm, close on *Mornington*. We'll try to put the Royals on her."

"Close on *Mornington*, aye, aye, sir." Since Harry was already linked to the ship, he failed to use the interface. The ship simply changed position.

"Royals away."

The small boarding sleds favoured by the Royal Marines leapt across the gap. Flares against the hull showed their presence.

"Boarding Unit Foxtrot Oscar now aboard. Estimate twenty boarders. Engaging."

"Keep them off the Control Centre, Lieutenant," ordered the Captain.

"They're attempting to disengage, sir."

"Switch target. I want those damned mother ships put out of action. Target their drives!"

"Target the drives. Yes, sir." The weapons officer hesitated. "Ships that lose their transit drive during transit have never been found, sir."

"I know, and they know. I've been watching them. They're targeting ours."

"Yes, sir." The weapons officer consulted his displays. "Main battery, target bearing horizontal three six degrees, negative bearing one fiver degrees. Lock to drives." He paused, waiting confirmation. "Fire."

"WELL DONE, *LEANDER*. WE LOST THREE OF THE CONVOY, but you secured *Mornington*, and they lost two mother ships and about forty remoras." The commanding officer of the *Aurora* paused. "That was a damned good spot, Greg. Opening fire when you did forced their hand."

"What convinced me were the reports that our ships were being damaged by internal assault, not by weapons fire. My Royals have now secured one of the remoras that attached to the *Mornington*. Very basic, they tell me, but damned effective to shift a full squad and attach to a hull with two access units, which allowed them to penetrate the target hull and gain access."

"Now that we're aware of this tactic, it will be easier to combat in future." The Senior Escort Captain paused. "*Penelope* took some damage, but *Hermione* returned the favour on their leader."

"We have no damage, though they tried to get four remoras on us. I don't think those motherships have much in the way of weapons, and the remoras we've captured only have defences against interceptors."

"That's good to know. What about that screening system?"

"They managed to destroy two of the three, but we got the third. I've had it extracted and secured so Fleet Research can study it. One less secret for them to use against us."

"BEACON FOR THE SERAPHIS SYSTEM LOCATED, SIR."

"Good. Prepare for dropout on the beacon."

"Prepare for dropout. Aye, aye, sir." Harry focussed on the task of preparing to decelerate and hold station so they could pick up the guidance beacons in the system and use them to bring the ship and the convoy to the desired orbit around the planet.

The brief engagement in hyperspace had been costly. Two of the lost ships carried vital equipment needed for the building of the new lift platforms under construction. Sheer luck had played a part as well, since the *Mornington* carried vital components needed for immediate use.

Captain Rafferty watched his displays and the relative positions of the other ships. "I shall be glad to get rid of our prisoners, Phil," he remarked to Commander Philippa Sönderburg "They knew exactly which ships to target, even had the damned manifests for them."

"Helms linked with *Aurora*, sir."

"Very good." Greg Rafferty gripped the arms of his command chair. "Here we go. The *Beagle* is already waiting for us." The 3D command display revealed the full glory of the system they had just entered.

"Unusual system and an unusual planet, Seraphis. The seas are quite shallow, and the landmasses are essentially large islands scattered all over it." The Executive Officer turned to Midshipman Sheoba. "Glad to be home, Mid?"

"It is good to return, yes, but we have our duty to our people. We must learn the ways of other worlds, and the way of defending our own." She made the gesture of respect. "One day I shall return to nest. Until then, I serve to defend it."

Surprised, the Exec hesitated. She'd not expected the frank reply. Then she remembered the history of human contact with the Lacertians. "Of course." She considered briefly. "Did the Consortium actually occupy your world with troops?"

"At first they came speaking of friendship and trade. Then more came and took what they desired, and when the Sersan objected, they killed some, seized many and took her and the council away. It will not happen again."

"No, it won't, not if we can prevent it."

"It is why we build our own ships, and train and serve with yours, Commander."

Chapter 28 – Diversion

"Squadron ready to depart, sir. The *Beagle* will be in position within ten minutes. She had a delay in recovering one of her survey barges."

"Ten minutes?" Captain Rafferty huffed in annoyance. "Well, that won't make a huge difference to us, but I bet the gate operator is fuming. Keeping their power cells hot doesn't do them a lot of good. We'll wait while the *Beagle* rounds up her missing pup."

"We've a choice?" *Naiad's* captain joined the conversation.

Harry watched the 3D display, the strange looking survey ship just visible above the darkened planet as she manoeuvred toward the waiting squadron. A large ship, her crew comprised a small number of specialists and officers, and a large contingent of scientists. The survey barges attached to her outer hull reminded him of a creature the Reverend Bentley had enthused over while on HMS *Spartan*, with all its young clinging to its fur.

Idly he wondered what it would be like to serve on such a ship then put it from his mind as the *Beagle* closed and his attention shifted to the task in hand

"WE'LL BE TRANSITING THROUGH HOSTILE TERRITORY. Our destination, the planet New Eden, is in a quadrant they have been operating in for a long time. I want the ship at defence stations from now on."

"That'll be tough on our people, sir."

"Being taken unaware will be fatal." Greg Rafferty tapped the arm of his chair. "Work out a schedule that gives everyone a reasonable rest period, and we'll run some drills to keep them on their toes."

"I suggest we run one immediately, sir. I did a check earlier and found half the watch didn't have their survival suits ready for use."

"Good plan. Do it, Phil. Nothing like a good shake-up to kick things off."

THE HULL BREACH ALARM SOUNDED THROUGHOUT THE SHIP, the urgent blare of the klaxon sending the crew scrambling for their survival suits.

"Damn, I must have left mine in my locker," was an exclamation heard far too frequently for the Executive Officer's liking.

Cancelling the alarm, she ordered a stand fast then sent her Damage Control team to every section of the ship with orders to take the names of everyone not properly rigged.

"This was a drill. The next time you hear that alarm, it may be the real thing, not a drill, and you will have less than two minutes to get your survival suit on and started." She paused. "We are entering enemy territory, and hostiles could be anywhere. These drills will not be announced. Anyone found who does not have their survival pack with them at all times can expect to have a session with the Captain. Carry on."

"Phew." Ferghal removed his survival suit, checked it, and stowed it properly for its next use. "Just lucky I was off duty. I usually forget to take it when I go on watch."

"Better not forget it in future." Harry's ears were still burning at the rollicking he'd got when the Exec had discovered he didn't have his survival suit to hand. If that weren't humiliating enough, the reprimand was made worse by the fact that he was currently on her Damage Control team. "The Exec has a list that includes Mama Behr, three other officers and over half the crew. She's very annoyed."

"I wager Mama isn't happy either."

Harry laughed. "No wager. She's on the warpath."

THE ROUTINE OF EXERCISES AND DRILLS, AND THE WATCH routine demanded by remaining at defence stations, meant sleep was sometimes at a premium. To Harry and Ferghal it was almost like returning to the decks of HMS *Spartan* with the constant calls for sail handling disturbing their sleep.

It also meant that the ship was settling into a finely tuned readiness for action by the time Captain Rafferty decided to scale back the exercises.

"We've got them on their toes now, Phil. From now on we'll exercise only the duty part of each watch and let the off duty part catch up on their sleep." He broke off as his link chirped.

"Rafferty."

"Greg, we're picking up a distress call." Captain Gratz's voice paused. "A freight liner, *Greenbay Orion*. She comes up in the database as carrying passengers and a high value cargo. Given where we are right now, it could be a trap."

Greg Rafferty studied the display provided by Lieutenant Orloff, the Navigation Officer. "I have her. Yes, right on the edge of the area we had word the Cons were active in. Damn. What do you want me to do?"

"Take a swing out to her position and investigate. I don't need to tell you not to take any chances, and if you don't like the situation, jump out again and yell for help. If you think it's safe to do so, see if you can render assistance and rendezvous with us at the next way point."

"Will do." Captain Rafferty studied the plot data. "I anticipate it will take us six hours to reach her coordinates. After that, we'll see." He broke the link. "Pilot, change course to intersect with the coordinates for the *Greenbay Orion*. I will want to drop out about a million clicks off the location, launch fighters and scan for hostiles then jump again and scan before I approach her. Understood?"

"Understood. We'll set the course accordingly, sir," replied Lieutenant Orloff.

LEANDER DROPPED OUT PRECISELY AS PLANNED, her fighters launching even as she slowed, her crew already at action stations.

"Fighters launched. Maximum scan, report contacts."

"One ship, sir. Reads as a freightliner. Her distress beacon is active." The operator paused to adjust his displays. "No other contacts, sir."

"Check the passive scanners."

"No hostiles on scan, sir," reported the weapons station. "Nothing on passive and nothing on active."

"Good, maintain scan and check visuals as well," the Weapons Commander reported. "System seems to be clean, sir, just the freighter on scan."

Captain Rafferty nodded. "Keep scanning. We'll approach in a series of short hyperbursts around the system to make sure."

Harry and the rest of the navigation team plotted the Captain's orders for an unpredictable approach. The *Leander* leapt past its target then off to one side and finally to a dropout directly alongside the freighter.

"Boarders away."

"Transit to the outer edge of the system. Keep us moving, Pilot."

THE BOARDING PARTY WERE CYCLED THROUGH the freighter's airlocks and into the ship even as the frigate made another leap to a remote part of the system.

"Thank God you're here." The officer who met them looked dishevelled. "We were hit two days ago. They shot the Captain and took the Chief of Engineering and his number two with them."

The Lieutenant leading the boarders wrinkled his nose at the unpleasant smell permeating the air. "What's happened to your enviro plant?"

"They wrecked it. Blew out the algae tanks and stripped out the recycling pumps for good measure — and they destroyed the engineering controls so we can't even manoeuvre."

Frowning, the Lieutenant nodded, aware the live link on his EVA suit meant his Captain was hearing the conversation and observing the situation. "What else did they take?"

"All of the engineering stores, part of the cargo and two of the passengers — besides our engineering people."

The Lieutenant stopped. "Better show me the damage. If we can't get her going, we may have to evacuate her."

STARING AT THE IMAGES RELAYED FROM *GREENBAY ORION*, Captain Rafferty gave an angry snort. "Looks like they intended these people to die rather unpleasantly. I wonder why?" He paused. "Okay, we'll dropout alongside in ten minutes and put an engineering team aboard to see what can be done. Have her crew and passengers ready to transfer to *Leander* as soon as we arrive. No baggage, just essential personal items, and make sure the passengers are all legitimate. We don't need any unwelcome surprises coming aboard."

"Understood, sir," came the response. "There are twenty people to bring aboard, most of them in a bad way. Some will need medical attention."

"Get them aboard and to the medics. We'll work out what to do with the rest." He turned to his Executive Commander. "Phil, make sure they're screened, and don't bring anything aboard that could compromise us. The officers can go into our spare Wardroom cabins, and the rest should probably go into the Senior TechRates' mess adjoining the Royals' barracks. Put the passengers in the Gunroom, and tell Sub-Lieutenant Isfahan to warn the Mids not to talk about our current assignment. The Royals can keep an eye on the crew. We'll tranship them to *Beagle* as soon as we can. She's more suitable for passengers if we have to fight."

"Shall I brief Mama Behr?"

"Do that. Thanks. Coms, get me a secure link to *Aurora*. This whole deal stinks."

When the squadron's senior officer responded to the link, Captain Rafferty got right to the point. "I suspect this is an ambush Captain. I'm taking the crew and passengers off and sending a team to see if we can jury rig something to get her to the squadron. The cargo is Fleet spares for Pangaea."

FERGHAL ACCOMPANIED LIEUTENANT GUZEWSKI to the damaged ship with several TechRates.

"Salvage that set of nodes, Mr O'Connor. We can use them to rebuild this station. Mech, give him a hand." The Lieutenant dismantled the damaged portion of the control station. Using the salvaged parts and some spares from *Leander*, he patched together a console from which the navigation could be run. Directing Ferghal to another, he said, "This business in merchant ships of having a combined Engineering and Command Control Centre makes this easier. Here we have Navigation and Drive control in one compartment — no need to run additional coms anywhere. Get that Engineering unit open and see what you can do with it."

"Aye, aye, sir." To Ferghal it seemed vaguely disquieting to know that they were alone on this semi-derelict ship, conscious that their own ship had jumped back into transit status to avoid showing up on any hostile scanners. Despite the assurance of the small fighter squadron now forming a defensive shield about them he worried that they might be attacked while helpless. This motivated him to work quickly but carefully to restore the systems as soon as possible.

Aware of the usual noise of an AI in his ears, he wondered if he could activate the engines of this ship. He asked the ship, "*Greenbay Orion, will you allow me to run your engineering controls, perhaps to operate your drives?*"

"You are cleared to bypass my controls." The AI paused. "You are not a standard mobile interface. Where do you come from? You have no manufacturer's engagement coding."

Ferghal's laugh drew the Lieutenant's attention. "What have you found?"

"Nothing, sir — or a solution, I'm thinking." Ferghal told the AI, "*A moment, please. I must explain this to my superior.*" After a moment's thought, he added, "*I am a human. Our ship calls me a mobile human node. I've been called many things in my life, but that was a new one on me!*"

Ferghal could've sworn he heard the AI chuckle. Back to business, he said to the Lieutenant, "Sir, this ship will allow me to control its drives through my link to its AI. Now, if we could have Harry as well, the two of us could run Engineering and Navigation.

The Lieutenant stared at him as he pondered this. "Sounds good. But we'll need a few more people. I'll talk to the Captain. You talk to the ship and see what else is needed."

HARRY DISEMBARKED FROM THE BARGE THEN GATHERED HIS equipment and cycled through the airlocks. Already the ship's AI was in his head as he made his way to the Command Bridge.

"We haven't a lot of time. Are you connected to the ship?" Lieutenant Orloff stared at the wrecked consoles. "Hell, I don't know if this is even possible!"

"I'm connected, ma'am. *Orion* says it will be helpful if some of the interfaces can be repaired, but is happy to accept instructions through us."

"Okay. What have we got to lose?" Over her shoulder, she shot "Don't answer that, Piotr!" knowing he was probably doing just that under his breath.

She contacted the Captain. "We are ready to run a trial, sir."

"Proceed."

"Right. Harry, set the helm to move us one astronomical unit from this position."

"Set, ma'am."

"Good. Ferghal, you have the drives ready?"

Ferghal nodded, his face a mask of concentration. "Aye, ma'am."

"Harry, action, please."

"Very good, ma'am." He concentrated. "*Greenbay Orion, let me speak to Ferghal.*" He waited for Ferghal to join him in the link. "*Ferghal, on my mark, ninety seconds at two-thirds power on the hyperdrive. Three, two, one, mark!*"

With the usual command displays destroyed, only Harry and Ferghal could see the result. Through the ship's external sensors, they watched as the view of the system vanished, was replaced by the grey fog of hyperspace, then returned into view, though now from a different aspect.

"On station, ma'am."

"That's a relief." She linked to the Captain. "It worked, sir. We're ready to go."

"Good. We'll collect you. Get Mr Heron to link the helm to us as soon as we drop out. Drives all functional?"

"Drives are functional, sir."

"Here we go then." *Leander* appeared, the fighters sweeping back to her as she closed the freighter. "Link your helm."

Harry reached into the program and ordered the link. "Helm linked. Drives standing by."

"Enter transit, match course and speed with *Leander*."

The pair of ships plunged into the singularity created by their drives and vanished, *Leander* leaving behind a small and unobtrusive drone.

"Piotr, we had better get to work on rebuilding at least two of these control positions. Can we get a visual display working? I hate flying blind like this."

"The consoles will take a couple of hours. The displays? Maybe. Give me a hand with the helm console. If we can get it working, only one of our mobile human nodes needs to be in constant contact with the AI."

The Engineering lieutenant glanced at Ferghal. "I agree, but Ferghal suggested something earlier that has me thinking. I want to rig a receiver unit that will make it possible for us to do this from *Leander*. Ferghal talked about towing a ship if it was disabled, and it makes sense."

"Good idea. If we can transfer the controls to *Leander*, we don't have to live in this foul atmosphere." She massaged her temples. "The carbon dioxide levels must be high. It's making my head thick."

"All the more reason to get off her then," said Lieutenant Guzewski from within a damaged console. "We can't scrub it out of the atmosphere, and I'm not sure of the water purity either."

IN THE EMPTY SPACE THE *GREENBAY ORION* HAD OCCUPIED, the small drone sent a stream of scrambled pre-recorded messages. The simulation of an on-going conversation between two ships was intended to create the illusion of an attempt at rescue or salvage. It achieved its purpose.

The Consortium ship dropped out where the freighter had been, her weapons ready to fire.

"No target, sir. The signal is from a drone."

"What the blazes? I thought that damned freight hauler was inoperable!" The Consortium Captain glared at his second in command. "You told me you'd destroyed all the controls for the drives and navigation."

"We did." The man frowned. "Those control units were stripped right down, and what we didn't need we smashed."

"Well, somehow they've got her going again." The Captain's fist pounded the arm of his chair. "And it was the frigate we wanted to catch." His anger boiled over as he thrust himself out of his chair. "Damn that clumsy moron Blatch. If he hadn't caused that feedback on the weapons controls, we'd have had them before they could shift that wreck."

His second-in-command shrugged. "He won't do it again."

"How the hell did he do it the first time? It's supposed to be impossible to create that sort of shunt."

Studying his fingers, the Executive Officer kept his face neutral. "It was deliberate. I've been watching Blatch for a while.

He had a score to settle, I believe. Now he's had a little disagreement with a personal plasma projector."

The Captain's mouth dropped open as this sank in. His executive officer was a cold fish, and a deadly one. With an effort he redirected his anger. "Blow that bloody drone to atoms, then set course for New Eden."

It didn't matter how the Fleet ship had managed to get the freighter going. They had done it, and at least he knew where she was going. *The Johnstone leeches can wait a little longer for their assets,* he mused in bitter frustration.

"DRONE HAS CEASED TRANSMISSIONS, SIR. Final transmission was interrupted, but we got an image of the attacker. Heavy cruiser of their Trader Class."

"So they were there. We're lucky she didn't jump us. I wonder why they didn't strike while we were fiddling about."

"Could be they've had their own problems to sort out. I've been wondering why they took some of the control modules intact."

"Could be, Phil, could be." His link chirped. "Captain."

"Sir, we think we've managed to rig up a system that will allow us to operate this ship from the *Leander*. Piotr has rigged receivers to the control consoles we've rebuilt. The atmosphere here is bad and deteriorating fast, as there are no circulation fans. We're having to use survival packs in Control."

"That's not good." Captain Rafferty frowned. "You're sure this will work?"

"Yes, sir. Piotr has everything rigged, and Heron and O'Connor have tested it. They can link to the *Orion* through the receivers as long as they're linked to an AI."

"What happens if we lose control of it? Is there a way we can get a backup?"

"I think we can set it up in about an hour. It really only needs the fitting of a multi-channel link and an interface to the AI network. Once that is in place, we can test it and run with it. If necessary, we can always fail the reactor containment. That will vaporise the entire ship."

"And everything nearby, but you've got a maximum of a half hour tops. We'll drop out in system GBB69774, pick you up and go hyper again as soon as Heron and O'Connor can connect."

"EVERYTHING READY? MR HERON? MR O'CONNOR?"

"Ready, sir." Harry glanced at Ferghal. "We're connected to both ships."

"Link helms. Transfer course and speed data."

"Done, sir."

"Activate."

The display showed the damaged freighter on station, proving to the Captain's relief, that the link between the frigate and the *Greenbay Orion* had held.

"Well done. Now, if it all works, we've a convoy and a squadron to catch. Can the *Orion* manage a sustained full power run? We'll need that capability if we're to catch up. Even then it'll be four days minimum."

"There was no damage to the drives, sir, and being a freightliner, her plant is designed to run at near full power on passage for sustained periods."

The Captain nodded. "True. It remains to be seen if we can drop out successfully."

"If the *Orion* decides not to, someone is going to get a nasty surprise one day in hyperspace," remarked Lieutenant Commander Dalziel as he watched their prize on the scanner.

"You're right," grinned Lieutenant Orloff from her console. She winked at Harry. "What would you fellows have done with a prize in your day, Mr Heron? I doubt you could have rigged it to sail itself, now could you?"

"No." Harry grinned. "We probably would have set her afire to make sure the French couldn't save her later."

"WE'RE IN CONTACT WITH OUR SQUADRON, SIR," the weapons officer reported. "Aurora acknowledges our pennant number."

"Good. Get Captain Gratz on a link for me."

"Welcome back, Greg. I see you've got the *Orion* with you. Well done." Captain Gratz paused. "Any problems?"

"I think they planned an ambush, but something went wrong. Greg Rafferty rubbed his eyes. Not having left his Command Centre for almost four days as they overhauled the squadron, he was exhausted. "A Trader Class heavy cruiser dropped out shortly after we departed and shot up the drone I left. The *Orion* is in a bad way. Her controls are destroyed and her environment section is completely inoperable."

"Bad. So how are her crew operating her?"

"They're not. We had to jury rig her and be a bit creative. We're hoping she'll drop out with us. If she doesn't, it's going to be an interesting chase."

"Creative?" The uncertainty in Captain Gratz's voice was plain "Never mind. What's your ETA for joining us?"

"My Navigation team tell me four hours."

"Good. Our ETA for New Eden is now forty-eight hours."

"COMING UP TO DROPOUT, SIR," LIEUTENANT ORLOFF reported

"Link helm to *Aurora*." The Lieutenant Commander looked at Harry. "Make sure our tow stays with us, please."

"Aye, aye, ma'am." Harry focussed on his link. *"Leander, please connect me directly with* Orion.*"*

"We are connected, Harry. Orion *hears you."*

*"*Thank you. Orion, *we are about to drop out of transit. Are you receiving the commands?"*

"I am." There was a moment's pause. *"Will I be repaired here?"*

"There are no repair facilities here, Orion, *but there may be an opportunity to restore at least some of your system while we wait for the* Beagle *to complete her surveys."*

"On the mark, sir. *Aurora* counting down."

On the display, each of the ships showed on station against the backdrop of the stars, with the damaged freightliner following on *Leander's* quarter.

FROM THEIR VANTAGE POINT IN SPACE, NEW EDEN seemed very similar to Earth.

"An odd place, it seems," Harry remarked, studying the planet "New Eden is smaller than Earth and about the size of Venus, *Leander* tells me. And the atmosphere is slightly richer in oxygen."

Ferghal grinned. Harry's constant quest for knowledge amused him, but there was no denying that it was often very useful. In contrast, he was satisfied with the essentials. After all, if he needed to know something, he had only to ask and the information would be there, as if he'd always known it. Now he decided to play Harry's game. "As you say, and the oceans are shallow affairs with creatures as unlike our fish as they could be."

The marine life, he'd learned, tended to invertebrates and the creatures that could eat them.

The flora and fauna of this strange world were radically different to anything Harry could have imagined. According to the files he had studied before landing on the planet, very large insect-like creatures abounded because of the higher oxygen levels. Alongside these, certain flora had evolved as flesh eaters, some of the varieties similar to certain species found on Earth, but others radically and savagely different.

"Small wonder the early colonists could not survive here," commented Harry. "The Protection of Native Life Treaties must have rendered defence against the flesh-eating flora difficult."

A surface scan of the settlements showed that these had not only been abandoned, but someone had very methodically stripped them of everything usable, and even the domes had been destroyed.

"I wonder why," mused Captain Rafferty when this was brought to his attention. "I would have thought they might have been left intact in case the mining operation needed to return."

Lieutenant Commander Dalziel offered an explanation. "I expect the location may have been a factor. They're not near the mines for the most part." He frowned as he studied the data from the *Beagle*'s scanning drones.

"There's a lot of life registering, and a few anomalies. Those could be some of the abandoned mines."

"Leave it to the scientists to do the exploration of that then." The Captain considered. "On second thought, flag the anomalies. We'll do a deep scan of them when we have a chance."

"Fleet wants to put a base somewhere in this area, and the mines would be a bonus, but I think they'll have to go for automated mining and orbital platforms."

The Executive Commander joined them.

"What should we do with the *Orion*, sir?"

"Put a repair team aboard her, Phil. We're to take up a patrol station beyond the asteroid belt. Let them try to get her environment system functioning again first. I'm not happy about her trundling along with no one aboard. If we lose contact, we'll have even bigger problems to deal with."

NECRS *BEAGLE*'S TASK WAS TO CONDUCT A FULL SURVEY of the planet to determine the viability of placing a permanent station there.

"This will serve as a base for maintenance and to provide a permanent protection squadron in the system," Captain Gratz told the other Captains. "Another aspect is the potential for mining the asteroids — which also needs a permanent station here."

"There are enough of the damned things," commented Lieutenant Commander Dalziel. "The presence of two gas giants this close to the sun has disrupted the formation of most of the probable inner planets. The debris field is massive — far worse than any other system I have seen so far."

"Agreed," said the Executive Commander as they sat in the Wardroom. "By the look of them, those two giants will tear each other apart or merge. The outer one's orbit brings it very close to the inner one, and each time they pass each other, the larger one strips atmospheric gases from the smaller. Give them a few thousand years and they'll either mutually destroy each other or merge, and this could become a binary star system, in which case New Eden will fry. "

"Not a bad thing given its current inhabitants," commented Lieutenant Orloff helping herself to a drink from the counter. "Pretty awful collection of life forms from the records."

"Come, come," chided the Commander. "WTO Directive on Preservation of Sensitive Environments and respect for Sentient Life Forms places us under an obligation to preserve all sentient life and defend its rights."

"Obviously written by some idiot bureaucrat who has never left his comfy office," she grumbled on her way to the door.

Chapter 29 – Ambushed

The attack was launched with precision, and the frigates had no warning of the impending strike. *Leander* reeled under the onslaught of the heavy weapons deployed by the Consortium cruiser that dropped out of hyperspace almost on top of them.

The general alarm sent the crew racing to their action stations. Harry and Ferghal sped in opposite directions to their posts. Just as Harry reached the entrance to the navigation control centre, the ship lurched heavily, flinging him violently against the doorframe.

He gasped as pain shot through his ribs. Driven by adrenalin, he staggered to his post and took his seat. Clumsily, he checked his survival suit was in its stowage as he scanned his display.

"Course plot closed up. Midshipman Heron on the plot." Hearing the acknowledgement, he completed the myriad tasks required to keep the ship moving and evade the attacker. Deliberately he pushed his fears aside and focussed on his work. Immersed in the AI, he could feel every blow the ship suffered.

"Where the hell did they come from?" Captain Rafferty asked, dropping into his command seat.

"There are three destroyer class vessels engaging the rest of the squadron, sir. *Naiad* is in trouble."

"As are we." The Captain winced as the ship shuddered under a hit from the cruiser's heavy weapons. "Weapons, target his launch bays. Our intel say they're vulnerable there. Pilot, keep him guessing until we can get some help. Coms, emergency broadcast to Fleet Command, copy to *Aurora* and her group. We're under attack by trader class cruisers and escorts. Require urgent support."

Their consorts, *Dragon*, *Danae* and *Naiad*, were faring little better as they fought off their larger attackers.

"*Naiad*'s gone, sir." Lieutenant Orloff stared at the command display, the fading flare of the lost ship just visible still. "Poor bastards. At least it was quick."

"Her attacker must have caught some of the flare as her reactors went. He's breaking away."

"*Danae* has powered up her hyperdrives and broken away," one of the ComsRates reported.

Harry concentrated on the calculations for the next jump.

"She's got off an engagement report and is calling for help," called the ComsRate.

"She's got her hands full," commented the Navigating Officer. "That cruiser is on top of her again."

The ship reeled and alarms sounded somewhere outside the compartment. Harry heard Damage Control directing a team to the forward end of the ship. There was another tremendous convulsion, and the ship seemed to lurch sideways with the sensation that the deck was tilted at a strange angle, something that should not happen with artificial gravity.

"Lieutenant Orloff, take charge here," the Navigation Commander ordered. "The Exec Commander has been injured in Environmental Engineering. I'm going to take over Damage Control."

Harry noticed the odour of smoke in the air around them. He was also aware, through his link to the AI, that there was something very wrong with that vital part of the ship.

At this point their luck turned.

"We have a clear shot at the bastards," came the voice of the weapons targeting officer on an open link. "Missiles away!" This was followed by a burst of cheering and the fragmented speech of someone in the Weapons Control Centre saying, "Direct hit! Eat that, you bastards." Followed by someone else ordering, "Concentrate on your tasks — the bastard isn't out of it yet. Only three of our missiles hit him. What happened to the rest?"

"Here he comes again."

The ship shuddered. Harry felt something like pain as the AI network lost parts of itself, and was unable to reroute its neural connections to regain contact with some of its nodes. The stench of smoke grew stronger. Through his internal link, Harry could hear damage reports streaming in. It didn't sound good.

He wondered if the survival suit would protect him if they had to abandon the ship. A burst of what sounded like cheering over the ship coms distracted him.

"We did it! The strays must have gone past the primary — they hit the other cruiser. Look at the bastards run."

Whatever damage their missiles had caused, it was sufficient for their attackers to break off and retreat into hyperspace, leaving the badly crippled frigates drifting and desperately trying to keep their life support functions operating.

"HARRY, I NEED SOME QUICK SOLUTIONS. WE HAVE TO manoeuvre clear of the gravity well of this gas giant."

Harry worked feverishly to calculate their trajectory. "I will have them in a moment, sir. Our AI has been damaged. Parts of it are not accessible."

"Damn. Do your best then. Are the manoeuvring and nav functions still operating?"

"Aye, sir." Harry hesitated, unsure how to explain what he was sensing through his link to the AI. "The ship is in pain, sir, and seems distressed."

"In pain?" The Captain frowned, not sure what to make of this observation. "We'll do our best to deal with that as soon as we can get to a safe orbit."

"*Beagle* went into transit as soon as the Consortium ships attacked. Hopefully she's clean away now."

"Hopefully she'll bring some help." The Captain stood mopping the trickle of blood from his forehead. That last hit had thrown them all around, dislodging some equipment and destroying the command display. Something was still burning, and the Damage Control crew were trying to find it. The smoke was making breathing difficult. "Evacuate the Command Bridge and find the source of this smoke. I'm going to the Emergency Control Centre. I hope we can hold together long enough for someone to get here."

"I have the calculations, sir. We can make it to New Eden if we can use the gravity of that planet's moon to alter our trajectory. A three-minute burst on the hyperdrives will put us in position to be drawn into orbit." Lieutenant Orloff straightened from where she'd been monitoring Harry's plot calculations. "We'll need to use the manoeuvring engines to put us on course for the moon."

"Thanks, Engineering. Can we manoeuvre?" His strides rapid, the Captain entered the Emergency Command Centre. After verifying that all stations were functioning, he wedged himself into a vacant seat.

"Manoeuvring is possible, but we'll need to use manual controls."

"I'll need the hyperdrives for a short burst. Can you give me that?"

"Two of the pods are destroyed, a third is damaged. As long as we don't try to transit anywhere, it'll hold up. I can give you no more than ten minutes' power on it though. Anything more than that and I can't guarantee the outcome." Mama Behr sounded tired.

"That'll be enough. Stand by for the manoeuvring orders. We need to position ourselves first." A thought occurred to him. "Is O'Connor available? I think I'm going to use an unorthodox method for this." Listening to the reply, he nodded. "Tell him to position himself wherever he needs to, and link up with Mr Heron I'll get Pilot to tell Mr Heron to do whatever it is they do and run the commands."

HARRY SEARCHED FOR FERGHAL IN THE AI NETWORK and found him doing the same thing he was doing.

"I am ordered to take us into New Eden's orbit. I have the helm. Have you the manoeuvring?"

"I do. Mama Behr has told me I'm to do as you instruct, but you must know we have only one usable drive pod, and some of the manoeuvring engines are not functioning either."

"Then let us do it. I will inform Lieutenant Orloff." To his lieutenant, Harry said, "We are able to do the manoeuvres, ma'am.

"Good. Mr Heron, lay in the course to get us to New Eden." She grimaced. "Not that I'm in a hurry to get there. The bloody place is a nightmare, but it's better than nothing."

"Aye, aye, ma'am." Harry was already coaxing the response he needed from the network. It appeared simultaneously on his screen and inside his eyes in jerks and jumps as the AI tried to circumvent the damage.

"Ma'am, I have the course," he advised Lieutenant Orloff.

"Good, send it to the helm, and let's hope Engineering can give us the power to get there quickly. We have about a week's worth of air on board, and it'll take three weeks to get there at normal speeds." She exhaled a heavy sigh of frustration.

The Communications Warrant Officer called across, "Lieutenant, *Danae* is signalling that she has critical damage to her hull and weapons, but her engines are serviceable, and she can stand by us while we approach the planet."

"Acknowledge. Tell them to stand by," snapped Lieutenant Orloff. "Orders, sir? Manoeuvring is restricted."

The Captain nodded. "I know."

"Sir, you're wounded—."

"Yes, I know that too, but it's not serious." He dabbed the last bit of blood from his forehead and applied an adhesive bandage that acted as a second-skin sealant infused with antibiotics for quick healing. "Right, that's done then." He faced Lieutenant Orloff. "Engineering say we have the power to get us to New Eden. Mr Heron, are you and Mr O'Connor ready?" He took the confirmation and nodded. "Good. Take us there, Pilot — best speed, please. We may not have a lot of time."

His link chirped. "Captain, we're losing the fields on the remaining pod, and I have a reactor going unstable as well. I'll need to shut it down if we can't stabilise it. I'm short handed as we lost a turbine room and control. I have a lot of casualties here."

"Do your best, Heather. We need to get close to New Eden so I can evacuate the ship. I want to carry out enough repairs to keep her together until we can get a repair ship here."

Harry's heart went cold when he heard part of this conversation and wondered who else among his friends was injured or dead. He moved awkwardly in an attempt to retrieve a tablet that had fallen during the battle, and winced as pain shot through his side. In the excitement he had forgotten his injury. Gritting his teeth until the pain subsided, he flexed his fingers to satisfy himself that nothing was broken.

A quick check of his arm and shoulder revealed a livid bruise on his upper arm and across his side. There seemed little else wrong so he focussed his attention on coaxing the crippled AI into providing the guidance necessary to get them safely into an orbit above the planet.

"Ferghal, are you ready? The Captain orders that we bring the ship to New Eden."

"Aye, Harry, what are your orders?"

"Use the manoeuvring units to bring us onto this bearing." He input a series of directional coordinates, and when he was satisfied that they had the ship on the exact heading, he said, "Give me a three-minute burst on the hyperdrive."

As the seconds ticked by, he ran several calculations until Ferghal advised him that the hyperdrive was shut down and the ship once more was drifting in normal space-time.

"Good. Now the manoeuvring engines, please." Harry gave Ferghal detailed instructions to alter the ship's direction and attitude. "That is well. Now the hyperdrive again, please. I require ninety seconds at three-quarter output."

Searching the sensor arrays, he was reassured to find their surviving consorts *Dragon* and *Danae* had managed to match their course and stay with them. As the ship reached the final point at which they could adopt an orbital "parking" position, Harry told Ferghal, "Shut down the hyperpods and activate the manoeuvring units We need to put her into a stationary orbit."

Watching as Harry brought the ship to a geostationary orbit, Captain Rafferty wondered what else this youth might be able to do through this connection to the ship's AI. He'd noticed that not once did Harry touch the interface. He simply sat staring ahead, and the ship responded.

"Well done, Mr Heron—you handle her like an expert." The Captain smiled. "Secure your station and get down to the hangar deck where you'll report to Lieutenant Harvey. I will want you and your fellow Mids to man the barges and get our non-essential people down to the surface. The sooner we can get them to safety, the sooner we can get started on emergency repairs."

THE HOURS THAT FOLLOWED WERE ALMOST AS HECTIC as some of the moments that Harry and Ferghal could recall aboard *Spartan* during drills to prepare the ship for action. It seemed that an incredible amount of equipment had to be checked, stripped for packing, packed and then loaded aboard the ship's barges for transport to the surface. The typically crowded hangars were conspicuously absent of their complement of strike fighters, as those had been early casualties in the surprise attack by the cruisers. The few that had struggled back aboard were badly damaged and unfit for further use.

The only consolation to their surviving pilots was that their Consortium opponents had not fared any better once the frigates' fighters had got away from their parent ships. And all the while there was the need to seek out and plug as many hull breaches as could be found and then to stabilise the ship's atmosphere.

"Mr Heron," called Lieutenant Commander Dalziel. "Take charge of Barge Two and set down on New Eden in the vicinity of these coordinates where you'll also set up the camp. I'll get down there as soon as I can, but if you find this site unsuitable, use your discretion and choose the best location for safety and protection."

"Aye, aye, sir." Harry saluted. He had just turned away to get suited up when the older man called him back.

"Remember, you'll be Beach Master until I can get down there, so use your discretion and let the Warrants do the running around and heavy lifting." He turned away to deal with the queue of people waiting for his orders, and Harry made his escape.

Chapter 30 – Survivors

"Gawd, the stench!" Master Warrant Officer Gottschalk clenched his nostrils as the barge shuttle's outer doors opened. "I hope we don't have to be here too long."

"It's warm enough, and extremely humid." Harry could feel the prickly heat on his skin, and his face glistened with sweat. In a memory flashback, he felt as if he was back in the oppressive heat of New South Wales. He wrinkled his nose. "And you're right about that stench. The data files failed to mention that! Damn me, Master, but it is worse than London in the heat of summer with the cesspits overflowing." Stepping out of the barge, he walked a short distance, lifting his boots with effort out of the suction of the fetid surface. "Looks like the ground is as foul as the London streets too."

The Master Warrant puzzled over this. His home city prided itself on being very clean. "Lunnon doesn't stink, sir." He sounded a little aggrieved. "Except near the recycle plant, and even that isn't anything as bad as this."

"Sorry, Master." Harry grinned. "I forget — you would not know the stench from the cesspits in my day." He glanced around. "Whoever named this place New Eden had a very strange sense of humour or never set foot upon it. Paradise it is not — Purgatory, perhaps, but not Paradise."

The Warrant Officer had a wry smile. "Glad I didn't have to grow up in your Lunnon then, sir, and I wouldn't know about any paradise — not in my old neighbourhood anyway, but it was tolerably clean what with health and safety and all their rules and regs." He broke off to bellow orders at the group unloading the barge. Turning back to Harry, he explained, "Grew up in a very mixed part, sir. Probably a bit different to when you were there."

Nodding, Harry grinned. "I expect so. In fact I should have been surprised if it had not been." Looking around, he consulted the survey map on his tablet. The chosen campsite was a long flattened ridge, the highest ground in this area, which at least offered a view of the surroundings. "We'll establish the camp on the rise over there, if you please."

"I'll see to it, sir. These survival shelters have a decent base to stand on." The Warrant Officer turned away issuing a string of orders, setting in motion the process of erecting several large emergency shelters.

Harry looked at the luridly coloured vegetation, noting several of what appeared to be pitcher plants. Recalling the data he had acquired in the history files, he recognised these as being flesh eaters.

"Master, keep our people away from those plants with the pot-like structures." Harry pointed from a safe distance. "They're colourful and have a unique beauty, but they consume flesh."

"They do what, sir?"

"They're flesh eaters, Master. Apparently they capture animals, draw them in and consume them in that pitcher-shaped part of the plant."

"Damn. Why couldn't we be stationed somewhere decent? As if it didn't stink bad enough here, now we've got to worry about being eaten by a plant," muttered the Master Warrant, shaking his head. A hard-bitten man, he had developed a qualified respect for Harry, and was glad he had him to deal with. "I'll get our people onto it and warn them away from the plants."

No sooner were the words out of his mouth than a scream followed by shouts of alarm drew his and Harry's startled attention. One of the TechRates had wandered too close to a large pitcher plant. He screamed again, and dropped his load as more of the plant's tendrils wrapped around his body and drew him toward the gaping pitcher.

"Bloody f**kin' hell!" The Master Warrant Officer lunged forward, coming perilously close to being gripped by the plant.

"No you bloody don't!" Drawing his projector, he blasted the tendrils close to the man's torso, then grabbed him and pulled him clear as the plant released its catch.

Harry listened awestruck as the Master Warrant told the TechRate, in language as pithy as it was colourful, what he thought of people who didn't consider where they were going and who they might inconvenience in rescuing them from their own stupidity. Admittedly, the Master Warrant had only just learned of the plant's deadly capabilities, but that didn't stop him from giving his crew a piece of his mind. They were used to it by now.

As the wounded man limped away, ignoring the jibes from his mates that a plant almost took him down, the Master Warrant got the situation under control and summoned a group of Marines to clear the area of all vegetation. Eager to comply, the Marines blasted the vicinity clean of anything that would burn, and within moments, all of it vanished in steaming blasts of plasma and flame for some distance around them.

"That'll teach the bastards, sir," the Master said as he squelched back over to where Harry stood to oversee the rest of the unloading.

"I hope so, Master." Harry studied the burnt remains. "But I suspect the WTO may disapprove of our killing too many of them. He grinned. "Even if they are trying to eat us."

The Master Warrant Officer snorted. "I don't plan on giving them the chance, sir, and as to the WTO, they can kiss my—." He paused, remembering his place. "They can come down here and give these meat-eaters a kiss in the face themselves. Bloody awful dump, this planet. I suggest we keep the domes on this high ground and put the landing area for the barges over there. Close enough for load handling, far enough to keep them clear of the camp."

"Good idea, Master. See to it please." Taking out his large drawing pad and a pen, Harry drew a rough sketch map. "As I am designated Beach Master, I shall establish myself here. Please be so good as to direct all new arrivals to me."

"Will do, sir."

The arrival of several more barges and smaller shuttles demanded Harry's attention. "I think I am in need of an assistant," he remarked to the barge pilot, a senior warrant officer.

"Want me to find you one, sir? I won't need the full team when I take her back aloft for the next load."

"That would be helpful, Warrant."

"I'll detail one of the lads, sir." He looked up as several more barges arrived. "Better make that two. I can pick up some handlers on *Leander*." Turning away, he signalled two of his crew. "Shan, Desiree, get over here. Mr Heron has a job for you." Saluting Harry, he added, "With your permission, sir, I'll get airborne."

Returning the salute, Harry nodded. "Carry on, Warrant. I think the first task is to arrange the traffic control." He glanced at a pair of TechRates who stood nearby. "Either of you any skill on that?"

"Yes, sir. Air Control handler when I'm not required on the barge crew, sir."

"Very well, Lead Rate. See Master Warrant Gottschalk over there, and get the equipment you need. Tech Patois, take this sketch plan to Warrant Thomas — he's somewhere over that way — and tell him I want the domes assigned as I've labelled them. Oh, and avoid any vegetation the Royals haven't blasted away. Some of these plants attack anything that passes too close. Get back as soon as you can."

The Lead Rate returned with the portable ship communications unit and made a second trip to fetch the power packs. When she had this connected, she tested the equipment then put out a general call. "Ready to go, sir."

"Commence, please. Is this the best position for you?"

"Highest point around, sir. Not perfect, but I can manage."

"Excellent." The stream of new arrivals drew his attention with demands for directions as to where additional domes were to be established, medical units placed, canteens located and supplies stored. With each new arrival he assigned a warrant officer the task of supervising some aspect of establishing the camp, but was very relieved when Lieutenant Commander Dalziel disembarked.

"Well done, Harry. Brief me quickly, and I'll relieve you of some of the workload."

Harry explained how he'd divided the site into four sectors with a medical dome and commissariat for each. During his recital Ferghal and several more officers and midshipmen joined them.

"Excellent. Yes, I like the way you've set it out. We'll keep to that." Bob Dalziel looked round. "Mr Bredon, take over the Aerial Control, please. Mr O'Connor, the Royals have a couple of digger units. See the QM and get a proper launch zone sorted out." After assigning other tasks, he said, "Mr Heron, you've already got a priorities schedule, I see. Take charge of coordinating the major equipment allocations. There'll be a lot of officers demanding it, and we've too few units to do it all immediately."

WITHIN A FEW DAYS, THE CAMP HAD TAKEN SHAPE. Laid out along the lines of Harry's rough plan, it formed a six-pointed star divided into four quadrants. He'd chosen the design based on his recollection of the star-shaped forts he'd seen at the Cape and in the East, and recognised the advantages for defence that such a design afforded. However, the defensive screens didn't seem to be working properly. The eight-legged creatures that wandered into the camp proved to be the least troublesome.

"These caterpillar things have a taste for plasmetal." An Engineer Lieutenant watched his squad herding one away from their equipment. "They've already damaged some of the survival domes. They started showing up as soon as we had built a few."

"Determined creatures, aren't they," commented Dalziel. "And the damn things stink — you can smell them through the background stench."

"One party say they were attacked by some sort of ambulant tree. It doesn't move very fast, but has whip-like tendrils it uses to grab something. The Royals destroyed it."

"Good. I better have a word with their senior officer. It sounds like we need a bit more than the usual screen to keep them out of our camp. No wonder the miners abandoned the bloody place." He caught sight of Harry using a sighting device attached to the top of a table to take bearings on various objects.

"What is Mr Heron doing?"

The Lieutenant shrugged. "Said he was making a plan of the camp, sir. He's using what he calls a plane table. Says it's how they mapped things back in his day. It's very accurate, and it's practically a work of art."

"That could be useful. Think I'll go and take a look." Walking across to where Harry worked, he watched the process, noting the pencil lines and bearings with neat notations of what the target was, but he couldn't see how this could become a map or a site plan. He was about to ask when Harry realised he was there.

"Sir, I beg pardon, I did not see you approach."

"No problem, Harry. What are you doing?"

"I'm making a plan of our camp, sir. This is the outline. I shall complete the detail later. As you can see, it is the plan of Sector Alpha. This is the commissariat dome, here the medical centre, these the sleeping accommodation, and here the wardroom."

To Lieutenant Commander Dalziel, it looked like a finished product. He said so.

"Oh no, sir." Retrieving a second sheet, Harry spread it out carefully. "I have yet to add the details. This is the landing area for the barges."

Staring at the clear outlines, the colour shading and detailed annotations — even some profile sketches of prominent features of the surrounding landscape — he asked, "When did you start on this?"

"Three days since, sir. In between the other tasks you gave me and when off watch. Midshipman Sheoba has taken many of the measurements, and Midshipman Kelly of the *Daring* has taken on the task of collating the sheets with Mr O'Connor."

"Was this your initiative, Mr Heron? What made you think of doing it?"

"As Beach Master, I thought it might be useful to have an accurate plan of the site, sir."

The Lieutenant Commander studied the finished plan of the landing area. The setting up of the camp, the constant movement and the landing and taking off of the various barges as they shuttled personnel between the surface and the damaged ships for repair work might draw attention from inhabitants that they were as yet unaware of. "You're right. It will be useful. I'll assign more people to assist you, and I want you to make it your task to complete it."

"Aye, aye, sir." Harry watched the Lieutenant Commander walk away, and was about to return to his task when he heard Midshipman Paula Sarbut exclaim, "Look at the size of that brute! Harry looked in the direction she pointed and saw a creature very similar to a large caterpillar, its grey and hairless skin undulating as it moved in a humping motion, its odour revolting and powerful enough to penetrate the entire area.

Paula looked about her for an unlucky volunteer. "Corporal, get some men and chase the damned thing out of here. Looks as if it could do some serious damage with that massive beak. I don't want it anywhere near our campsite!"

"Will do, ma'am," exclaimed the corporal, muttering that he always got stuck with the rotten jobs.

Midshipman Sarbut heard him. "Well, if you hadn't been standing around looking like you needed something to do, I wouldn't have volunteered you!"

Harry struggled to suppress a smile at that comment, and was reminded of a few of his fellow officers on the *Spartan*.

THE ROYAL MARINE CAPTAIN DELIVERED HIS REPORT of the surrounding area. "We aren't the only humans here. I sent out some scouting parties, and they found evidence that could suggest another group somewhere. Since all our people are accounted for, it can only mean some of the Consortium's people are here, or this planet has inhabitants that none of us are aware of."

Lieutenant Commander Dalziel nodded. "If they're survivors, they may need help. If they're part of a garrison, they will be a problem."

"I'd like to strengthen our perimeter defences — just in case." The Marine Major laughed. "That Mid you appointed as Beach Master laid out an interesting perimeter, the classic concept of defence in depth for an area such as a base or a camp. Says he based it on a defensive design he'd seen in Africa and what he calls the Dutch East Indies. Had to look that one up to realise he meant Indonesia. He said the concept was from some French chappie named Vaubon. Looked him up too — military engineer. Europe is still littered with examples of his work. Heron's sketch plan made sense, so I've had my lads dig ditches and build berms, and it seems to be working, at least against some of the creatures here."

"If we've got Consortium troops here, will it work against them?" asked Dalziel.

"Probably, but they'd have to get past those pitcher plants first."

"Yeah, there's that bit of fun, isn't there?" Bob Dalziel would not be sorry to leave this dump of a planet. "To make things even more interesting, our defence screen doesn't seem to have much effect on them. Some of the damned things seem to like the kick it gives them."

LIEUTENANT COMMANDER VALLANCE WAS DISAPPOINTED to find Bob Dalziel alive and well, since Bob was his senior on the Fleet List. When he'd learned that two of the Executive Commanders were dead and one was in a medical unit, he'd hoped to be the senior officer in the camp. That would have put him in a position to ensure the survivors would offer little resistance when his paymasters arrived to deal with them. "Bloody awful place this," he remarked. Lifting his ranging optics, he swept the distant line of a ridge. "Hopefully we won't have to sit here much longer."

Bob Dalziel shrugged. "A question of what comes first, the relief force or the Consortium squadron that attacked us." It hadn't escaped his notice that Vallance was the sole survivor of *Naiad*, and the fact that Vallance was reluctant to talk about it made Bob even more suspicious of the man, but he didn't let this show. Catching sight of Harry, he said, "Ah, Mr Heron. Got the latest plans of our defences?"

"These are the completed ones, sir." Harry laid the plans out on the table. "We are almost done now, sir." He acknowledged Lieutenant Commander Vallance then continued. "We have one area left to complete — the south western quadrant." He hesitated, choosing his words with care. "There is something odd in that direction, sir — a curious anomaly that affects my compass."

"Your compass? That thing you use to draw circles?" Bob noted that Harry seemed reluctant to speak freely in Vallance's presence, and he wondered why.

Harry hesitated again, uncertain of how to explain the erratic way the small handheld magnetic compass reacted in the presence of a powerful magnetic field. "No, sir. This one. It has a magnetised needle that aligns to the north-south polarity of the Earth's magnetic field. I thought perhaps it would function in the same manner on this planet, but here on New Eden, the poles seem unrelated to the axis, so the compass is of little use except in giving an orientation for the plan."

Bob Dalziel studied the small device Harry held, his mind considering the implications of magnetic fields on any electrical system or force field. "Useful to know. I want to walk along that part of the perimeter anyway. We may as well take a look at this anomaly of yours while we're at it. Hold the fort here, will you, Vallance? Come on, Harry, let's see what your compass does then."

When they had walked a short distance away, Bob said, "I've been meaning to ask, Harry. When you set up the initial layout, why did you divide the resources as you did? Why separate the commissariat into three locations, and also the medical units and even our engineering support? And why this star shape? The Marines like it, but it does pose some restrictions. Some of the people grumble about it."

"Sir, we know not who or what may inhabit this place. If we are attacked, this design makes it unlikely they can so easily destroy all of our resources at one time. The star layout was something I saw when I visited the Cape, and later, Batavia. The fortresses there followed the pattern set out by General Vauban. His principle was to create defensible units within units." Grinning, he added, "It seemed a good principle to follow, sir."

"Very good thinking, Harry," replied the Lieutenant Commander, walking in silence a few paces. "But why do you think there may be other inhabitants?"

"I cannot be certain, sir. But when I am near an AI network, it seems as if someone is whispering in my head. Here, we have no AI and very few uplink modules to any AI, yet every time I am on the western edge of the camp, I can sense a very faint voice as if there were a large network somewhere in this vicinity."

"Is that so?" Bob Dalziel frowned. "Is this what your compass indicates? A magnetic field where there shouldn't be one?" He looked at Harry, a thoughtful expression in his eyes, and asked, "Does Ferghal feel it as well?"

"I believe so, sir. He mentioned it to me during supper yesterday evening, and there is another thing. Yon tree appears to be leading others toward us." Lapsing into the speech pattern of his childhood, Harry indicated a strange-looking copse of trees.

"Tree? What? Oh! Yes — the one that looks as if it's standing on its head. Damn, a whole lot of them are coming this way."

"That's correct, sir. I believe they are moving toward us with deliberate intent. Half an hour ago they were a mile or so from here, and now they are barely a quarter mile from us."

"Damn." The Lieutenant Commander glanced about him then called to a Royal Marine passing with a load of bedding piled in his arms. "Royal! Where is your Sergeant? Fetch him or your officer at the double please."

A Royal Marine Lieutenant and a Sergeant arrived at a fast walk. "Lieutenant Harding, sir, of the *Dragon*," said the Lieutenant, saluting, "and Sergeant Bateman."

Returning the salute, Bob Dalziel identified himself. "Lieutenant, take a good look at those trees — yes, your eyes don't deceive you. We've determined that they're moving toward us. According to our information, these damned plants eat flesh, and they think they've just scored a bonanza of a feast. I want them discouraged permanently. And that goes for any others that attempt to come anywhere near us. And Lieutenant, two things are important about them: one is that they must be totally destroyed, and second, tell your people to stay at least fifty metres away from them. We've already had to pry one man loose, and we don't want to go through that again."

"Very good, sir." Saluting, the Lieutenant turned to the NCO. "Sergeant, bring up our field plasma projector. We'll have to give these tree creatures a very swift distaste for this life."

"Right you are, sir." The Sergeant strode away, already bellowing orders at a group of Marines nearby.

Harry noted the way the base of each tree was comprised of a mass of writhing roots that moved it steadily forward. Strange cocoon-shaped bundles dangled from some of the branches, which suggested the idea of a massive insect carrying its young in sacs, ready to deliver them at any moment. The hairs on the back of his neck rose as he watched the largest tree advance about twenty feet, and his every instinct screamed a warning.

He quickly calculated how long it would take to get to their position, and glanced at the Lieutenant Commander, wondering if he was also aware they had little time to prepare. Evidently, Bob had been doing the same thing, because he spoke again to the Marine Lieutenant.

"Lieutenant Harding, I suggest that you get your men to shift themselves, or that damned tree will be among us before you can set up your field projector." The tree was now close enough for the full horror of it to be visible, including what appeared to be the remains of a large animal tightly wrapped in the tendrils dangling from one of its branches. "I calculate we have eight minutes before it's within the estimated range of its striking shoots, as the botanists called them."

"Yes, sir," responded the Lieutenant, who turned to speak to the Sergeant, who, having glanced at the advancing tree with an expert eye, ordered the field projector wheeled about and set in. A few seconds of adjustment and correction and the sighting laser sprang into view on the tree's lower trunk.

"Projector ready. Permission to fire?"

"Granted."

"Fire!"

The incandescent bolt of plasma blazed across the intervening gap and stuck the tree exactly at the aim point. Harry winced as a high-pitched scream filled his head. He tried to block his ears then realised it was in his mind. Worse, no one else seemed to hear it.

The projector fired again, and this time the centre of the tree burst open in a great gout of steam and flaming splinters, even as it lunged toward its attackers. A third burst of plasma struck it as it lashed out at them with long whip-like tendrils, striking the ground only yards from where they stood. Then, the tree erupted in flames as the projector sent bolt after incandescent bolt, each producing a further burst of steam and splinters as the tree toppled.

The tendril writhed as if trying to reach them, and Harry, suddenly aware of Sheoba between him and the tendril, clearly saw the sharp needle thorns at its tip, the means by which it obviously injected poison into its victim.

"Shift target right to the next nearest tree," the Lieutenant ordered. "Sergeant, call for battery support. The damn things aren't stopping. We need the full battery."

"Lieutenant, according to our information, they reproduce by splitting off sections, which means any splinter can become a new tree. Make damned sure it is completely destroyed or we'll have them swarming all over us in no time."

"Yes, sir!"

Turning to Harry, Lieutenant Commander Dalziel said, "Mid, get a message to all officers. I want everyone in the Sector Alpha commissariat dome in ten minutes. We need to figure out how to keep these damned trees at bay — quickly."

Chapter 31 – Consortium Strikes

"Impressive." Bob Dalziel surveyed the newly completed system of moats and berms that surrounded the ridge on which the camp and the landing area were situated. "I see what you mean about the overlapping fire zones."

"They stop most of the local beasties as well. Those tree things don't cross them, nor do those caterpillar creatures. The spider critters love 'em. Apparently we've created an environment for their favourite food." The Marine Major laughed.

Harry joined them, his ever-present folder of plans slung over his shoulder. "Sir, Lieutenant Orloff's compliments. Captain Rafferty has sent a message. The deep scan carried out by the *Danaea* confirms there is an installation to our southwest. They are unsure of the extent, as it is heavily screened, but it appears to be in a mine of some kind."

"So your feeling was right, Mr Heron." The Lieutenant Commander paused. "That would explain Lieutenant Sci'Girac's team having seen vehicles exiting a tunnel. Anything else, Mr Heron?"

"Aye, sir. The Captain advises that a squadron is underway to retrieve us, expected within a fortnight, but he hopes sooner." Harry smiled. "And my guardian is promoted to Rear-Admiral in command of the Fourth Fleet."

Bob Dalziel laughed. "Excellent. A fighting admiral for our Fleet at last."

THE ATTACK CAME AT SUNRISE, PRESAGED BY THE SHRIEK of a pair of aerial strike units that came in low over the landing area. Catching one of the barges in the act of rising from its pad with the reliefs for the working party on *Danae*, the leader opened fire, breaking away as the barge plunged to the ground, ploughing into two more, one for *Daring* and the other unmanned.

The Royals recovered quickly, their plasma projectors swinging rapidly to meet the circling strike craft and delivering a wall of plasma streams.

"Man the berms!" The order sent Techs and Marines racing to their allotted positions on the substantial dykes the Marines had constructed to Harry's sketch. "Commander Dalziel!" The Marine Captain spoke into his link. "We have ground forces supported by armour approaching from the southeast. Delta Sector. They're aiming for the landing area."

"Hold them off. *Leander* and *Daring* are scrambling their remaining strike craft. They need thirty minutes to get here."

The shriek of the enemy aerial craft drowned out the reply, and Bob Dalziel ducked as explosions hurled debris into the air.

"Bastards have hit Med Dome Delta, sir!"

"Tell the medics at Unit Charlie to send help." To Sci'Anatha he said, "You may deploy your people, Lieutenant. Just make sure they stay out of our firing lines. Good luck."

The Lacertian made her gesture of salute and strode away, her own people joining her.

"We need all the luck we can get now," said Bob Dalziel to himself. He settled down to listen to the reports flowing in, and issued instructions as needed.

The Marine Captain studied the attackers. "They've taken the outlier position." He gave a harsh laugh. "They've discovered the problem with that, though. Bastards are evacuating it again. That Vaubon chappie of yours was a bloody genius, Mr Heron."

"They're trying to use the moats to approach, sir."

"They'll soon discover their mistake." He handed a set of ranging optics to Harry. "Take a look through these. See that ridge to the right? There's a command post, or something that looks like one, on the back slope of it. Report to Commander Dalziel and tell him I would like to send a raiding party to take them out." He grinned as Harry took the optical device. "I suspect they've got a listening post over there, so we'll communicate the old fashioned way — your way."

Harry studied the ridge and made out what appeared to be masts just visible above it. "I shall tell him, sir." He grinned. "Perhaps we should adopt flag signals and port fires by night, sir." He watched as a figure moved into view, studying the defences. "Barclay? Here? Changed sides, has he? Or was he always on their side?" Harry lowered the optics. "I shall inform the Lieutenant Commander, sir."

He nodded distractedly, his attention focused on the latest attempt to smash a way past the tiered defences, each succeeding berm dyke higher than the next and providing arcs of fire that covered all approaches from those in front of it or to those on either side. He raised his ranging optics and studied the attacking troops.

The Marine Captain snorted a wry laugh. "Don't those fools realise they're walking straight into kill zones?"

IN ORBIT ABOVE THE PLANET, THE STRUGGLE TO STABILISE the damaged *Leander* went on without pause.

"All the bodies are recovered, sir. We've placed them in the holds on the *Orion* for shipping back to Earth. With her holds not under atmosphere, it saves power to keep them—"

"Quite. How about the loss of atmosphere from the Weapons Control?"

"We've found the leak and sealed it, sir." Mama Behr paused. "We've sorted out two of the drive pods and sealed off the leaks in the forward end. Portside hangars are still open to space. It will need a major rebuild to solve that, and the AG forward of Frame 47 is another dockside job." She stopped as a chirp sounded from the Captain's link.

"Captain."

"Base Camp reports being under attack by surface forces, sir. The attackers are targeting the barges and landing area, and have hit one of the med units and the commissariat in one sector."

"Damn, so Bob Dalziel was right. They are having a go." He hesitated. "Get Captain Gratz on link for me, and send me the Flight Officer on board."

"I'll get my team ready to power up the weapons and support for launching the strike craft."

"Do that, please. Damn, the *DGK* and her group aren't due for another twenty-four!"

WATCHING FROM HIS COMMAND POST AT THE CENTRE of the camp, Bob Dalziel lowered his ranging optics. "They're pulling back." He glanced up as the roar of several strike craft filled the air "Ours. That'll change the score a little." He contacted the Marine officer now hastening the departure of the last Consortium troops. "What's your assessment of their intentions?"

"They've fallen back to positions just outside the range of our heavy weapons." The Marine officer hesitated. "They may be regrouping or waiting for reinforcement. I don't think they've much in reserve though. This lot seem to be no more than a garrison, not a full brigade even. They started to pull back as soon as we hit whatever was behind that ridge."

"I think it was some sort of observation post." Bob Dalziel stopped as Lieutenant Sci'Anatha arrived. "I think I'm about to find out what it was and what happened to the occupants. I'll get back to you."

"We found a Command Post, sir. They had this." She presented him with the decoder unit.

"What?" He looked more closely at the unit. "Well, I'll be damned." He whistled softly. "So that's how they're doing it. They're reading every damned signal we make." Turning, he spotted Harry. "Get a launch, and get this aloft to the Captain. Don't send any messages, and don't mention what you are bringing aboard if you're asked. In fact, disguise it now, and don't tell anyone what it is. We'll need to warn the ships and the Fleet."

To Lieutenant Sci'Anatha, he said, "What happened to the men manning that post?"

She told him.

"No prisoners? Did they resist?" He stopped, correctly reading the alien's expression. "I see. How many of them?"

"Six guarding, four in the vehicle, and two observing from the hill. Some left before we struck. They did not see us. Their compatriots have sent a patrol, but I assigned two of my people to follow and learn the strength of the main group."

Bob Dalziel nodded, silently thankful the Lacertians were on his side. "Very well." He stopped himself from asking if two would be enough. These Lacertians seemed more than capable of taking care of themselves. "Better tell me what you've learned from this excursion then."

HARRY HURRIED TOWARD THE LANDING AREA, AND WAS relieved to see the fires already out, but concerned that several of the larger barges were damaged or destroyed. He slowed his pace when Lt-Cdr Vallance stepped out of a dome and asked where he was going.

"I am ordered to take a report to Captain Rafferty, sir." His senses prickled for no apparent reason. "The destruction of the Delta sector commissariat has cost us the culture plant for a third of our meat supplies," he improvised. "If I cannot bring back a fresh culture and replacement culture tanks, we will have to impose rationing."

"Ah." Ari Vallance knew the commissariat had been damaged, so he bought the story. "Better get on then. Can't let the troops go hungry." Watching Harry retreat, he cursed his luck. His plan to grab the kid as soon as it was dark enough and then to work his way out of the camp on a pretext was obviously a non-starter now. At least he'd managed to acquire a Consortium comlink from a fallen trooper. Now all he could do was sit it out and wait for them to send in reinforcements.

HARRY SLEPT THROUGH THE RIDE TO THE DAMAGED *LEANDER* He hadn't realised how tired he was. He disembarked with the decoder under his arm and reported to Lieutenant Mariam Isfahan, the gangway officer. "I am ordered to report to the Captain."

Mariam returned his salute. "He's in the Command Centre, Harry. I'll let him know you're on your way." She noticed the carefully wrapped package, and her curiosity was piqued. "So, what have you got there? How are things going on the surface? Are the Royals holding the attackers off?"

Harry grinned. "Where shall I begin? Flesh-eating plants, walking trees, and yes, the Royals have held the defences."

This elicited a laugh from Mariam.

"And this," Harry added, tapping the package, "is for the Captain's eyes only."

When Harry entered the Captain's office, the Captain wasted no time getting right to business. "Mr Heron, Commander Dalziel tells me you have an important package for me."

"Aye, sir. It was recovered from the Consortium Command Unit — a fleet signal decrypter. Lieutenant Commander Dalziel believes they may have full access to all our signal traffic."

"That explains a lot." Rising from his seat, Greg Rafferty took the package, unwrapped it, and turned it this way and that to examine it. "I'll be double damned. So that's how they're always aware of what we're planning and doing. It's so damned obvious, our people should have spotted it. Now we've got a bigger problem They'll know exactly when the *DGK* and her escort will get here, and what our condition is."

"Aye, sir. Commander Dalziel thinks the troops here are waiting for reinforcement. They're regrouping on our perimeter, and have divided their forces, possibly in preparation for a fresh assault as soon as these reinforcements arrive."

The Captain hesitated. "Right. I need to warn the other Captains. Coms are out, so we'll have to send a message in person. Activating his link, he ordered, "Lieutenant Isfahan, send the nearest midshipman to me immediately. Have Mr Heron's launch placed on standby for immediate departure, and place my launch on immediate readiness."

Listening, Harry wondered what his Captain planned. He wasn't left in doubt for long.

"You have that pad you always carry with you, Mr Heron?"

"Aye, sir."

"I'll make use of it, if you don't mind."

"My pleasure, sir." Harry handed over his pad just as Ferghal joined them.

"Gentlemen, I'm writing a note to Captain Gratz and Captain O'Shea. I want you to take the launches and deliver them for me, in person, please. Mr Heron, explain the problem to Mr O'Connor while I write this."

Chapter 32 – Engage the Enemy

The Consortium Commodore studied the 3D display of the system. "Three frigates and the freighter." He paused. "The freighter is unmanned, the same one we disabled as bait for the *Leander*."

"They must have done something unusual to get her here." As a member of the boarding party, the Lieutenant had seen the destruction of the control interfaces.

Commodore Ellerton shrugged. "Immaterial. She's no threat, and the cargo she carries will be useful. We have twelve hours to deal with these wrecks, destroy their survivors and withdraw our forces. I want the landing barges away as soon as we close the planet."

"Commodore, as you're aware, our stealth screen is still inoperable. They'll be able to scan and target us as soon as we drop out."

"Yes, but if the damage assessment is accurate, it won't make any difference." The Commodore was aware that his flagship, a converted freight and passenger carrier, carried a heavier armament than the majority of the Fleet cruisers. Her conversion made her a formidable opponent for anything smaller or of equal size, but not for a heavy cruiser such as *Der Grosse Kurfürst*. He touched his link. "Captain Doerries, drop out on the blind side of the planet and take us through the low orbit arc. I want to attack these ships from the planet. Confirm my intention with the escorts

Tell them to mop up once we've disabled them." He paused. "The landing barges are to launch as soon as we have contact with the targets."

HARRY EXPLORED THE *LEANDER*'S MANOEUVRING FUNCTIONS again. There was a worrying lag in relays that controlled the operation of firing the multiple thrust generators that the ship relied on to change direction and orientation. Some had been destroyed, others damaged, but before the ship could be moved anywhere, these command and control circuits had to be fully operational.

"All hands, all hands, battle stations, battle stations, one heavy cruiser and two frigates closing. Prepare for manoeuvring and engagement."

This was followed by the Captain's calm voice. "Attention all hands. This is the Captain. We are completely outgunned, and you all know that we are in a damaged state. All hands are to rig in EVA suits as quickly as you can and take your posts. Should the opportunity be offered, I will attempt to ram the cruiser, and I will want the ship evacuated as soon as I give the order. Make sure you are fully prepared to leave the ship as rapidly as possible. Our companions on New Eden must be given every chance to survive, and those of you who can abandon the ship when the moment comes may be able to join them. Good luck, and thank you all for what you have done. That is all. Captain out."

The signal of the general alarm sounded with shrill urgency, and the men ran to obey the order. The scramble to rig in suits and get to their action stations slowed the ship's response, but soon enough all stations reported ready. Harry noted that a number of men and officers made no attempt to get their EVA suits rigged, apparently determined to go down with the ship.

Harry asked one of them, "Sir, why do you not rig for EVA?"

The Lieutenant lifted his shoulders in a brief shrug of nonchalance. "If I have to go, I'll go this way, quick, spectacular and taking as many of the bastards with me as I can. Now lad, head for Navigation — they'll need you there."

Harry made his way to Navigation Control where he was welcomed by Lieutenant Orloff and a Master Warrant Officer. "Welcome, Harry, glad to see you are properly rigged," greeted the Lieutenant even as Harry noted that neither of them was rigged for EVA. "Take the Navigation Station, please, and plot us an intercept. Then get ready to run like hell for the escape hatches. We'll take it from there."

"Aye, aye, ma'am." Harry seated himself awkwardly in the bulky suit and linked to the AI network. As he did so he remembered that Ferghal was also aboard the ship. He said a silent prayer then prepared to do his part for the ship.

"WE'VE GOT A PROBLEM." BOB DALZIEL LOWERED HIS ranging optics. "They've got reinforcements alright. Looks like a full detachment landing and disembarking. And we can expect no help from the ships. There's a Consortium cruiser and her escort in system."

"Full landing force by the look of it — must be a heavy cruiser by the numbers. The Marine Major deactivated his optics. "Damn, that means they'll use strike craft on us once they've dealt with our ships." The Marine officer shrugged. "Well, we'll give them a taste of hell and make them pay as heavily as we can."

Bob nodded slowly, pondering their situation. "Yes. I wonder why they are here. Sci'Anatha says there's a very intricate set of uplink projectors very well hidden around twenty kilometres from here. She got me an image, and they look like hypercom relays, but why here? Those damned giant caterpillars eat plasmetal, so they'll be after those relays."

"Perhaps we'll get it sorted out once we've beaten this lot."

Bob grinned at the Major. "Damn right. Come on, let's make them regret coming here." He contacted his strike craft pilots. "We've four strike craft against their God knows how many. Let's get started."

THE HUGE CRUISER MADE AN IMPRESSIVE SIGHT WITH her frigates close and a swarm of strike fighters preceding her.

"Damn. We're outgunned, out classed and damn near sitting ducks." Greg Rafferty winced as the first plasma bursts struck the damaged *Danea*. "He's going to try to finish us off one at a time. Pilot, can you plot us a micro transit past *Danea* and *Dragon* so I can position the old girl to ram him?"

"Will do my best, sir."

"Fine." He contacted Heather Behr. "Mama, this is going to be tricky. I need those hyperpods online, and I'm going to be demanding some tricky manoeuvres. Can you do it?"

Listening to this exchange and already engaged in plotting the Navigator's solutions, Harry had a sudden thought. He linked to his friend swiftly. *"Ferghal, are you ready to evacuate?"*

"Aye, Harry, that I am — to be sure we have little hope either way, it seems."

"We cannot give up without a fight, and we may have a better chance this way." Harry paused to search the AI network. *"Ferghal, the link to the* Greenbay Orion *is still active. Can we start her engines? Can she use her hyperdrives?"*

"They were still online when we parked her, and no one has been aboard her except to secure her atmosphere and some equipment from her holds. Why?"

"She will not show as a live ship on the Consortium scanners. They will not expect her to move. Help me quickly. Use the link with me. Get her hyperpods ready while I programme her for an interception course. Hurry — we have little time."

"Should we not ask the Captain's permission?"

"There is no time."

Harry accessed the *Greenbay Orion*'s navigation system and swiftly did the calculations for the interception coordinates. Several precious seconds were lost persuading the *Orion* to sacrifice itself to save the squadron.

"It is the same ship that attacked me and left me crippled. I will help you, Harry. Set the course I must follow."

Harry contacted Ferghal. *"Ready? Good, then let's do it. Activate the engines on my signal."* He paused for a microsecond count, listening to the network clock in his head. *"Now!"*

THERE WAS A MOMENT OF CONSTERNATION ABOARD the Consortium's heavy cruiser as the apparently abandoned freighter came to life, her hyperpods lighting up in a great flare of energy. The weapons scanners reported, "Freighter attempting to escape."

"Ignore it," ordered his Officer. "We can deal with it later. Concentrate on the frigates."

In the Command Centre, Commodore Ellerton was equally surprised, but the entire ship had only seconds left to its existence.

Aboard *Leander*, Captain Rafferty watched his targeting scanners and the navigation plot with impatience. Like the Consortium officers, he was startled by the sudden disappearance of the *Greenbay Orion*. "What the hell? I thought that ship was unmanned and in stand-by mode." He realised that no course solution had been transmitted to his own ship's helm. "Pilot? Where's that nav solution? They're going to be on us any minute now."

THE *GREENBAY ORION* LEAPT OUT OF HER STATIONARY ORBIT, vanished from the screens for ten seconds then re-materialised, dropping out exactly inside the space occupied by the mid-ship section of the massive cruiser.

The image of two ships sharing the same space lasted a nanosecond before a great flower of flame and debris erupted as the pair mutually destroyed each other. The nearest Consortium frigate shared the fate of her senior ship as the cruiser's reactors ruptured. The second frigate was luckier or her navigation officer quicker to respond. She leapt out of danger, vanishing into hyperspace even as her consorts disintegrated.

"Got you," shouted Harry into his comlink, his excitement overcoming his normal restraint. His amplified voice, heard by everyone on board, brought instantaneous silence. He too fell silent as he watched the cloud of vaporising debris expanding where the two ships had been. A cold chill clutched his heart when he realised what he had just done.

He stared in horror as the last fragments vanished from the display and lost their incandescence. He had not expected the ship to be totally destroyed; after all, the freighter was smaller than the ship she had rammed. He had expected to see the cruiser break in half, or perhaps lose a part of its hull. What he had not expected was this total annihilation of not one but two enemy vessels.

In his head he heard Ferghal's equally shocked response. *"Holy Mother of God, what have we done?"*

"Saved our ships and our friends," responded Harry, suddenly uneasy about how easily and quickly he had caused such mass destruction. *"We did what our Captain intended to do with our ship. We have only forestalled him, but the destruction is far greater than I expected."*

"Mr Heron." The voice of Captain Rafferty was flat and emotionless in Harry's comlink. "If, as I suspect, that was your doing, perhaps you will be good enough to explain what has just happened. In my quarters please, as soon as you have extracted yourself from your EVA suit." After a slight pause, he added, "As fast as you can."

"Aye, aye, sir." Harry suddenly felt hot then cold, and his hands trembled. "Right away, sir." Conscious of the quietness around him and the fact that Lieutenant Orloff and the Master Warrant Officer were very carefully avoiding his eye, he excused himself and hurried to the dressing station, exchanging his suit for his normal uniform, now very aware there seemed to be a clear space around him even in the crowded confines of the dressing station.

WHEN HARRY REPORTED TO CAPTAIN RAFFERTY, HE WAS worried about the responses of the crew, and he felt somewhat defiant and on the defensive, but he composed his expression. He entered on command and stood to attention in front of the Captain's desk.

"You called for me, sir?"

Captain Rafferty studied him, his face unreadable. "Mr Heron, I don't know whether I should commend you or charge you. You were ordered to lay in a course for *this* ship to intercept the cruiser, and you did not. Instead you activated the *Greenbay Orion* and smashed her into the enemy." Holding Harry's gaze, he said, "Why did you disobey an order, Mr Heron? I hope you have a good reason."

Standing at attention, Harry held his ground. "Sir, I realised that many of my fellow officers and the men had not rigged for EVA and intended to die with you, sir. Then I found that we still had access to the *Greenbay Orion* controls, and Mr O'Connor was able to activate her engines. I should have sought permission, sir, but there was not the time, so I acted, and I believe correctly, to save this ship and her crew, and I launched the *Greenbay Orion* into the enemy." He kept his eyes fixed over the Captain's shoulder.

"Do you now?" Greg Rafferty exhaled slowly. "Damn it all, Harry, sit down." He waited until Harry was seated. "You disobeyed an order, but you saved the ship. The one doesn't cancel the other, but I have to admit that in your position I would have done the same. Next time get permission." He held up a hand "I know, there probably wasn't a lot of time, and your action was correct in these circumstances. You saw an opportunity, and you took it, but you could, and should, have advised me or your officer first."

The reaction to what he had done made his knees feel weak, and he clenched his fists to stop the tremor. "I shall, sir."

"Good." The Captain paused. "I will report this exactly as it has happened and credit you with the decision and the action — and endorse the fact I approve of the action. Do you wish to say anything else about it?"

Harry hesitated. "I did not expect such destruction, sir. Complete and immediate annihilation was not possible when we engaged the enemy in the year 1804. The sight of it troubled Ferghal, and I shall not easily put it aside either." He raised his chin and held his head higher. "It troubles me greatly to know that I have killed so many people in this one action, but faced with the same threat and choice, I would do it again to protect my friends and to defeat an enemy I have no cause to love, sir."

The Captain rubbed his hand across his face, his exhaustion showing. "None of us enjoys seeing death or destruction on any scale. Even one man's death for someone else's gain is too many."

"Yes, sir."

Summoning his android steward, the Captain looked at Harry and said, "Tea? Or perhaps something stronger."

"Tea if I may, sir." Harry watched as the steward set a steaming cup before him. "Thank you, Lee One."

"A pleasure, Mr Heron." The android placed a second cup in front of the Captain. "Will you have your meal now, sir?"

"Meal? No." He hesitated. "Have you eaten, Mr Heron?"

"No, sir." Harry's stomach growled as if supplying a more urgent answer to the Captain's query. "We were to return to the Eden base camp for our dinner this evening."

"Then stay and eat with me. Two meals, steward." He hesitated. "What did Mr Heron call you?"

"Lee One, Captain. He abbreviates our ship designations. I am GP dash Leander dash Zero One. My programming is to maintain your quarters and attend to your meals and uniforms, sir."

Speechless for a moment, Greg Rafferty glanced at Harry. "Thank you, Lee One." After the steward departed, the Captain said, "Do you know all our droid stewards by name, Mr Heron?"

It was Harry's turn to pause. It hadn't occurred to him that this might be unusual. "Not all, sir, but those I encounter regularly." He paused. "And the ship, of course. *Leander* considers himself fortunate to have survived the latest encounter, but is saddened by the death of the *Orion*."

Greg Rafferty watched the steward prepare the table and lay out the meal. He'd never considered that there might be some deeper relationship between the ship and these unusual midshipmen, Heron and O'Connor. Moving to the table, he asked, "So you are telling me the ship and each of the stewards has a personality, and they experience emotions as we do?"

Harry took his place at the table. "Yes, sir. *Leander* feels his damage in the same manner that we feel an injury." Hesitating, he added, "And *Orion* died willingly, knowing that in doing so, he saved our squadron further injury."

The Captain leaned back, studying his guest. "I suppose I shouldn't be surprised." Making a mental note to explore the matter further when he had a chance, he decided to enjoy his meal and changed the subject by asking about Harry's early life.

Chapter 33 – Farewell to Hell

The planet-side assault was being driven home with determination.

"They've pushed right up to our inner berm in Alpha sector, but we're holding them."

"Good. The ships are in trouble. There's a heavy cruiser and an escort closing on them." Bob Dalziel cast his eyes about the barren landscape. "There must be something here for them to be this determined to protect it. Have we enough people to hold Alpha? They're pushing into Bravo sector as well."

"We're holding them for now. They haven't brought up anything heavier than the plasma projectors, and we've countered most of those. It's the aerials the cruiser must have that worry me."

"Yes." Bob raised his ranging optics. "Hallo. There's a new group gathered on that hill. See them?"

"Looks like a command group. Now what?" The Marine officer pointed to the Delta sector. "They're pulling back. It's a damn slaughterhouse." He shook his head. "You know, I begin to understand why these star defences changed warfare — I wouldn't want to lead an assault on one. The defenders have all the advantage."

An explosion drew their attention to the sector behind them. "Lieutenant Bradley? Report, please."

"We bagged two armoured units, sir. Trapped them in the crossfire between the bastions." Cheering erupted from the direction of Bravo sector, and moments later, from Delta and then the others.

"They've had enough for the moment. They're pulling back." The Marine officer pointed. "That command group are in one hell of a hurry to get out of here. I wonder why?"

A ComsRate hurried up. "Sir! Commander! Message from Captain Gratz. They've beaten the cruiser, sir. Took her out completely."

"What? Our three wrecks took out a cruiser? You sure?"

"I'd say they must have — look, the Cons are pulling back." Raising his ranging optics, the Marine officer shook his head. "Looks like they're regrouping for a major push. I wonder if they know their cruiser is down, or is there another one around?"

THE LULL IN THE FIGHTING GAVE AN OPPORTUNITY for the repair crews to return. Disgorging from the landing barges, they hurried into the defended areas as the barges lifted off again. Their arrival coincided with a renewed assault, sending the tired men racing to defensive positions. Harry found himself on Bastion Charlie with a Royal Marine sergeant above and behind a heavy projector and its crew.

"Welcome to the party, sir. We heard the wrecks managed to send a cruiser to hell. Damn good work." He raised his ranging optics. "Damn, they're not giving up. If the *DGK* can put troops down as soon as she arrives, we'll have them beat, sir." The Royal Marine sergeant sounded cheerful despite his damaged armour and the evidence of several wounds.

"She should be here at any moment, but we won't know immediately, I suspect. Everyone is being very careful about using the signals transmissions."

Focussing his ranging optics, Harry drew a sharp breath. "What is he doing here?"

"Who, sir?"

"A fellow who gave us a lot of trouble at the College last year, Eon Barclay is his name. Damned fool, I heard he'd left the Fleet. Looks like he turned his coat!" There was little time to say more as several heavy projectors opened fire on the bastion. "Damn, here they come again." Harry slid behind the parapet, and when he rolled over, he found himself staring at the weapon held by Lieutenant Commander Vallance.

"Sir?"

"Keep your hands where I can see them. You and I are going over the top. You have a date with a certain research foundation, and I have a reward to collect." Vallance quickly relieved Harry of his weapons. "Now get up and walk in front of me, and don't even think about pulling any of your usual stunts. I have a transport ready to take you off-world."

"Then you'd best shoot me now, sir. I will not surrender myself to those people under any circumstances." Harry rolled quickly, scrambling to gain his feet. The armour deflected the first blast of plasma, but he felt the sting of the heat. With no weapon he tried to close the traitor, but his feet slipped.

The disturbance drew attention.

"Drop the weapon, Commander." The order came from a Marine Lieutenant flanked by two Marines, their weapons steady.

"Damn you, Heron," snarled Vallance. "Why couldn't you just come quietly? Why did you have to force me to do this?" He raised the projector and Harry stared, mesmerised by the obvious anguish in the man's face.

"I don't understand, sir. What have I done to distress you?"

"No, you wouldn't understand," said Vallance, bitter and spiteful. "None of you would understand what it is like to watch someone you love be destroyed because you can't afford the treatment they need. The reward for capturing you was my last hope." He straightened and swung round to face the men hurrying toward them. "Damn you, Heron, damn all of you," he muttered, and in that moment, a Marine sprang forward to grab the projector.

The blast made Harry wince, and he stared down at the still body of the man he had just been talking to, his stomach turning at the sight of the ugly wound in the head.

The sound of firing and the blast of explosives drew their attention, and he joined the battle for the defence, the sour taste of vomit in his throat.

When the Consortium troops withdrew from fighting, Harry stood atop the berm and focussed his range taker on the distant hill where he'd seen his old adversary Barclay, and was surprised to see the Consortium troops still there, apparently waiting for something. Several gave the appearance of watching for some signal from the camp, and he felt sick again as he realised what they were waiting for.

Scanning the area around them, he noticed a stealthy movement. "Lieutenant," he called to the Marine officer near the big plasma projector that dominated this part of the bastion. "I see a target. Bearing right, five degrees, range five hundred meters." He waited while the officer focussed on the group.

"What? That group on the hillside? We don't shoot at individuals with this weapon, Mid."

"Not the group, sir. Just to the right and behind them. That tree creature is stalking them. Enemy they may be, sir, but I hope we draw the line at consigning them to that fate, not even a Barclay!"

The Lieutenant refocussed. "Damn, you're right. Bloody hell, it's almost up to them. Sergeant!" He gave his targeting directions quickly.

The big weapon pulsed. Harry saw the group of Consortium officers dive for cover as the incandescent stream lanced past their position. Two more pulses followed as the Consortium group raced to their transport.

"Cease fire. Damn tree won't be doing any more stalking now. I hope our Consortium friends appreciate the favour, but I doubt it."

DEEP INSIDE THE CONSORTIUM HEADQUARTERS, THE BASE Commander made an emergency call.

"We're being evacuated. There will be a flying pickup, but this base must be destroyed completely. The Fleet must not be able to recover anything." He glanced around, his expression bitter. "All that bloody effort wasted because someone got careless and let three bloody wrecks survive."

"Is there no chance we could come back and finish setting up the operation later?"

"None. The stuff we've installed already would give them too many indicators of what we were planning. No, it will all have to be destroyed. Use a fission bomb. Use as many as we have. Make sure they can't salvage a damned thing."

"That'll have an impact on the local life, sir."

"Serve them bloody right. We've lost too many of our people to them. Time for some payback." He looked about him in anger.

He'd put a lot of effort into building this base and the mining operation associated with it. It would have gone undetected if the idiots at Head Office hadn't insisted on their attacking the base camp to recover two midshipmen they called research assets.

Working fast, he packed his personal items into a small holdall. He'd chosen to work for the Consortium for altruistic reasons, not to fight wars, but as an opportunity to earn a better wage and explore new horizons while shedding what he considered the burdens of bureaucracy that strangled his home nation and government.

"We have very little time," he told his assembled staff. "A ship is on its way to collect us, but the Fleet has a squadron on its way as well. It will be touch and go as to who gets here first. And now that our presence is known, they will be looking to capture us."

The Commander noticed Eon Barclay making an effort to get his attention. Still shaken by the narrowness of his escape on the hillside earlier, Barclay didn't wait for permission to speak.

"The two we want are still here and may be on the surface. If we capture them, we might win some points with the Board. Heron and O'Connor won't expect a small raiding party." He stopped when he suddenly became aware of the angry stares of the men around him.

He wondered why the Fleet had turned the weapon on the tree creature that had stalked them. He had been watching the defenders and had seen Heron. He had also seen him turn and direct someone else's attention to the tree, and had dismissed it as unimportant until the Royals' field piece blasted the damned thing just as it sent its snare toward them. He couldn't help but wonder why Heron would save his life and the lives of the very people who were out to get him.

The Commander just stared at him. "You may have noticed we haven't exactly had a great deal of success capturing those two on the ground or in orbit."

"Whatever," huffed Barclay, and he stomped off in the direction of the transport barges.

"THE FLEET IS HERE!" ANNOUNCED A MIDSHIPMAN, who hurried over to Lieutenant Commander Dalziel. "The *DGK* and her battle group have arrived, sir." She paused for breath. They've launched their landing barges. *Dragon*'s message says they'll be with us in thirty minutes."

"Thank heaven for that." Bob Dalziel focussed his ranging optics on the distant enemy position. "They must have received word as well. They're pulling back. Find Major Ryan. He's over in the Alpha sector. Tell him negative pursuit, and to stand by for reinforcements." Looking round, he spotted Harry. "Mr Heron, over here, please."

"Aye, aye, sir." Harry joined the Lieutenant Commander.

"As you heard, we're about to get reinforcements. Tell the command posts. When you've done that, I've another job for you."

THE ARRIVAL OF THE LANDING BARGES AND THEIR STRIKE fighter escorts brought an immediate change. Several units of the Consortium forces surrendered and others withdrew to their hidden base.

Bob Dalziel stood with the landing force Marine Major observing the enemy.

"They're preparing something. They have drawn their troops into a defensive perimeter, but it doesn't look as if they're planning to stay long."

Dalziel nodded. "Looks like they're planning to evacuate it. How long before your people can get here in the sort of strength you need to disrupt this little exercise?"

"We need another hour to bring up the weapons to crack this place. What have you got in mind?"

"I want to know what they have here. It must be important to have this level of screening, garrison and support from their fleet." He activated his link. "Lieutenant Sci'Anatha?"

The Lacertian appeared near an outcrop and strolled toward the human pair. "You wish to speak to me, Commander?"

"Ah," Bob Dalziel said with a casual air, attempting to cover his surprise. "I didn't see you there. Are any of your people able to get close enough to this base to find out what they are doing there?"

She considered. "We have reached the entrance, Commander, but we cannot go within." Hesitating, she added, "Have you not asked the Navigator or the Sword Wielder? They will hear the brain of this place, and may tell you what it thinks."

"Of course. Damn. I should have thought of that." He activated his link. "Mr Heron, what is your location?"

"At our base, sir."

"Get a transport and join me — make that an aerial. I need you here as soon as possible."

The Marine Major rubbed his chin. "Mind telling me what that was all about?"

Bob Dalziel grinned. "Let me put it this way: our Mr Heron has an unusual ability with AI systems. He can hear them." Seeing the sceptical look, he explained, "He was fitted with an internal link, but something has changed it in some way, so now he is more or less a mobile node of any AI he's near. I'm hoping he can link to this one sufficiently enough to tell me what it is doing here."

"CAN YOU HEAR IT, HARRY?"

"Aye, sir, but it is a strange system. It does nothing concerning navigation, and only a small part is running the base. It seems largely about some accounting function, trading in currencies and something related to the ownership of companies."

"Odd. Why would they have something like that here?"

"Commander!" The Marine Major's voice was sharp. "Their people are pulling out. There go the first transport barges!"

"We must leave, sir!" Harry listened again. "They have set some devices to destroy this facility, a fission weapon, they called it."

"Fission weapons?" The Lieutenant Commander turned away. "Get our people back to our camp. Now. Pull back. We don't have a lot of time before this whole place is blown to hell."

"SHIP'S IN DROPOUT IN LOW ORBIT, SOUTHERN HEMISPHERE."

"Show in Command display. Sound action stations. Alert the *Goethe*, *Foch* and *Ariadne*. Engineering to stand by. Navigation, plot intercept." The orders flowed from Captain Haakon aboard the *DGK*.

"Sir, two frigates, one transport. Identified as Consortium. They're just clear of the atmosphere."

"Navigation, set a course for intercept. Link to the frigates. I want to cut them off before they can insert reinforcements for their people."

"Shuttles coming from the surface, sir. Six large troop carriers.

"So that's what they're here for. Interceptor Group, prepare to engage. I want those barges disabled. Weapons, target the transport."

Watching his display, the Captain tapped the armrest of his chair. This close to the atmosphere and the targets he dared not risk a micro transit. Even the smallest error by any of the ships — his or those he was pursuing — could bring disaster. The targets were moving, matching velocity with his ship and staying just out of range of his weapons. He watched as his interceptors met a squadron launched by the enemy.

"The transport's done a micro transit. He must be desperate or very determined. He's made a flying recovery of four of the shuttles — there they go. Damn. I want those remaining transport barges captured." He thrust himself out of his seat. "Send the frigates after them and the interceptors. Navigation, get us back to the *Dragon*'s position."

The Navigator executed the commands. "That transport was well handled, sir. He took a hell of a chance to pick them up. Did you see the heat signature? He was inside the atmosphere when he took them aboard. No wonder he couldn't wait for the other two."

"You're right, Hans. A risky manoeuvre." The Captain frowned. "They must have had someone on one of those shuttles they had to recover. Let's hope we can find out who when we talk to those we've captured."

THE GROUND TREMBLED BENEATH THEIR FEET.

"Damn." Bob Dalziel shook his head in disbelief. "They really meant to destroy everyone and everything, didn't they?"

The Marine officer nodded. "Just as well young Heron tipped us off." He indicated a rising column of smoke in the distance. "It must have been close to the surface." His expression changed. "Everyone down! Here comes the shockwave!"

Harry felt the hot breath of the wind as it passed. It brought back memories of the sensation that followed the firing of a large cannon, though this was more like a sudden squall of wind presaging a storm. He looked in the direction of the distant Consortium base and stared at the rising cloud atop the towering column of dust and smoke.

"Thanks to you, Harry, we're alive to watch this from a safe distance. Otherwise, we'd be in bits and pieces tumbling around in that mushroom cloud."

"What is that weapon, sir?"

"You've never seen a fission bomb? No, of course not. That, Mr Heron is an old weapon, but probably one of the nastiest that mankind has ever come up with."

Harry considered this, watching the cloud towering on the skyline. "I see, sir." In his opinion, the plasma projectors and particle beam weapons fell into the same category, but he held his peace. "Permission to begin the evacuation, sir?"

"WE'VE DETECTED A NUCLEAR DETONATION ON THE PLANET, sir."

Captain Rafferty frowned. "Is it on the surface? Anywhere near our camp?"

"Negative surface, sir. It is at a hundred metres below the surface. From the signature, looks like a range of mining galleries and levels. About thirty miles from the camp, sir."

"Are our people near it?" Not waiting for a reply, he said, "Get me Bob Dalziel, pronto."

The communications officer scrambled to get the link. "Lieutenant Commander Dalziel on link, sir."

"Bob! We've detected a nuclear event down there, about thirty miles from you. Any of our people involved?"

"Negative, sir. We had sufficient warning and pulled our people away. Afraid we'll get nothing out of there though. They did a thorough job of it. Everything is gone, and there's nothing but a bloody great crater where their base was."

"Well, that's someone else's problem. Suggests they had something there they definitely wanted hidden." The Captain frowned. "How about radiation?"

"For the moment quite low, but it's set off a lot of earthquake activity. I'd like to get our people off here ASAP."

"I'll talk to Captain Haakon and get back to you with the distribution. Make a start on getting set for immediate evacuation.

Chapter 34 – Breakthrough

The survivors of the *Leander* disembarked in the *DGK*'s large hangar deck, their battered barge work stained and in need of repair among the cruiser's near pristine craft. Lieutenant Orloff saluted the Lieutenant Commander who met them. "Navigator Lieutenant Orloff and party, sir, transferring to this command."

"*Willkommen.*" The Lieutenant Commander returned the salute. He noticed the Lacertians emerging from the barge. "Ah, so these are the Lacertians who have been with you." He indicated a group disembarking on the other side of the hangar from a shuttle surrounded by Marines. "Our guests over there will not be pleased to see them."

Lieutenant Orloff followed his gaze. "I expect not. Frankly we aren't too happy to see that lot here either. I hope you've got some good holding cells for them."

"Don't worry, they will be well guarded." The Lieutenant Commander glanced round. "Is everyone here? *Sehr gut!* Come with me, please. We will get you signed in."

Harry watched as a sullen file of Consortium prisoners shuffled past. Ferghal gave a sharp intake of breath. "Harry, look — there! That man, he is one of those I saw in the access panel for the network node of this ship when they sabotaged it during our training cruise."

Ferghal stepped forward and confronted the man. "Hey, you there. I know you. You and your friend sabotaged this ship when we were last aboard her."

The man stared at Ferghal then at Harry. The whole file came to a stop, and everyone stared at Ferghal. He was only getting started. "Yes, I remember you well. You pretended you could not speak English, yet here you are among English speakers. What do you say now?"

The man scowled. "You've got me mixed up with someone else."

"*Ich weiß ganz genau, wer Sie sind,*" came the voice of the Lieutenant Commander. He summoned the nearest guard. "Keep this man separate. He is a traitor and a deserter."

The man grabbed the nearest person and threw him into the guard then dove among the group from *Leander*. What he intended he alone knew, but he made the mistake of going for Harry, whose fist caught him a stunning blow on the side of his face. He staggered and turned with a snarl of rage, his second mistake as Harry's uppercut lifted him off the floor a few inches. His eyes glazed and he crashed to the deck unconscious.

"Ouch." Harry shook his fist to ease the throbbing pain. "His jaw was harder than I anticipated," he said with wry humour, nursing his throbbing fingers.

Ariadne looked at the fallen man, then at Harry. "That was some punch," she said in an awed voice.

"You had better get your hand seen to by a medic, Herr Heron," said the Lieutenant Commander before he ordered the removal of the man Harry had knocked out.

Ferghal watched, half amused by Harry's felling of the man and half annoyed with himself for allowing it to happen. "Good milling there, Harry. A bit showy for the ring though." He grinned and clapped Harry on the back. "You need to wrap your hands for the bare knuckle work, as you should know!"

THE EVACUATION OF NEW EDEN MEANT A REDISTRIBUTION of survivors to the relief squadron since the damaged frigates could not support their full complements during the transit back to Pangaea and the repair facilities they needed. The *Leander* officers were assigned to the *DGK* for the journey, and Harry and Ferghal were assigned to Navigation and Engineering.

Ferghal arrived at the Engineering Office to hear the Commander venting his anger.

"*Der verdammt Glasfiend*! He listens to no one. You cannot reason with the man." He paused, reining in his anger. "Der Käpitan is correct though. This infernal machine will make it possible to see through the Consortium screen. He wants me to work with this maniac to solve the problems with power surges and feedback loops."

A lieutenant noticed Ferghal, and cleared his throat to get his attention.

"Ja? Ach, Mr O'Connor. You are assigned to my branch?"

Ferghal saluted. "Aye, sir. I am ordered to join your department, sir."

The Lieutenant Commander hesitated, and the other officers watched him, bracing themselves for a volatile response. Then he smiled. "You still speak no German?"

Surprised, Ferghal shook his head. "No, sir. No German."

"Good. Very good! The Herr Doktor speaks little English." He laughed. "Especially your English! Herr O'Connor, I have just the task for you."

"Aye, sir?" Ferghal noticed that the others were struggling to hide their amusement. "I shall do my best to meet your expectations, sir."

"You will, Herr O'Connor. You will." Briefly he explained the task.

"So you wish me to build a means to prevent this device from overloading the rest of the system, sir? May I see the machine?"

"Naturlich." To one of the Lieutenants, he said, "Take Herr O'Connor to the Herr Doktor's workroom. Tell Glasfiend I will see him shortly, and let Herr O'Connor see the machine."

AFTER AN AWKWARD START, FERGHAL ENGROSSED HIMSELF in work, and soon had built a surge management unit to regulate the power flows created by Dr Glasfiend's device. The doctor's mercurial temper and passion for his work drove the group to despair and frenzied activity. Building the control unit and regulators involved a huge amount of work, but at least Ferghal could largely ignore the doctor for the most part, since neither of them understood the other.

The scientist assigned to liaise between them shook her head as she watched the doctor stalk away, yet again frustrated by the blank expression Ferghal used whenever the doctor tried to browbeat him. "He does not know what to make of you, Herr O'Connor." She hesitated. "And sometimes I think you pretend that you do not understand him."

Ferghal glanced up. "Sure, and with Frederick-Wilhelm's help I understand the doctor just fine." Grinning, he added, "But if he knew that, I'd be deprived of your company."

She looked around, her expression puzzled. "*Sie sprache Deutsch*? Who is Frederick-Wilhelm?"

Ferghal paused in his work and pushed up his visor. "Frederick-Wilhelm? The ship. He tells me what the doctor is saying. It is our little secret. The ship tells me what is said, and it checks my work as I do it."

"The ship talks to you?" Her puzzled expression mingled with disbelief. "But the ship is named *Der Grosser Kurfürst. Wie sind* — who is this Frederick-Wilhelm?"

"Was that not the name of the Elector of Brandenburg?" Realising she didn't understand his meaning, Ferghal shrugged and turned up the charm. "It is a secret that the ship and I are able to communicate, but I trust you with this information. The Herr Doktor doesn't know I understand him." He winked and made her blush. Giving her his most disarming look, he added, "If my secret got out, I'd have to find who did the telling and teach her a lesson." He grinned.

For a long moment, she didn't respond, but her eyes grew wide, and she smiled as she gathered the meaning of his tease. Then she laughed. "So all my translations — you've known what he's been saying all along?"

"I had to find some excuse to keep you nearby."

Ferghal's Irish charm had just ratcheted up a notch. "You're impossible, Herr . . . I don't even know your name other than Herr O'Connor!"

"Call me Ferghal." He grinned. "He does get worked up over nothing, doesn't he? He thinks me stupid, so I encourage him. It keeps him out of my way."

"Ferghal? *Sehr gut.* Call me Ingrid, please."

"Ingrid . . . oh, yes, please."

She laughed out loud at that bold response, and it took a few minutes to get back to the business at hand. "Okay, Ferghal, so what do you want me to do?"

"Could you do all the tests and checks on the components and the interfaces as I complete the units? That will be a huge help — and keep the doctor off my back, please, Ingrid!"

WHEN THE SCANNER AND ITS CONTROLS WERE INSTALLED, Ferghal reported to the lab, now converted to a control room for Dr Glasfiend's system. Ingrid Groznic smiled a welcome and steered him to a monitoring station she'd set up. "We can watch from here in safety."

Glancing to where Dr Glasfiend and Lieutenant Commander Reuter seemed to be in a state of imminent eruption, Ferghal grinned. "Aye, best stay clear of them, and hope nothing fails!"

"Is it likely? Everything tested perfectly, and you over rated quite a lot of it."

"Aye, my blacksmithing, the commander called it." Ferghal's laugh fell into one of those inexplicable silences that occur in crowded situations, and drew the attention of both Dr Glasfiend and the Lieutenant Commander.

"Gut!" the doctor said. "You are here." He fired off a string of instructions at his team then turned to Ferghal, demanding in German, "Are you certain everything is correctly assembled?"

"Aye, sir," Ferghal replied, letting the implied suggestion that he might have got it wrong pass, and forgetting he was listening to the ship translating. "Everything is installed and ready for the test."

The doctor failed to notice that Ferghal didn't wait for Ingrid's translation, and he dashed away to another part of the compartment.

The Lieutenant Commander watched him carefully. "Herr O'Connor, your German seems to be getting very good. You have been teaching him, Frau-Doktor?" To Ferghal's surprise, he smiled then winked. *"Gut gemacht!"*

Ferghal watched him walk away and grinned. "Now I'm in the soup!"

Ingrid laughed. "Maybe, maybe not. I think he is impressed." They watched the system being prepared. Now that his part was done, Ferghal felt a little left out of the proceedings, but then he saw Lieutenant Commander Reuter standing to one side similarly excluded, and that made him feel better.

The system charged up as he watched, praying to all the saints he could think of that nothing would fail. To his own and Lieutenant Commander Reuter's surprise and satisfaction, the equipment powered up without mishap, although the atmosphere took on the taste of tin once more.

"So far so good, Herr O'Connor," the older man acknowledged him.

"Aye, sir," responded Ferghal, and then, unable to resist the temptation, added, "Perhaps my blacksmithing work was necessary after all?"

Lieutenant Commander Reuter's face froze for a moment as he turned a haughty gaze on Ferghal. Then slowly his eyes betrayed his amusement, and a smile spread across his face. "So it would seem, Midshipman, so it would seem."

Doktor Glasfiend seemed to be everywhere as the final checks and adjustments were made by his team of assistants and their technicians, his voice sometimes strident as he chased those he considered to be slow or obstinate in carrying out his directions. Finally, all was ready. The moment of truth had arrived.

Ferghal watched as his readings leapt up the scale then subsided. He breathed out again as nothing tripped, blew out or failed. The pulse repeated, again nothing failed, nor on any of the subsequent pulses, but his heart stopped as an outburst of excited German from the monitoring console end of the compartment broke the breathless silence.

"*Es funktioniert! Da ist das Shuttle! Die Röntgenbeugung funktioniert tatsächlich — das kristalline Metall im Rumpf und in den Maschinen ist deutlich erkennbar. Jetzt haben wir ihn!*" The jubilant doctor was suddenly transformed, becoming as playful and gregarious as a small boy who has just won the biggest prize at the county fair. Ferghal watched, amused, until he was startled by a hand on his shoulder, and the voice of Lieutenant Commander Reuter broke his idleness.

"Good work, Herr O'Connor. It seems that you were right. Your blacksmith work has provided us with the sort of connection we needed for this device." He smiled at the surprise in Ferghal's face. "*Alles in Ordnung, Herr O'Connor.* And if you stay with us much longer, you will learn to speak our language as efficiently as you have learned to adapt our technology." He winked. "Now I must go and make sure the madman does not attempt any so-called improvement on his equipment. I do not think even your ingenuity can overcome every problem with this device."

Thank you, sir," replied Ferghal, flattered by the compliment. "I just hope it works when we need it, sir."

"So do I, Herr O'Connor. So do I!" He walked away leaving Ferghal to thank Ingrid for her assistance. They'd formed a good friendship, one he hoped to continue.

As if reading his thoughts, Ingrid said, "It has been fun working with you, Ferghal. May we have dinner together sometime, perhaps?"

"It has been that!" Ferghal grinned. "I'll ask the Gunroom Senior if I may invite a guest."

Chapter 35 – Surprise

"*Danae* to *DGK*. We are losing our remaining transit drive. We need to drop out on the Beacon Bravo-Bravo-Sigma 449 and carry out repairs."

"Understood, *Danae*," replied Captain Haakon. "All ships, the entire squadron will drop out on my mark at the beacon. It provides an opportunity to carry out any other emergency repairs to *Leander* and *Dragon*. *Leander*, we will dock with you and do an atmosphere refreshment."

"Thanks, *DGK*. Our air is pretty foul now even with the emergency scrubbers at full power. We'll follow you in."

Manning the Engineers' desk in the Command Centre, Ferghal grimaced as he heard this. The ship's atmosphere had been topped up from New Eden, so he had some idea of how bad the smell would be when the exchange took place.

AWARE THAT CONSORTIUM SHIPS HAD RECENTLY conducted raids on orbital platforms and ships in this general area, Captain Haakon ordered, "I want that new scanner in operation as soon as we drop out. Notify Herr Doktor Glasfiend, please."

"*Jawohl, Herr Kapitän*," responded the Chief ScanRate, a senior Master Warrant Officer who busied himself with the comlink.

At his station in Navigation, Harry updated the navigation of the other ships as the *DGK* approached dropout.

"Sound Action Stations. Stand by to drop out."

The tone of the general alarm sent the crew racing for their stations in the Command Centre where personnel changed and reported their readiness.

"Dropout at three, two, one. Initiate."

The display filled with the scattered planets of a dying sun in the distance.

"Emitter ready." The scanning officer checked the newly installed displays.

"Initiate the scan," ordered the Captain. "Everything else says the sector is empty. Let's see what the doctor's machine can show us."

The first pulse returned a positive echo.

"Weapons, lock to the coordinates from the difraction scan," ordered the Captain. He opened his Command link. "All ships, lock to the coordinates provided. We have contacts with screened ships." He waited for confirmation. "Navigation, coordinate all ships. I want a hyperburst to put us on the range."

"Navigation linked," responded Commander Pösen as the general alarm sounded throughout the ship.

Harry checked his survival suit was handy and switched his monitors to battle mode, suddenly conscious of the feeling that someone or something was following his every action. He glanced round the navigation centre, but everyone was engaged in activity.

Aft, in Engineering Control, Ferghal had the same feeling, but could not find a reason. With his typical Irish humour, he dismissed it as leprechauns and set about his task of monitoring the power management for the ship's hyperpods.

The squadron leapt toward their targets in a coordinated phalanx, the damaged frigates behind them, dropping out precisely in range of their heavy weapons.

"Open fire," ordered Captain Haakon.

Explosions erupted, and a group of ships appeared, flashing up their own weapons in response.

"All ships, take independent action," ordered the Captain. "Engage independent targets." His own ship closed rapidly on the leading enemy, the fury of her fire tearing great chunks of plating from the target as the enemy ship desperately tried to take evasive action. Hemmed in by her consorts engaged by the *Swiftsure* and the two destroyers, her movement was severely restricted.

Even the damaged *Dragon* added her weight, swinging beneath the Consortium leader and scoring hits on her hyperpods. The *DGK* swung wide, opening her arcs of fire, and her weapons team took full advantage. *Dragon* danced clear as the enemy's after end disintegrated, torn open by some internal explosion. Immediately the ship switched target and joined the *Bristol* in attacking the third ship in the group.

Emden launched her missiles at close range, swinging beneath the second ship in line even as *Swiftsure* switched targets to engage the fourth. *Emden*'s missiles found their target, and Harry winced as he caught a glimpse of the scanner image of the ship tearing herself in two.

The fury of the exchange, and the fact that the Fleet ships had apparently been able to see them through their screens, was enough for the two survivors to make a desperate effort, and they successfully accelerated into transit and hyperspace, though not without suffering serious damage.

"They won't get far," remarked Commander Pösen with a note of satisfaction in his voice.

"It will have shaken them badly," replied the Captain. He paused to order the launch of the ship's barges to rescue survivors. "They thought they were invisible to us right up to the moment we fired." Opening the Command link again, he ordered, "*Swiftsure*, escort *Dragon*, *Danae* and *Leander* to the inner orbit we selected and commence the repairs on *Danae*. We'll join you as soon as we've secured all survivors and prisoners, and then we can attend to *Leander*'s atmosphere."

THE LAST OF THE SURVIVORS WERE BEING DISEMBARKED from the barges when a large freighter dropped out almost alongside. Instantly she was challenged and the ship's weapons locked to her.

"Unknown ship, you are under weapons lock. Surrender or I will open fire."

There was a moment of silence, and then a voice. "This is the freighter *Twee Jonge Gezellen*. We surrender, sir. We are unarmed and protest strongly at this unwarranted threat."

"Identify yourself," ordered Captain Haakon. "According to our records your ship is registered as having been seized. My boarding party will require access to all compartments and the holds. If your authorizations are in order, you have nothing to fear from us."

A Lieutenant signalled then held up his hand indicating the Command display where two large barges were alongside the freighter, and a swarm of strike craft held position ready to fire.

Captain Haakon frowned. "My boarding party is alongside. Open the boarding locks, please." He watched the boarding ports open and the Marines enter. *"Etwas stimmt nicht mit das."*

"Agreed, sir. The *Twee Jong Gezellen* was taken by pirates several months ago. The crew were dumped out of the airlocks without EVA or life support."

"Hmm. Lieutenant Orloff, assemble a passage crew to bring her to the rendezvous with *Danae* and *Leander*. We'll take a closer look at her there while we deal with *Danae*."

"Sir, we have the crew secured. The ship is carrying contraband, and her destination is a planet on our embargoed list, reported the Marine Lieutenant through the comlink. "Her crew appears to be small for a ship of this size. Her Captain says he had hoped to get some extra hands from the ships he expected to meet here."

"Lieutenant Orloff is on her way to bring the ship to our rendezvous with the others," replied the Captain. "When she gets there, leave four of your squad to assist the prize crew and return to the ship with your prisoners. We'll go over her thoroughly at the rendezvous."

"HARRY, FERGHAL, SHEOBA — YOU'RE WITH ME. Warrant Carolan is rounding up some TechRates. We can sort out our personal effects later if necessary. Right now, we're just moving her across the system to the rendezvous." Lieutenant Orloff checked her list. "Harry, you'll take the Navigation role. Ferghal, the drives. Sheoba can assist you."

The Warrant Officer approached and saluted. "I've got the TechRates together, ma'am. The barge is ready when you are."

"Let's go then." She glanced at Harry and Ferghal. "Got everything you need?"

"Aye, ma'am." Harry tucked a long bundle under his arm and grinned. "Ready."

THE *TWEE JONG GEZELLEN* WAS DESIGNED TO CARRY a small number of passengers and a large amount of freight. The passenger accommodation was not occupied, but the crew space was. The Marine officer greeted them in the navigation centre.

"She's all yours. My orders are to leave you four of my men as guards, and to take the ship's officers and crew back to the *DGK*. We've searched the ship. Couple of oddities — they were disturbed at their meal, and there are more places set than there are crew. But unless they have managed to jump ship, they're not aboard."

"Okay. We'll stay alert, but the transit across to the rendezvous should be no more than half an hour anyway. See you there."

Busy at the navigation console, Harry didn't see the Marine leave. "Course plotted, ma'am."

"Good." She touched her comlink. "Got the drives sorted, Ferghal?"

"Aye, ma'am. We're ready."

The Lieutenant frowned. "Harry, can you access the AI?"

"Already linked to it, ma'am. It seems frightened of someone."

"Frightened? Of us?"

"No, ma'am — frightened of its Captain."

"Well, he's no longer aboard." She hesitated. "Tell it to seal all access from the cargo spaces and all unoccupied accommodation. I want just the crew space, our control rooms and the Marines accessible."

Harry nodded. "It is done, ma'am."

"Good, and one more thing. Check the crew lists. I want to know exactly how many crew she had, when they left her, and all the officers' names. Something is not right, but I don't know what the hell it is."

ABOARD THE *DGK*, CAPTAIN HAAKON LISTENED to the report and checked the manifest. "This ship has an interesting cargo. Commander Pösen, I want her thoroughly searched as soon as we are at the rendezvous."

"Yes, sir. I'll arrange it." The Executive Officer shook his head. "Even with the people taken from the damaged ships, we're short-handed with the need to guard prisoners."

"I know. We'll have to make some adjustments. As soon as we have the barges recovered, take us to the rendezvous."

LIEUTENANT ORLOFF LOOKED ROUND AT HER TEAM. Warrant Carolan at the helm, Harry at Navigation, two TechRates, Mann and Weimar on the Coms and scanners; in the Engineering Control, she had Ferghal, Sheoba and TechRates Jürgen Sørenson and Horst Werner. "We're an international mix alright, and interspecies including Sheoba. Everyone ready?" Receiving their confirmation, she smiled. "I'll get movement clearance from the Captain. They've still got us under a weapons lock. Wouldn't want to get shot up for attempting to move without clearance!"

She looked up as Harry attracted her attention. "Yes, Mr Heron?"

"Ma'am, the crew list has been amended in the last hour. It lists only twelve now, but it also seems to show a change of Captain. I'll have to see if I can persuade the ship to show the erased files somehow, but it may take a while."

"Well done, keep digging. There was a change of Captain? When did that happen?"

"According to the ship, just as the Marines boarded. The new Captain is the man the Royals took away with them, but the old Captain signed the log just before they dropped out, and he has a different name entirely."

"The hell you say," breathed the Lieutenant. "I knew we should have kept the Bootnecks aboard! Where the hell are they?" She glared with irritation when her link chirped.

"Lieutenant Orloff."

"Ma'am," came Ferghal's voice, "someone is accessing the engineering controls from outside this space. They are trying to engage the hyperpods. I have blocked them so far, but I need Mr Heron to trace them while I block their efforts to take control."

"I heard it, ma'am."

Harry focussed his attention on the neural flow of the AI. Within seconds he found the source, then another loophole that someone else was using to input navigation data. He acted quickly, locking both terminals and instructing the AI to refuse all commands.

"I have them, ma'am. The terminals are portable, engaged through ports in the cargo bay. I have locked the ports against access, but I am not sure that will hold if they can connect another node in that area."

"Right, isolate all terminals and ports in that part of the ship." She contacted the Marines. "Corporal, have we got the cargo areas completely locked down?"

"Yes, ma'am. I have lock indicators on all internal access ports."

"Good. Sheoba, see if you can turn on the flood lighting in those spaces and record everything in sight. If we have passengers, I want to know who they are. Weimar, contact the *DGK* and tell them we have stowaways. Harry, you and Mann will stay here and monitor the network. Tell Ferghal to do the same in Engineering, and send Sheoba to me." She paused to think. "What is the atmosphere status in the holds? Are they under atmosphere?"

Warrant Officer Carolan checked his console. "They register as under atmosphere ma'am, but this system doesn't respond as it should."

"Right, that does it." She contacted Engineering. "Mr O'Connor, shut down the gravity field generators in the holds, please, then bang them back on at twice normal. Let's see what that shakes out. Warrant, monitor your console and tell me if that registers. Harry, what about you? Can you see anything unusual in there?"

"There's a lot that is not right with this AI, ma'am. It does not recognise any command not given with a key prefix. I think I can access that and disable it. With your permission, ma'am, I will disable every terminal outside this Control Centre and Engineering."

"Do it, Harry. What about the holds, Warrant? Anything show up?"

"Nothing, ma'am."

"Mr O'Connor, have you done as I asked?"

"Aye, ma'am. Gravity in holds One to Eight is now at two G."

"Keep it there. That will slow down anyone in there until we can deal with them." She turned to Harry. "Do what you can to sort out the network please. Sheoba, take over Navigation and keep station on the *DGK*. I want to stay close to her until we can sort ourselves out here." To TechRate Mann she ordered, "Open up a channel to Captain Haakon. We need to keep him in the picture."

"Captain on link for you, Lieutenant." Warrant Carolan signalled.

"Captain Haakon, we have a problem. Someone aboard this ship is trying to access Navigation and the drives from portable terminals. We're blocking them, but I need backup to find these people."

"Very good, Lieutenant, I will send a detachment of Marines to you immediately. Keep things locked down until they get there."

Chapter 36 – Unwelcome Passengers

Harry isolated and disabled every terminal and access port outside of the control centres. Then he scanned the data nodes and discovered that the network had been instructed to withhold certain functions and information.

He changed his approach, projecting into the AI's programs the idea that he, being part of it, should be given access. Then he reversed the blocks.

"I've found the blocks and removed them, ma'am, but—"

Everything lurched as the hyperpods burst into life and the ship dived into hyperspace.

"That's torn it. Damn." The Lieutenant huffed in irritation. "Mr O'Connor, shut the drives down, please. Harry, where are we headed?"

"I have no idea, ma'am!" exclaimed Harry. "The ship's own system is not guiding us. In fact, it seems unaware we're in transit."

"My controls are not responding, ma'am," Ferghal replied on the comlink. "And the AI is unable to access the drives."

"Damn! Mr Heron, try to get a navigational reading please. Mr O'Connor, track down the loss of communication with the hyperpods and manoeuvring. See if you can bypass it somehow."

The Lieutenant broke off as a voice interrupted the ship's communication system.

"Attention Fleet boarders. We have taken control of the drives and the navigation system. You are to surrender immediately and return this ship to my control. I am taking this ship to meet our main fleet, and if you fail to hand her back to me as a representative of the owners, I will have you shot by our troops when we arrive. Do I make myself clear?"

"Who are you?" demanded the Lieutenant, aware that Harry was concentrating on the AI. She played for time in the hope that he was doing what she thought. "Identify yourselves."

"I don't need to identify myself to you. I am the Master of this vessel, and you have no business attempting to take her. Lieutenant, you have a simple choice: we have control of the ship, and you and your people can surrender or die. Surrender now and I'll think about letting your people stay alive until I can hand you over to Consortium troopers. Interfere, and my people will cut you down without blinking."

The Lieutenant looked across to where Harry was holding up a page torn from the notebook he always carried. In large block letters he had written, I HAVE AMENDED THE COURSE AND LOCKED THEM OUT. He turned the sheet over to show her the other side: I DO NOT THINK THEY WILL NOTICE FOR A WHILE. Lieutenant Orloff opened her mouth to ask how when she realised that the comlink was still active. She stalled. "I will have to consider my position," she said to the man who called himself the master of the ship. "Give me some time to think on this."

"Think all you like," he mocked. "You aren't in control. Try anything clever and you'll regret it. I don't know how you locked us out of the ship's systems before, but you'd better unlock them and surrender or it'll be the worse for all of you. I'll give you thirty minutes to talk to your people. I expect compliance. "

Lieutenant Orloff looked at Harry and raised her eyebrows in a question.

Harry nodded. "The audio system is disengaged, ma'am. I have amended the course they set. The ship is now on a heading that will take us to Earth. I couldn't alter toward Pangaea or anywhere we could return to our squadron. That would have been a major shift of course, which they would have noticed immediately. As it is, they will notice the change of heading and the coordinates as soon as they think to check their progress. Do you wish me to leave it, or should I return control to them, ma'am?

"Leave it as you have set it. Have you got a name on the Captain yet?"

"Aye, ma'am. It is the original Captain. His name is Heemstra, Hendrik Heemstra. He is wanted for a war crime, but I am unable to discover what it was."

"Heemstra?" Lieutenant Orloff nodded. "Yes, you're correct on the war crime. I know all about that bastard. He had something to do with the capture of a freighter last year." She frowned as she recalled the incident. "This ship in fact! He ordered the captured crew confined in a hold then he vented the atmosphere. We have a problem here. He won't be happy when he discovers you've changed the course." Pausing to think, she asked, "Can you eavesdrop on them without their knowing? And how did you get into their network? I thought they'd isolated it from the neural net.

"Aye, ma'am," replied Harry. "They had, but by opening the communications they gave me a way in. I can listen to them at any time. Right now they are discussing how they will split up and work their way round the doors we have locked down." He gave a tight smile. "There seems to be some disagreement."

IN THE COMMAND CENTRE ABOARD THE *DGK* there was a moment of consternation as the *Twee Jonge Gezellen's* hyperpods lit up and the ship vanished into the singularity she had just opened.

"What?" exclaimed Captain Haakon when he lost communication with his prize crew. "Navigation, secure a trace on her, *schnell!* Follow her into transit, and try to get a lock on her track."

The ship lurched into her own singularity and entered transit on roughly the same bearing as the escaping freighter. The ScanRates worked like men possessed as they tried to locate and lock onto a trace for the freighter.

"No contact, sir. She may have doubled back on entry. There is too much background noise, and the power traces disperse rapidly. If she is not in sight, we have no way of finding her."

Harry's adjustment to the course had compounded the problem for the *DGK* since it put the ship on a course a full one hundred and eighty degrees away from the heading of the searching cruiser.

"*Verdammt!*" Captain Haakon glared at the blank displays, the swirling grey mists of hyperspace the only thing visible.

"Navigation, return us to the squadron rendezvous." Seating himself again, he paused to gather his thoughts. "Contact Fleet. Report our capture of the *Twee Jong Gezellen* and her escape with our prize crew."

He could only hope the ship would be intercepted and his people retrieved.

"Rheinhard, send the Marine Lieutenant to me. I want to know how they could hide a crew!"

Commander Pösen nodded. "It is done, sir. We have done everything possible for the ship to be found."

"I do not hold out any great hopes for that, Rheinhard. With Heemstra possibly still aboard, we can only hope that our prize crew will be safe when she arrives at her destination, wherever that may be."

"YOU SAY THEY'RE ARGUING AMONG THEMSELVES? That could be helpful." Lieutenant Orloff considered. "How did you get into their system? Can't you return us to where the *DGK* is?"

"To speak to us, they had to link into the ship's neural net, ma'am. That link allowed me to go back through their system, as we were to be linked to the *DGK*'s helm for the transit that they had not provided the coordinates to yet, ma'am." Harry hesitated. "They are using a small semi-portable system that must be from a shuttle. It is not very sophisticated and cannot control the ship's fusion reactors. If you desire it, Ferghal could shut down the reactors and deprive the ship of all power."

"Now that's a thought, but it would deprive us of power as well. No one actually knows what happens when you lose power to the drives in hyperspace, and I don't think I want to find out just yet." She paused, thinking fast. "We'll keep that one up our sleeves for now. Can you identify where they are exactly?"

"Aye, ma'am," replied Harry. "The ship has several concealed spaces that show up on the ship's schematic in the networl if you search the hidden data. The after end of each of the holds has a false bulkhead with an access from the hold, but I cannot tell exactly what that is. There is quite a large space behind each of these, and four of the eight are equipped for accommodation. Captain Heemstra and his people are in the spaces in holds six, seven and eight, ma'am."

"Okay, so if they are hiding there, how do we get access to them or smoke them out?"

"Ma'am?"

"Sorry, I meant is there some way we could get them out into the open, something we could initiate so we know where they are likely to come out?"

"I can check with Ferghal, ma'am. He may have some ideas since all the services run through the service tunnels between holds one and eight, and the backup systems between four and five on the other side. Perhaps we could reroute all the power and command systems to the alternate tunnel."

"Ask Ferghal. You concentrate on what they are planning. Sheoba, contact Ferghal and see what he can do about Harry's suggestion."

While Sheoba spoke to Ferghal, Harry concentrated on the AI again and listened to a heated debate between the Consortium crewmen.

THE ARGUMENT OVER CAPTAIN HEEMSTRA'S PLAN to dispose the Fleet personnel continued. Several of his people were aware of the Captain's previous record and were unwilling to be party to another such event. Listening to them, Harry searched for clues as to where the entry and exit points from these concealed spaces might be hidden. Eventually he was rewarded when one of the Captain's supporters ordered several men to leave the compartment via the exit to the main service tube to seize the Command Centre.

Alerted to the fact the hidden compartments all connected to the service tube, he warned Lieutenant Orloff of the intended attack.

"Right, now we know where they are and how they got there." She thrust herself out of her chair and stood with hands on hips, her expression angry. "Time to lay a little surprise for them." Looking around, she ordered, "Warrant, you, Weimar and Mann come with me, and tell the corporal and his people to meet us at Hatch Alpha Papa Two Zebra. That should allow us to get into the tube where they won't be able to see us, and it will put us in a position to give them a nasty surprise."

"Lieutenant," Sheoba interjected. "If you will permit, I may hide, and when they pass, I will disable the rearmost."

"That's a thought too. Right, we'll try it." She turned to Harry. "What's their status? Have they entered the tube yet?" She realised something. "Damn, I was forgetting. How much time before this Heemstra fellow expects our surrender?"

"We have twelve minutes, ma'am," replied Harry. "They're opening the tunnel access now, but must first transit the hold, ma'am."

"If he wants to talk to me, will I be able to reply from the tunnel?"

"I think so, ma'am. The tunnels are equipped with communication links. If it is not functioning, I can try to make an excuse for your absence, ma'am."

"Good, let's move people! I want to get in there before they have a chance to get started. Got the weapons, Warrant? Excellent. Let's go."

HARRY CONNECTED WITH FERGHAL THROUGH THE AI. *"The Lieutenant is going to try to intercept our stowaways in the service tunnels."*

"We had best hope she succeeds. There are more of them than we can muster, I think."

"I believe you are right, my friend. I cannot access the portable AI they are using to control the drives. It has no connection to the main system. Only the navigation system is accessible."

"They must have disconnected the drives completely from the ship or stowed them in a part of the ship that is heavily shielded, because I cannot sense them at all."

"Aye, and the man who leads them is in the mould of the worst pirates we heard stories of in our day. Listen to him on the audio links!"

From what he could hear over the link to the hidden control centre, Captain Heemstra was definitely not a man to tolerate resistance or opposition. His impatient and sarcastic manner was evident in the way he gave his orders and dealt with his own people. From what Harry could hear of them, they were no better either.

"I do not think I wish to deal with this man on any level. Let us hope he can be overcome before their plans can be put into effect."

This Captain Heemstra was exactly the sort of person that Harry loathed — bombastic, intolerant and abusive. Knowing that he was also a mass murderer did not improve Harry's opinion of him.

Lieutenant Orloff and her small force deployed quickly. The tube provided a number of options for concealment, and they took full advantage. Sheoba's ability to disappear against the background astonished the Lieutenant, as she had never seen her do this before. They took their positions just out of sight of the entry hatch where the Consortium men would enter the tube, and they settled in to wait.

They heard the hatch open then the sound of several people clambering through it. Lieutenant Orloff smiled when she realised they would have some difficulty because they were passing through an area currently bearing twice the normal gravity, and the switch back to normal would throw them off balance.

Signalling her team, she whispered this information to those closest to her. Noises in the near distance suggested the leaders were moving toward her position. *Damn. Wish I knew how many of you bastards there are*, she thought. She tried her infrared scanner. Not much help. There seemed to be six figures other than her team members, but one might be Sheoba. The first man passed her, his vision hampered by the low lighting. She felt a little relief when she registered that he wasn't using any vision enhancement optics. Letting him pass, she prepared to attack the second man when all hell broke loose around the corner as Sheoba acted.

A blast of plasma struck the deckhead, and Lieutenant Orloff ducked. Raising her weapon, she fired at the nearest figure's weapon arm. At near point blank, she couldn't miss. The plasma burned the man's suit away and his arm to the bone. His weapon clattered to the deck as he screamed in agony.

To her right TechRate Mann disabled the leader, clubbing him to the deck with a vicious blow. Weimar immobilised the man the Lieutenant had shot, and now he lay writhing on the floor, desperately trying to find relief from the agony in what remained of his arm. Lieutenant Orloff jumped over the struggling pair and dived around the corner to find herself facing an open hatch and one dazed figure struggling weakly to reach his fallen weapon, one arm broken and useless.

She stepped forward, noting that the man's face showed signs of having met the bulkhead with considerable force. She used her boot to push the weapon out of reach. About to investigate the hatch, she jumped back as Sheoba shot through it and dropped to her battle stance in front of her.

The Lacertian's eyes slowly resumed their normal mild appearance as the battle rage drained from her. "Two have fled to their hiding place, Lieutenant. Do you wish me to pursue them?"

Recovering her composure, though her pulse still raced, the Lieutenant shook her head. "No, I think we should secure these three, and then you had better keep watch for any others." To the men with her, she said, "Patch them up and secure them somewhere they can't communicate with their pals."

Contacting the Marines, she ordered, "Corporal, we have three prisoners to bring out. Set up your team to monitor the access points to the holds from the accommodation."

Listening to the acknowledgement, she switched channel. "Harry, have you managed to find out how many of these bastards are down there?"

Chapter 37 – Fight or Die

Captain Heemstra's rage made the ship's AI cringe as Harry eavesdropped. He did his best to soothe it, but was relieved when the Lieutenant returned with just two minutes to the deadline. She took the command chair again.

"That spoiled their little plan. We have three of their people out of the way and locked up where they won't be able to do anything for a while. God, that Sheoba is fast! She almost got the other two as well, but they made it back to their hiding place."

"So now they know we have a Lacertian with us." Harry paused. "I hope they don't have IR visors."

"Damn, I hadn't thought of that." She stopped as the communications system came to life.

"So, Lieutenant, you have chosen to fight," Captain Heemstra drawled. "Good, that will make this much more enjoyable for me."

"I didn't realise you were sincere in offering safe surrender for me and my crew, Captain Heemstra. Your reputation suggests that anyone who surrenders to you is unlikely to survive to enjoy anyone's hospitality." Lieutenant Orloff could barely suppress her smirk.

At first there was no response. Then, the indifference gone, he snarled, "So you have learned my name. Then you know I don't play games. I am taking this ship back. The Fleet can't help you. We outnumber you and have sufficient weapons to do it whichever way you want it. Surrender and your deaths will be quick and painless, but make me do this the hard way, and I'll make sure every one of your people dies as unpleasantly as possible."

Her pulse quickening, the Lieutenant replied, "Thank you for your offer, but I don't accept it. And now that the odds are in our favour, you may find us a tougher prospect than your last victims." She hesitated. "I will make you an offer, Captain. Surrender yourselves now and accept defeat, and I will guarantee that no one will be harmed or injured. We don't kill prisoners of war. If you force me to, we will find ways to reach you and to make sure that you are neutralised and made prisoner. This ship is under my command, and it will stay that way. If you attempt to leave your hiding place, we will know, and I will be forced to take action against you."

Monitoring the AI, Harry became aware of an attempt on one of the airtight doors he had disabled. He resorted to his pad and pencil and passed a note to the Lieutenant.

Heemstra was gathering steam. "Lieutenant, you are a fool. I shall take personal pleasure in killing you myself. No more games. You and your people will die, because that is the only option you've chosen."

There was an audible click as the comlink closed, as if someone had used considerable force to deactivate the link.

The Lieutenant looked across to Harry. "I think we'll have some angry visitors shortly. Are you still monitoring their end? What is happening at that airtight door they were trying break through?"

"I think they may be attempting to use the manual system, ma'am. Captain Heemstra just ordered his men to work their way through to Hold Four and access the service tunnel on that side."

"Damn, that makes things difficult. We can't afford to watch two access points. Are the holds on that side under atmosphere?"

Harry checked. "No, but I think they will go through the hidden compartments, and those are almost certainly under atmosphere, ma'am."

"See if you can depressurise the ones that give access to the second tunnel, and warn Sheoba if you do. That will at least slow them down. Do it gradually so that anyone in the tunnel has a chance to escape to a pressurised one."

"Aye, aye, ma'am." Harry searched the network and found what he wanted. After verifying that no one was in the compartments when he vented them — he had already seen the result of a compartment being vented and knew it was not a pleasant way to die — he started the process.

A check of the sensors showed the access hatches were secure, so he withdrew the atmosphere in the compartments adjoining holds four and five. Satisfied that the process was complete, he turned his full attention to the communication system and heard the Consortium captain ordering his men into EVA suits.

Realising the danger and guessing what the enemy was planning, he contacted the Lieutenant. "Ma'am, they are rigging in EVA gear. I think they may plan to break through the bulkhead, or perhaps they think we will deprive them of air in their compartment."

"Thanks. Any indication of where?"

"They are in Holds Three and Seven, ma'am. Those adjoin the crew galley and the galley stores for the passenger galley."

"Hmm. From there they have access to all the corridors and decks. Damn." She paused. "I want you to stay in the Command Centre and take control of the ship. Tell Ferghal to stay in Engineering. Your ability to work the ship with that link of yours and to keep us informed is our best asset. Keep me updated. I'll take everyone else with me and try to stop this."

"Aye, aye, ma'am." Harry contacted Ferghal and conveyed their orders. *"I think the Lieutenant has forgotten we can work with the AI from anywhere."*

"I believe you're right, my friend, but orders are orders — even if we cannot, at present, do much more than listen to it," replied Ferghal. *"I'm trying to find a means to reroute the control, but they must have uncoupled the drives somewhere aft of the holds. I have my cutlass to hand, and I know that Warrant Carolan has one as well. He has been learning its use for some months now."*

"Good," responded Harry. *"I have my dirk and a projector should they approach us. I fear this will be a no quarter affair, my friend."*

"I think they may have more than one way to leave those compartments, Harry, and I am unsure of how we can monitor it," Ferghal confided. *"They seem to be far better prepared for this than seems possible unless they planned in advance."*

"You are right, Ferghal. We must be prepared. I disabled their network but left it giving the responses they would expect to see if all was in order. What I could not do was transfer the control of the propulsion back to your Centre. They have a separate unit controlling the drives. It is not connected to the unit I have accessed."

"I have seen it," replied Ferghal. "A unit suited to a barge, nothing more. It will not be able to manage the ship's transit pods for long. Can they surprise us?"

"All the door and airlock controls are disabled now except on my command, so I think we can be certain they can only escape through some new hole in a bulkhead or by manually opening a door, all of which we can monitor."

Harry heard Captain Heemstra leave the compartment. "Heemstra is making for the men in Hold Three, ma'am. They are planning to cut the bulkhead from there."

"Well done, Harry. We'll see if we can head them off and deal with them. Keep me posted on any other developments!"

"Aye, aye, ma'am. What do you want me to do if they succeed in breaking through?"

"Whatever is necessary, Harry. Don't let them take control of either Command Centre. Block the access or whatever it takes, but don't let anyone take them."

"Aye, aye, ma'am, I understand you perfectly. I shall tell Ferghal the same."

"Do that. Here they come, Harry. The bastards have a plasma cutter and are slicing through the bulkheads with it."

IN THE PASSENGER STORES DECK, LIEUTENANT ORLOFF checked the disposition of her people.

"Corporal? What's the situation at your station?"

"They're using a plasma cutter to cut the door, sir. We're ready for them."

Shutting off the link, she remarked to Paul Carolan, "I hope they don't have grenades, but just in case, we'll pull back behind those cabinets. That'll put us behind them and between the door to the passenger lounge and them."

"With you, ma'am." He glanced at the smoking bulkhead. "They'll be through any time now."

Taking her position, she signalled her team. "Let them show. Then give them hell." Even after reducing the Consortium crew by three and taking into account that they would probably have to leave some of their people to run the ship from their improvised control room, her team were heavily outnumbered.

The intense flame of the cutter completed its final cut, and the section of the bulkhead slowly fell into the companionway.

Two grenades were hurled, and the detonations were shattering, but their preparations protected them. The first figure dived through amidst a hail of plasma fire, the second took several hits and fell, but the next pair made it through the gap covered by a storm of fire from behind.

"Damn, there's too many of them. And they've got armoured EVA." She signalled the others as the smoke thickened from a fire started by the plasma bursts. "Pull back to the lounge." Firing off a series of rapid bursts, she had the satisfaction of seeing another of the attackers fall.

"Go, Lieutenant. I'll cover." Paul Carolan laid down a series of bursts and saw at least one of the suited figures take a hit. He dove through the door seconds before it closed.

"It won't hold them long." The Lieutenant contacted Harry. "We've a fire in the passenger stores, Harry. Can you activate the suppression system?"

"Yes, ma'am." Satisfied the system had operated, he checked the disposition of the intruders. "Ma'am, there are eleven of us, but there are sixteen of their people, two in their hiding place, six engaged with our Marines, and eight at yours."

"Make that six. I think we got two of theirs." She ended the connection. "Get this place ready for a hot defence, Warrant. Here they come." Shifting as much of the furniture the five defenders could move to form a barrier, she watched as the incandescent glow revealed the progress of the cutter. "They'll pull the same trick with the grenades. We'll fall back to the bar area and wait for them there."

Grenades bounced into the lounge, the detonations ear shattering, followed by the attackers, who were unable to find their targets at first. Then the firing became desperate.

The defenders shifted position in short dashes in the former passenger lounge and dining space. There was only one opening through which the attackers could approach.

"If we hold them here, we have them contained."

"We've a problem if they cut another opening, ma'am."

"Doubt they'll use the cutter in here, Warrant. Let's hope not anyway."

She was wrong. A second opening appeared in the bulkhead.

"No you don't, you spailpin!" bellowed Warrant Carolan, using an old Irish insult, and he blasted the man before destroying the cutter itself with a well-aimed discharge of plasma.

Another grenade burst, the shrapnel ricocheting off the bulkheads, and everyone ducked for cover. "Bastards are trying to split us up," yelled the Lieutenant. A pair of Consortium men managed to get to a position from which they could target her. She changed position and ran straight into a bolt that burned away most of her leg. She heard herself scream in agony even as she blacked out.

THE MEN IN THE SECRET CONTROL COMPARTMENT LOOKED up when the door opened. No one entered, and nothing further happened. The senior man said, "Must be a short in the door circuit. Bloody thing was a jury rig anyway. See if you can sort it, Max."

Max levered himself out of his seat. "Hope the Captain deals with these Fleet idiots fast. These AI units aren't up to running a ship this big for much longer."

Moving toward the door, he studied the control unit. There appeared to be something odd about it, but he could not see what. Reaching for the door control he gasped as something seized him. He got a brief glimpse of a grinning reptilian face and then he was airborne.

The other two leapt to their feet as their companion smashed into the bulkhead behind them. Both froze as they saw the reptilian intruder, its mouth slightly open and its eyes blazing yellow as it struck. Sheoba seized their weapons and broke them, tossing them to the deck as if they were toy guns.

"On the deck," she hissed. "Any other move, and I will kill you."

Their pain and the immobility of their companion warned that this creature did not make idle threats. With no regard for their injuries, Sheoba secured them using cargo straps she had removed from somewhere on her way to their lair.

Chapter 38 – No Quarter Asked, None Given

"It goes badly for our people," Harry told Ferghal. "I fear the enemy is at an advantage. They know this ship well."

"It would seem so," responded Ferghal. "I too am following it on the monitoring system. I hate this sitting idle when there is fighting to be done."

"I can find no sign of Sheoba," Harry said. "Can you hear her?"

"Nothing — I have no sign of her, but they will have a watch for her now, I'm thinking." Ferghal added, "The Lieutenant is down. I heard her fall. Sounded like she was in a lot of pain, and then she was silent. Our people are divided and in retreat."

Harry's expression was grim. "I thought I heard her fall as well. I will contact the rest of the crew and direct them to assault from behind the Consortium men. See if you can find out if the Lieutenant survived, and the state of her health if she did."

Harry searched the AI and found the second part of the prize crew. "Corporal, the Lieutenant has fallen. I need you to assist Warrant Carolan."

"On my way, sir. We've taken out three of their people. The other two made a break to join their mates."

"Do your best, Corporal."

Harry contacted Jürgen Sørensen. "TechRate Sørensen, the enemy have Warrant Carolan and the Lieutenant trapped in the passenger lounge on Deck Three, Corridor Port Alpha. Take your people through the dining area and attack the Consortium people from behind."

Paul Carolan reported, "We can't get to the Lieutenant to get her out, and the bastards are pushing us back, sir."

"Do your best, Warrant, The Marines are on their way." Hesitating, he added, "I'll see if we can give you some help."

With the Lieutenant down, Harry realised that he was now technically the senior officer. He made a decision. Contacting Ferghal, he said, *"How did we deal with an attempt to recapture a prize ship in our time?"*

Harry listened to the response and nodded. *"Then let us do the same in kind. Destroy every control panel and make sure it cannot be repaired. Then join me, my friend. It is time to show these scum how we fight."*

He stood and looked about him. Collecting a heavy lever from the emergency locker, he smashed every console, tearing out the innards and methodically destroying every part.

FERGHAL JOINED HARRY WITH HIS CUTLASS IN ONE HAND and a plasma projector in the other, and a second projector tucked into his waistband. Giving him a grim smile, he said quietly, "I have laid a few traps for any who attempt to come this way. Do we give quarter if it is cried for?"

Harry returned the smile. "Only if it does not endanger us to do so. Leave no one standing who can use a weapon, as old Mr Treliving was wont to say — and he was a wise tutor. Now, my friend, I think it is time we showed these scum a taste of cold steel."

Ferghal snorted. "Sounds good to me. Which way?"

"If we go this way, we can strike at them from the flank as they pass the officers' lounge." Hesitating, Harry added, "I wish I could see their faces when they see the control centres, but there will be time enough for that when we deal with them." He gave Ferghal a grin. "Cold steel, I think. They are in armoured EVA suits. The suit will rupture and the systems malfunction, and the armour is designed to deflect plasma bursts, not blades."

Ferghal nodded. "Aye, and if the malfunction sets off the alarms, they will be unable to retaliate for a few seconds and may even act as our shields if the others try to intervene."

"So I hope."

They went down two decks and into the short companionway that led to the officers' lounge.

Cutting across this space side by side, they reached a door that opened into another short corridor that connected to the main one that ran the length of the accommodation deck. They opened the door with caution, standing on either side of it to listen to the fighting to determine the positions of the two parties.

Ferghal peered round the edge of the door then darted out, his cutlass thrusting as he cut open the fabric joint in the suit of the crouching enemy sheltering in the entrance to the corridor.

Harry used his dirk on a second man, driving it through his uniform and wrenching it hard across, evidently finding flesh and bone. The man staggered back, his face twisted in shock, and the suit's controls shorted out in a bright flash. Wrenching his dirk free, Harry made sure of his victim by slashing at the man's fingers as he tried desperately to open the fastenings on the suit. Pressing the attack, Harry drove him over the first man, who was struggling to free himself from a suit that had been slashed in several places by Ferghal's skill with a cutlass and was leaking fluids amidst bursts of sparks as the systems destroyed themselves.

Leaving the helpless and disarmed pair in a tangle of arms and legs, Ferghal took off to deal with more enemy combatants, and Harry hurled himself into the lobby across the corridor, colliding with another figure in an EVA suit. The man's weapon swung downward, and Harry rolled aside as a bolt of plasma burned the deck where he had stood moments before. He rolled to his knees and slashed desperately at the man's legs with his dirk, and had the satisfaction of seeing the suit rip, the edge of the tear turning red as escaping air and coolant drew blood with it.

The man tried to train his plasma projector on him, but Harry was too quick. The dirk stabbed upward into the suit's exposed arm joint and sank home, the man's face registering shock and pain as the projector fell from his paralysed hand. Harry wrenched the blade free and smashed the hilt hard across the suit's control panel. The blow was rewarded by a satisfactory signal of malfunction.

He aimed another stab at the other arm as the man desperately tried to grab Harry's blade. Fending this off, Harry stepped back and watched as the man slowly collapsed against the bulkhead and slid to the deck. There was another burst of fire in the corridor and then Ferghal's voice bellowing, "No you don't, you scum!" followed by the sound of steel striking something hard.

Harry leapt out into the main companionway to see Ferghal driving an EVA-suited figure back to where Warrant Carolan had emerged from another lobby, his cutlass slashing at yet another retreating man while he held the first at bay. Ferghal's combatant desperately tried to set his plasma projector to a bearing he could use to shoot his attacker while warding off the slashing attack of that lethal blade, and he failed miserably at both. His suit bore signs of the damage Ferghal had inflicted, and he was obviously aware of the danger behind him.

Harry checked the opposite direction and found the corridor clear except for three more suited figures lying motionless. Behind him he heard the sound of a struggle and turned to see the Warrant Officer force the Consortium man to the deck and then rip the suit open, no mean feat, and a clear indication, Harry thought, of how angry the Warrant must be.

Sheoba materialised beside him. "Navigator, are you well?"

"Yes, I am well, but we have several of their people here, and I know not how many more at large. Do you have news of the rest of them?"

"They have gone to the control centres, Navigator. They did not see me, but they are not pleased with what you have done, and I could not surprise them this time."

"At least we know they are there. Do they have the Lieutenant with them? Has she survived? She is not among those here." He turned as Warrant Officer Carolan joined him. "Where is Lieutenant Orloff?" Harry asked him.

"I think she's with them, sir, but I don't know if she survived. She got hit by a plasma bolt in the passenger lounge where these bastards came through the bulkhead and jumped us." He looked troubled. "We had to leave her in the lounge, and when I tried to get to her so that we could bring her with us, they grabbed her and pulled her out."

"You did your best, Warrant. What has become of the others in our crew? Where are Sørensen, Werner and Mann?"

"All with us now, sir. I detailed them to take charge of the wounded prisoners."

"Very well. Ferghal, take Warrant Carolan, Werner, Mann and Sheoba and search this deck and the control centres. Have a care, my friend, for this Captain Heemstra is a man entirely without honour." Addressing the Corporal, he said, "Your men took down three, but two escaped?"

"Yes, sir, but we got them. They are all here in this group. They'll be no trouble now, sir."

"Very well. Come with me, and bring two of your people. The others had best stay here and secure the prisoners. If any are dead, leave them secured. See what you can do for the injured, and place them with our earlier captives. I will check on the Captain's quarters while you search the control deck."

Satisfied that the prisoners were secure, and ashamed to find himself sorry that none were dead, Harry checked the AI for traces of the missing Captain and his companions.

"You have inflicted damage to my manual interfaces. How will I know what they want of me?"

"We will repair them. It was necessary to prevent the man who stole you from your original Captain from taking control again. Now I need you to help me find him."

"He is in the Captain's quarters attempting to use the interface to access me. Should I allow it?"

"No! Where are his companions?"

"They are in Engineering Control."

Harry set off at a run, going up a deck to where the Captain's spacious quarters occupied half the forward end of the ship.

Approaching the head of the companionway stairs with caution, he found the corridor empty and the doors closed to the Captain's quarters and the Chief Engineer's, which occupied the other half of this part of the deck. He approached the Captain's door and checked the access log.

A grim smile spread on his face when he saw that the door was open, and the occupant of these quarters was attempting to bypass Harry's blocking codes on the console. Harry was smugly satisfied when he heard Captain Heemstra swearing at the network when it refused to respond to his efforts.

Harry heard someone groan in pain, and Heemstra snarled, "I am finished with you, Lieutenant. Your people have destroyed my ship and caused me more trouble than any of you are worth."

A blast of sound made Harry wince, and he stepped back to one side of the door, ready to activate it and rush in when he realised Captain Heemstra was about to open it from the other side.

Harry braced himself, his dirk at the ready, and as Heemstra cleared the opening, he leapt forward and drove the dirk deep through the suit and into the man's side.

"Take that, you damned murderer," he snarled as he wrenched the blade clear and slashed again at the figure's swinging arm, the projector clutched in the gloved hand sending a burst of plasma that burned the bulkhead.

Harry's blade found the charger unit on the projector. A burst of incandescent heat engulfed a section of the blade and the gloved hand holding the projector. He swung again, this time directing the blow at the control unit on the front of the suit. There was a satisfying burst of sparks as the controls were torn apart and the figure staggered backward, desperate to escape this hard-eyed youth with murder in his heart and a blade in his hand to deliver it. Harry drove him back, his blade poised, the killing lust running high in his veins. This murderous bastard would not escape him now. Nothing mattered as he focussed all his attention on the terror in the man's eyes as he retreated.

Captain Hendrik Heemstra stumbled backward in the rapidly failing EVA suit and saw death grinning at him behind the grim youth with the antique weapon in his hand. Turning, he scurried behind the desk and console that occupied one end of what had been his quarters. Desperately tearing loose the latches on the suit with his uninjured hand, he ripped it open, suddenly aware that he was bleeding profusely, and his hand was burned down to the bone.

"Don't kill me!" he screamed. "I surrender. I surrender. Please don't kill me! I'm hurt. I'm bleeding. Help me...." His voice trailed off with a whimper.

"Help you?" Harry felt the bloodlust draining out of him. Suddenly he felt sick. Here was a man pleading for his life, but this man had taken many more lives without a thought. A memory of the torn and burned corpses on New Eden, and the disfigured and distorted corpses retrieved from the destroyed compartments on *Leander* swam before Harry's eyes. His gaze took in the body of his Lieutenant, one leg and most of her head burned away. "You ask *me* for mercy? What mercy did you show my Lieutenant? What mercy did you show the original crew of this ship? Yes, *Captain*

Heemstra, I do know about the original crew and how you came to be her Captain." He stared with contempt at the whimpering man. "If I were like you, I should do to you what you have done to so many. I would place you in the airlock and send you out into space But I am not as you are, and I will not sully my name or the Fleet's with such action."

He lowered the blade as Ferghal and Sheoba rushed into the cabin. To Ferghal he said, "Call TechRate Sørensen to render first aid. Then lock this murderous pirate in isolation. We will hand him over to the authorities as soon as we reach Fleet headquarters in Earth orbit."

Rallying slightly, Captain Heemstra laughed weakly. "You'll be lucky! How do you plan to control the ship without the control centres? Fleet may think they're God almighty, but even he couldn't control this ship without the network." He glared at Harry and said with an air of triumph, "You have been too clever by half, my young friend. With the controls gone, we're all as good as dead now."

"Really?" Harry turned his eyes on the scowling Captain. "Would you care to look at the console display in front of you?" He waited until the man, somewhat reluctantly, looked at the screen. "Now let me see," Harry mused with nonchalance. "Here is the ship's log, and here is the manifest, notable by the absence of certain items you have in the real manifest, coming up now. Oh yes, and here is the modified Watch and Station Bill you so thoughtfully provided, and the course and destination you fed in from your little rat hole."

His contempt for the visibly shaken man boiled to the surface. "Do you really think for one moment, Captain Heemstra, that I would have ordered the destruction of those control consoles if I did not have another means at my disposal to control the ship?"

To Jürgen Sørensen, he said, "Take him away, please, Mr Sørensen. Keep him alive and ensure that he is kept isolated from everyone else. Get Mr Werner to assist you in making sure he has no weapons hidden, no means to access any network and no means with which to deprive the courts of their opportunity to hear his crimes. Then send Mr Mann and Warrant Carolan to me here. The Lieutenant will need to be accorded a decent burial in due course."

"*Jawohl*, Herr Heron," replied Sørensen, his voice rumbling from deep within his tall, solid frame. Then, as if he were merely picking up a ragdoll, he dragged Captain Heemstra to his feet and almost tore the man out of his EVA suit before propelling him to the door.

To Ferghal and Sheoba, Harry said, "Have you captured the remaining men?"

"One has escaped and is hiding somewhere," said Ferghal. "Warrant Carolan is searching the ship for him."

Harry nodded. "Then we must find him quickly. I want the drives returned to the control of the ship's network as soon as possible. Navigation too, but we must secure the ship first."

Chapter 39 – Taking Command

The search was painfully slow business. It seemed incredible that there could be so many spaces where a person could conceal him or herself. On Harry's orders they searched each deck sealing each door as they did so. As they completed the main deck, TechRate Mann found an abandoned EVA suit, and for Harry the whole picture changed when he realised the suit was designed for a woman's use. His notions of propriety and chivalry clouded his thinking. "A woman, you say? But this is unconscionable! We must find her quickly. If she is injured, she may need help. She may be in fear of us, and I would not wish her injured further."

It was almost his undoing when he opened the next door without caution, his mind filled with the need to find a possibly injured woman.

Sheoba's lightning responses saved him. The bolt of plasma singed his cheek as she threw him aside. A scream of rage and fear followed the sound of a brief struggle. The Lacertian emerged, her prisoner screaming obscenities, helpless in the iron grip of her captor.

Harry picked himself up off the deck and retrieved his fallen dirk, momentarily unable to believe his ears. Surely no lady used language such as this! He had certainly heard this and worse on a woman's lips, but they had been trollops and fish sellers. No woman of any breeding would behave so.

His temper flared as the narrowness of his escape boiled up inside him.

"Silence!" he roared, his voice filling the compartment and echoing along the corridors.

Everyone froze. For several seconds no one moved. Then the woman sneered and said, "Well, well, look who we have here." She eyed him from head to toe and back again. "If it isn't the escaped lab rat. I enjoyed experimenting on your body, Heron." Her smirk was positively vile.

Harry's Irish temper had reached its limit. "Lab rat, am I?" his voice now ominously quiet.

Ferghal, who alone had witnessed Harry's fury and knew that the quietness of his voice meant he was only just barely in control, moved to where he could intervene if necessary.

Harry's eyes blazed, and the woman found herself looking into pools of white-hot fury. "Oh yes, I recognise you, Katerina de Vries, dragon queen of the Johnstone torturers," Harry said, remembering how she had taunted, teased and flirted with him to entrap him in the lab on Pangaea two years earlier. "You are no woman. You are nothing but a beast from the deepest pits of hell. You are unfit to breathe the same air as decent folk. You are unfit to share the name of humankind. You consort with the devil, and you shall suffer with the devil. You are filth in my eyes and an insult to womanhood."

Katerina opened her mouth to protest then stopped when the tip of the antique blade touched her nose.

Harry shook Ferghal's restraining hand from his arm as his friend intervened. His voice almost a whisper, he said, "My blade is carried with honour. I will not soil it with your blood. I will not sully my name nor even the name of any of my crew by destroying you as you destroyed those who had the misfortune to be your lab rats." He could smell her fear now and saw it in her eyes. "Yes, I am the lab rat who escaped, so I guess that makes me the better man, doesn't it? I managed to get out of your lair and trap you and several others in it. But you would do well to remember that rats also bite, and their bite may be fatal. Take care you do not get bitten. After you and your people had done with me, I felt I had been demeaned as a human being. I felt violated, dirty and ashamed. Though it cost me my soul, I will destroy every last one of you."

He let the sword point indent her skin just enough to show her that he meant what he said.

Finally, he stepped back, and Katerina let out a visibly shaky breath.

"Get her out of my sight," he ordered. "Keep her from the others, and let Sheoba be with whoever attends her. If she makes any attempt upon any one of you, I shall kill her myself."

He stalked out of the compartment shaking with the effort to control his fury. He paused out of sight to lean against the bulkhead and say a silent prayer for help and forgiveness for his murderous desires.

Ferghal and Sheoba found him a short while later, seated in the command chair amidst the destroyed controls, his damaged dirk resting in his hands. He was still shaking, his face white with rage. He looked up, his eyes bright. "Sheoba, thank you for saving me from my stupidity. I will not make that mistake again."

Sheoba bowed, making her gesture of respect, slightly awed by this new Harry she was seeing.

"Damnation," he muttered. "These scum make me feel unclean! Damn the lot of them to the eternal pit of fire!" He calmed himself, forcing his mind to address the problems of running this ship. "Sheoba, show Ferghal where the access is for the hidden control centre. I will transfer the Navigation system. We have a ship to deliver to the Fleet. Let us make a start." He looked at the blade of his dirk, the metal discoloured with blood and the edge partly destroyed were it had made contact with the plasma projector's charger unit. "I fear my dirk now bears the record of our fight. I shall have to acquire something of less personal importance should we have to fight again lest I destroy it utterly."

"Fear not, Harry." Ferghal felt relieved to see his friend returning to his normal controlled self. "I know I can repair it for you, but I recommend a cutlass for the future. It is truly a working man's weapon, but effective nonetheless." To himself he thought *Neither a dirk nor a cutlass is the weapon a Captain carries. As our Captain now, you shall have a sword. I shall see to it as soon as we have this ship secured.*

THEIR DETERMINATION TO PREVENT HEEMSTRA AND HIS crew retaking the ship had perhaps been over enthusiastic. And now there was a further problem.

"The shuttle controls they used to operate the drives are failing," Ferghal told Harry. "We must reconnect it to the AI as soon as possible. The only way to regain control is to dismantle the connections and return them to their proper links. I have tried to link the shuttle unit back to the ship, but it cannot be done."

"But that will shut down the drives, will it not?" asked Harry.

"So will the failure of the current arrangement. And that is already showing signs of it." Ferghal paused. "Uncoupling the drives while in operation will shut them down unless I can hold them in operation by acting as a bridge until the connections can be restored. It will be difficult, but it should work."

Harry shook his head as he considered the severity of the situation. "They must have known this when they set it up."

"True. But I don't think they intended to continue with it. They perhaps planned to drop out of hyperspace again as soon as they were clear and then restore the link, but we do not have that luxury. The unit they used is failing rapidly."

Harry considered their options. The lieutenant was dead, her murderer under lock and key and tranquillised because of his injuries. Harry had his own people to save, and several prisoners. If he left this situation, they could all die. If he ordered Ferghal to go ahead and it failed, they would certainly die.

"Very well, my friend, see what you can do to prepare, and then we will have to attempt it as soon as possible," agreed Harry. "Advise me when you are ready."

FERGHAL WORKED OUT THE STEPS AND THE SEQUENCE. Then he assigned each of his team members a task, and rehearsed exactly how it must be done.

Left to himself, Harry checked the star charts and databases and found there was nowhere they could safely drop out while the reconnection was made. It seemed they had no option but to attempt this while in transit. It represented a huge risk, but he could see no alternative.

His thoughts were interrupted when Ferghal connected with him through the AI.

"Harry, if I take control of the drives, can you link to me and help me stay in contact with the network while Sheoba and TechRate Mann switch over the circuitry? I must keep the control circuits active while this is done or the drives will shut down."

"Of course. I have transferred the navigation already, so I am free to assist." Harry hesitated, suddenly conscious of another presence in the AI. "Ferghal, there is something or someone else in the system. Do you sense them?"

"I do, but we have little time to waste. Help me do this quickly lest they seek to prevent it."

Taking a position where he could signal his intentions, Ferghal nodded. To Sheoba and the waiting TechRate, he said, "Watch for my signal. I may not be able to speak once I take control of the drives. Get those circuits moved as fast as you can."

Linking to Harry, he whispered a prayer as he sought out the drive controls and immersed himself in the complex stream of commands that kept the drives operating and stable. He sensed Harry supporting and helping to hold circuits and systems in operation, then suddenly felt a third presence. He was about to withdraw and alert Harry when he felt a sense of calmness descend and somehow, he knew that whoever it was wished to help. He checked the circuits again, and when he was sure he had everything, he made a slight gesture, which Sheoba spotted and correctly interpreted as the signal.

"Now, Mr Mann, quickly," she hissed.

The transfer took mere minutes, but for Ferghal it was the longest few minutes of his life. He struggled to hold his concentration on the multiple links simultaneously. At one point, he sensed the third presence intervening through his own failing grasp on the circuits.

Then it was finished. The transfer was complete.

He staggered as he removed himself from the system and sat down with his head in his hands, a splitting headache pounding his temples.

Drawing a sobbing breath, he gasped, "One minute more and my head must have exploded. It is done, my friend. The system will now function on automatic until we tell it not to. It was not a minute too soon, either — the multitask processor in their unit was overloaded and would have failed within the next hour. It had not the capacity for a plant of this size and complexity."

Harry nodded. "They could not have had much time to arrange it."

His headache worsening, Ferghal agreed. "Lieutenant Orloff's precautions must have frustrated their intention of making a brief transit while they dealt with us." He hesitated then said quietly, "Something was assisting me, not unlike the time the Siddhiche guided me on the *Vanguard*. I wonder why they help us?"

"I felt it too. Perhaps they want to assist us in this. But why are they here? I wonder what they seek? And why with us?" Harry paused. "Perhaps we shall have time to learn this, for I do not think we shall be told." Indicating the wrecked controls, he grimaced. "Now that we have the ship, we must bring her under control." His mind had already moved on to their next problem. "I have a problem with the navigation. If I attempt to put us on a course for Pangaea, we must needs pass directly through an area where we will almost certainly encounter the Consortium ships in force. To turn back and seek the company of the *DGK* and the others runs a similar, although lesser, risk. That leaves us but one option: we must press on and take the ship directly to Earth."

"Aye, that would make a deal of sense," replied Ferghal wearily. "How long would we have to remain in transit to do that?"

"I estimate three months." Harry rechecked his figures. "Yes, about three months and some days. And for almost all of that we will have to stand watch since only we can operate the controls should that be required." He smiled. "We were too efficient in our cutting the sheets and halyards, my friend. We cut the tiller ropes and the stays as well!"

Despite his headache, Ferghal grinned. "And now we must face a problem of our own devising."

Harry nodded. "Precisely." He drew in a deep breath. "I have considered, and I think that some of the essential displays can be rerouted to screens we could salvage from elsewhere on the ship, provided my Engineering Commander agrees."

"Engineering Commander? But we have ... ah." Ferghal smiled. "What do you intend, Captain?"

Chapter 40 – Long Way Home

It took a great deal of coaxing by Harry to convince the AI that he intended it no further damage. Cautious at first, the AI was reluctant to do more than answer his questions. It was even reluctant to accept his commands.

Harry decided to set the record straight. *"We cannot continue like this, suspicious of one another. How would you prefer me to address you? If we are to be joined in this way, you may address me as Harry through my link. If we use the audio system, I would prefer Mr Heron."*

"My teacher was Nikolaus. I liked his name. You and the other, Ferghal, are human, yet you are part of my databanks and programming. I do not understand this."

"Neither do we, but it gives us the ability to know each other and to work together more efficiently. May I call you Nikolaus?"

The AI concurred, and when Harry finally withdrew from the system, he was confident they could now safely navigate the ship home. In the process he'd learned a great deal about the ship's original capture and the manner Heemstra and his men had used it.

HARRY LOOKED UP WHEN FERGHAL ENTERED THE COMMAND centre carrying a long bundle under his arm. "Two hours before our change of watch, my friend," he said. "What is the problem?"

"Mere hours from dropout, and you ask what the problem is?" Ferghal grinned. His mood lightened as he produced the long object carefully wrapped in a heavy cloth. Ferghal had spent many hours painstakingly making this gift for his friend. It was, he felt, the very least he could do to show his appreciation for all that Harry had done for him before and since their arrival in this new age. Handing it to Harry, he said, "This is for you, Captain Heron. I hope you will use it well."

Accepting the parcel, Harry carefully unfolded the wrappings to reveal a new officer's sword. Drawing the blade from the scabbard, he studied it with pride.

"Ferghal, you should not have done this," he said, admiring its gleaming beauty, but he was secretly pleased. Sheathing the weapon again, he laid it carefully aside then dug into his pocket. "A blade must be paid for, and I have no coin!"

Ferghal laughed. "A pledge will suffice. Weyland the Smith takes payment in kind when necessary."

Seeing the puzzled expressions on the faces of the others, Harry explained, "In the old legends, Weyland was a fairy blacksmith — his blades were reputed to be the finest forged, and he was said to be the hand that forged all blades. Those who fail to pay him suffer injury from the same blade."

"A strange legend, Navigator," Sheoba commented. "This Way-land worked metal? Iron only? Or other metals?"

"In our time, a blacksmith worked iron, but some had secret means to make their work superior, and others knew the secret of making steel." Harry found what he was looking for. Placing it in Ferghal's hand, he continued. "I pledge before these witnesses to redeem this token at Scrabo with the price of this blade."

Grinning, Ferghal accepted the small metal token. "Let it be the silver penny of tradition."

"WE WILL BE IN POSITION TO DETECT THE TRANSIT GATE beacon in two hours," Harry said, rising from the command chair. "I shall be very pleased to bring this passage to a close, my friend."

"And I." Ferghal glanced at the displays. "Should we not give warning of our approach?"

"Aye, we should, but we have nothing with which to do so." Harry let out a weary sigh. "My concern is that while we can see ships converging on the gate, anything coming toward us may not be visible in time for us to avoid hitting it. I am counting on the gate sensors detecting our approach and preventing any other from entering transit on a collision course."

Staring at the display, Ferghal paused. "Aye, that would not end well." Settling himself into the chair, he began the process of allowing himself to become an extension of the AI. "It will be complex enough without that."

THE *TWEE JONGE GEZELLEN* DROPPED OUT, JUST AS HARRY intended, through the Near Earth Gate Southern Hemisphere Indian Ocean, and decelerated swiftly. Only the members of the prize crew on the ship were aware that it was being controlled by the mental link between Harry, Ferghal and the ship. The effort required all their concentration. Perforce Harry ignored the demands for identification from the Gate Controllers on Orbit Three, and they were now closing the docking station rapidly.

Realising the seriousness of this, Warrant Officer Paul Carolan took the initiative and opened a communication channel from his station. "Gate Control, Gate Control, this is the Prize *Twee Jonge Gezellen*, Midshipman Heron of the *Der Großer Curfirst* in command. We have damaged controls, and Mr Heron is unable to speak to you at the moment. Hypercoms are out. We have only our ship-to-ship coms. We need assistance urgently and a security team. We have prisoners aboard."

"*Twee Jonge Gezellen*, you are ordered to take up a stationary orbit at one thousand miles from Orbit Three and prepare to be boarded. Acknowledge compliance immediately."

"Received and understood. We will have the boarding airlock open to receive you. *Twee Jonge Gezellen* out." Paul Carolan turned to Harry. "Mr Heron, I hope you heard that." He saw Harry's almost imperceptible nod, and breathed a sigh of relief.

Immersed in the network, Harry told Ferghal, *"Cut the drives. We will need the manoeuvring engines in two minutes."* He waited, conscious of Ferghal operating the circuitry to cut one set of engines and bring others online.

"Done. Manoeuvring online when you need them."
"On my order then. Give me the braking sequence starting now."
"Aye, aye. Braking sequence in progress."
"In fifteen seconds bring us to this bearing . . . five, four, three, two, one, now."

The observers on the approaching corvette saw the flares as the freighter fired her braking jets sequentially, slowing imperceptibly. Then her manoeuvring engines fired, which turned the ship onto her final bearing before finally, the flare as her braking engines brought her to a geo-stationary orbit.

The corvette's commander placed his ship alongside the freighter and launched his boarding party across the intervening space, noting with satisfaction that the other ship's airlock was already opening as they approached. The first boarders passed through the opening and the hatch closed behind them.

"Ship is secure, sir," the Marine Lieutenant reported. "It is the prize *Twee Jonge Gezellen* under command of Midshipman Heron."

"Why didn't they report themselves?"

"Hypercoms are out, sir."

"Give me a full report as soon as you can."

THE MARINE LIEUTENANT ENTERED THE CONTROL CENTRE and stopped in amazement, his Sergeant and another Marine colliding with his back.

"Good God," he exclaimed. "How the blazes did you guys get this thing here?"

"It's a long story," replied Harry, his tiredness showing in his face. "Perhaps you could secure our prisoners first, and then I'll explain it. Warrant Carolan, would you show these gentlemen where we have the former crew bottled up? Thank you."

"With pleasure, sir." Paul grinned. "I think they may be glad to see you fellows. Their quarters have been a bit basic, and some need a little medical help."

"Deal with that, Sergeant." Signalling his Sergeant to follow, the Lieutenant opened his helmet and looked round. The damaged and destroyed control consoles showed their uselessness now that he could see them clearly. The ship should not have been capable of maintaining transit, never mind the dropout and then the neat manoeuvring that brought her to this parking orbit.

"When did this happen?" he asked. "You couldn't have controlled this wreck from here."

"As I said, it's a long story." Harry sank into the command chair. The relief at having safely delivered his crew and the ship was beginning to have an effect on his legs. "We took this prize in the Sirius sector when the *DGK* and her squadron caught her escorts flat footed and she dropped out right alongside us. She surrendered under our weapons — they had no choice really." He glanced about him. "What we didn't know when we came aboard was that the bulk of her crew were concealed in hidden holds. They tried to take her back."

"So how did you stop them?"

Harry shook his head. "Their Captain Heemstra killed Lieutenant Orloff. She had been wounded, and he executed her when he saw what we had done to the Control Centre. They outnumbered us and came close to succeeding in their enterprise."

"Obviously they didn't, but are you saying that *you* tore these controls apart?"

"We did," admitted Harry, glancing at Ferghal for support. "I wasn't going to let them take the ship anywhere, and only Ferghal and I could do it with these control interfaces destroyed, so we destroyed them."

"Where the hell did you guys get that idea?" demanded the Lieutenant.

"Well, it's sort of an old idea in a new guise," replied Ferghal, his exhaustion showing. "You see, in our time, if you wanted to disable a prize ship while you took another, you cut her rigging so she could not be sailed. Mr Heron simply did the same here, and I did it to the engineering control interfaces. Without the interfaces they could not manoeuvre her — him."

"But how the hell did you control the ship after destroying all this?"

"Well, we can get into the network another way," explained Harry. He was about to elaborate when the Marine cut in.

"Right, so you had a backup interface hidden somewhere." The Lieutenant grinned, falling for the ruse. "Good plan. Right, I better report in." He busied himself contacting the corvette while Harry and Ferghal carefully avoided each other's eyes in case they gave away their enjoyment of the misunderstanding of their actual means of controlling the ship.

THE DOOR OPENED, AND THE SERGEANT ENTERED accompanied by the Marine Corporal.

The Corporal saluted. "Corporal Nielsen, sir. *Der Große Kurfürst* detachment. We've got prisoners to hand over, sir."

"Thank you, Corporal. Sergeant, arrange transport."

"In hand, sir. We've got a right prize here." The Sergeant glanced at Harry. "These gentlemen have brought in Heemstra and Katerina de Vries — both top of the wanted list for murder and sabotage." Pausing, he added, "Heemstra lost most of his right hand while attacking the Mid — sorry, the Acting Captain, and de Vries says she wants to lay charges against Mr Heron for threatening to kill her."

The Lieutenant looked at Harry in disbelief. "You guys captured Heemstra and de Vries? Do you know how dangerous that pair are?"

"We certainly found out," agreed Harry. Standing, he picked up his sword. "As for Miss de Vries, she may lay all the complaints she wishes. It is no concern of mine. I am perfectly happy to have the ship's own logs opened for inspection. Her behaviour and actions will condemn her. Personally, I have no desire to see or speak to that creature now or ever again. She had her chance to kill me — twice. She missed it both times. My own mistake gave it her, but I will not be so foolish again. I could have killed her. I had the opportunity and the desire, but I would not permit myself to stoop that low, not for any purpose."

Harry's face told the Lieutenant that, as far as he was concerned, the matter was closed, and he let it drop.

"You chaps have done a fantastic job," said the Lieutenant. "Nineteen of them against twelve of you, and most of your people not trained for this kind of combat. Those are pretty serious odds even for my squaddies." He watched the prisoners being herded toward the airlock, Captain Heemstra and the former medical technician under separate guard. "What did you guys do to them? They all seem to have stab or cut wounds." He looked at Harry. "Your people haven't been abusing them while in transit, have they?"

Harry turned a cold eye on the Lieutenant. The atmosphere developed a distinct chill. "Most certainly not. They chose to fight, and we met them hand to hand. Mr O'Connor and Warrant Carolan are extremely handy with a cutlass, and I made use of my dirk during the battle. In close quarters a blade is more effective than a pistol if wielded by someone who knows the art, and when plasma projectors malfunction, a blade is your only resource. As far as this scum is concerned—" He waved a hand over the prisoners. "They showed no mercy when they seized the ship from its original crew, and would have shown, indeed did not show, any mercy in their attempt to take it from us. My Lieutenant's body lies in the hold as proof. The wounds you see are the result of our fight sir, and if any man or woman . . . " he glared at Katerina " . . . says otherwise, they are liars. We did our best to give them aid with the medical resources available to us once they had surrendered and the ship was secure, which is far more than can be said of their plans for us."

He looked the Lieutenant directly in the eye. "If you doubt me, sir, you may take with you the ship's own record of the fight and the monitoring of the cells throughout the voyage."

The Lieutenant noted the anger etched in Harry's face and the fire in his eyes. "I don't think that will be necessary. I merely had to ask the question. I am sure that everything you've said will be confirmed by the ship's log and the medics. Now, sir," he accorded Harry the courtesy of his temporary position as commander of a ship. "My people will take the prisoners across to our ship for now. We can send tugs out to fetch you in, or you can wait here to receive berthing instructions."

Harry relaxed slightly. "Thank you. I will signal for berthing instructions, and I must report to the Station Admiral for further orders. Is there any word on the *Der Größe Kurfürst* or the squadron we were with?"

"I'm afraid I don't know the movement orders, sir, so I can't say if your ships are en route."

The Lieutenant finally noticed the sheathed sword attached to Ferghal's belt. *So this is the infamous cutlass*, he mused. He looked again at Harry and realised that he had overlooked a similar weapon sheathed in his belt.

The Lieutenant looked from Harry to Ferghal and back again as understanding dawned. "Wait a moment. You talked about cutting rigging earlier. And you said your name was Heron? Are you the guys who got caught in that time slip everyone was talking about?"

"We are," responded Harry.

"So you took them on with these swords?" He looked from Ferghal to Harry. "May I see one?"

"Certainly," said Harry. "Mr O'Connor, would you show the Lieutenant your cutlass, please?"

Ferghal drew his cutlass and passed it to the Lieutenant, taking care to present it in a manner that made clear it was not being surrendered.

The Lieutenant studied it briefly and tested the weight and the edge. He looked at Harry. "You took on men in EVA suits and modern weapons with this?"

"We did," replied Harry. "A man in an EVA suit is very vulnerable to a determined man with a bladed weapon at close quarters, especially if that man thinks a cutlass is a toy. It is not a mistake he makes twice and survives."

"THE NEWS JUST IN IS THAT THE FREIGHTLINER *Twee Jonge Gezellen*, captured by the Consortium eighteen months ago, and the centre of a major criminal investigation when the bodies of her crew were found drifting in space without protective suits, arrived today at the Southern Hemisphere Indian Ocean Gate. She has been brought in by a small group of Fleet personnel, bringing with them the persons wanted for the murder of her original crew and several other crimes. We cross live to Orbit Three where our reporter has obtained permission to board the vessel and meet the young men who brought her home."

Niamh L'Estrange glanced up at the screen to see what the excitement was about, her needlework idle in her lap. The camera angle changed, and the view focussed on an outer door opening for an airlock. A grinning face appeared, his hair a deep russet, his uniform that of a Fleet Warrant Officer. Beyond him several more figures could be seen as the Warrant Officer said, "Our Captain is waiting for you, gentlemen. If you'll follow me, please."

The commentator began a running dialogue of what he could see and deduce from the route he was following and the evidence of fierce fighting visible in burn marks, holes and blast damage as they moved.

"Certainly been a battle aboard her," commented Theo from his comfortable chair. "Amazing that they managed to get her here by the look of it."

The commentator was saying, "And the notorious Captain Heemstra and his partner, Katerina de Vries, led a party that outnumbered the Fleet prize crew. Grand Admiral Cunningham has given us a full statement, and expressed his admiration for the achievement of the young men who took charge and brought the ship back after their officer, Lieutenant Orloff, was killed during the fighting. And now we are entering the Command Centre to meet the man who led this crew."

Niamh let out a shriek of joy, her needlework flying across the room as she leapt to her feet. "Harry! And Ferghal! They're home! They're safe! I shall give them such a talking to when I get them home," she declared. "Why couldn't they have let us know they were safe?" She collapsed into her chair again with tears of joy running down her face.

"I expect they had good reason," Theo said, his eyes on the projected image of the damaged control consoles in the ship. "Very good reason."

THE GRAND ADMIRAL RETURNED THE SALUTE AND STUDIED Harry and Ferghal across his desk. "At ease, gentlemen." Walking round the desk he held out his hand. "Gentlemen, you have, between you, logged quite a record of achievement. Three ships destroyed, a prize brought in under very difficult conditions and in the face of a superior and hostile force aboard. Well done."

"Thank you, sir."

"I've read your report, Mr Heron. Very good indeed." He paused, regarding them, a smile playing on his lips. "It seems to me there is only one thing to do with the pair of you. It is a little irregular because you are technically both too young and too old. But these are irregular times. Mr Heron, as of this moment you are promoted to the rank of Sub-Lieutenant with seniority backdated to the moment you took command of the *Twee Jonge Gezellen*." He turned to Ferghal. "Mr O'Connor, I am promoting you to Sub-Lieutenant as well, effective immediately and I am according you the same seniority."

Their surprise and pleasure showed as they chorused, "Yes, sir. Thank you, sir."

"Gentlemen, that ship is proving to be a goldmine. Her holds were crammed with equipment and information that is invaluable to us. Very well done to you both."

"Thank you, sir," replied Harry, flushed with pleasure as the Flag Lieutenant clipped his new insignia to his uniform. As the officer moved to do the same for Ferghal, he asked, "What news of *Leander*, sir?"

The Admiral smiled. "Decommissioned for a rebuild, I'm afraid. I expect the Drafting Office will re-assign you as soon as you have completed some well-earned leave. Good luck, gentlemen."

HAVING ENDURED HARRY'S TEASING OVER AN ENERGETIC tryst with Ingrid on their last night on the dock station, Ferghal watched his friend paying very stilted and old-fashioned court to the young woman he'd fallen head over ears for as soon as he met her upon their return home to Ireland. For her part, Mary seemed to be enjoying it, and to be very attracted to Harry.

When she wasn't on the concert touring circuit, she enjoyed being home in County Down, and often participated in musical evenings at the local pub, playing Irish folk songs along with other musicians for the pure fun of it. It was there one brisk, cold night that she had first spotted Harry watching her with fascination as she sat at the piano while he and Ferghal enjoyed the music and a pint together.

He smiled to himself as he remembered that evening, and how he'd teased his friend on the walk home about love at first sight. They were an unlikely pair, he thought, as he strolled down to the family home, Mary a headstrong and extremely talented concert pianist, and Harry the artist who loved music but couldn't make it.

Wrapped in their own conversation, neither Mary nor Harry noticed when Ferghal left them alone on the hillside surrounded by the most beautiful scenery on Earth, in his opinion.

"What now, Harry?" Mary asked. She found him intriguing, a mix of very talented artist, endlessly curious and creative, his manners and courtesy matching his very old fashioned ideas of honour and correct behaviour, sometimes reckless and even ruthless, yet very rigid in his principles. The combination fascinated her. She enjoyed his company, finding it comforting and pleasant, and he was never far from her thoughts when they were apart. "After your latest adventures, where will you go next?"

"I expect we'll be posted to a new ship soon." He smiled. "I should not be sorry if it were to the Home System Patrol. After New Eden, a spell in a quieter and more pleasant neighbourhood would be nice."

She laughed, a delightful rippling trill of laughter that sounded musical to Harry. "And boring, I should think! I expect you'd be complaining within weeks that there was no excitement in chasing asteroids, inspecting freighters and monitoring mining operations."

"Perhaps, but if I know your concert schedule, I can take my planet leaves to attend some of your performances."

"I'd like that." Her hand found his, and she squeezed it gently. She studied it on her knee, surprised yet again at the delicate shape of his hand that belied the strength of his grip. "I will arrange tickets for you — and Ferghal, of course."

"I should like that indeed."

Printed in Great Britain
by Amazon